THE LUKARILLA AFFAIR

By

Jerry Banks

To Chuck
with best wishes
Jerry Banks

Printed in the United States of America.

For information address:
Durban House Publishing Company, Inc.
7502 Greenville Avenue, Suite 500, Dallas, Texas 75231

Library of Congress Cataloging-in-Publication Data
Banks, Jerry, 1938 –

The Lukarilla Affair / Jerry Banks

Library of Congress Control Number: 2004107753

p. cm.

ISBN 1930754590

First Edition

10 9 8 7 6 5 4 3 2 1

Visit our Web site at
http://www.durbanhouse.com

THE LUKARILLA AFFAIR

To Janet, my wife and best friend and
companion for over fifty years.

ACKNOWLEDGEMENTS

This is my first novel, and there are a number of people who made this publication possible. There was Bill Greenleaf. He provided early professional help and gave me the name of Karen Lewis in my search for an agent and a publisher. Karen liked the story, saw the need for more professional help and referred me to Kay Garrett. Kay became my editor and truly changed the focus and presentation of the story, so that when it was rewritten it got the attention of Karen's husband, John Lewis, and the publisher Durban House Publishing Company. Durban House's marvelous editor, Robert Middlemiss, provided the finishing touches with the assistance of its proofreader, Jennifer Adkins. Thank you all. I am indebted to each of you.

I also fondly thank my wife Janet, my younger daughter Sarah, and my grandson Brian for putting up with my chatter and for being my early test readers.

PROLOGUE

Wednesday morning, September 25, 1991.

Hugh Chalmers was at home finishing his breakfast when he opened *The Oregonian*. His eyes widened at the front-page headline: "WOMEN CLAIM SEXUAL ASSAULT AT MALE RETREAT." The article reported that three women, who asked to remain anonymous, alleged they were sexually assaulted at a male retreat in the Coast Range Mountains last Sunday night. It said that an early investigation revealed that each year a small group of political and financial leaders from across the nation meet for a retreat at a camp owned by local lumberman Hugh Chalmers, who has yet to be questioned, and that the camp is located beside the Nehalem River, several miles south of Highway 26. It explained that the group calls themselves the Lukarillas, and that there is no known list of its members, but a source advised that they range from U.S. senators, congressmen, and governors, to some of the most influential business executives. The article concluded that no names had been released and no arrests made, but the Clatsop County District Attorney was investigating.

"Damn it." Chalmers picked up the phone and dialed his lawyer, Jake Marion.

"Jake, have you read the morning paper about our retreat?" Chalmers asked.

Marion responded that he had.

Chalmers said, "What the hell is going on? I was at the retreat. Nothing like that happened! We've been holding the retreats for more than forty years without a hitch, and the last thing we need is publicity, especially if it's bad."

"Take it easy, Hugh," Marion said. "I know the DA. I'll talk to him and get back to you."

About a week later Marion called back. "The district attorney's dropping the sexual assault claims. Your members deny what the women claim, and the DA couldn't find any evidence to corroborate their allegations. Do you want to issue a press release?"

"God, no," Chalmers replied. "We don't want any more publicity."

⚤

Thursday evening, December 5.

Chalmers had finished a tough week and decided to catch the evening news before heading home. He filled a short glass with ice and a couple of jiggers of Scotch and turned on the television set to KPOR, the Empire Broadcasting Company's Portland affiliate.

The EBC's anchorman stared at the camera. "EBC has just completed an investigation into the charges of sexual assault by members of a group called the Lukarillas Sunday night, September twenty-second. The findings were shocking."

Chalmers refilled his drink, and his gaze fixed on the screen.

Two women appeared on the screen, one of whom had her face blurred. The other woman introduced herself as an investigator for EBC and turned to the Jane Doe. "Are you one of the women a Portland newspaper reported was sexually assaulted by members of the Lukarillas back in September?"

"I am," the woman said.

"Tell the viewers what happened," the reporter said.

"Senator Shepard made me have oral sex with him." The woman choked back a sob. "Another member of the Lukarillas, Alex Lovejoy, forced me to have sex with the senator."

The anchorman came back on the screen. "EBC will carry a full report of the findings of the investigation on Dorothy Watters' show later this evening."

Chalmers switched off the TV. He dialed Jake Marion. "Jake, thank God you're still in your office. I've been watching EBC's *Evening News*, and you won't believe what they're saying. The Watters show comes on at ten; you gotta watch it. I'll call tomorrow morning. We need to talk."

Chapter 1

Friday morning, December 6.

Barry O'Shea left home for the office at seven-thirty. It was a clear, cold morning. *Most people outside of Oregon don't believe we have days like this,* he thought. *They think it rains all the time. But that's good, it keeps the throngs away.* Barry was a partner in the law firm of Swift, Wyman & Wiggins. The firm had offices in a downtown tower. He exited the elevator on the twenty-first floor and headed for his office in the southwest corner. From there he had a breathtaking view of the city, the Willamette River to the east and the green foliage of Portland's West Hills to the south.

As he was approaching his office, he heard a phone ringing. "I'm sure that's mine," he muttered. By the time he got to his office and picked up the receiver, there was only a dial tone, and "VM" stared at him on the display window. He dialed into his mailbox and got his partner Jake Marion's voice.

"Barry," Jake said. "One of my best clients, Hugh Chalmers, called me last night. He's really upset. EBC did an expose on an organization he belongs to. I saw the program, and he's got a major problem. He's coming in early this morning. I know this'll get into court, so I need you with me. Give me a call or come up to my office when you get in."

Jake Marion and Barry had practiced together for more than thirty years. They were classmates in law school. Marion was the firm's senior corporate lawyer, and Barry headed the trial lawyers. When they joined the firm in the late fifties, there were only about fifteen lawyers. It was up to about one hundred eighty now.

Marion's office was on the twenty-third floor in the northeast corner. As usual he was on the phone, so when Barry entered, he remained standing, taking in the view out the corner windows. He always said that, if he'd lost out on the southwest corner, this was where he'd want his office. The downtown streets and buildings were in the foreground with the West Hills in the distance. If he squinted a little, he could see the river to the north, winding its way toward its meeting with the Columbia.

With his full head of white hair and his brown glen plaid suit, Marion was a portrait of a corporate lawyer. He ended his call. "That was a lawyer in New York, Howard Sugerman with Bellman & Swett. His firm represents a guy named Alex Lovejoy and his company, Silex Petroleum. Lovejoy's involved. I told him we'd call him later today, after we've met with Hugh." Marion then told Barry about Chalmers' call the night before and about the TV special that they'd watched. "He'll be here anytime now," Marion said. "He went down to KPOR to get a video of the program. I hope you've got time to meet with us and watch the video."

That was music to Barry's ears. He'd been in trial all week. It had settled suddenly the morning before, and he had been at loose ends. "I've got all day. While we're waiting, fill me in on Hugh. I know he's big in lumber, and I've seen him some socially, but I'm vague about his background."

"Good idea," Jake agreed. "Hugh grew up in McMinnville, the son of a logger, and later a lumber mill operator. He worked for his dad all through school. After college, he joined the Navy and served in the South Pacific during the war. Around forty-five, he rejoined his dad in the lumber business. By then his dad had amassed timber holdings in Washington and Oregon, and he was operating several mills. He called his company Chalmers Lumber Company, and Jerry Swift was his lawyer.

"Hugh took over management in forty-six, when his dad was killed in a mill accident. Hugh changed the company's name to Chalmers Forest Products. I became CFP's and Hugh's lawyer when Jerry retired. He's always been an ambitious man, a good athlete in high school and college, more because of mental drive than physique.

"Sometime in the late forties, he came up with an idea of bringing together a bunch of business leaders, political figures and entertainers for an annual retreat at a camp he built on the Nehalem River in the mountains on the way to the coast. It was kind of a think tank. The group's held these every year in late September. They call themselves the Lukarillas. Hugh can tell you more about them."

Barry shook his head. "You've got my attention already." As he turned to leave, he added, "I'll be down in my office. Why don't we meet in the large conference room on our floor? There's a VCR and TV in there."

A little over an hour later, Marion stood with Hugh Chalmers at Barry's door and said, "Barry, you know Hugh."

Barry shook Chalmers' hand. "Sure do, hi, Hugh."

Chalmers was about six feet, well conditioned, and wore his gray hair cropped short. His rugged appearance belied his seventy-two years.

"Let's go down to the conference room," Barry said.

In the conference room Marion said, "Hugh, why don't you give Barry some background, while I set up the VCR and television set?"

"Okay. Well, I don't know what Jake's told you, but I came up with this retreat idea in nineteen forty-eight," Chalmers began. "I felt the group should be small. I passed the idea by our lawyer in Los Angeles, our accountant and a congressman I knew from the Navy, and they liked it. Together we went after twenty well-known guys in all parts of the country. We told them about my idea to get together anonymously and share ideas and experiences, while relaxing in the mountains with home cooking, horses and a great fishing stream. Surprisingly, twelve joined us, making a group of sixteen with me, the LA lawyer, our accountant and the congressman. We met the first time on Friday, September twenty-fourth in nineteen forty-eight, the anniversary of my father's death. The retreat lasted until the following Monday. We've held them every year since then on a weekend in late September.

"We've now got twenty members. We've kept the group about that size, and the members have stayed until they died or resigned. The prominence of our members increased over the years. Replacements have always been unanimous and usually from the same kind of business or profession. We called ourselves the Lukarillas after a small town nearby. It was actually only a few houses, and it doesn't exist anymore. We've stayed away from any kind of publicity. Almost no one knew we existed, until this happened."

"Were you all men?" Barry asked.

"Always," Chalmers answered.

Marion interrupted, "Barry, I've got the videotape ready to go. Here's what Dorothy Watters had to say."

Marion turned on the television.

The picture showed Dorothy Watters in a studio setting. "It's December ninth, time for 'You Heard It Here,'" she said. "Back in September EBC reported that three waitresses claimed they were sexually assaulted during an all male retreat in the remote mountains of Oregon. We learned that the local district attorney refused to prosecute, so we conducted our own investigation into the charges to find out why. Tonight we report on the results of that investigation.

"From the waitresses we learned that they were sexually assaulted by several members of a group called the Lukarillas. The Lukarillas we found is an association of some of the most powerful men in the nation. There are about twenty of them, including U.S. senators, congressmen, governors, business executives and entertainers. At least one of the members has been mentioned as a possible presidential candidate. For the last forty years the group has been meeting once a year in the Oregon Coast Range Mountains without anyone knowing that it existed. It was during the most recent meeting that the alleged sexual assaults occurred."

At this point four women joined Watters in the studio. Watters introduced one of them. "This is Susan Silver, one of our most experienced investigators. The other three women with me are the waitresses. We have distorted their faces and will refer to them with fictitious names to protect their identities. I must warn you to use your discretion on who should remain watching this segment of the program as what will follow will involve some crude language. Susan, please tell our viewers what you discovered."

"Thank you, Dorothy," Susan replied and addressed one of the other women. "This is Jane Doe. Jane, tell the audience what you told me when we first met."

Without hesitation, Jane Doe said, "Me and two of my friends were working for West Portland Catering. It had a catering job for the Lukarillas. The job was at a camp a few miles off Highway 26. It was really out in the boondocks, so we were staying in one of the cabins at the camp. Sunday night, after we'd finished cleaning up, we was walking back to our cabin, when Abe Sumas asked us in for a nightcap. He was sittin on the porch of the cabin next-door. He seemed like a nice guy, so we went along.

"When we got in the cabin, Alex Lovejoy and the senator were there too. We had some drinks and shot the bull. It seemed like the senator had had more than his share, and he tried to start a game of strip poker. I cut him off. 'No way, count us out,' I told him, and then I motioned to the other gals and said, 'Let's get out of here.'

"Alex told me to calm down. He said the senator wasn't serious, and he suggested we have another drink. We believed him and had a couple more drinks. Then all of a sudden Senator Shepard put his arms around me and asked me to unzip his pants. I was stunned. I said something like, 'What for?' and he said, 'I want you to meet Pete in there.' I'd had enough. I pushed him back and shouted, 'No way!' I tried to back away, but he grabbed me and pushed my head down. His penis was out of his pants, and he tried to force it into my mouth."

She started to sob and said, "Abe grabbed Rita and was doing the same thing to her."

She paused briefly and then said, "Alex yelled at them and told them to stop. He told the senator and Abe that what they were doing wasn't fair. I'll never forget what he said then. 'Use those things for screwing. Then everyone has fun.' I said, 'No way. Let's get out of here.' But Alex continued to press us. He said, 'Oh, come on now. Don't play hard to get. All we want is a little fucking. What's wrong with that?' Then Alex grabbed Linda, Abe grabbed Rita, and the senator pushed me down on the couch. Alex threatened us. 'You'd better cooperate or we'll tell the cops you tried to sell us sex. We've checked you out and we know you've done this for money before.'"

Again starting to sob, she said, "We was scared. We knew what guys like them could do to us. The police was sure to believe them over us, so we gave in and screwed them."

"Did you tell the district attorney what you've told us?" asked Susan.

Angrily, Jane Doe replied, "You're damn right I did. And I told him I'd never sold myself for sex. I told him I knew what big shots those guys were, and I was afraid, if they said I did, he'd believe 'em."

The camera turned back to Susan and then to the second woman, whom she introduced as Rita Roe. "Rita, you heard what Jane Doe has just said, tell us what happened to you."

"Abe grabbed hold of my head," Rita Roe said. "He took his cock out, shoved my head down and tried to put his cock in my mouth. I jerked from side to side and got his cock out. Then I spit, and Alex called him off. Alex threatened us, and I let Abe screw me, like Jane told you, but I didn't want to do it."

"Had you ever charged for sex as Lovejoy claimed?"

"Never, but like Jane said, I was afraid. I come from a rough neighborhood, and I knew who the cops'd believe."

Finally, Susan introduced the third woman as Linda Loe. "Linda, is what Jane and Rita have said true?"

"Yeah, I had sex with Alex, but I'd never done it if he hadn't threatened us with the cops."

Susan Silver came back on camera. "The men involved are Abe Sumas, an owner and general manager of the NFL's Los Angeles Stars, Alex Lovejoy, the chief executive officer of Silex Petroleum, and Lionel Shepard, the junior United States senator from Illinois."

The television picture switched to an old courthouse in a small community. Susan explained, "This is the Clatsop County Courthouse in Astoria, Oregon. We took our television crew there to interview the district attorney,

Owen Persell."

The picture showed Susan entering the courthouse and approaching the receptionist in the district attorney's office. "I'm Susan Silver," she said. "I'm the one who called you earlier and told you I'd like to interview the district attorney about the Lukarilla matter."

The receptionist apologized, "I'm sorry, Mr. Persell is not available, but he told me to tell you that he has no comment at this time."

The scene then changed to a low commercial building in a suburban neighborhood of Portland. "This is West Portland Catering," Susan said.

Shortly after Susan entered, the waitresses' supervisor, Marlene Smyth, greeted her.

Susan said, "I'd like to talk about your waitresses and the incident that happened at the Lukarilla retreat. And I want you to identify them as Jane Doe, Linda Loe and Rita Roe."

"I've got no problem with that," Smyth responded. "The gals joined me last July, just after I took over this business. I purchased it in June. Jane, Linda and Rita came highly recommended by a friend of mine down in LA. They'd been working for a catering outfit in Corona Del Mar that she used. She said they were reliable and good workers."

"Tell me how your company happened to be working at the Chalmers place last September."

"Hugh Chalmers hired us to cater the meals Friday night, Saturday, Sunday and Monday morning. Since the camp was so far from Portland, Chalmers gave us a cabin to stay in. There were four of us, the three gals waited on tables and I was the cook."

"When did you first realize something had gone wrong?" Susan asked.

"Around midnight Sunday morning, all three gals came into the cabin crying. Jane's blouse was torn and hanging open. After I calmed 'em down some, they told me that Abe Sumas, Alex Lovejoy and Senator Shepard had raped them. They said they'd been threatened, or they wouldn't have let them do it."

"Is there anything in these women's records indicating that they'd previously sold themselves for sex?"

Symth responded abruptly, "Absolutely not! They wouldn't be working for me if that were true."

The scene shifted to Susan in a studio. "We tried to interview Sumas, Lovejoy and the senator, but they wouldn't talk to us. Under these circumstances it's hard to understand why the DA didn't press charges, but the next chapter in this amazing story may still be in court. EBC has learned that Jane, Rita and Linda have sought legal advice."

Chapter 2

Marion turned off the television, and Chalmers said, "You can see we need help, and badly."

"I don't need convincing," Barry said. "Let's go back to my office and talk."

As they walked down the hall, Chalmers reflected. He agreed with Dorothy Watters, this was going to be in court, and he was sure he was in the right hands. Jake Marion had been his lawyer and close confidant for more than twenty years. Chalmers would follow Marion's advice religiously on any business matter. He knew the firm. His dad had used them since the thirties, when there were just four lawyers. He only knew Barry socially, but what he'd seen impressed him: an imposing man, about six-four, receding short gray hair, who seemed in charge, and before they'd joined Barry earlier, he'd asked Marion about his reputation.

"He's done trial work from the start," Marion told him. "You've seen those ads on television from fellas who call themselves trial lawyers and brag about astounding win-loss ratios. Well, that's a bunch of bologna. Barry's learned that being on the losing side is part of the learning process, which any good trial lawyer has to experience many times. He's a real trial lawyer, the kind you want and need. Some probably say his success in court is because he's tall, glib and imposing. That's partially true, I'm sure, but he's earned his gray hair, what's left of it, and he knows his way around the court as well as anyone. Just ask anyone who works at the courthouse and they'll tell you that you can't do better. We know he's the best.

"I should also tell you that he's married to your banker and friend Steve Murdock's daughter, Sarah. But don't think that bogs him down with social functions. To the contrary, Sarah's more devoted to the law than society. In fact she was once a legal secretary here in our firm, and she's Barry's biggest supporter when it comes to the law."

That was all Chalmers had needed to hear, so, as he entered Barry's office, he turned his attention to his surroundings. He saw Mt. Hood with its 11,000 feet commanding the Cascade Mountains to the east and the blue Willamette River in the foreground. But what he noticed the most was that the office itself seemed to fit the man. Instead of fancy wood paneled walls, the walls were plain white. The furnishings were comfortable, but not ornate. A brown leather couch, two matching chairs, a large desk and a table occupied the space. From his impression so far, he doubted that Barry ever used the couch, but it gave the office the look of a senior partner. On one wall was a Haitian version of a Rousseau jungle scene with two jaguars and a leopard. Fitting for the fighting man he wanted.

"What the hell did you guys do to piss off EBC?" Barry asked. "It looks like they're just getting started on you. You're probably in for more TV blasts, and I'm sure you're going to get sued. Those waitresses can smell blood. The Watters woman is right. They've been steered to lawyers, so you'd better start preparing to defend yourselves.

"You must have known about this before this week. Tell me what was going on?"

Chalmers nodded. "You're right, it hit the papers the Wednesday morning after the retreat. EBC and other networks reported on it that evening, but it was EBC that did the follow-up. I called Sumas, Shepard and Lovejoy right away. Obviously, they were shook up and mad as hell. Their stories were consistent. They were in their cabin Sunday night after dinner playing cards. The waitresses came to the cabin to see if they needed ice. They asked the girls in for a drink, and one thing led to another. But they emphatically deny that they forced themselves on the girls.

They said that the girls came looking for sex, and that's what happened."

"Who hired the girls?" Barry asked.

"I hired West Portland Catering, not the girls. I've used that outfit for several years. Usually the cook was a man, this time it was a woman. The waitresses have always been women."

Barry asked how old the girls were. Chalmers said, "I'd say between mid-thirties and early forties. Ginny Lane and Peg House appeared older than the Marcellas girl, she was in her twenties, and she's Mexican."

Marion interrupted, "I don't want to cut this short, but I've got another client coming in, and you guys will want to spend a lot of time on this. Let's get that lawyer in New York on the phone."

Barry dialed the number. "Mr. Sugerman, this is Jake Marion's partner, Barry O'Shea. I have you on a speakerphone, because Jake and Hugh Chalmers are here with me."

"Thanks for calling me back," Howard Sugerman said. "Now that you've had a chance to talk to Mr. Chalmers, you may appreciate why I called this morning. Alex wants the Lukarillas' lawyers communicating and coordinating. He's wondering about Mr. Chalmers' reaction to the program and whether he plans to take any action. Alex thinks there's more to this than just three disgruntled waitresses, and he wanted me to convey his thoughts about why EBC's involved.

"Silex is in a running battle with EBC about its employment policies, specifically the advancement of women executives. EBC aired an expose naming both Silex and Alex. The battle is in court, because both Silex and Alex have sued EBC for defamation. We suspect that EBC's motive with this program is somehow involved with this lawsuit."

Chalmers said, "You want my reaction? I'm *pissed*."

"I certainly understand," Sugerman replied, "but I think we have to look at this calmly and plan our actions, because I know we've not heard the end of EBC or the waitresses."

"We agree with you," Barry said. "We're forming a team here to begin an investigation. We'll keep you advised. Do you know if the others have lawyers? If they do, we should be discussing our strategy with them, too."

"I think Alex can find that out," Sugerman said. "When I talked to him earlier, he said he was going to get in touch with Sumas and Shepard. I'm pretty sure the Parker & James firm in D.C. represents the senator, but I'll let you know what Alex finds out. Maybe Mr. Chalmers should check with them too. Why don't we get back together Monday? Why don't I call you at one your time to check in? Is that satisfactory?"

"Sounds fine. We'll talk to you then," Barry agreed, and he ended the call.

Barry then turned to Chalmers and said, "Hugh, why don't you try to reach Sumas and Shepard later today and see who their lawyers are. Let's meet again here Monday, say at about ten-thirty, and take up where we left off. By that time we'll have had time to digest this a little more, and we can share thoughts. That'll also give me some time to gather our resources."

"That's fine. But come over to my place. We're just a few blocks away," Chalmers replied.

"I'll see you there," Barry said, and the meeting ended.

Barry went next-door to see if Becky Cohen was in her office. She was there working at her computer. Becky was one of the firm's younger partners, and she often teamed with Barry on his big cases.

"Clear your desk," Barry told her. "We've got a wild one on our hands. It's right up your alley, so don't tell me you're too busy."

"You know better than that," she said with a smile. "What's it about?"

"Come on into the conference room, and I'll show you." They went down the hall, and Becky watched a repeat of the video.

"Wow!" she exclaimed. "Who's our client?"

"Right now, it's the founder of the Lukarillas. He's Hugh Chalmers, the head of Chalmers Forest Products, and he was just here. There isn't any lawsuit yet, but sure as hell it's coming, so we've got to get organized and find out what has been going on. We'll need Mary Jo and Ben Lorenzo for sure. I want to talk to them right after lunch. See if you can get them together in my office at one. They should see the video before then."

"Will do," she responded.

Mary Jo was Mary Jo Knight, one of the firm's senior legal assistants. She'd been with them for a little more than fifteen years. She was with a couple of other firms before that, and she'd been to all the paralegal schools and had their degrees. She was a whiz with the computer and litigation software. She never missed a deadline and could organize a herd of frightened antelopes. Trying a lawsuit with her in his corner left Barry free to do the lawyering the client needed. Exhibits were where he wanted them, and everything on his side of the courtroom was always in order.

Barry used Ben Lorenzo for investigation and gofer work. He'd been with the firm for eighteen years. He was fascinated with computers and had made them one of his primary tools for investigation and document production. Lorenzo had been in police work before joining the firm, and he still retained his contacts.

Becky was in Barry's office, waiting for him to return from lunch. Mary Jo and Ben arrived first. Becky greeted them and learned that they'd just seen the video and were as excited as she was. She couldn't wait to get more details. When Barry entered the room, Becky said, "We're all ready to go, chief."

"What's this chief shit?" Barry chided. "There's no chief in this group, but I'm glad you're all available. Has everyone seen the video?"

They all had.

"We know a lawsuit's coming, and you know my thinking. While tradition says lay low and maybe the thing'll go away, it rarely does, and it's not worth giving up early preparation to risk that it might. It's almost sure that the women have a lawyer, and that lawyer is already ahead of us in developing the facts. Our factual defense has to start right now, and it's got to be aggressive. Let's start with what we can do now. We need to find out what's been going on. The newspaper and KPOR are the places to start. Ben, you know the reporters there, so that should be easy. We know EBC has been out here. See what the local reporters know about what they were doing. The DA in Clatsop County made an investigation and apparently dropped the matter. Why?"

Barry looked at Becky and said, "See if you can talk to him. His name is Owen Persell. You better go to Astoria, there may be others there who need to be interviewed. I think you can also help us with KPOR. Remember our tower case. As I recall, you were in pretty tight with KPOR's chief engineer. Go see him; maybe he can open a door or two."

Then talking again to all three, he said, "We'd better stay away from the catering company for now. They're obviously adverse, and we don't want to stir up the lawsuit, even though we know it's coming. You're on your own, those are just suggestions. I'd like as much as you can find out by early next week."

Barry asked Becky to stay for a minute. When they were alone, he said, "I want you to meet Hugh Chalmers. I'm going to his office Monday at ten-thirty to follow up on my meeting with him this morning. I'd like you to come along, so we can learn together about the Lukarillas, its members and the retreats. We'll find out who else was at those retreats."

Chapter 3

Monday morning, April 4, 1988.

Susan Silver was approaching Central Park in her jogging suit, and she saw Angie Lawrence waiting for her at the traffic light at Fifth Avenue and Seventy-second. Susan admired Angie's figure. Her height, five-ten, was accented by her shoulder-length brunette hair, which was tied behind her head.

It was a beautiful April morning in New York. The sky was clear, the temperature was near fifty and the sun was about to appear. The drab texture of winter was gone and replaced by crocus, daffodils and fruit trees in bloom. All of the trees were sprouting their leaves.

As they started running into the park, Susan asked, "Are congratulations in order? I heard Friday that George Mendenhall is giving up as CEO at Silex. You must be next in line."

"Ha! Don't kid yourself," Angie replied. "Remember, I'm still a woman, and just a vice president. Andy Schwartz is Executive VP and COO."

"Oh, come on, Angie," Susan said. "Everyone, including the board, knows you're George's brains. Andy's over sixty. You're the only choice, and the fact that you're a woman shouldn't have anything to do with it."

"We'll see, but don't hold your breath."

Monday morning, April 18

A *Wall Street Journal* headline read, "SILEX GOES OUTIDE FOR NEW CEO." The article reported that in a somewhat surprise move late Friday, Silex's board had appointed Alexander Lovejoy president and chief executive officer of the company. It described Lovejoy as a fifty-three-year-old former Texan who'd risen from an operations manager at New Brunswick Corporation to president and chief operating officer. It pointed out that most observers believed the CEO post at Silex would go to the Executive VP, Andrew Schwartz, or the bright young vice president, Angie Lawrence, who had been so prominent in the success of Silex in recent years.

That Friday, right after the board meeting, Lovejoy called Angie and asked her to meet him after work at the Dorset Bar on fifty-fourth. Lovejoy had never met Angie, although he was well aware of her accomplishments and had seen her a couple of times at social affairs. At the Dorset Bar, he got right to the point. "I know our situation is somewhat awkward, but I had to meet you away from the office. I've had the experience of meeting a new boss for the first time on the other side of a desk. It's not the way to introduce yourself to someone you need as a partner. From everything I know about the company, it needs you badly, probably a lot more than it needs me. I want to learn from and plan the company's future with you."

"You're very kind," Angie said, "but I really haven't had time to assimilate the board's decision. I don't know what I'll be doing, so I can't talk about plans."

"I realize that," he said, "but I hope that doesn't mean you're thinking of leaving Silex. I don't want that to happen. I wanted to meet and chat socially, before any decisions like that were made. Can we just talk? Then maybe we can go somewhere for dinner?"

"That's okay, but I don't know about dinner. It's Friday. Don't you have a train to catch?"

"I've talked to my wife and told her that if I didn't spook you, we might have dinner together. She approves, so I can go home late with safety."

That was how it worked out. They got along surprisingly well. After several hours sharing their likes and dislikes, they stayed right there for dinner. Lovejoy took Angie home in a cab and spent the night at the Park Lane, where New Brunswick kept a suite for its executives.

⚤

The following Monday, Lovejoy was on the job at Silex as CEO. His first order of business was an executive committee meeting to start the transition. He asked each member to continue in his or her position. A disappointed Andy Schwartz announced that he had decided to accept the company's early retirement. Angie and the other committee members agreed to stay on. For the present the committee decided to leave the positions of executive vice president and chief operating officer vacant. Alex agreed to hold both the CEO and COO jobs, until he felt comfortable as CEO.

So things went that way at Silex for the next few months. Lovejoy worked closely with Angie, just as George Mendenhall had. There was a difference, however. Alex was fifty-three, while Mendenhall had been sixty-eight. Although Angie and Lovejoy had no intimate exchanges, they became very close friends. Whenever work kept them into the evening hours, they would dine together. Angie continued her active social life, and while she was fond of Lovejoy and respected him enormously, she didn't have any romantic feelings toward him, and she didn't recognize that their closeness was beginning to affect him.

One evening, after they had worked late, had consumed a few drinks and had finished dinner, Lovejoy couldn't keep his feelings to himself. He leaned across the table, looked into her eyes, and softly said, "Angie, I'm very fond of you."

"I'm fond of you, too, Alex."

"What I mean, Angie, is I want to spend the night with you."

Angie straightened. "You can't be serious," she said. "I like you, Alex, but I won't get personally involved. You're married and have a family. I won't disrupt that."

He insisted, "But I am serious. We can work around the family. Arrangements like this go on all the time with married men who have to stay in town a lot."

"Hold it right there! Do you really think I'd be someone's town girl?"

"I didn't mean that, Angie. You know that. We're going to be spending a lot more time together. The company needs a chief operating officer, and I think you're the one. The company needs you, and I need you. I know it's something we can work out together."

She was visibly mad. "That's enough. I'm not giving you sex to be COO. End of conversation. It's late. I'll get my own cab." Angie left.

They continued to work together, although very seldom in the evenings, and when they did, there was no socializing.

Monday morning, August 7, 1989

Lovejoy made a decision that changed everything, a decision he didn't discuss with Angie. At the executive committee meeting, he announced that it was time for him to give up the COO duties. "I've given the matter a great deal of thought and decided to ask the board to appoint Lou Ierulli chief operating officer. Does anyone have a comment?"

There were none.

After the meeting Lovejoy and Ierulli were greeted with handshakes from all in attendance, except Angie, who quietly slipped out into the hall.

The next morning, Lovejoy found Angie's resignation on his desk. He called her office, but her secretary told him Angie had left the office without any word as to when she would return.

Angie never came back. She never spoke to Lovejoy again. After she left the note in Lovejoy's office, she called Susan Silver and told her what had happened.

Susan could tell Angie was terribly upset. "You get right over here," she said, "so we can talk."

Susan's office was on the thirty-first floor of the EBC building. When Angie arrived, she didn't wait to be announced. She went right to Susan's office. The door was open.

Susan greeted her. "Angie, you've been fucked, and I don't mean literally. After all you've done for Silex, and that prima donna shits on you like this."

"I guess it's my own fault," Angie said. "If I'd played along with him, I'd have been COO a year ago."

"What the hell are you talking about?"

Then Angie told her about the evening when Lovejoy came on to her after dinner.

Susan stared at her. "What he did was sexual harassment in spades! He was trading sex for advancement. That's a classic. You need a lawyer. The company owes you plenty for that."

"I don't want their money," Angie said. "I can get another job. I'm just disappointed, and, I guess, pissed off as well."

"Come on, keep your options open. Sleep on what I've told you. Now let's get out of here and go get drunk."

On Friday, August 10, the *Wall Street Journal* reported on the new appointment at Silex and that Angie had left.

Later that day Angie got a call from her former secretary. Elmer Russell of Citrus Publishing Company in Los Angeles had called. He left a message: "I want you to join my company as president and chief operating officer. Call me right away."

To Angie, Southern California appeared inviting and the offer attractive. Her mentor and friend George

Mendenhall sat on the Citrus' board. She returned the call and was on a plane to Los Angeles the following Tuesday. She met with Russell and signed an employment contract that same day, agreeing to come to work officially on October 1. Angie never made a complaint against Silex or Lovejoy.

Meanwhile Susan Silver didn't let Silex's treatment of Angie drop. She decided a deeper look into Silex's female policies was in order. She told her boss at EBC that she had a tip that Silex might be discriminating, and she got the green light to investigate.

Three months later EBC did an expose on Silex's policies. While Silex had been a leader during the sixties in hiring women executives, Angie, it turned out, was the only one who had advanced beyond middle management. It also turned out that there were a number of fairly serious sexual harassment and racial discrimination complaints against Silex in the Department of Labor files. Silex fought back with a libel suit in federal court. The suit had been viciously contested and was not yet set for trial.

Chapter 4

Monday morning, December 9, 1991.

It was clear and cool, so Barry and Becky decided to walk to Chalmers' office.

"This should be an interesting morning," Barry said. "I always think the first several days of a new case, finding out what happened, are usually the most fascinating. You get a foundation that sets the stage for what happens later. My guess is that when we talk to Hugh we'll learn a lot about what's ahead of us."

They got there a few minutes early, because of Barry's watch. It was four minutes fast, a habit he started as a young lawyer after an experience in one of his trials. The afternoon session was scheduled for one o'clock. Barry and his client were on time. So was the opponent, but the opponent's lawyer was not. The judge took the bench and brought in the jury. The other lawyer finally entered the courtroom ten minutes late. What the lawyer saw was his client, Barry and his client, the judge, and the jury all seated and waiting. What the lawyer heard was the judge saying, "It's nice of you to join us, Mr. Lawyer." Barry never wanted that to happen to him in or out of court, thus the extra four minutes on his watch.

Barry and Becky were shown directly to Chalmers' office on the east side of the building. It had that gorgeous view of the river and mountains.

"Jake figured it was time for him to beg off, but I brought Becky Cohen with me," Barry said, introducing Becky. "She works with me as a team on matters like this."

"Very glad to meet you, Becky," Chalmers said, shaking her hand firmly. "If Barry vouches for you, I'm sure we'll get along fine."

"You're going to see a lot of her," Barry told him. "She's tough, but if she needs to, she can sweet talk anyone. Thankfully, I latched on to her early in her career with the firm."

"Like I say, Becky, it's good to have you on board." Chalmers turned to Barry. "I talked to Shepard and Sumas, as you suggested. They hadn't involved their lawyers, but they will now. Hopson & Hill in LA are Sumas' lawyers, and Shepard's are Parker & James in DC. They said they'd have one of the lawyers call you this week. They're both livid about the Watters show. To quote Sumas, 'It's a bunch of horseshit. Nobody did anything to 'em they didn't ask for.' He also reminded me that he's had past problems with EBC. I seem to remember it had something to do with a black female reporter in the Stars' locker room. He said his lawyer would give you the details."

"I'll wait for their calls," Barry said, "and then we'll get all the lawyers together on a conference call to talk strategy. For now let's take a few moments and have you repeat what you told Jake and me about the Lukarillas for Becky's benefit."

Chalmers did that.

"Who are the Lukarillas' members?" Becky asked.

"Here are two lists I had my secretary make up," Chalmers answered. "One is a list of the present members, and the other is all the past members." He handed the lists to Becky.

On the first list the members, other than Chalmers, Lovejoy, Shepard and Sumas were:

Hilton Jones, managing partner of a NYC law firm, Stevens & Sherman

Max Pepper, a senior partner in a LA law firm, Newman & Levine

Cecil Upshaw, president of MJK&L, a national accounting firm

Parker Price, well known pop singer, movie star and golf celebrity

Edward Thomas, U.S. representative from Vermont
Julian Epstein, senior U.S. senator from Texas
H.P. "Smokie" Goodenough, U.S. representative from Tennessee
Nelson Beecham, governor of Wyoming
Vincent Grady, governor of Virginia
John Quincy Ames, chairman of the board of Southern & Eastern Railroad
Ezra Livingston, chairman of the board of the National Bank of the South
William Churchill, president of Random Electronics
Mason Rutledge, president of Marion University
James "Hook" Van Dyke, former NBA star and philanthropist
Stephen Weinstein, chairman of the board of S-Mart Stores
Rex Smith, president of Universal Airlines

"Which ones were at the retreat last September?" Becky asked.

"As I remember it, there were fourteen of us. For sure there was Abe, Alex, Shep and I. Then, let's see, I know Hilton wasn't there. Neither were Ed Thomas, Vince Grady, J.Q., Mason Rutledge or Rex Smith," Chalmers said, looking at the list. "I'm sure the rest were there, so that makes fourteen. But you'd better check with Sven to make sure."

"Who's Sven?" Barry asked.

"He's the caretaker for the camp. He and his family mind it for us. They live on a place about a half-mile downriver. We gave them the land as part of their compensation. There's Sven Larson, his wife Emma, their son Thor, and his wife Judy and their two kids. When we have people using the camp, Sven and Thor handle the horses and the work at the camp. Emma and Judy do the housekeeping. All four were around that weekend."

"Who else was around?" Becky asked.

Chalmers thought about it. "Sometimes there're fishermen and boaters in the river, but I don't remember any that weekend. The neighbors upriver are about a mile away. We hardly ever see them. No one's across the road for several miles either way. I don't think there was anyone."

Barry looked at Becky and said, "You need to talk to the Larsons. Can you arrange it while we're here, Hugh?"

Chalmers asked his secretary to get Sven Larson and put him on speakerphone. When Sven came on the line, Chalmers introduced Barry and Becky as his lawyers handling the EBC matter. "Becky would like to come to the camp and interview you and your family about the retreat. Any problem with the timing?"

Larson replied, "No problem, except we're going to visit relatives tomorrow and won't be back till just before Christmas. That week should be okay, if she don't mind traveling so close to Christmas. We'll all be here then."

Becky looked at her pocket calendar. "How about Monday morning the twenty-third, at around eleven. That'll give us some traveling time that morning."

Larson said that was fine.

Chalmers turned to Becky. "Then it's set. Make sure you take a four-wheeler in case it snows in the mountains. It's early, but you never know this time of year."

On the way back to the office, Becky said, "When I get back, I'll call Owen Persell and see if he'll meet with us in Astoria Monday after we visit the Larsons. Hopefully, he'll show us what he has and tell why he dropped the matter." She had her secretary set up the appointment.

Tuesday morning, December 10

Becky, Mary Jo and Lorenzo gathered in Barry's office. "What'd you find out?" Barry asked Lorenzo.

"I talked to the people at the paper and at KPOR. There's been nothing in the paper since the first article back in September. From KPOR I got two other videos. The first is the EBC *Evening Report* of September twenty-fifth. It doesn't say much more than the AP news release, except that the anchorman promised the viewers a follow-up. The second contains the Clatsop County DA's press conference on October second and parts of EBC's *Evening Report* that night. I think you should see that one."

Lorenzo had the VCR ready to go. When he turned it on the scene was an office with the district attorney, Owen Persell, seated behind his desk. He addressed the media representatives, "I've asked you here today to discuss the complaints made by three women who claimed to have been sexually assaulted two Sundays ago at a camp on the Nehalem River off Highway 26. My office has made a thorough investigation into the charges, and we have found that there is insufficient evidence to proceed any further in the matter. I'm sorry that I have time for only a few questions."

Persell recognized Amy McCormick, a reporter for television station KPOR.

She asked, "You said the complaints were made, not by one, but by three women. Just what did you find that causes you to discount what three women have said? What is it that makes their statements insufficient evidence?"

"I gave every benefit to what the women said," Persell said, "but I couldn't find any evidence to corroborate their statements."

Ms. McCormick followed up, "Do you usually dismiss matters like this, when you have three persons complaining? Why don't they corroborate each other?"

"I've already adequately answered those questions. I'll take one more question," he said, pointing to a reporter representing Cable TV.

"Is it true then that your office will take no action against the men?" that reporter asked.

Persell answered, "That's correct," and he motioned to the operator to turn off the camera.

Lorenzo then put a second tape in the VCR and turned it on. This was the video of part of EBC's news program on October second.

The anchorman said, "Earlier today the district attorney in Astoria, Oregon dropped all charges against the members of the Lukarillas alleged to have sexually assaulted three waitresses last September. Here's what he said." The video then showed parts of the press conference and the questions and answers between Amy McCormick and Owen Persell. "EBC can't understand why the district attorney took that extraordinary action. So we've decided to launch our own investigation, and we'll report our findings at a later date."

"Boy, that tells us where last week's program came from," Barry said. "EBC's sure as hell been out our way. What did the KPOR folks say about that, Ben?"

"They didn't. I asked what the follow-up was, and they stonewalled me. We need to talk to someone higher up who's not afraid to talk."

Then Becky spoke up. "I've got a meeting with Burt Anderson at KPOR later today. He was chief engineer when we did the tower case. Now he's a VP. Hopefully, I can find out more."

That afternoon, when Becky met with Anderson, she said, "Thanks for agreeing to talk to me. I thought there might be some scuttlebutt around here about the Lukarillas matter. I guess the way to start is to ask directly, what's being said?"

"That's what I've always liked about you, Becky," Anderson grinned. "You always cut right to the chase. But I don't know how I can help. I know Amy McCormick thought she got the runaround from the DA in Astoria. I also heard Susan Silver of EBC talking to Amy, and it was clear she had an agenda when it comes to Lovejoy and maybe Sumas. She told Amy that they'd had trouble with those two before. She was real interested in the Lukarillas, and she said they were going to keep digging. I also heard her say she thought a lawsuit would give her some leads. That's about all I can tell you."

"Well, that tells me Ms. Silver paid the station a visit," Becky said.

"You bet she did. That's when I heard her talking to Amy. She was out here talking to the girls, and who knows who else."

"I appreciate your talking with me, Burt. As usual, you've been a big help."

Wednesday, December 11

Barry heard from the lawyers for all of the accused Lukarillas.

From Bellman & Swett, Joan Dixon called and told him she was the litigation partner who'd be handling the matter for Alex Lovejoy.

Paul Shumanski, of Fleming, Rose & Krause in Cleveland, telephoned next. Parker & James had hired him to represent Senator Shepard.

Barry recognized Shumanski's name. He was one of the nation's most publicized trial lawyers. Whenever a high-profile public figure had a media court problem, Shumanski was on the list of whom he or she would want to hire. The final call came from Lou Miles of Hopson & Hill in Los Angeles. He was representing Sumas.

Barry brought each lawyer up to date on his firm's activities. They were all in agreement that he had the matter well in hand. They agreed that a lawsuit was coming and that they would get back together when that occurred.

Barry ended each call the same way. "Don't wait for the complaint to call, if you have any ideas. The earlier we follow up on leads, the better."

Chapter 5

December 1990.

Abe Sumas' confrontation with EBC had been a year earlier. Sumas was president and one of the owners of the Los Angeles Stars professional football team. He was born in 1930 and raised on a dairy farm in Wisconsin. After four years as a linebacker for Wisconsin, second-string All America the last two, he played nine years for the Chicago Cardinals. His doctors refused to operate again on his right knee, so he retired as a player and went directly into coaching. He ended up with the Stars and was their head coach from 1976 to 1983, when he was elevated to general manager. The Stars was a private corporation, and during those years, Sumas acquired stock. He was elected president in 1986.

Sumas was still a big guy, six-four and around three hundred pounds. He'd aged a little, evidenced by his bald head surrounded by a halo of white hair and a gray tint to his thin mustache. Married three times, he had five children, all from his first wife, who was still probably his best friend. Sumas was never hesitant to speak his mind, and profanity was usually involved.

During the 1990 season, he got embroiled in an ugly controversy with Rachel Jacobs, a black sports reporter for KEBC, the Los Angeles affiliate of EBC. It was in December, and the Stars were in the hunt for first place in the Western Division. Rumors were rampant about a rift between Alonzo Green, the team's All Star wide receiver, and Joe Marshall, the quarterback.

Jacobs was in her mid-thirties at the time and on the rise at KEBC. Tall and athletic, her complexion was light and her features sharp.

She appeared in the Stars' dressing room to interview Green and Marshall after the team had suffered an embarrassing loss. She was told that Marshall had left, but Green was showering, so she headed that way.

Just as she entered the shower anteroom, where several naked players were toweling themselves, Sumas grabbed her from behind and shouted, "Where the hell do you think you're going?"

"Take your hands off me!" she demanded, and then calmly added, "I'm here to interview Alonzo Green."

"Not in the showers, you won't. Now get your ass out of here."

"Don't cuss me," she said. "You know the league rules. I've got a right to do interviews in the locker room."

"This ain't the locker room," he told her. "You're in the shower getting kicks out of staring at my nude players."

"Why don't you grow up," she sneered. "I've got two big brothers and lots of boyfriends. I see 'em nude all the time. My guess is if anyone's getting a kick out of my being here, it's those players."

Sumas said, "I don't give a damn about your background. You're not going to bother my players, casting your eyes about in here. Now get your butt out of here before I have to throw you out." He took her by the arm and started ushering her toward the door.

She freed herself and exploded, "I told you before. Take your big white paws off me, you cocksucker. You'll hear about this from the league office." She slammed the door as she left.

Jacobs was good for her word. The league office heard about the episode immediately. The complaint came from EBC Sports producer Grant Slade. Slade also went on EBC Sports' *Sunday Sports Roundup* that night with a blistering editorial, charging Sumas and the Stars with sexual and racial discrimination. He implied that Sumas was a racist for barring Jacobs from her interview and manhandling her. All of the other networks and many of the nation's sport pages chimed in.

Sumas held a press conference and defended his actions. He demanded privacy for his players. "I don't understand where everybody's coming from," he told the reporters. "Aren't you entitled to privacy in your bathrooms and showers? Well, Rachel Jacobs doesn't think so. She's always had complete access to our players in the locker room, but that wasn't good enough. Does she think she's entitled to talk to them when they're on the head?"

A female reporter asked, "What do you say about Slade's implication that you're sexist and a racist?"

"I've never had problems with women," Sumas responded. "Even my ex-wives are my friends. How many divorced guys can say that? Some of my best and closest pals are women, and some are black, including one of my wives. I've worked and played with blacks all my life. Can the pious Mr. Slade say that?"

It didn't get any better during the rest of the question-and-answer session. Finally, the Stars public relations guy called a halt. The matter is still under investigation by the league, and several of the players have had to bite their tongues to answer the media's questions with a straight face.

At the Winter League meeting in early 1991, the NFL didn't renew EBC's television contract. The Commissioner's office issued a statement that the decision was based on money and other factors. Speculation had it that the other factors might include the Stars' locker room incident. Sumas wasn't bashful about it. To anyone who asked, he made it plain that he made a big stink about EBC at the meeting.

Several days after the television contract award, Grant Slade called the Subcommittee on Antitrust, Business Rights and Competition of the United States Senate's Judiciary Committee and asked to speak to the chairman, Senator Lionel Shepard. He was referred to another number. When he called that number, the subcommittee's majority chief counsel answered and asked what he could do for the caller.

Slade explained, "I'm Grant Slade, executive producer of EBC Sports, and I called to speak to Senator Shepard."

"This is not Senator Shepard's office," was the reply.

"I know that," Slade said. "I called the Subcommittee on Antitrust, Business Rights and Competition, and after I told them why I was calling and that I wanted to speak to Senator Shepard, they told me to call this number."

"I see. Well, Senator Shepard just left. Can I help you? I'm the Subcommittee's chief counsel."

"No, I have a matter that I want to discuss with Shep personally."

His use of the familiar name must have helped, because the chief counsel retreated. "Hold on a minute, Mr. Slade, let me see if the senator is still in the building."

A few seconds later, the senator came on the line. "Grant, this is Shep, what can I do for you?"

"I need you to kick some butt, the LA Stars and Abe Sumas for a start," Slade said. "The bastards have worked behind the scenes and caused the NFL to cancel our TV contract. There's got to be some sort of unfair trade practice tag you can put on it. I want you to tell them that you'll drag their asses before your committee if they don't come to their senses."

"Settle down, Grant. I can't do that, and you know it. I'll look into the matter, but you've got to give me more to go on."

Slade told the senator what had happened. "We've had that contract for the last eleven years," he said. "Add to that, Sumas has been bragging about how he blackballed us at the League meeting."

"Okay, Grant, I'll have the staff look into it. That's all I can do for now."

"Well, all right, but will I hear from you soon?"

"Someone from the chief counsel's office will be in touch with you. I've got to go now. They got me out of a meeting I'm chairing."

After numerous calls by Slade over several weeks, Senator Shepard finally called him back. "Grant, I'm sorry to be so long in getting back to you, but it has taken some time to look into this. We've found that you lost the contract because ABC made a better offer. You're right that Sumas was bragging, but he didn't swing the deal. Money did. We just can't do anything about it."

"Horseshit, Shep! What you mean is you won't do anything about it. I guess I understand. You've gotta look at your future and getting into this now probably wouldn't help. But I'll tell you this, I'm not letting this thing lie, and neither is EBC. Somebody's ass is going to burn before this is over."

"Do what you have to do, Grant, but the Senate can't help you. Sorry."

Several weeks later Slade was talking to Rachel Jacobs. She was in the running for a network sports job. As an aside, he mentioned the NFL contract and said, "I tried to put some pressure on the league through Congress, but Senator Lionel Shepard, whom I thought was a buddy, turned me down."

Jacobs called him back the following Monday. "Grant, I told my boyfriend over the weekend about your call to the senator. My boyfriend was already pissed at Sumas, because they're supposed to be friends. He says Sumas knows we're living together, and he thinks what Sumas did to me was a slap in his face. My boyfriend knows the senator, too, now he's pissed at him also. They all belong to some group he called the Lukarillas. My boyfriend told me he's been a member since 1976, when he took the place of some guy who won an Oscar back in the forties. I don't know much else about the group, but I gather it's a close-knit bunch. I thought you ought to know."

"Who's your boyfriend?" Slade asked.

"Parker Price."

"Very interesting," Slade said. "Apparently Shep has a better friend, but I'm not forgetting this screwing, no way."

Chapter 6

Thursday Morning, October 3, 1991.

EBC's anchorman arrived at Mike Ballard's office at a quarter past seven. Ballard was president and CEO of EBC News. The anchorman knew Ballard would come in at about seven-thirty, and he needed his help. He intended to find out why the Astoria district attorney had dropped the Lukarilla matter, and he wanted Susan Silver, EBC's best investigative reporter.

The anchorman knew Susan, but before he left work the night before he'd dug out her resumé. She was a New-Year's baby, born on January 1, 1956. She'd worked her way through NYU and got a degree in journalism, and then she served five tough years at the *Daily News* as a reporter, covering almost every beat. That's when television got her. She worked at WEBC, EBC's New York affiliate, for more than four years, joining the network in 1985. She'd been a rising star ever since.

When Ballard got off the elevator, the anchorman approached him. "Mike, I've got a problem. Last night on the *Evening Report* I got a little carried away and made a commitment that needs your support."

"I saw the program," Ballard said. "You sounded angry, but that's why you work for us. People like that. If you hadn't made that commitment, a follow-up wouldn't have had any impact, so don't apologize. But how can I help?"

"I want Susan Silver to do the investigation, and I know it takes you to get her on short notice."

"I'm not sure of that, but we'll see," he said. "I'll get her up here."

Susan was there in a matter of minutes. She wore a short navy skirt and an open-collar, white short-sleeve blouse. With her Mediterranean complexion and dark hair falling below her shoulders, she was a striking woman.

"Did you see his *Evening Report* last night?" Ballard asked.

"I sure did," she said.

"EBC News wants to do a follow-up investigation. Are you free?"

Without hesitation she replied, "You bet. When do I start?"

After Susan returned to her office, she turned to one of her mirrored walls and gave herself a high-five. "Just what I needed!" she said. She'd been getting bored with the regular EBC job. Her peak had been stirring up the Silex-Lovejoy expose. With the lawsuit that followed still working its way to trial, the proceedings were taking too much of her time. She was a reporter. She thrived on new projects, especially those involving women's rights. This one was made to order.

It took her about two weeks to organize her other work. She would need help in Portland, and Julius Sanchez, whom everyone called Julie, was her choice. They'd worked together since her days at the *Daily News*. He'd spent thirteen years with the NYPD, rising to the rank of detective, before the booze got to him. After several years of drifting nowhere with the bottle, a mission priest got to him, and Sanchez took the cure. Susan met him at the mission while she was investigating a lead that the mob was using the mission as a front for drug traffic. Sanchez set her straight. From his police days, he knew what the mob was doing and where it was doing it. He fed her the names of a couple of informers. The informers helped her with her story, and indebted, Susan convinced her boss to hire Sanchez as an investigator. The relationship grew from there.

Susan loved the way Sanchez operated. Slight and wiry, with a shadow mustache, tight curly hair and an angular face, he could fit in anywhere without attracting attention. Now in his mid-forties, he knew how to appear older or younger, depending upon the need. He fit in wherever Susan wanted him to pry.

⚥

Tuesday, October 15.

For the first trip to Portland, Susan decided to take Sanchez along. She called Amy McCormick at KPOR. McCormick told her that she'd done some preliminary investigation. She would fill Susan in when she arrived in Portland. McCormick agreed to arrange for working space and accommodations and to meet Susan and Sanchez at the airport.

The KPOR building was located on the west side of the Willamette River in a district called John's Landing. Once inside, McCormick told Susan and Sanchez that she'd identified the catering company and the waitresses. The company, West Portland Catering, was located nearby. The waitresses' names were Virginia Lane, Peggy House, and Tina Marcellas.

Susan explained their plans. "Julie and I are going to split up. I want to do interviews with the caterer, and Julie's going to concentrate on Chalmers, the Lukarillas, and the DA. He'll stay here in Oregon after I leave and do more legwork.

"While I contact the caterer, can you tell Julie what you know about Chalmers and the Lukarillas?"

"Sure," McCormick answered, and she took Sanchez into her office.

After they left, Susan picked up the telephone and called West Portland Catering. Marlene Smyth answered the phone. "Ms. Smyth, I'm Susan Silver of Empire Broadcasting Company. I'm here in Portland investigating the problem at the Lukarillas' retreat last September. I need to talk to the waitresses involved. Can you help me locate them?"

"Just call me Marlene," she answered. "Sure, in fact, Ginny's here right now, and Peg and Tina are due in at about four. Come on over. They'll talk to you."

Susan and Amy McCormick arrived at West Portland Catering just before three. They parked in front, and as they entered the front door, a bell sounded somewhere in the back of the building. In a few minutes a stocky middle-aged woman appeared through the door that accessed the back of the building.

"I'm Marlene," she said.

"Hi," Susan responded, "I'm Susan Silver, and this is Amy McCormick from KPOR."

"Glad to meet you. You don't know how happy I am that someone's finally looking into this terrible mess. We told the newspaper and the cops about it, but the DA just pushed us aside. Fuckin' little peas in a pod is what we are against those big shots. Come on back here. I've got the girls waiting to meet you."

She led them to the back of the building. "Girls," she said, "meet Susan and Amy. They're the ones from the TV station I told you about. They wanna talk to you about the Lukarillas and what happened." She introduced Ginny Lane, Peggy House and Tina Marcellas.

Ginny Lane was in her early thirties. Plain, but attractive, she had straight brown hair and was about average height and weight, with a big bust and stocky legs. She was Jane Doe on the television broadcast. Peggy House was much smaller, younger and prettier. Her hair was bleached blonde and cut short. She had a good figure. She was Rita Roe. Tina Marcellas was Hispanic and was thin and taller than the other two, about five-seven. In her early twenties, she was Linda Loe.

Susan explained that she wanted to interview them about what happened last September. She asked if they objected to her recording the interviews.

They did not.

Susan talked to each woman separately, starting with Ginny and ending with Tina. Amy McCormick just listened.

What they said conformed to what they would later say on the Dorothy Watters show in December.

Finally, Susan interviewed Marlene. After the individual interviews were completed, Susan talked to them all together. "EBC's investigation is continuing, and I'll be back later to video interviews with you. Have you talked to a lawyer about this?"

"Marlene told us we should," Ginny replied, "but we don't want to. Yeah, we're mad and pissed off, but we're big girls, and we don't want trouble. These guys got lots of money, lawyers and probably even hoods to back 'em up. We don't want no part of that. Besides, we're scared of courts, and we can't afford a lawyer, anyhow. Ain't that right, girls?"

Peg and Tina nodded.

Susan didn't like Ginny's answer. "You're being too hasty. It's a lot easier than you think. Yes, they're powerful men, but this is the nineteen-nineties. The courts have grown up. The laws have changed. Men don't get away with harassing women anymore, no matter how important they are. All kinds of women, just like you, have taken guys like this to court and won lots of money as payback for being treated like you were. You've got a hell of a case. It could be worth millions. Most lawyers won't charge you a thing, unless they get you some money, and then they'll take a cut. Listen to Marlene, go see a lawyer, and have the lawyer call me. I think we can help. Okay?"

"You make it sound okay, but I don't know no lawyers," Peg said.

Ginny added, "'Cept for divorce lawyers, none of us do."

Marlene spoke up. "Well, I do. I know just the guy. He got me a big settlement when an asshole hit me with his Caddie. I wasn't even hurt that much. Oscar Bellows, that's his name. Like Susan said, he didn't charge me a dime till he got me the settlement. Then he took a percent."

"Maybe we'll call him," Ginny said.

"You do that," Susan said. "Thanks for your time. Here's my card." She handed one to each of them. "If you think of anything more, please call me. We won't be filming interviews for several weeks, but call if you want to talk. Also tell your lawyer to call me. Marlene, could I talk to you some more before I leave?"

The girls left, and Susan asked Marlene about Chalmers and the Lukarillas.

"West Portland catered retreats for Chalmers when Bill Lattanzi owned it," Marlene said. "I bought him out last June and got the job, although at the time Chalmers didn't know about the change of ownership. Other than that, I can't tell you anything more about Chalmers or the Lukarillas."

Susan asked, "How did the police get involved?"

"After the girls came back to our cabin Sunday night, Ginny wanted to go to Mr. Chalmers for help. I told her no. I was convinced the three men weren't about to say anything, at least right away, so I told the girls to keep quiet until we got out of there on Monday. We did some planning, and that seemed to compose them. We decided to serve breakfast in the morning, as if nothing had happened, then clean up and leave.

"As soon as we got out of there, we headed toward the coast, looking for the police. As it turned out, we spotted a sheriff's patrol car at the bottom of the big hill where there's a road going off to Saddle Mountain State Park. Later someone told me that there's always a cop there because people come off that hill doing a pretty clip. Anyway, we stopped and told the deputy what had happened. He had us follow him to a sheriff's office, where he took the girls' statements."

Susan thanked Marlene and left.

When Susan got to the Marriott, she called Sanchez's room. He'd left a message to meet him in the bar, which she did. Susan filled him in and asked, "What did you find out?"

He told her some history about the Chalmers family and their lumber operation that he'd gotten from the KPOR files and those at the local paper, *The Oregonian*. "I talked to a guy at the newspaper. Earl's his name. Your old boss at the *Daily News* gave me the introduction. Earl told me they got the story when Marlene Smyth called them on September twenty-fourth. They printed it and gave it to the AP. Then television took over. There may be more, though.

Earl said they were at the DA's press conference. Afterwards, one of their reporters approached a secretary in the DA's office. She acted afraid to talk. The reporter wanted to know why the DA gave up so easy. She still wouldn't talk. He kept pressing, and she said, 'Maybe you should ask Chalmers.'"

"Did he give you the name of the secretary?" Susan asked.

"Yup, I got it, Beth Erickson."

"I won't say any more," Susan said. "I know where you're headed."

⚥

Wednesday, October 16.

The next morning Susan was on her way back to New York, and Sanchez was off to the Oregon Coast. He didn't leave Portland until early afternoon, however. He spent the morning at *The Oregonian*, going through old newspapers. Then he headed west on Highway 26, arriving in Astoria three hours later. It usually took a little over two hours from Portland to Astoria, but Sanchez took a detour. He wanted to see where the retreat had been held. The site of the Lukarillas' camp was just a few miles off the highway, about sixty miles out of Portland. Amy McCormick mapped the route for him. She told him to turn left on an unnumbered road, just before the little town of Elsie.

As was usual for Oregon in early October, the day was sunny and mild. The highway traveled through the Coast Range Mountains. The fall colors made the mountains a beautiful sight to behold.

When Sanchez got to Elsie, he knew he'd missed the turn, so he backtracked, found it and made a right turn. The road followed the picturesque Nehalem River south, and about seven miles later he spotted the camp on the right next to the river. On the map, it was just beyond a town called Lukarilla, but the town was no longer there. No one seemed to be around. There was a chain across a gravel driveway. He parked alongside the road, stepped over the chain and entered the property. There were no signs of any kind. That was true throughout the property. The camp consisted of seven buildings, all constructed the same: one story with pitched, wood-shingled roofs. The exteriors were wood in natural color. Each building had a brick chimney and a wood-decked porch. The largest building was clearly a mess hall. Through its windows he could see a restaurant-style kitchen and a rectangular room with long tables stacked against the far wall. It had a larger chimney than the rest.

Another building was distinct. It resembled a more permanent residence, larger, but designed the same. It was divided into several rooms, one of which was its own kitchen. He bet that it was where Chalmers lived. The other five buildings were identical, and he learned, after peering through their windows, that they were sleeping cabins, each with three bedrooms, two bathrooms and a living area. Near the river was an additional building, a barn. It actually looked more like a stable, but there were no animals around. The stable look was enhanced by several natural wood corrals. A quaint dock stretched out into the river, and several boats were hung from davits, dry-docked above the water.

Looking around, he noticed that the grounds were well maintained, the wild grass was cut and the remains of annual flowers were still growing neatly in beds. An open area with benches, surrounding a large fire pit, looked like a picnic area in a park. An exception, however, was the lack of any apparatus for youngsters.

When Sanchez finally got to Astoria, it was approaching evening, so he decided to first find a place to stay and to then scout around. He found a motel near the waterfront, just east of the bridge that spans the river and carries Coast Highway 101 over into Washington. He pulled off the highway, went into the office and registered.

Around five Sanchez walked over to the motel office and asked for directions to the nearest bar. He wanted a drink, but more important, he needed to rub elbows with some locals. He was directed to The Ship Inn, a restaurant and lounge, about three blocks east and one block north, and directly on the water. He followed the easy directions and went into the lounge, taking a seat at the bar. As the name suggested, the décor was aboard ship. The lounge was enclosed, but the restaurant looked out over the Columbia River's wide mouth. He ordered a Bud Light. It wasn't long before he'd isolated a conversation between a couple of old-timers to his right. They were discussing whether there'd be a commercial salmon season the coming year.

"I hope you don't mind my interruption," Sanchez said to the man closest to him, "but why wouldn't you have a salmon season?"

The man didn't mind at all, and before long Sanchez was being educated. "In recent years," the man said, "the Injun's fishing rights and them environment people have nearly wiped out the fishing industry down here. There's only so many fish, and the commercials don't get no priority. But say, the way yah talk, I betcha come from the East Coast. What'cha doing way out here in this dead old town?"

"You're right, I'm a New Yorker," Sanchez replied, "and I guess I sound like one. I'm a history buff, and right now I'm into courts. I'm doing research, hoping to write a book about historic courthouses across the country. I've been in Oregon about two weeks now examining, taking notes and photographing some classics. I was told you've got a real old one right here in Astoria that dates back to the early nineteen hundreds. So I drove down from Portland this afternoon to take a look."

"Sure do," the other local agreed. "It's 'bout six blocks from here on Commercial between Seventh and Eighth."

"Thanks! I'll get over there and check it out. I'd like to talk to someone who's spent some years around it and can tell me some of its lore. You know anyone like that?"

"Sure do, Beth Erickson'd be the one," he replied. "She's worked at the courthouse for better than sixty years. Started working there for her grandpappy, old Judge Erickson, when she was jest a teenager. T'was back in the thirties. She's in her eighties now, but she's still on the payroll. They list her as a secretary, I think. She's a landmark, knows everything, 'cept what she's forgot. She's usually in here by now," he added. "Comes in almost every day after work. Likes her booze. She lives over the store on the corner, a few blocks from here."

The name rang a bell. Sanchez remembered that was the name Earl at the paper had given him. "She sounds perfect," he said. "If she comes in, introduce me. My name's Julie Sanchez."

The first local chuckled. "That sounds like a gal's name," he said.

Sanchez was used to the kidding. "Yeah," he said. "That's what my folks called me when I was little, and it stuck. But it's probably better than Julius, which is what it's short for."

They continued talking for another twenty minutes or so, when Beth showed up. She came into the lounge, hung up her blue raincoat and came right to the bar. Except for her black laced working shoes, she was dressed mostly in gray, a pleated skirt and a cardigan sweater with a white silk blouse peeking out in front.

The guy closest to Sanchez called her over. "Beth, there's a guy here we'd like yah to meet. This here is Julie. He's from New York. He's writing about old courthouses and wants the low-down on ours. We told him where it is, and that you're the one knows most about it."

"There ain't much I don't know about it," she said. "You're right about that. Glad to know yah. I'll perch right here next to yah. That way yah'll be on my good side. Hearing, you know," she said, pointing to her left ear.

"Nice to know you, as well. What'll you have to drink? It's on me," Sanchez said.

"Mike," she said to the bartender. "The usual. This fella says he's buying."

They talked for more than an hour. Sanchez started by telling her what he was doing and looking for. That set her off. During that hour, he heard a lifetime of stories about the old courthouse and its occupants.

When she paused to begin her fourth drink, Sanchez decided to get more pointed. "You know so much about the history of this region, maybe you can tell me about a place I saw on the way down here." He described how beautiful the scenery was on the trip down, and how he decided to go off the main highway to look around. He told her about the road near Elsie, the river the road followed, and the camp he came upon. "It's magnificent in there, those quaint cabins, the huge trees, and the river. Where was I, what is that place?"

"No doubt about it," she replied. "It's the Lukarillas' camp. With all the news and stuff, I'd think you'd heard of that."

"I don't recall that I have."

"Well, it's a camp that belongs to Hugh Chalmers. He's one of the richest timber guys in these parts. Was a big scandal up there 'round the end of September. Hit the papers and national TV. Three women claim they got molested by three of Hugh's buddies. They's part of a bunch that call themselves the Lukarillas. The gals say they got raped. Camp's in our county, so the charges came to the courthouse we've been talking 'bout. But the DA wouldn't press charges, and that really pissed off the press."

"What do you mean, he wouldn't press charges?" Sanchez asked. "Why not?"

By now Beth was a bit looser than she would have been had this conversation been going while she was on the job at the courthouse. "He told 'em he was dropping charges at a press conference 'bout a week after them gals complained."

"I don't get it. What happened?"

"Well, as I told you, I work in the DA's office. Not much goes on in there I don't know something 'bout. I probably shouldn't say this, but you're not from 'round here, so what the hell. Day before the press conference, a couple of slick-looking guys in courtroom suits spent an hour or so behind closed doors with the DA. Whatever business they was on didn't last past that day, 'cause I never saw 'em again."

"That's strange," Sanchez agreed. "You've got my interest up. Is the DA's file public?"

"Sure is. Want to see it?"

"I don't know, maybe."

"Well, you'll be comin' over to see the courthouse tomorrow. You can't miss me when you're walking around. My desk's right inside the DA's office on the second floor.

Gimme a holler. The file's closed and stored, but I'll get it, and you can take a look."

"Thanks. Want another?"

"Nope. I gotta walk home," she said. "I'd better get going. I gotta get sompen else in this belly. See yah tomorrow. And thanks for the drinks." She got up and staggered out the door.

"Don't worry about her," the guy to Sanchez's right said. "She just had her usual."

Thursday morning, October 17.

Sanchez drove east from the motel, and as he turned off Commercial on Seventh he saw the courthouse. Constructed of stone in 1904, it occupied a full city block. He parked and went in the back entrance. Then he toured the building, took some pictures and made sure everyone thought he was doing a thorough examination.

Inside, the floors were marble, and the plaster walls and ceilings were framed with decorative local lumber, stained brown. The clerk's office and the tax department were on the first floor. The main courtroom and the district attorney's offices were on the second.

Sanchez went up to the district attorney's office. Beth was seated at a desk in the reception area. He told her he'd decided to look at the file.

She paused for a moment, almost forgetting that she'd extended the invitation. Then she took him down to the clerk's office, found the file and left him with it. "When you're done, just leave it on the counter," she said.

He examined the file carefully. It contained the complaint from Virginia Lane, Peggy House and Tina Marcellas, with short statements of each attached, and summaries of four telephone interviews with Chalmers, Lovejoy, Sumas and Shepard. Lovejoy, Sumas and Shepard didn't deny that they'd had sex with the women, but they claimed it was consensual. That was all, no investigator's report or correspondence. Sanchez took notes and left. He checked out of his motel, drove to Portland and caught the red-eye back to New York.

Chapter 7

Wednesday morning, October 16.

"Well, what's this all about?" Amanda Johnson asked Ginny, Peg and Tina. Amanda was a lawyer in her early forties. She was seated behind her desk, and Herb Goodman, her investigator, sat beside her.

Peg and Tina looked at Ginny, expecting her to start.

"As Marlene told you," Ginny said, "we work for her at West Portland Catering, and when we were on a job in the mountains last month three guys raped us." She told Amanda the details of what had happened that Sunday night, becoming agitated as she proceeded. "And no matter what anyone else says, we're not hookers. We didn't go up there to get laid. Marlene would can us if we got involved with the customers."

"That's a good start," Amanda said. "By the way, this is Herb Goodwin, our investigator. I practice with a partner, Oscar Bellows, and we specialize in representing people like you in lawsuits. We do personal injury cases and criminal work. We've both had lots of trial experience. And so we know how to take care of ordinary people who got fucked by the establishment. Now, I want to talk to each of you separately. Let's start with you, Ginny. You two wait out in the reception area," she said to Peg and Tina.

"I want to know something about your background," Amanda said to Ginny, "where you come from, how you've been employed, your social life and marital status, things like that."

"Well, I was born and raised in Southern California, Glendale. I've been married twice, no kids. I never graduated from high school, as I had to work. I worked mostly in bars and did some bit parts in the movies, until I got into catering. I moved up here to work for Marlene."

"That's enough," Amanda said. "I'll get more details on a questionnaire I'll have you fill out if you decide to hire us. Had you ever met any of these men before?"

"Not the ones who raped us, but I knew two of the others, Max Pepper and Park Price. They were at some of the parties I catered in Newport Beach."

"Did you socialize or spend time with them at the retreat?"

"No, other than to say 'hello' and things like that."

"Were there any witnesses to what happened Sunday night?"

"No."

Amanda's questions of the other two were along the same lines. She recorded the conversations, and then she brought all three back together.

"I understand the Clatsop County District Attorney looked into this, is that right?" Amanda asked.

Ginny said, "That son-of-a-bitch, he didn't do a damn thing!"

"Didn't he take your statements?"

"Yeah, if you can call it that. Monday we reported what happened to a sheriff's deputy in Seaside. A woman there gave us a form to fill out. Said it was a complaint. She gave us each a sheet labeled Statement and told us to write out a brief description of what happened. She emphasized to make it brief, 'cause it all had to go on that one sheet. That's all. We never saw the DA, never talked to him, just the deputy and that woman in the sheriff's office."

Amanda was astounded. "That's hard to believe."

"Well, it's the truth, damn it," Peg shouted at her. "When is someone going to believe us?"

"Take it easy," Amanda said. "I meant it's hard to believe what the DA did." Then she explained what being their lawyer meant, and what she and Bellows would do if they got hired. "We'd handle the case on the basis of a contingent fee. That means that you don't owe us anything unless we collect you some money. We'll take a third of whatever we get for you as our fee. The details are all on these printed papers that I'm handing you. Read them carefully, and after you've done that, if you decide you want to hire us, sign on the line at the end and date it. You can read those here and make your decision, or you can take them with you and let us know later what you want to do."

All three were ready to go. Again Ginny was the spokesperson. "We'll read and sign now."

They did, although how much they read and understood was questionable.

After the agreements were signed, Amanda asked, "Is there anything else I should know, before we get started on this?"

Tina looked at the other two and asked, "Shouldn't we tell her about the EBC gal?"

"What EBC gal?" Amanda asked.

Tina told her about the meeting the day before with Susan Silver, and she gave Amanda Susan's card. "She told us to tell our lawyer to call her, that she would help."

"Thanks, I'm glad you told me. We'll need all the help we can get. I'll call her." Then speaking to all three of them, Amanda said, "I want you to know you did the right thing, coming here. You can't let men get away with abuse like this. If the authorities won't do anything about it, then the only way left is to sue and make them pay big dollars for what they did. That's our job.

"We'll do some investigation and put together a complaint. That's how a lawsuit starts." Amanda knew, however, that to make a credible case in court, the women had to have sustained some damage, so she told them, "But there's something more you need to do. I know this whole thing has been very upsetting. Attacks like this can cause shock and damage your system. I wouldn't be surprised if you've had some real nightmares since this happened. You need to see a doctor and get counseling. Here's a card for Dr. Bentley. She specializes in these kinds of problems. I want each of you to call her and make an appointment. I'll write her a letter introducing you and telling her what this is all about. She needs to see you before we can file your complaint, so try to get an appointment within the next couple of weeks. Okay?"

What Amanda said made sense, so they agreed and thanked her. After arriving scared to death, they left "ready to take the bastards on."

After they left, Amanda called EBC in New York. Susan Silver was out, so Amanda left her name and number and a message that she was a lawyer representing Ginny Lane, Peg House and Tina Marcellas. Then she dictated a letter to Dr. Martha Bentley. Dr. Bentley practiced "forensic psychology," jargon for a Ph.D. who treats patients involved in lawsuits.

Wednesday afternoon.

That afternoon, Susan called Amanda back. "Thanks for calling," Susan said, and she explained how she and EBC had gotten involved and what they'd done and were doing in their investigation of the women's complaints against the Lukarilla members. "Something about what happened stinks," she added. "Behind the Lukarillas and the attacks on your clients may be a major story. I can feel it in my bones. Whether our investigation will help you, I can't say, but I thought we should talk and work together."

"I couldn't agree more," Amanda replied. "And we want all the help we can get. I know we'll be up against a lot of high-priced lawyers. They'll try to dry us up financially, but we've been through that before. Anyway, what do you propose?"

"A lawsuit by the girls could be a big help to us," Susan replied. "You can get discovery, and what you learn can open doors for our investigator. What we find could be bombshells for your case. Here's where I see this going. We'll finish our initial investigation in a few weeks. Then we'll go on the air with a special report. I've got enough material right now, but I want a report from my investigator, and we need to do video interviews with your clients. We should be ready to air the report no later than early December. We'd like you to lay low until after that show. Then hit them with a big-dollar complaint and a demand for information. We'll help you with the demand. When they give you the information, our investigator will go to work. The only problem I see is how we keep what we're doing for each other confidential. We don't want the Lukarillas or their lawyers to know we're talking, much less cooperating. Do you have any ideas?"

"I think I do," Amanda answered. "We don't want your cooperation exposed in the lawsuit either. What if you hire us as your local lawyers in connection with your investigation of the Lukarillas? Then we can claim that our communications are confidential under the lawyer-client privilege. If your fees coincidently help us to serve certain other clients, so be it. You get the drift?"

"I sure do," Susan answered. "You're hired, subject to my boss firing me. Send me what you propose for a fee agreement. Our legal guys will make some modifications, I'm sure, they always do, but I don't see why we can't start working right now, if that's okay with you."

"Fine. What's next?"

"Videotaping your clients and Marlene at West Portland Catering. I'll be in touch probably on Monday to set it up. We'll probably do it through KPOR. Incidentally, Amy McCormick is our contact there, so she may be calling you. When I find out what my investigator has been up to, we'll decide if there's more videotaping needed. You go ahead with plans for the lawsuit, but hold up filing. Call me immediately if any problems arise, and I'll do likewise."

Chapter 8

Thursday morning, October 17.

EBC's legal department was on the thirty-second floor. Susan left the elevator and went directly to Mike Clarke's office, where she found him immersed in a pile of papers. She sat, and he pushed the papers aside. She told him what transpired in Oregon and asked, "What can we do to help them?"

"Get them together with the trial lawyers at Levinson & Wood," he replied. "They'll know what the complaint should say. Fashioning discovery for a case like this is right up their alley. These facts call for more than just a sexual assault complaint. We need to see what an expert would put in there."

Levinson & Wood was a large New York City law firm Susan had worked with before. They were EBC's outside lawyers.

"Great idea, Mike," Susan said. "I always know when I come up here that I'll leave better off. Who should I call there?"

"Either Matt Lipinski or Ryan O'Donnell. You know them from the Silex Petroleum case. I'll see if I can get one of them right now."

O'Donnell answered the call. Clarke put him on a speakerphone and said, "Susan Silver's in my office, she needs your help with a lawsuit out in Oregon. It involves several sexual assaults by some high-profile men that EBC had been investigating. The women have a lawyer, and they're going to sue the men and get discovery that Susan hopes will help EBC's investigation. One of the men is our old friend Alexander Lovejoy. The men all belong to an exclusive Oregon group called the Lukarillas, and Susan wants to find out who else belongs to the group."

"My, my," O'Donnell said. "Why don't I come over to EBC and talk to Susan today?"

"That's fine," Susan said. "Come over anytime after lunch."

When they met, O'Donnell started the conversation. "After Mike called, I checked Oregon procedure and found it doesn't allow interrogatories in state court. So, if they file the case in state court, they'll have a devil of a time getting information, such as names of witnesses, or in this case the names of the members of the Lukarillas. The lawsuit would be a lot better off in federal court, where you can get that information. Also, the lawyer I talked to says that the judges in the federal court are tougher and less likely to get pushed around by expensive lawyers, like Lovejoy and his buddies will have.

"The question is, how do we get the case into federal court? That could be a problem. The usual way to get private litigation there is by diversity of citizenship. That means that the plaintiffs and defendants are from different states. If one plaintiff and one defendant are from the same state, there's no diversity. You don't have it here, because we have Oregon plaintiffs and at least one potential Oregon defendant, the Lukarillas. If you only sued Lovejoy and his buddies, leaving the Lukarillas out, then the case could be brought in federal court, but I don't think you want to leave the Lukarillas out. The real potential for this case could well revolve around that group. Also, you need that defendant in to get the discovery you want. So, we need to come up with some other way to get to federal court. Other ways to make a federal case are if the case concerns a constitutional question or if a federal statute's involved. Now, I've got an idea, but I need to do some research before I suggest it, and I'll need more of the facts. Do we have time?"

"A little," she answered. "I've got statements from the women and their boss, and I'll give you copies before you leave. Do your research. But we should call the Oregon lawyer and let her know what we're doing. Then maybe you can work directly with her to set this case up right."

"Good idea."

Susan put her phone on speaker and dialed Amanda Johnson's direct number. Amanda answered.

"Amanda, I'm on a speakerphone," Susan said, "and I've got a friend with me who's a lawyer with a big firm here in New York. He's Ryan O'Donnell. I'm filling Ryan in on your case, and he has some ideas. I think it might be a good idea for the two of you to chat."

"Wonderful," Amanda responded. "Hi, Ryan."

"Hello, Amanda," Ryan said and then he explained his ideas. "Give me your number, and I'll call you directly after we've finished our research."

⚥

Tuesday, October 22.

O'Donnell called Amanda. "I've got good news. You're clients have a civil rights case," he said. "Those statutes provide for a private right of action and give the federal court jurisdiction. According to your clients, the sexual assaults were made in connection with threats to have them charged with prostitution. That amounts to depriving them of their civil rights under color of a statute, which would violate the Civil Rights Act. It might sound like a stretch, but it's enough to get federal jurisdiction. You can throw in a conspiracy claim to get the Lukarillas in the middle of it. Why don't you let us draft a complaint, setting up the theories, and FedEx it out to you? After you've looked it over, call me and we'll talk some more."

"Great," Amanda replied. "I'll look forward to receiving it. We'll review it and get back to you right away."

"I don't want to be presumptuous," O'Donnell added, "but I'll also give initial discovery some thought and send along a draft of some suggestions in that area too?"

"Wonderful, we can use all the help you can give us."

⚥

Tuesday, November 12

The drafts of a complaint, a few interrogatories and twenty-three requests for documents arrived at Amanda's office by Federal Express. The interrogatories were simple, seeking the names and pertinent information about the present and past members of the Lukarillas. The requests for documents were addressed to each defendant. They were much broader. They requested that the defendants produce anything they had that related to the retreats, and their contacts with each other, other Lukarilla members or the plaintiffs. They also wanted copies of organizational documents of the Lukarillas and financial records of all defendants.

Not surprisingly, the complaint, the interrogatories and the requests for documents filed by Amanda in December contained almost the identical language of these drafts.

Tuesday, December 10.

Susan called Amanda. "Did you see the *Evening Report* on Friday?"

Amanda had been expecting the call. "We sure did," she said. "Great job. We can hardly wait to get going out here."

"Wait for at least a week. That'll give the program a chance to sink in. The two-week gap will allow the complaint to make its own news. It won't be just an afterthought of the program."

"That fits perfectly with our plans, because I'm waiting to hear from the girls' doctor, and I can't file until I hear her findings," Amanda said. "I'm sure she's seen them and will give me preliminary thoughts about their psychological damage, so I'll call her today. Why don't we target filing it on Thursday, the nineteenth? Thursday's a good news day out here."

"That's just fine. I assume you have all you need for now from the New York lawyers."

"We do. They did a great job."

Amanda called Dr. Bentley. She was seeing patients.

"Please have her call me," Amanda told the receptionist, "and tell her I'm calling about Ginny Lane, Peggy House and Tina Marcellas."

Wednesday, December 11.

When Dr. Bentley returned the call, Amanda asked, "Tell me about your examinations of Ginny Lane, Peg House and Tina Marcellas."

"I saw them separately on Tuesday, November twelfth," Dr. Bentley began. "You told me you didn't want a written report at this time, so I'll read and paraphrase from my notes.

"I took histories, which confirmed pretty much what you told me in your letter. I examined each of them and performed some tests. In varying degrees, they all have feelings of humiliation and degradation as a result of the events, and they're extremely depressed. They each express anger and frustration, a desire for revenge, guilt, and some shame at their loss of control. Again in varying degrees, they all complained of nightmares, of general disturbance of their sleep patterns and of impairment of concentration and memory. Their symptoms are consistent with the diagnosis of post-traumatic stress disorder. My prognosis is that some of these symptoms in each of these patients will be chronic and require an indefinite course of treatment and counseling. Some of these symptoms may well be permanent in nature.

"In serious cases like these, the patients should also have the benefit of a psychiatrist, so I had them seen by Alan Schapiro. He agrees with my diagnosis, and we developed a course of treatment. You might want to talk to Dr. Schapiro yourself.

"Your clients will require treatment for at least the next several months. I have set up a series of counseling sessions with each of them. After those sessions, I can probably give you a better prognosis for their chances of recovery."

"Thank you, Dr. Bentley," Amanda said. "I appreciate your prompt response. I'll check back with you next spring."

Chapter 9

Thursday afternoon, December 19.

The complaint was filed in federal court in Portland. The plaintiffs were identified as Virginia Lane, Peggy House and Tina Marcellas. Lionel Shepard, Abraham Sumas, Alexander Lovejoy, and the Lukarillas were named as defendants. The case was assigned civil number 91-5067LL.

Friday morning, December 20

Barry picked up *The Oregonian* from his front porch and began reading as he walked toward the kitchen, where his breakfast was waiting. Once seated at the kitchen table, he spotted the headline at the bottom of the first page, "U.S. Senator Charged with sexual assault." The story that followed confirmed that it was The Lukarillas matter. He grabbed the phone and called Chalmers at his condo in the Portland Center. "Have you seen the paper?" he asked.

"I have now," Chalmers replied, "but not before I answered the front door a little while ago and was greeted by a US marshal with a summons and the complaint. It's the shits! They want a million apiece and a hundred million in punitive damages. How the hell they think they can get that from the Lukarillas is beyond me. I'm about to leave, should I bring the papers by your office?"

"Yes. I'll leave right now. Wait for me, if you get there first."

About fifteen minutes later, Barry and Chalmers were sitting in Barry's office while Barry read the complaint. It was a standard federal complaint, not a lot of facts, just legal conclusions. It charged that the plaintiffs were victims of rape and sodomy, and it made claims against the defendants for assault and battery, sexual discrimination, and violations of their civil rights. It also alleged a conspiracy. It claimed the Lukarillas were liable for negligence. Each plaintiff claimed mental suffering and permanent post-traumatic stress disorder as a result of the defendants' wrongful acts. In addition to the damages Chalmers had mentioned, the complaint asked to have defendants pay plaintiffs' attorney fees. Amanda Johnson signed the complaint.

After Barry finished with the complaint, he looked at the rest of the papers. As he expected, there were some interrogatories and a number of requests for documents. Before he could explain, Chalmers asked him, "I know what rape and sodomy are, but what's assault and battery got to do with it?"

"That's the technical legal term," Barry said. "It means an unwanted touching. That's what rape is, but sodomy, that could go either way. The civil rights claim is a real stretch. Rape and sodomy aren't what Congress had in mind when it passed the Civil Rights Laws. They do make a colorable showing of a violation, however, when they allege that they were forced to give sex by threats to turn them in for prostitution. That claim's probably there to get them into federal court and to get attorneys' fees as damages.

"The claim against the Lukarillas is a little troubling. You see that they claim you hired women to cater the retreat when you knew, or should have known, that they would be subjected to unwanted sexual attacks and that you were negligent in not supervising the retreat to ensure that improper sexual attacks would not occur. Do they know something about some of your members' pasts?"

"That's a bunch of crap," Chalmers replied. "These guys aren't sex maniacs. I've never heard of any of them having problems like this."

"All right, but this complaint looks like there's more to this lawsuit than the emotional distress of the waitresses. Maybe Sugerman's right. There may be a larger agenda here than rape and sodomy. These discovery requests seem to bear that out. Did you look at them?" Barry asked Chalmers, showing him the discovery requests.

"Yeah, do we have to give them names of the members?" Chalmers asked.

"Probably, but let's not worry about that now. When Becky gets in, we'll try to get a conference call with the other lawyers. Then she'll get back in touch with you about those requests and what you have to give them."

"I can tell you right now, we don't have most of what they want," Chalmers said as he was leaving.

When Becky arrived, Barry gave her a copy of the complaint and discovery requests. "These were served this morning. We knew the lawsuit was coming. Set up a conference call with Joan Dixon, Paul Shumanski and Lou Miles. I'm sure their clients have aroused them, so they should be reachable. I'll call Amanda, tell her we've got the complaint and see if I can get us some extra time to respond."

After Becky left, Barry called Amanda.

"Hello," she answered.

"This is Barry O'Shea at Swift, Wyman & Wiggins. I've been retained by the Lukarillas in the lawsuit you just filed."

"Glad to have you aboard," Amanda replied.

"I've read the complaint. What's it all about?"

"The three girls came to see us about a month ago," she said. "They'd had a problem at your client's retreat back in September. Several of the members got out of hand and raped them. We sent them for some counseling. When they came back earlier this month, they wanted to sue, so we took the case, and you've read the rest."

Barry had been told that Amanda Johnson liked to make her opponents dig and scratch with court discovery to learn what was going on. He knew that tactic wouldn't help either side. He'd learned long ago that free exchange of facts saved clients money and made a case easier to resolve, so he decided to give it a try. "Yeah," he said, "but you must have had more than that before filing. Tell me who you've talked to and what you've learned."

"Sure we looked into it," she answered. "However, at the present time I'm not at liberty to tell you more. After we get the stuff we've asked your client for, maybe I can expand. We'll see."

She wants to play hardball, he thought. "All right," he said, "then let's talk about what you've asked for. It's way too broad. Narrow it down. Tell us what you really want. I'm sure you don't want to bother the judge with haggling over discovery, so let's try to work together. Why don't you drop me a line, setting forth your realistic needs? Then I'll let you know what we can and can't give you.

"Also we'll need the usual indefinite extension to answer both the complaint and the request for documents, so confirm that you agree to it in the letter."

"Frankly, I think the request is pretty well worded, and we want what we've asked for," she countered. "I'll write you the letter and try to cooperate, but don't think by doing so I am waiving what's in the request. From what I've learned, some of your client's members are pretty nasty guys. Nasty guys are likely to have nasty lawyers, and I don't want to get run over by them. Furthermore, I can't give you an indefinite extension on the request. You can hold off answering it until after I write the letter and you respond. But, if we can't work things out that way, I want the request answered in thirty days. Since we're in federal court, you'd better send me a stipulation for an extension of time to answer the complaint that we can file with the court. With all of these parties involved, I don't want that to be indefinite either, so make it for sixty days."

Barry really couldn't ask for more, but he didn't want Amanda to think she'd satisfied him. "I guess that's the best we can do for now, but please reconsider and tell us what you know. The more we both know about what's going on, the better we can resolve this matter for our clients. By the way, have you heard from any other lawyers?"

"I haven't," she replied.

Barry said, "Well, I have, and I'll be talking to them soon. I'll tell them what we've agreed upon and that they have the same extensions. We'll prepare the stipulation for everyone and put February fourteenth in it for the date to answer. It'll be your Valentine."

"Very funny," she said. "The date's fine."

"I'll look for your letter," Barry said.

⚤

The conference call was set for noon West Coast time. Before they placed the call Barry met with Becky to set an agenda. "We need to take the lead in preparing the case," Barry said. "You know the reasons. Plaintiffs' lawyers are local, so we're in the best position to deal with them. The same is true for the judge and the jury, when we get into the courtroom. If we take the lead in developing the facts, my experience tells me that we'll keep that position throughout the case. We've already started that, so let's plan to stay in charge as we talk with the other lawyers."

"I'm fine with that," Becky said.

"Then I'm going to suggest to the lawyers that we have an early face-to-face meeting and that it be here in our offices," Barry continued. "I've reviewed my calendar, and with the holidays coming up, I suggest we try for January seventh. How does that strike you?"

"That day is fine," she replied.

"Okay, but we need more investigation before the meeting, and I want us to do it. You should interview the Larsons, and someone should visit the DA's office in Astoria. You know about my wife's friend Pam Hall. She's the best *sub rosa* investigator around. I'll get her to do some background work on the waitresses, Marlene Smyth, Bill Lattanzi and West Portland Catering."

After Becky agreed, he said, "Let's get the lawyers on the phone."

Joan Dixon, Paul Shumanski and Lou Miles were all on the line and the speakerphone was connected. The call proceeded just as Barry had planned. The meeting in his office on January seventh was agreed to, and the other lawyers were happy to have Barry and Becky continuing with the investigations.

"Don't forget the document request responses are due by February fourteenth," Barry said. "We'll plan to work on those at the meeting."

Becky went back to her office. It was smaller and just two away from Barry's on the east side of the building. She called Chalmers, but he was out. She made an appointment with his secretary for Saturday morning, and she told the secretary that she would fax a brief agenda of what she wanted to talk about. She turned to her computer and prepared the fax with the agenda and confirming the appointment. In it she told Chalmers to gather together everything he had responsive to plaintiffs' discovery request so they could discuss responses at the meeting.

Barry called home. "Hi, honey," he said. "I need Pam Hall's help on the Lukarilla case. We need her to do some background investigation on the plaintiffs and the catering people. Please find her and get her on board right away. I'll bring written instructions for her home tonight."

Pam Hall was an investigator whom Barry's mentor, Elmer Wiggens, first discovered before Barry joined the firm. Actually, Barry's wife, Sarah, was the one who told Wiggens about Hall and the service she was developing. Sarah was Wiggen's secretary then. Hall specialized in *sub rosa* work, but she demanded total anonymity. She would not testify, and in fact would not identify herself in person to her clients. She used Sarah as her contact with all clients.

She claimed that her incognito approach to interviews relaxed the interviewee and made it easier to discover the truth. Over the years Wiggens found this was so. Barry and Sarah were married several years after he joined the firm, so when he used Hall he always went through Sarah for the arrangements and reports. If what Hall discovered later needed to be presented in court, Barry always found an alternative way to introduce it without revealing Hall.

Saturday morning, December 21

Becky took a cab to Chalmers' office because the weather in the Pacific Northwest was back to normal, low clouds and a steady rain. They met in Chalmers' office and began the discussion about the request for documents and the interrogatories.

Chalmers gestured toward a small stack of papers on his desk and said, "Here's what we've put together so far. Frankly, there aren't many documents to answer these requests. The Lukarillas is a very informal group. We don't have any organizational or financial documents. There is some correspondence. I think most of it's here, but we're still looking. There are some West Portland Catering documents, a few letters confirming arrangements. We don't have documents concerning our members or the girls. We don't have any statements from anyone or any photographs or videos. So far as I know, no one talked to the DA or any other authority.

"Of course, we do have lists of our present and past members. They're the same ones we gave you earlier. But I hate to give them up. We try to keep that sort of information confidential."

Becky answered his concern. "We'll have to produce them, but there are ways we can get the court to protect the lists from disclosure. We'll do that before we produce them."

Chapter 10

Monday morning, December 23.

Becky and Lorenzo left for the Lukarillas' camp in Lorenzo's Ford Explorer. During the trip over the Coast Range the sky was overcast, but the temperature was in the fifties. They arrived at the camp about twenty minutes early. The chain was down, so they drove in and parked near one of the larger cabins. As they were getting out of the Explorer, a man came out on the porch and approached the Explorer.

"Howdy, I'm Sven Larson," he said. "Come on inside and I'll introduce you to my wife, Emma, my son, Thor, and his wife, Judy."

They met in the entry hall of the cabin.

Sven Larson was a Scandinavian in his late sixties. He was heavy-set with a full head of gray hair, but there was no sign that he couldn't still do a hard day's work. Thor was almost the twin of his father, except for his age, brown hair and a mustache. Both had worked in logging most of their lives, although that work had been hard to find since the mid-eighties. All of the Larsons lived in a mountain cabin on the river just south of the Lukarillas camp. Sven had built the cabin just before he and Emma married.

The entry hall was narrow and long, extending nearly two-thirds the depth of the cabin and leading to the living room, which, together with the master bedroom suite, occupied the entire width of the back of the cabin. On the left near the end of the hall was the dining room that looked out over a porch toward the river.

Sven led them into the dining room, and they sat around the table. "This is Hugh's cabin," he said. "He uses it most of the year, but more in the spring and summer. What can we do to help?"

Becky answered, "Hugh's already told us what you do here at the camp. What we want to talk about is the retreat last September. I understand you were all here, is that right?"

"Yes, we were," Sven replied.

"You may know all of this, but let me cover what's going on," Becky continued. Then she went through briefly the newspaper story, the TV programs, the complaint that had been filed, and what they'd learned so far. "We want to know if any of you saw or heard anything that might help us determine what happened."

"The answer to that is yes, we did," Sven responded. "Thor, why don't you start, tell them what you know."

"Okay," Thor said. "I guess you know that the retreat started Friday evening. After everyone arrived, they had drinks and a big dinner. It was a night to kind of unwind. Like several years before, Hugh hired West Portland Catering to take care of the food. But this time it was a new group. Before, a guy named Bill Lattanzi was West Portland Catering. He always did the cooking, and he brought several different women as waitresses. There never was a problem. This year the cook was a woman. Her name was Marlene. She had three gals with her. They'd never been here before.

"Anyway, Saturday morning, about five, I was down at the stable feeding the horses, and I saw one of those girls coming out of one of the men's cabins. That didn't make sense to me at that time of the morning, so I watched her. It was the one they called Peg. She crossed the yard and went into the women's cabin. About that time, out came another one of 'em. This time it was Ginny. She looked around, like she was trying to sneak away. Then she hightailed it over to their cabin and kind of slipped in the door. That evening I was telling Judy about what I saw, and she looked at me kind of strange and asked, 'What cabin was that?' I told her, and she said, 'That solves the mystery. When I was making up that cabin this morning, I emptied the wastebaskets, and there were used condoms in two of 'em. It surprised me, and I think I said out loud, 'I'll be damned' or something like that."

"Whose cabin was it?" Lorenzo asked.

"The one where Max Pepper, Steve Weinstein and Park Price stayed," Thor answered.

Becky asked, "Do you remember how many of the members attended that retreat?"

"Sure," Judy replied. "There were fourteen, including Hugh." She verified the fourteen Chalmers had named, and further told them that Chalmers and Smokie Goodenough were in his house. Abe Sumas, Senator Shepard and Alex Lovejoy had one cabin. Senator Epstein was in another one with Bill Churchill and Ezra Livingston. Cece Upshaw, Nels Beecham and Hook Van Dyke were in the last cabin.

"This is all very helpful. Is there anything else you can tell us?" Becky asked.

Sven answered, "We didn't notice anything unusual the rest of the weekend. In fact, we didn't know anything had happened Sunday night. Come to think of it, that's unusual. The retreat ended after breakfast on Monday. The men were gone before noon. The caterer worked with us Monday afternoon cleaning up. If those girls had been attacked Sunday night, I can't believe someone wouldn't have said something. Especially since they apparently went to the sheriff later that day. Everyone seemed normal all day Monday."

Then Emma spoke up. "I talked to Marlene and the girls several times Monday afternoon. They acted calm as can be."

Judy agreed.

"There's another thing you should know," Emma added. "About a month later, a man drove up to the camp. The chain was across the driveway. He parked his car, got out, stepped over the chain and walked down the driveway to the cabins. I was with our dog down by the river, where he probably didn't notice me. I saw him go around the mess hall, looking in the windows. He did the same thing with Hugh's cabin and a couple of the sleeping cabins. Then he went back to the car and drove back toward Highway 26."

Becky and Lorenzo thanked the Larsons, left and headed for Astoria. They also got there early, but they went up directly to the district attorney's office anyway. Owen Persell was there and invited them into his office.

Becky and Lorenzo sat in two wooden chairs facing Persell's large desk. "We want to hear about your investigation into the assault complaints from the waitresses at the Lukarillas' camp," Becky asked. "In particular, what prompted you to drop the matter?"

"Sure," Persell said. "The complaints from the women were sent to us by the sheriff's department. It contained written statements of each of them. I personally called the men, questioned them, and recorded what they said. They flatly denied any sexual assaults. According to the men the women came to their cabin looking for sex, and the men admitted they had it with them, but claimed it was consensual.

"Because it was the waitresses' words against the men's, with no corroboration, I felt I had to drop the matter. With that kind of standoff, going forward would not lead to convictions, and I didn't want to damage reputations."

"Did you interview anyone else?" Becky asked.

"No I did not. If you'd like to see my file, you may." He called out his door, "Beth, will you bring me the Lane-Lovejoy file?"

"It's in the storeroom. I'll git it," was the answer from the other room.

In about five minutes Beth Erickson came in and handed the file to Persell. "This's the second time since we closed it that I've fetched it," she said.

"What are you talking about?" Persell asked.

"There was a fella here in mid-October, a New Yorker. Claimed he was studying old courthouses. I guessed he'd seen Hugh Chalmers' place on the way down here, 'cause he asked me 'bout it. I told him 'bout the Lukarillas, the TV and the gals' claims. He wanted ta know why yah didn't charge those fellas. I told him the file didn't have enough in it. He wanted ta see it, so I showed it to him."

"You did? I know it's a public record, but you should have asked me first," Persell said.

"I guess so, but you wasn't around. Later I forgot 'bout it. I jest don't 'member things like I used ta."

Becky and Lorenzo looked through the file and saw that it was just what Persell had represented. They left Lorenzo's card with the secretary, with a request that she call if she or Persell thought of anything else.

As they left the courthouse, Lorenzo said, "Sounds like the mysterious New Yorker was two months ahead of us. I'll bet he's part of that EBC investigation team. When we get back, I'll do some checking around and see what I can come up with."

Becky was confused. "I'm surprised that Persell didn't interview the Larsons. It doesn't make sense that he would take statements from both sides and not follow through. What about the other members who were at the retreat? Why didn't he try to talk to any of them? There's something about this that doesn't smell right."

Tuesday morning, December 24

Becky called Chalmers.

He was in a conference, but after Becky identified herself, he came on the line.

"Hi, Becky," Chalmers said. "I know it's only Christmas Eve, but let me wish you a very merry Christmas."

"And the same to you, Hugh." Becky told him about their visit to the camp and the DA's office. "We need to talk to everyone who was at that retreat. We'll hear from Lovejoy, Sumas and Shepard through their lawyers, but how do we get in touch with the rest of the Lukarillas, and particularly Pepper, Weinstein and Price?" she asked.

"It'll be easier than you may think. Our meetings have been so successful in exchanging ideas and producing innovation that several years ago we began discussing ways we could communicate privately between retreats. Last year Bill Churchill of Random Electronics presented us with a novel idea, where we could network computers and send messages back and forth over the phone lines. It involves a new concept in the computer world that they're calling electronic mail. All we had to do was each get computers and take training. It sounded so great that everyone signed on. Bill's technicians designed the system and had it installed on each of our computers. We tested the system last September, and it really works. I can type in a message to one or all of the fellas, send it, and he or they can reply the same way. I'll send a message to everyone who was there, except for Alex, Abe and Shep. In the message I'll introduce you, and ask them to cooperate when you call. Do you want to talk to them individually on the phone or arrange meetings?"

Becky thought about it briefly and then said, "I'm not sure right now. It might be better if we don't try to set this up with everyone at once. Why don't we start with Pepper, Weinstein and Price?"

Becky then took a legal pad and did some composing. She drafted the message for him. It asked Pepper, Weinstein and Price if they knew anything about what the waitresses were claiming in their lawsuit or anything else about the waitresses' activities at the retreat.

"I'll send it right away," Chalmers said. "Pepper and Price are in LA and, while Weinstein's office is in Miami, he's a horse nut and has a small ranch in Rancho Santa Fe north of San Diego. He spends lots of time there. We can probably set a meeting or meetings for you in Southern California."

Thursday morning, December 26

Even though it was the day after Christmas, Becky was in her office. The telephone rang. It was Chalmers.

"I'm glad I found you at work," he said. "We've got a problem, and it may be a serious one. I got answers from Max, Steve and Parker. They all claim that they don't know anything about the lawsuit or the waitresses, and they won't meet. I called Max at his home. I know him better than the others; he's been one of my lawyers for several years. His reception really took me by surprise. He said, 'I've told you all I can. I don't want to talk about it anymore.' For someone who's supposed to be your lawyer, that's pretty curt, don't you think?"

"It sure is. We do have a problem," Becky agreed. "I'll talk to Barry and see what he wants to do."

Becky went into Barry's office and found him talking to his secretary. "Barry, I just talked with Hugh. Something has come up, and I need your input." Becky brought him up to date on her conversations with Chalmers.

"Chalmers needs to contact the others," Barry said. "I'll compose the message and fax it to him."

The fax said, "Hugh, you need to communicate with the rest of the Lukarillas right away. Ask them if they know anything about any unusual activities of the waitresses at the retreat. Tell them that Pepper, Weinstein and Price won't talk about the waitresses and ask if they know why. Finally, say that if they know anything, you need to get them in touch with one of your lawyers right away. Call me as soon as you hear from them. We've got a meeting with all the defendants' lawyers here in Portland on January seventh, and we need their responses before then. If we decide to contact them, we can do it quicker using all three firms."

Tuesday afternoon, December 31

Barry had just returned from his annual New Years Eve lunch with some old high school buddies, when Chalmers called.

"I've got a bunch of replies to my message last Thursday," Chalmers said. "Everyone's heard about the suit. They either saw the TV or were told about it. They all say that they'll talk to you whenever. None of them heard anything about the girls being attacked, until it came out on the TV. No one said anything that weekend. Ezra Livingston thinks he knows why Steve won't talk to us. He talked to him after the TV program. Ezra and Bill Churchill knew that a couple of girls had been in Steve and Max's cabin, and Ezra called Steve to see what he thought of the women's claims. Steve told him he couldn't talk because his lawyer told him not to. Ezra asked him why he went to a lawyer, and all Steve would say was that he was afraid he might be next. Churchill also said he knew the girls had been in the cabin next to them earlier, but he didn't know or ask what was going on. Hook Van Dyke responded that he didn't know anything, except it was his impression that the girls were looking for action. Nels Beecham had the same impression. I'll fax you copies of their replies."

"Thanks, Hugh," Barry said. "I'll let Becky know."

Friday, January 3, 1992

Ben Lorenzo reported to Becky. "I just learned that the DA in Astoria had some visitors before his press conference. You remember that secretary, Beth Erickson, who we talked to at the courthouse? Well, she called me this morning and said she had forgot to tell us about these visitors." Then he reported what Erickson had told him about the two men who visited the district attorney the day before his press conference.

When Barry arrived home that evening, Sarah gave him a report from Pam Hall.

"What she found out is preliminary. She says all three girls are from the Los Angeles region. They went to work for West Portland Catering sometime last summer. She couldn't find any criminal records on them, either in California or Oregon. According to local county records, Marlene Symth and J & L Investment Company own West Portland Catering. They bought it last June. J & L Investment Company is a California corporation, and its place of business is a lawyer's office in Orange County, California. Hall hasn't done any further follow-up on the company yet. Since as usual Pam's report was oral, I've prepared a written report for her."

"That's a big help," Barry said. "At least we've got a little more to tell the lawyers at our meeting Tuesday. Tell Pam to hold up on further checking until we've taken the plaintiffs' depositions. I'm sure there'll be plenty of follow-ups to do then."

Chapter 11

Tuesday morning, January 7, 1992.

Just before nine, in preparation for the defense counsel meeting, Barry, Becky and Mary Jo gathered in the small conference room just down the hall from Barry's office. Boxes with some of the Christmas decorations taken down over the weekend were still stacked in one corner. A blackboard with a drawing pad was mounted on the opposite wall of the room, and Barry wrote a rough agenda on it. About nine Howard Sugerman, Paul Shumanski and Lou Miles were shown into the conference room, along with Joan Dixon, whom Sugerman introduced as a senior trial lawyer in his firm. Barry offered them coffee.

When introductions and the general chitchat had concluded, Barry stood by the white pad and said, "Since I set up this meeting, I guess I should start." Pointing to the white pad, he said, "I've roughed out an agenda. It's not intended to be complete, just someplace to start. We've been doing some things since we last talked, so I've written 'What We Know Now' as item number 1. Number 2, I'm sure you want to know about the plaintiffs' lawyers, the court and the jury potential. I've called that 'The Locale.' Next, we want to hear what your clients have to say, whatever you can tell us; I've listed as number 3, 'Defendants' Versions.' We think there may be an EBC connection here, so I added 'EBC Connection' as number 4. Do your clients' past dealings with that network have a connection with this lawsuit? For number 5, I've written 'Strategy.' Can our clients join together? If not, where do we divide, and what can we do as a unit? Finally, number

6 is the important item, 'General Pretrial Planning.' What do we do next, who does it? I also wrote February 14 here, because that's the date we owe appearances and the answers to the plaintiffs' first discovery requests.

"Those are just beginning thoughts. We'll expand the agenda as anyone wants. I'll start with what we've done and what we know now." He brought them up to date on the progress they'd made so far, including his conversations with Amanda, and Becky and Lorenzo's visits to the camp and the DA. He told them about the investigations they'd started, and he concluded with the mysteries that had surfaced about some of the Lukarillas members.

Starting the discussion of the locale, Barry introduced them to Johnson & Bellows. "They don't have much experience with high-profile cases. I suspect from reading the complaint and the discovery requests that they are getting help."

He turned to Sugerman and said, "Howard, in our first telephone conversation you asked about the court and its rules. You'll note the case number on the complaint. The number contains the initials LL. Those are the initials of the judge to whom the case has been assigned. LL stands for U.S. Magistrate Walter Lloyd. Since Judge Lloyd is a magistrate, you know he can only handle pretrial matters, unless all parties agree that he can act throughout the case, as if he were a federal judge. I know that seldom happens in most districts. But in this district, because all of our magistrates either have strong judicial or practicing lawyer backgrounds, they're usually accepted in cases for all purposes as a federal judge. So, when a magistrate's initials appear after the case number, early on the clerk's office asks the parties whether they will stipulate to the magistrate for all purposes. Your clients probably got that request with the papers that were served upon them.

"Whether to stipulate is an important decision, so let me tell you about Judge Lloyd. First of all he's black, which is somewhat unusual for this district, because we have a very small black population. He was a basketball star at Oregon State University, and he served in Vietnam. He was discharged from the Army as a captain. His law degree is from Stanford, so as you would expect, he's bright. After a successful trial practice with a local firm, he served for several years as a state court trial judge. The President appointed him to the U.S. magistrate position three years ago. He's a dedicated civic leader, and he has a strong reputation in our legal community as a superior judge.

"We don't have to decide now, but we will have to make that decision and notify the clerk before we complete the pretrial phase of this case. After you have had a chance to see Judge Lloyd in action, I suggest we give serious consideration to accepting him. I think he'd be great for this case. The earlier we make our decision the better, so he knows what his role will be.

"Turning to potential jurors, I'd say Portland is very similar to other large metropolitan areas, with an important exception. It's more provincial than New York, Los Angeles or Washington, D.C. Federal jurors in this district are more conservative when it comes to awarding big money. But that's not to say that they don't get swayed and render large verdicts when they've been convinced that someone was clearly wronged."

"How do they react to out-of-town lawyers?" Joan asked.

"That shouldn't be a problem," Barry replied. Then smiling, he added, "You'll have Becky and me to supply local color."

Barry then pointed to the table at the side of the room. "Before we continue, you may want a refill on your coffee, and help yourselves to the donuts. They are fresh from the restaurant downstairs."

After the cups were full and the donuts tested, Barry sat and said, "Howard, what can you tell us about Alex Lovejoy?"

Sugerman replied, "I'm going to turn this over to Joan. She's the trial lawyer, and she's here to take over the case."

Joan Dixon had intrigued Barry from the moment of Silverman's earlier introduction. A tall heavy woman in her mid-fifties, her complexion was ruddy, her hair was short and gray, and something about her presence was imposing. She had earned the reputation as a bright, tough litigator in New York both while with the district attorney's office and with Bellman & Swift.

"Obviously," Joan said, "we haven't done anywhere near as much as you have, and we thank you for moving so quickly. Alex Lovejoy, as you know, gave a statement to the district attorney. That's pretty much what he has to say, although I'm sure he'll be willing to expand as necessary. When Howard told me what you said to him on the telephone about Pepper, Weinstein and Price, a little red flag popped up in my mind, because Alex and Pepper had a nasty run-in a few years ago. Let me explain. Pepper used to be with Boldt, Benjamin & Spruce in Boston. He was a business trial lawyer there. At that time Alex was with New Brunswick and had been instrumental in building that company into a strong diversified conglomerate. A client of Pepper's decided to make a tender offer to Brunswick's stockholders. It was a classic unfriendly takeover attempt that immediately erupted into serious litigation, as they all do. It was a messy, mean case, with Alex successfully fighting off Pepper and his client. There've been hard feelings on both sides ever since. So strong that I'm surprised Pepper got into the Lukarillas over Alex's objections.

"Anyway, I called Alex and told him Pepper's attitude. He said he's been keeping an eye on Pepper, and he recently found out that Pepper and a woman named Angie Lawrence were living together out in Los Angeles. They're both divorced." Joan brought them up to date on the Lawrence/Lovejoy scenario at Silex. "Alex thinks she bears a grudge. I don't know if this means anything, but it is one more unusual fact involving Pepper and Alex.

"As far as I know, Alex doesn't have anything to hide. He thinks they were set up, and he wants to fight. The bad publicity isn't a factor, because it's already happened. You've already started the sort of investigation I was going to urge. Yes, we want a joint defense. I guess that's where we are. I know you will bring up EBC later, but here's a tantalizing fact: Angie Lawrence's got a connection there too."

Barry thanked Joan and asked Lou Miles to speak.

Miles, from Los Angeles, had the reputation of one of Southern California's premier civil trial lawyers, particularly when entertainers or sports figures had courtroom problems. He leaned forward casually with his elbows on the table. "Abe also gave the DA a statement," he said. "I've talked to him at length, and I'm convinced he's telling the truth. Abe's not bashful about himself or the life he leads. He calls it as it is, publicly lots of the time. He admits having sex with one of the girls, but I can't see him getting involved in rape. He's had three wives. But none of his divorces have involved any physical troubles. He claims to be pals with all his ex-wives. He suspects a setup, and particularly if EBC's involved. He's had trouble with EBC in the past. I'll explain that later when we get to that item on your agenda."

"I'll be damned," Barry interrupted. "Everything seems headed for that item on the agenda."

Paul Shumanski was next. He was one of the nation's high profile trial lawyers. "I can't add a lot to what Shep told the district attorney," he said. "Like the others, I think Shep's been straight with me. Somebody's obviously out to get him, along with the others, but we don't have any idea who or why."

Joan asked, "Are we ready to talk about EBC?"

"That's just where I was going," Barry replied. "Can you give us the background on the Silex matter and report on the status of the lawsuit?"

"I'll do my best," she said. She described EBC's November 1990 expose' of Silex's alleged discriminatory practices, including the details of the Department of Labor complaints. She was adamant that the TV show had blown the facts completely out of proportion and had included a number of actual lies, which produced a libel suit about a month later. The case was still in the discovery phase in federal court in New York City. "Silex has by discovery and other means of investigation been trying to find out what prompted EBC's vicious attack, but so far we've not been successful."

"It's hard to believe that two exposes about a year apart by the same network, one directed at Silex and the other at its chief executive officer, are simply a coincidence," Barry inserted. "Somewhere there's got to be a connection. Who was the reporter in the Silex broadcast?"

"Oh, there's a connection," Joan replied. "Susan Silver. She's the investigative reporter in both cases, but we still don't know what got her riled up."

"Then that puts Ms. Silver on our deposition list," Miles said. "Now let me explain Sumas' troubles with EBC." He described the 1990 problems that Sumas had with Rachel Jacobs and the subsequent editorial by EBC Sports. He pointed out that EBC subsequently lost its bid to renew its television contract with the NFL and that there were lots of rumors that Sumas was behind it. "In truth Sumas probably prompted some of these rumors with his public statements. He isn't shy about saying that he made a big stink about EBC at the league's meeting."

Joan shook her head. "EBC can't seem to get discrimination and sex out of its mind."

"Did EBC do anything more after losing the contract?" Barry asked.

"Not that we know of," Miles answered. "But to be frank, after the way Abe shot his mouth off, we were prepared for more. We have our suspicion that the recent Lukarillas program is the follow-up.

"And that brings up another thing. I told Abe about Parker Price's stonewalling. He thinks that bears looking into carefully. He tells me that Price is real close to Rachel Jacobs and that Price was pissed about the way Abe treated her."

Barry turned to Shumanski. "Does the senator have any problems with EBC?"

"I didn't talk to him about that," Shumanski said, "but I don't know of any. I'm sure they've made comments about him, just as the other networks have, but that's just part of being a U.S. Senator. Certainly, I never heard them charge him with discrimination or any sex problems until this broadcast."

They moved onto the next agenda item, a joint defense.

"Plaintiffs would love to have us fighting among ourselves. We've got to avoid that if we can," Joan said. "At least at this point we all have the same interest. Defeat the claims!"

They all agreed.

"I should point out, however," Barry said, "that the Lukarillas might be in a different position somewhere down the line, but that certainly doesn't present a problem at this time."

Barry leaned forward and said, "Okay, let's talk strategy. I say we go on the offense. Favorable facts are better developed by defendants when they go on the offense. Too many cases are lost when the defendants sit back and let the plaintiff take command of discovery and pretrial planning. Of course, Amanda has already made some requests. They have to be dealt with, and we'll do that today, but let's use today to get started ourselves. Let's plan our own discovery and send it out as early as tomorrow or the next day."

"I agree one hundred percent," said Joan. "You've echoed an in-house lecture I give to our young trial lawyers."

Miles said, "That makes two of us." And he added, "Let's go over their requests and then get out of the box ourselves."

Barry stood and went to the white pad, where he flipped over the agenda sheet. "Becky's been working on answers to the requests. She'll give you some ideas."

Becky said, "It's obvious that some of plaintiffs' requests are objectionable, but the Lukarillas have little to produce anyway, so it's probably a waste of time to file many objections. Hugh Chalmers has given us the Lukarillas' responses, and I've taken the liberty of putting them and a few objections in draft form. Mary Jo is handing you a copy of the draft."

The other lawyers reviewed the draft. Since most of the requests were directed at the Lukarillas, they approved them as is.

In addition to the few documents Chalmers had supplied, the only documents that the individual defendants had were the ones responsive to their travel records and their dealings with EBC.

Lovejoy and Sumas had some documents relating to their dealings with EBC. Joan said, "I suggest that for now we object to this request as not being material to the claims made in the complaint."

"That's my thought as well," Miles said.

"All right," Joan continued, "let's produce copies of the travel records for Lovejoy, Sumas and Shepard with their answers and our objections."

"But don't give them to Amanda before the fourteenth," Becky added.

"Okay, now comes the fun part," Barry said, "what we send the other way. Becky, tell them what you've been doing on that."

Mary Jo passed out some more documents.

"This is a draft of a first request to produce documents and other things," Becky said. "It's just a starter. We know we'll want more as we go along, but this seemed like enough to get us on the offensive."

The group worked the draft over for about an hour before deciding on a final product. They decided on what they needed: tax returns, employment histories, documents supporting plaintiffs' contentions in their complaint, evidences of criminal records and things relating to the retreat. Then they agreed upon a document to submit that was brief, but to the point.

"Okay, we should also request some depositions," Barry suggested. "Assuming we get those discovery requests out by Thursday, plaintiffs will have thirty days to respond, which takes us to Monday, February tenth, by my count. Let's tell them we want to take the depositions of the plaintiffs starting on Tuesday, February eighteenth. That's after they've received our answers to the complaint and their document requests. We should also depose Marlene Smyth during that week. The depositions of the plaintiffs can be done on Tuesday and Wednesday, so we'll take Smyth on Thursday."

"Don't forget Susan Silver," Joan said, "and the EBC investigator. How about deposing them in early March in New York? Our firm'll serve the subpoenas on them."

"We've got an investigator working on identifying that EBC guy," Barry said. "Hopefully we'll know who he is in time to subpoena him."

"Don't worry. We have ways of finding him," Joan said. "We'll know who he is in plenty of time."

"Our local custom requires us to write the plaintiffs' lawyer, giving her some flexibility on the dates," Barry said, "particularly for her clients, but we should be firm that we want these depositions no later than late February. I'll send the letter making the requests, with dates certain for plaintiffs and Ms. Smyth for the week of February eighteenth and for the New York depositions the first week in March. In the letter I'll tell her that we'll agree to reschedule for the convenience of the witnesses, so long as we stay in February and early March. That'll keep the pressure on.

"I expect Amanda'll complain that the depositions are too early, but we should insist. If she formally objects and takes us before Judge Lloyd, we'll be on good grounds because we didn't schedule the depositions until after we answered the complaint and plaintiffs' document requests. The judge'll want discovery done reasonably early, and taking the plaintiffs' depositions is a logical early step." Barry paused, and then added, "Actually, I hope she does object and forces us to see the judge. I always like my first exposure with the court to be one where we're acting reasonably and within our clients' rights. Our judges don't like arguments over discovery, so it'd be good to have her as the objector the first time we see the judge."

The lawyers reviewed their calendars and discussed the logistics. Joan summed up their plans. "Okay, then that's how we'll proceed. Our office will take care of the details in New York, and I assume Barry and Becky will cover Portland and send out the request for production. Does everyone agree?"

Everyone did.

Barry reminded them about the apparent problem with Pepper, Weinstein, and Price.

"Let's put that on the back burner for the moment," Joan said, "although I think that Swift, Wyman's investigator, should keep digging."

Chapter 12

Thursday, January 9

Barry sent Amanda a letter enclosing the document requests, the requests for the depositions of the three plaintiffs and Marlene Smyth, and a notice setting the deposition of Susan Silver and the EBC investigator on March twenty-fourth, which was the date picked by Joan Dixon. In the letter he offered to accommodate the witnesses, but made it clear that the plaintiffs' depositions needed to be taken before March.

Friday morning, January 10

Amanda called Barry. "You can't be serious about your deposition schedule. We can't be ready in February or early March. We haven't even received your answers to the complaint or to our initial discovery requests."

"You'll have those by February fourteenth," Barry said, "but you shouldn't need them anyway. Your clients filed this case. I assume they can answer questions about it without defendants' answers or discovery responses. Aren't they available? We can adjust a day or two, but we need to get going.

"As for the March depositions, Susan Silver is obviously also a key player in this case. We need to know what she and her investigator know. We'll delay their depositions for a week or so, if there's a really good reason, but we can't wait longer. Remember, you wouldn't voluntarily share what you know about this case, so we have to find out ourselves."

"I haven't talked to the girls," Amanda said, "so I don't know if they're available. But you're pushing too fast, and you know it."

But that was just what Barry wanted, to be on the offense. And he planned to stay there. "I don't think so. Unless there's some serious inconvenience involved, we plan to follow this schedule, and we're prepared to go to the court if you try to get a protective order."

"We may do just that," she said. "You'll hear from me one way or the other by Monday."

Monday morning, January 13

A Motion for a Protective Order was delivered. It asked that the depositions be postponed until at least April and for an expedited hearing.

Wednesday morning, January 15

The sky was overcast, except for a clear narrow patch over the Cascades, which revealed snow-covered peaks. Barry was staring out his window at Mt. Hood, wondering why he hadn't heard from the judge on Amanda's motion, when the mail clerk dropped the mail on his desk, and there it was, a postcard from Judge Lloyd's clerk setting the motion for hearing at nine-thirty, next Monday morning.

He hustled the notice into Becky's office. "The motion's set for next Monday morning," he said, handing her the post- card. "Let's get our brief in opposition filed by Friday, even though I'll bet the judge won't hear the motion. He's sure to suggest a discovery conference instead, and Amanda won't object. We need a conference call with the other lawyers this afternoon or tomorrow morning to discuss the brief we'll file and to discuss strategy in case we get a discovery conference.

"While the things Amanda has asked for are way too broad, our clients don't have most of them anyway, so why object? The most important thing is to get the discovery we want. We need to convince the other lawyers of that."

"I'll set up the conference call right away," Becky responded. "And I'll work on the opposition brief and fax them a draft before the call." She didn't reach any of them directly, but she was able to schedule a conference call for Thursday morning. She and Mary Jo worked the rest of the day on the opposition brief and faxed a draft to Joan, Shumanski and Miles that evening.

⚥

Thursday morning, January 16

It was dark out when Becky and Barry met at five forty-five their time. They placed the conference call at six. Barry explained his thinking about what would most likely happen on Monday, and there was general agreement to answer Amanda's requests without objection. They talked about Becky's draft opposition brief.

"I like Becky's approach," Joan said. "Let's file one brief jointly on Friday."

They all agreed.

"I'll be at the hearing on Monday," Joan said. "I want to meet the judge early on."

"I will too," Miles said.

"Unfortunately, I'll be in trial," Shumanski said. "So you all will have to appear for me and the senator."

⚥

Monday morning, January 20

Becky and Barry met with Joan and Miles at eight before the hearing.

"If the judge turns it into a discovery conference, he'll ask one lawyer on each side to give him a brief statement about the case and the status of discovery," Barry explained.

"Then you're our spokesman," Joan said.

Miles agreed.

Plaintiffs' motion was just one of many items on Judge Lloyd's Monday morning civil calendar. After several hours of arguments by lawyers and comments and rulings by the judge in the other cases, it was finally time for *Lane et al. vs. Lovejoy et al.* The clerk called the case and the lawyers came forward to the tables in front of the judge. Amanda and Bellows used the table to the right. Barry, Becky, Joan and Miles lined up behind the table to the left.

Barry addressed the court first. "Your Honor, before we get started, I want to introduce Joan Dixon, a member of the New York Bar, and Lou Miles, a member of the California Bar, and move their admission to this court for the purposes of this case. Ms. Dixon represents Alex Lovejoy and Mr. Miles represents Abraham Sumas. I am handing the clerk the written motions and the affidavits required by the court rules."

"Thank you, Mr. O'Shea," Judge Lloyd said. "I'm sure the papers are in order. Welcome to Oregon, Ms. Dixon and Mr. Miles. You are admitted. What about the other defendant?"

"Paul Shumanski, an Ohio lawyer, represents Senator Shepard," Barry said. "He could not be present because he was presently in trial in Texas. I have a similar motion and supporting papers to have him admitted."

"Thank you," the judge said. "Mr. Shumanski will be admitted as well."

The judge then leaned forward and took command. "I purposely left this case for last. I'm sorry you had to wait, but I'm going to make up for that by saving your clients a lot of money. We're here on a discovery motion, but rather than hearing arguments, since almost all of the parties' lawyers are here, our time will be better served if we convert this into our first discovery conference. If I have to,

I'll decide the motion, but we can accomplish more with a conference, and that'll probably make the motion moot. Does anyone disagree with that approach?"

All the lawyers replied that they did not.

"All right then, the court is in recess for the next fifteen minutes. We'll reconvene at eleven forty-five in my chambers. I'm sure that none of you will mind having a late lunch today." The judge stood and left the courtroom.

The lawyers were in the judge's chambers, seated around his conference table, when he came in at ten minutes to twelve.

"I see we're all here," the judge began. "Mr. Bellows and Ms. Johnson, I'd like one of you to give me a brief, and I stress brief, background about this case and tell me where you are with discovery. Then I want a similar statement from one of the defense lawyers."

Amanda spoke for the plaintiffs. She told the judge about the Lukarillas and what she called their secret meetings, hidden away in a remote region of the Coast Range. She emotionally explained what had happened to her clients. She told him about the status of the discovery requests she'd made.

"They say they'll answer them by February fourteenth," she said, "but frankly I don't expect complete answers, because Mr. O'Shea told me he felt the requests for documents were too broad and objectionable." Then she addressed defendants' discovery requests. "I was shocked," she said, "when I opened my mail, less than two weeks ago, on Friday, to find that the defendants had requested depositions of our clients and another person for the week of February eighteenth. No one called me in advance, they just sent me a formal notice. Again without the courtesy of a telephone call, they also demanded some depositions in New York in March." She related her version of the telephone conversation she'd had with Barry on this subject. "He told me that he would not delay the schedule," she said. "So we had no choice but to file for a protective order. That's where we are, judge."

"I don't like the way this case is starting," Judge Lloyd said, "but let me hear from the defendants."

"I've been assigned to be the spokesman for the defendants," Barry said. "I can't comment on much of what Amanda has told you by way of background because we frankly are in the dark about what, if anything, happened last September, except that defendants Lovejoy, Sumas and Shepard emphatically deny that they assaulted anyone. But, I do take issue with what Ms. Johnson has told you about the discovery so far. She is correct that she stipulated to an extension to answer the discovery requests until February fourteenth, but she's not correct about when she'll have the responses. I told her that she'd have the answers and discovery responses by that date, when we talked on January tenth. I have since conferred with the other lawyers, and I can advise the court and counsel that, except for the requests for the defendants' financial statements, we will not object to any of these requests and will answer them fully by February fourteenth. With respect to the financial statement requests, we object to producing them until plaintiffs have made a showing that punitive damages are involved. We don't believe they can make that showing.

"I agree with your Honor that this proceeding appears to be getting off to an adversarial start, but it doesn't need to. Plaintiffs' outstanding discovery will be answered promptly and fully. I asked Amanda, when I called her back in December, right after my client was served with the complaint, to tell me what she knew about the case beyond the complaint. She said, and I can almost quote her, that at the present time she was not at liberty to tell what she knew. I'm sure you can appreciate that the defendants, and particularly Alex Lovejoy, Abe Sumas and Senator Shepard, are very concerned about the charges made against them in this case and are very anxious to learn what's behind them. The claims have been aired on television and in the newspaper. Under the circumstances, they need immediate discovery from the plaintiffs and certain others, who we suspect may be involved in the making of these allegations.

"I told Ms. Johnson that we would be reasonable about people's schedules, but we did not want to postpone these depositions for more than a week or so. I asked her if her clients had any availability problems. Back on January tenth she said that she didn't know, but I've heard of no problems since. I should also say that on January tenth we also served plaintiffs with some requests for documents, six in number. They shouldn't have any problem responding to them in the usual thirty days, but again we are willing to be reasonable.

"Judge, our clients need to find out what's behind this complaint. They need that now so they can prepare a defense. All we're asking for is prompt depositions of the plaintiffs, their employer and the two people at the Empire Broadcasting Company. That's the television network that investigated the matter for the television show that probably led to this lawsuit. We want to start next month. That's all we're asking."

Amanda started to respond' but the judge interrupted her. "Wait a minute, Amanda. I don't want this conference to turn into an argument. I've heard from both of you, and I think I see where we are, so let me ask some questions. It's my guess that we can resolve this without any more arguments. Barry, can't you get the responses to Amanda before the fourteenth?"

"I think we can, judge, at least some of them. We'll get as much as we can to her by next Monday."

The judge turned to Amanda. "That being said, why can't your clients be ready for depositions the following week? You and Oscar wouldn't have brought this case without good reason and a sound investigation to back it up. Your clients know what happened. That's what the defendants want to ask them about. I frankly don't see why you need discovery before their depositions. Are your clients and the employer witness available the week of February eighteenth?"

"They're here, your Honor," Amanda said, "but I would just feel more comfortable, and I know they would as well, with more time. I don't know why we can't put this off until late March."

The judge gave her his answer promptly. "We can, but we're not going to," he said. "I respect the defendants' wishes to get the information as early as possible. I think that should be true for both sides. The earlier both of you know what's involved, the earlier you can evaluate your clients' positions in this matter, and the earlier this case can be disposed of, either by settlement or trial. The depositions and other discovery will proceed as scheduled.

"While we're on this subject, let me make a few comments on the procedures I want observed in these depositions. We've got four defendants here, and I don't want depositions to go on for days because each lawyer thinks he or she has to ask his or her share of questions. The defendants will choose a lead lawyer for each deposition, and I expect that lawyer to cover most of the questions. The rest of you can inquire, but only to a limited degree and in areas not already covered. Each deposition should be done in less than four hours, and, while I'm not ordering such a limitation, I want the lawyers taking the depositions to keep this in mind. Is everyone clear about how we are going to proceed?"

"I understand," Amanda said. "But it would really help, Barry, if the list of the Lukarillas members could be one of the things we could get next Monday."

"I'm sure we can do that," Barry replied, knowing that he already had it. "Judge, that brings up another matter. My client has tried to remain anonymous over the years, and it has a policy to keep the names of its members confidential. Could we have an order that the list of names will only be used for purposes of this case and will be returned at the end of the case with any copies that have been made?"

"Yes, you may," he said. "As a matter of fact, to save any further requests, I'm ordering that all documents produced in this matter only be used for the purposes of this case without further order of this court. I don't want discovery in this case to be conducted to support an agenda not connected to this case.

"Now, let's review where we are. The plaintiffs will have responses to their discovery by February fourteenth, most of it by next Monday. The defendants will take depositions and receive responses to their discovery as scheduled in their requests. I know this discovery will lead to more, but since we're getting an early start with this case, let's take advantage of it and set some schedules. I'm giving you a discovery cutoff date for May fifth. That means no depositions or other discovery after that date, unless we modify my order. I will modify it if you both agree that you need a little more time, but we're going to try this case by next fall, so there will be no significant discovery delays. I'll make myself available if there are any discovery problems, but I hope there won't be any.

"I said a trial by next fall." He looked down at the table and started turning pages on something before him. "I'm looking at my calendar. It shouldn't take more than two weeks to try this case. It'll probably take less time than that, but I have the middle of September open. I'm going to tentatively give you a trial date of Tuesday, September fifteenth. If you stipulate, I'll be your judge for that date, otherwise, we'll get a district judge, but the date will most likely stay the same. I want each of you to check your calendars, after you leave here, and call my clerk back today, if you have any problems with that. Let's try to accommodate that date or one close to it. I'll be reasonable with you, but only within limits. I think you all know what I mean. Now is there anything else we need to talk about?"

"The financial information," Barry replied.

"That's right. We'll abide by our usual practice. No financial information need be produced until plaintiffs have shown that the jury is entitled to consider punitive damages. If that happens, defendants should be prepared to immediately give plaintiffs' lawyer the appropriate documents. Is that understood?"

Amanda and Barry replied that it was.

The judge, as usual, had the last word. "Assuming you all stipulate that I'm to be your judge, I'll revisit later the timing of when we'll meet for the final pretrial conference. You'll hear from the clerk about that and other trial matters later in the summer. Is there anything further?"

Miles and Joan were speechless. They'd never experienced a pretrial proceeding like this. Everyone understood that the judge's question was asking for a unanimous no, and that's what he got. They also understood that they'd better have a good reason not to stipulate. The conference ended.

Chapter 13

Monday afternoon, January 20

The defendants' lawyers reassembled in Barry's office.

"I don't believe what I just went through," Joan said. "When I tell them, no one at Bellman will believe me. 'You can't live with that schedule. You can't possibly try it in September,' they'll say. In New York City this case wouldn't be tried for at least two years. But it's great for Alex, the sooner the better. If he can win this case or get the plaintiffs to back off, the momentum will be a big boost to the EBC case. However, I know when I get home someone's going to question how we can depose all the people we'll need by May."

This led to a discussion of whether this fast pace was really the course the defendants wanted. It seemed to fit right into the tactics the lawyers had planned. It put them on the offensive. The judge was giving them every opportunity. The limited time schedule would make it hard for plaintiffs to get the offensive back. While Barry's deposition planning was a bit foreign to Joan and Miles, they were willing to go along, particularly in light of the philosophy of Judge Lloyd.

"I like Walter Lloyd," Joan said. "He's my choice for trial judge."

"I agree," Miles said. "I say we sign the stipulation and make him our judge."

"Amanda and Oscar wouldn't dare object," Barry said.

In fact they also filed a stipulation a week later. Judge Lloyd became the trial judge.

Amanda called Susan Silver as soon as she got back to her office. "We've got a problem. The judge ruled in defendants' favor. The depositions will proceed as scheduled by defendants. The judge also set May fifth as a cutoff for any more discovery and September fifteenth for the trial."

"You've got to be kidding." Susan arched an eyebrow. "That's impossible. No case can get to trial that fast. How can you get all the depositions you need in about three months? There's no way! How do we change his mind?"

"I don't know what you mean by we," Amanda answered. "If you mean 'How do I do it?' the answer is I don't. Judge Lloyd's not an anomaly. He's the norm. That's the way things are done in this court. We'll have to limit our depositions to the ones we really need. We know we have to depose Chalmers, Lovejoy, Sumas and Shepard. Given the schedule he's approved, we'll have to schedule them for later in March or early April. The judge did give us some help. We'll have most of the discovery we requested by next Monday. Defendants have agreed to respond without objections, and they have agreed to provide the list of the Lukarillas in the Monday delivery. He also put limits on the depositions. He doesn't want them protracted. He made it plain that he expects each one done in at least a day.

"As soon as we get the discovery, and particularly the list, we can start our investigation. Then we can make more meaningful decisions on other depositions. But we'd better get the investigation done soon, because we don't have much time to schedule additional ones. My hunch is that we'll use the investigation in place of depositions for the most part. Can you get the investigation going and completed on this short notice?"

Susan got the message and returned to her normal aggressive mode. "Julie's available, or he will be," she replied. "But we need a meeting soon, next week, if possible. Since our resources are in New York, why don't we meet here? You say you'll have the discovery Monday.

Could you leave after you get it and meet in my office Tuesday morning?"

"Sure," Amanda replied, "but I'll need someplace to get some sleep after I arrive."

"I'll get you a room near our building on Sixth. Let's meet in my office at ten Tuesday morning."

"Great," Amanda said, adding, "I'll be there, unless you hear back from me today that there's a problem."

Tuesday morning, January 21

In the Metro section of *The Oregonian* was a small article headed, LAWYERS MEET WITH JUDGE IN LUKARILLAS CASE. The article reported that the trial was set to start September fifteenth.

Tuesday morning, January 28

Amanda arrived at the hotel at four a.m. A cold front from the north was on the way, and as she stepped from the cab, she was confronted with a wind chill in the teens. She checked in, went to her room, and left a wake-up call for eight. By the time she left for the EBC building, snow was starting to fall.

She was glad for the short walk. A receptionist directed her to Susan's office, where Susan greeted her and introduced Sanchez and Ryan O'Donnell.

They apologized for the weather, and O'Donnell asked, "What did they give you?"

"Except for the list of the Lukarillas, not much," Amanda answered. She handed them each several sheets of paper. "Here's the list of members. They promise the list of the past members by February fourteenth. The documents from the Lukarillas also included a few pieces of correspondence between Barry O'Shea's partner, Jake Marion, and the Secretary of State's office, and a name registration form filed with the state. There's no correspondence or other communications between the Lukarillas and its members. Whatever there was has been discarded. The same is true about their retreats. They produced the current correspondence with West Portland Catering, concerning the 1991 job. All defendants claim they don't have the other documents, except Lovejoy, Sumas and Shepard did send copies of their travel documents for the retreat. I guess I'm not surprised. Everything I've heard so far about this group is that it's very informal, exclusive and confidential. I didn't expect much of a paper trail. And we do know who's involved.

"That leads me to another matter. At the conference the judge entered an order that these and any other documents produced in this case are to be kept confidential and used only for the purposes of this case, unless he orders otherwise. So you can't use these at this time for any project not related to the prosecution of this case."

Susan and O'Donnell nodded casually, and then quickly started looking at the list.

"What a list!" Susan said. "Somewhere I heard that they've been meeting for over forty years. How could these people gather for that long without anyone knowing about it?"

"Well, it's sure a good place to start," O'Donnell said. "I'm not concerned about the confidentiality. Once the case goes to trial, the names will all be public anyway. We'll do a background check on each of them. The public members will be the easiest, but even there we'll dig as deep as we can. What we're looking for is not likely to be very public. There're twenty of them, six politicians, two lawyers, an accountant, three guys involved in sports and entertainment, an educator, and seven business executives, all across the country. Can you handle all of them in this short time, Julie?"

"Sure," he replied. "I know what you're after. I've got contacts in most of those places, and where I don't, I'll find connections. How fast do you need it?"

"Like tomorrow," Amanda said. "Seriously though, how about March third? It'll make your job easier if you concentrate on just those who were at this retreat. I'll talk to Barry before I leave here and get those names. The way the judge acted, I know he'll cooperate."

Susan knew that it would be no big problem for Sanchez, but she expected him to give a word of caution, and he did.

"That's pretty quick, but I'll get it done. I may need to do some follow-up later, but I'll get you a pretty good picture of these guys by then, including the kind of dirt you need."

When Amanda returned to Portland, as she suspected, Barry gave her the information on who had been at the September retreat informally. She faxed it directly to Sanchez, with copies to Susan and O'Donnell.

Wednesday, January 29.

Sanchez went right to work, concentrating first on Lovejoy, Sumas and Shepard. Sanchez already knew that Lovejoy had been the second-in-command at New Brunswick before he joined Silex in 1988. He called a friend in Boston. "I'm checking on a guy who used to be high up with New Brunswick Corporation. He left the company back in eighty-eight. I need to talk to someone who can give me some background on him."

"I know a VP who's been with them for almost thirty years," said the friend. "He owes me, and he likes to talk. I'll give him a call."

Several days later, the friend called Sanchez. "I talked to the New Brunswick guy. His name is P.C. Givens. He'll talk to you. Can you get up here this week?"

Alex Lovejoy

Sanchez met Givens in a hotel bar near Logan Airport on Friday afternoon.

"I work for a private investigating firm," Sanchez said. "We've been hired to do a background check on Alex Lovejoy for a headhunting firm in New York."

"I worked with him for years," said Givens. "I probably know as much about him as anyone still with the company. What kind of stuff are you interested in?"

"Where he's from, the kind of guy he is, things like that. But more important, any problems he's had."

"He's originally from the Southwest, Texas I think. He's got kind of a drawl. He came with New Brunswick in the early sixties and worked his way up to next to the top. I know he has a good home. He and his wife have a couple of kids, girls as I remember. In Boston he was pretty much a model citizen and socially prominent. The only controversy he was involved in was a takeover fight. A New York buy-out firm tried to take over the company in eighty-four, and it got messy. Injunction suits were filed in both our state and federal court, seeking injunctions for alleged illegal tactics and fraud. There were counter suits against Lovejoy and our board alleging the same thing. I remember Lovejoy made quite a splash in the papers when he walked out on a deposition. One of Boston's high profile litigators, a guy named Max Pepper, was taking Alex's deposition at the time. Apparently the questions got nasty, Alex got mad, and left. He had to be ordered back to the deposition by a federal judge. Alex had it in for Pepper after that, and I know for a fact that he sidetracked Pepper's ambitions with Boston society. I even heard that Pepper blamed Alex for Pepper's divorce. Pepper left town and moved to Los Angeles just before Alex joined Silex."

The interview put Pepper on top of Sanchez's list. He'd investigate Pepper after he finished with the defendants.

What Sanchez found out about Abe Sumas was much juicier. From Susan he already knew about Sumas' three marriages and the divorces, but he learned a lot more from some ex pro football players he ran into in a midtown bar on New York's West Side. Their names were Ernie and Gene. Sanchez again used the headhunter firm as his client. "A major charity is thinking about asking Sumas to be on their board," he said, "but the principals had heard some rumors about his past."

"They probably heard right," Gene said. "Ernie and I was teammates of his back in the late fifties and early sixties. Back then there was always babes hanging around our locker rooms and hotels when we was on the road. There was hardly a night that Abe didn't end up with one of 'em in bed."

"Yeah," Ernie said. "And don't forget the problems he had in Pittsburgh, Baltimore and Philadelphia."

"What problems?" Sanchez asked.

"In Pittsburgh the local paper claimed that one Saturday night before our game, Sumas had a gal up in his hotel room and tried to force her into oral sex, you know, a blow job."

"Did the authorities get involved?" Sumas asked.

"They sure did," Ernie replied. "The DA charged him with sexual assault, but it never went nowhere. The charge was dropped when the gal refused to testify."

"What about Baltimore?" Sanchez asked.

"Gene'd better tell you 'bout that, he has first hand knowledge."

Gene said, "That also came out in a newspaper. The paper claimed that Sumas and some other teammates tried to get some broads at a party we was having there to blow 'em. I was there but wasn't one of the guys charged. The charges got dropped again cause they couldn't find the broads to testify.

"I guess you want to know about Philly too. Another newspaper story, but the facts was different. It was just before Abe retired at the end of the sixty-four season. We'd won the game and was celebrating in the bar off the lobby of our hotel. The paper claimed that Abe tried to get a blowjob off one of the waitresses just after closing time. He'd been making out with her in a dark corner booth. Same thing, the case got dismissed."

Then Ernie said, "You gotta say one thing for Abe, though. After he got married, no one ever made any claims like that again."

Sanchez found that digging into the private life of Senator Shepard was another matter. The senator had the boy scout image that every politician envied. He'd served his country as a Marine in the Korean War and was a Democratic member of the House of Representatives from East St. Louis for six years before being elected to the U.S. Senate in 1970. Several political pundits had mentioned him as a possible challenger for the presidential nomination. His colleagues, even those from the Republican side of the aisle, held him in high regard.

Sanchez's break came in East St. Louis. He was entertaining an insurance agent who'd been active in local Republican campaigns. The agent was a major contributor to the Republican candidate who opposed the senator during his reelection campaign in 1982.

"We discovered that Shepard had made a sexual pass at a maid in a hotel in Springfield. It was supposed to have happened one morning when the maid came in to clean his room. We dropped it when our source proved unreliable."

"Don't suppose you'd be willing to give the name of the hotel and the time when the source claimed it happened?" Sanchez asked.

"Sure," said the insurance agent. "It was the Royal, and it was sometime in eighty-one."

In Springfield Sanchez talked to the hotel's personnel manager. "I know about the pass Senator Shepard made on one of your maids back in eighty-one. I'm investigating the senator, and I don't want to get you or the hotel involved. I just need the name of the maid and her address if you know it."

"You heard that from the Republicans. It never happened," said the personnel manager.

"Oh, I think it did," said Sanchez, as he pulled out a hundred dollar bill and held it in front of the manager.

"Like I said, it never happened, but I sure don't want any more publicity like that for the hotel," the personnel manager said, as he took possession of the bill. "The maid's name was Judy Filcher. That's her married name, she married one of our waiters. The last I knew they had a small bar and restaurant in Evansville, Indiana."

Sanchez left Springfield for Evansville. He found the establishment after a day of checking around. Judy Filcher was tending bar. He was the only customer, and he ordered a beer and engaged her in a conversation. He was upfront with her. "I'm investigating a sexual assault claim against Senator Shepard, and I heard you had a similar problem."

"I told those people in Springfield that it didn't happen, and that's all there is to it," she said.

"I hear there's more to it than that. I'm just trying to find out if this guy has those tendencies, so I can tell if my client is telling me the truth. I promise I'll keep it confidential."

She relaxed a little. "I don't want to be involved, and I'd never testify, but he did offer me a hundred if I'd put his penis in my mouth. But don't ask me to repeat it. I'll deny it just like I did before."

"Do you know if he ever did anything like that again or before?" Sanchez asked.

"Yeah, I know. A woman on his staff, Sheila Workman, came to see me after it came out that he'd done that to me. She told me the senator had made a similar offer to her and some others on the staff, but I'd better deny what he'd asked me to do. She told me no one would believe me, just like no one would believe her. She said that the senator and the press would dig into our pasts and dredge up minor things and turn them into unsavory activities. That's why I decided to deny it."

Sanchez found Sheila Workman working for the state in Springfield. He used the same pitch.

"I won't deny it," Workman said. "He made that offer to me, but I turned him down. He did the same thing to several other female staffers, and at least one told me she took his money. I won't give you their names, and I'd appreciate it if this would stay just between us."

Monday, February 3

Sanchez called Amanda. "I've investigated Lovejoy, Sumas and Shepard and have found out that both Sumas and Shepard get kicks out of oral sex. They've used their status to get blowjobs. Sumas used coercion to get his, and the senator bought 'em. Sounds familiar, wouldn't you say? I'll send you a report with the details.

"There's nothing like that in Lovejoy's background, but he and another Lukarilla ain't the closest of pals. In fact, it looks like Lovejoy hates Max Pepper's guts. I don't know how this bears on your case, but my experience tells me that we should check out Mr. Pepper next. What do you think?"

Amanda was stunned. "I'll be damned," she exclaimed. "You told us you'd work fast, but I never expected you'd find anything like this. I'm glad you're on our side. I agree, put Pepper to the top of your list. Can you cover the other eleven in your time frame?"

"I think so. Anyway, I'll give it my best shot. Be back to you soon."

Amanda dialed Susan Silver in New York.

Susan had already talked to Sanchez. "I also told Julie to put Pepper next on his list. You know, I wondered if Pepper might be Alex Lovejoy's Achilles' heel."

An associate at KEBC did the investigation of Pepper for Sanchez. "I think I've got what you want," the associate said when Sanchez called for a status report. "Do you want a written report?"

"Yeah, but for now just tell me orally what you've found out."

"All right. I got most of this from a guy I know at the firm where Pepper now works. He's good friends with

Pepper, but he owes me, and I promised to keep his name out of this.

"Pepper got his legal education at Harvard and started out as an associate in a New York firm. In the mid-seventies he moved to Boston to fill a litigator gap for a premier firm in that city. He married the daughter of a senior partner, and by 1980 he was pushing forty and already the firm's head litigator. He and his wife were starting to get a foothold in the bottom tiers of Boston society, when big litigation over a buy-out of New Brunswick Corporation began."

"I know all about that," Sanchez interrupted.

"Okay, but anyway, Pepper soon found that his tenacity with Alex Lovejoy in the lawsuit had its price. People important to the Peppers began avoiding them and leaving them out when invitations were being assembled. Their marriage took a turn for the worse, and a divorce followed. Pepper was unhappy and saw no reason to remain in Boston. A law school friend encouraged him to look west, and, with the help of the headhunter who had recruited him for the Boston firm, he received an offer to become a partner in the Los Angeles firm of Newman & Levine.

"Pepper joined Newman & Levine in 1981 and was soon assigned as the backup partner to one of the firm's founders, Sam Levine. Levine had successfully defended Chalmers Lumber Company in an antitrust suit brought by the California Attorney General in the late forties. The suit charged several lumber companies, including Chalmers, with price fixing in connection with lumber and sawmill operations in Northern California. After the case, Levine became one of Hugh Chalmers' closest legal advisers. Pepper worked closely with Levine, who began to rely on Pepper in representing Chalmers. Soon Pepper was handling personally a number of matters for Chalmers Forest Products and Chalmers. In February 1989, Sam Levine died of cancer, and Pepper took over the account.

"I think you'll like the next part. Pepper also took over the Citrus Publishing Company account. That company owned one of Los Angeles' major newspapers, *The Express*. On a visit with Citrus' chairman in October 1989, Pepper was introduced to the company's new president and chief operating officer, Angie Lawrence, who he was told would be in charge of the company's legal affairs. Both being divorced and about the same age, Lawrence and Pepper hit it off from the start. Pepper took her to dinner later that week, and by mid-October they were dating steadily. I think they're living together now, at least part time."

Sanchez had investigators in various states looking into the backgrounds of the other Lukarillas who were at the September 1991 retreat. From these he learned that Cecil Upshaw was the president of a national accounting firm that had among its clients several companies associated with Lukarillas members, such as Silex Petroleum, Random Electronics and Universal Airlines; that Parker Price was a good friend, and sometime roommate, of Abe Sumas' nemesis and Angie Lawrence's new friend, Rachel Jacobs; and that "Smokie" Goodenough and "Hook" Van Dyke had lifestyles similar to the senator and Sumas. Goodenough was reputed throughout the halls of the House office buildings to be a fanny-pincher and chaser of female staff members, although no one had formally complained about him. Van Dyke had a reputation during his playing days for playing with girls who hung around before and after road games, but nothing much had surfaced in recent years. He also learned that Ezra Livingston, although in his sixties, spent lots of time in singles bars since his divorce five years ago.

Sanchez used Vince Romero, an ex vice cop from the Miami police force, to check on Stephen Weinstein.

Romero's initial report was by telephone. "Weinstein grew up in Miami and attended the University of South Florida in Tampa for two years before being drafted," he said. "He served in Vietnam and was discharged when he was wounded after serving a little over a year. He returned to Miami in 1964 and started the discount grocery and drug business called S-Mart. In the next seven years he established additional stores in Ft. Lauderdale, Orlando, Jacksonville and Tampa. During those years his product line expanded to include hardware, furniture, appliances, entertainment items and gardening.

"I couldn't find out where he got the funds to grow so fast, but I soon learned an interesting thing about his future financing. As the early seventies progressed so did the S-Mart stores. They popped up in Atlanta, Birmingham, Charleston, Charlotte and New Orleans, and by 1975 the over-expansion had the company in deep financial trouble. Weinstein was about to declare bankruptcy, when Julio Boccini approached him. Boccini offered to provide the needed funds for an unknown percent of the ownership. Weinstein quickly accepted the proposal. After the Boccini investment, the company flourished again and went public in 1986.

"You need to know about Boccini. He calls himself an investor, but he's really the head of a Mafia clan in Miami. I had lots of dealings with him and his boys when I was on the force. I couldn't find any evidence that Weinstein has had any more dealings with Boccini since the company went public."

While Hilton Jones was not at the retreat, Sanchez checked the national legal directory, Martindale-Hubbell, and found that among the clients listed for Stevens & Sherman were Silex Petroleum, S-Mart and Random Electronics.

Chapter 14

Wednesday morning, February 12

When Barry arrived at his office, "VM" was glaring at him from his phone. He dialed for messages and found that Joan Dixon had called earlier. *She probably wants to talk about the depos next week,* he thought. He returned the call.

It was a direct line, and she answered. "Paul, Lou and I conferred yesterday, and we decided we won't present for the plaintiffs' depositions. We've hired local firms to attend for our clients. We feel it's better to save ourselves for the trial."

"You make a good point," Barry said.

"There's more," she continued. "We want to be sure that you'll do the main questioning. We've got confidence in our local firms, but your ideas and strategy are key to the defense of this case. Please get together ahead of time and give them your guidance."

"I appreciate your confidence. We'll take the lead.

"Also I've decided to send Becky to New York. She's a pro at depositions," Barry said. "While I assume you'll take the lead with Susan Silver because of your experience with her, Becky could lead with the EBC investigator, particularly since she and Ben made the visits to the camp and Astoria."

"That's fine with me," Joan agreed.

Saturday morning, February 15

The local lawyers joined Barry in the small conference room down the hall from his office. Mary Jo was with him. Saturday in the office was a precursor to the casual Fridays of the late nineties. It was a dress-down day, and everyone was participating.

After coffee had been poured and everyone was seated, Joan's local spoke up. "Barry, you've got a solid handle on this case. We assume you'll take the lead and share your ideas on how we should participate, if at all."

"I'm prepared to do that," Barry said. "Just so you'll know what I've got planned, here are my present thoughts. We haven't picked up much about the plaintiffs from our investigation to date, so they're going to have to be basic discovery depositions. I'll use them to learn about each of these women and their backgrounds, to find out and pin down exactly what they claim happened, and to get a good look at them and evaluate how they handle questions. Then we can follow up with investigation based on what we learn. If the investigation uncovers some gems that didn't come up in the depositions, we'll face plaintiffs with them at trial. I don't plan to test them with helpful things we already know. It's better to have key witnesses face tough facts for the first time when they're asked about them at trial. That usually happens if you're patient and keep those facts to yourself.

"However, there is one specific thing I'll cover with each of them. That'll be to pin down their versions of the visits to the other cabin the night before. They'll probably deny it, but we need to know what they're going to say, so we can make our plans to prove they're liars. I'll have to be a little indirect with Tina, because we don't know if she was involved. She may deny that anything went on that night, which is fine. But the indirect approach may unsettle her, and she may say more than she wants.

"That brings me to the subject of who we should depose first. The logical choice is to start with the one named first in the complaint, but I've got another suggestion. I suspect Virginia Lane's the smart one and tells the story best. That's why EBC chose her to do most of the talking on television. That's also probably why Amanda named her first in the complaint. She wants her to be the spokesperson. She'll want the other girls to hear her and me too their answers. I say we depose Ginny last. We've got an advantage in this case, because the plaintiffs have already been on TV. They've told us who the weak one is. It's the one who said almost nothing except to confirm what the others said was true. That's Tina. I'll take her first. Make her be the spokesperson, no telling what she'll say."

"Do we have a reporter?" Paul's local asked.

"I've already talked to Amanda about that," Barry replied. "We agreed that we should use the same firm for all the depositions. That way there won't be a new learning curve for the reporter each time. We decided on Ruth Mason & Associates. I called Ruth, and she is on board. She'll handle them herself. She'll give us daily transcripts of the testimony as we go along. She'll also provide a disk of the testimony so Mary Jo can program the deposition into our computer for later compilations and summaries.

"Also, we plan to video all of the depositions. We can use the videotapes at trial, either as a part of our opening statements or on cross-examination, to show the plaintiffs as they told their stories in response to our questions. That'll take away some of the impact of their testimony when Amanda tries on direct-examination to present them as innocent little lambs."

"Amanda may object to videos," Joan's local predicted.

"She didn't in court. In the requests for depositions, which we served on her in January, we reserved the right to use a video camera. Maybe she overlooked it, but I doubt it. She and Oscar have been videoing defendants' depositions recently. I think she'll want to do it herself."

"Do you want any questions from us?" Lou's local asked.

"I want your help," Barry answered. "Consistent with the approach I've outlined, if you think I overlooked an area we should know about, please fill in the gap. But don't test them about things we already know.

"One final thing. We'll need a legal assistant to help with documents, arrangements and other details. That's the reason I asked Mary Jo to be with us this morning. I assume you don't have any objections to having her do this."

They all agreed that Mary Jo was fine for the job.

Monday morning, February 17

"Have any of you ever had your deposition taken or given testimony in a trial?" Amanda asked, as she met with Ginny, Peg, Tina and Marlene Symth in her conference room.

None of them had.

"Then I need to tell you something about a deposition and how you should conduct yourselves. A deposition is just like testifying in trial, except it's more informal in its setting. It'll be done here in this conference room, and there'll be no judge or jury. One of the other lawyers will ask you questions, and you give the answers. I'll be with you. You'll be under oath, just like in court, so you must tell the truth. And I emphasize, *tell the truth*, no fudging. This is not a game. Since the questions will come from an adverse lawyer, you have to be careful. He'll lead you, use his own words, phrase them to get the answer he wants, so here are some guidelines you must follow.

"The most important one is *never answer any question you don't understand.* I don't mean just understanding the words of the question. I mean you must understand what's being asked. When you guess at what a question means and then try to answer it, you get in trouble at trial. A clever lawyer can change the question just enough at trial to make it appear that you're changing your answer. Then the lawyer'll read the deposition back to you, and put you on the spot, when he asks, 'Isn't that what you said under oath at the time of your deposition?' Of course, the answer is yes. The jurors don't know there's been a misunderstanding. They think you've changed your testimony, and they'll distrust your credibility. That won't happen if you make sure you understand what the question means before you answer. If you don't know what the question means, simply tell the lawyer that you don't understand it and keep doing that until you know what he's asking for. Next to telling the truth, this is your main job during the deposition. Listen to the question and make sure you understand it.

"Doing this will become harder the longer the deposition lasts, but you must continue to remind yourself to listen and understand. If I think you're missing the point, I'll say something like 'Just listen to the question.' If I do, pay attention, it's a signal, but I can't get away with doing it too often, so watch the questions carefully.

"That brings me to point number two. *Never guess.* Just don't do it. You can make an estimate, if the question calls for an estimate. An estimate is based on facts; a guess is based on speculation." She emphasized again, "*Never guess.* Nine times out of ten a guess will get you in trouble, just like I explained a minute ago.

"The third point is *don't volunteer.* Just answer the question. If it can be answered with yes or no, then answer it yes or no. Every time you add an unnecessary explanation, it just gives the lawyer more information than he asked for. That'll lead to another line of questioning that you probably wouldn't have been exposed to, if you'd just answered the question. If a question simply can't be answered yes or no without an explanation, the better answer is 'no, but I have to explain.' The lawyer phrased the question and probably did so to get an affirmative answer, so answering 'no, but' is usually safer. However, when you explain, make it brief.

"There are other things I'll discuss with you as we go along, but if you keep these three points in mind, you'll probably stay out of trouble at trial.

"Before we talk about what questions to expect, do any of you have any problems in your background that you want to tell me about? I need to know about the bad things ahead of time, so I can protect you and prepare you."

They all said there was nothing.

Then speaking just to Ginny, Peg and Tina, she said, "You've made this case about sex, so you'll get asked about your sex lives. The lawyers will want to know if you're loose with men, whether you've been a prostitute, charged for sex, things like that. If there's anything in your pasts like that, for Chrissakes share them now, so I can help. Is there anything I should know?"

They said there was not.

She then worked with each of them, including Smyth, going over the questions she expected and helping them with their answers. The session lasted all morning and several hours into the afternoon.

Chapter 15

Tuesday morning, February 18

Barry and Mary Jo arrived at Amanda's office for the plaintiffs' depositions. The other local lawyers were already there. Ruth Mason was set up in the conference room with her machine at the near end of the conference table. The video cameraman and his equipment were at the far end.

Amanda entered with her clients. She introduced them. "Ginny," she said, "you sit in the witness chair there to the left of Ruth."

Barry immediately corrected her. "No, have Ms. Marcellas take that chair. We want to start with her."

"But I assumed you'd start with Ginny. She's named first in the complaint," Amanda replied.

"Our deposition requests indicated a starting time of nine for each of them," Barry pointed out, "and it fits our schedule better if we start with Ms. Marcellas."

Amanda wasn't happy, but she knew she had to comply. "Tina, sit next to Ruth." Amanda sat next to her and instructed Ginny and Peg to sit in the chairs to Amanda's left.

Barry saw that Ginny was upset. He took the chair to Ruth Mason's right, directly opposite Tina. Mary Jo sat next to him. The other lawyers were down at the other end of the table near the cameraman. Barry wanted them to be where they could see the witness as the camera did.

Ruth Mason began the proceeding, addressing Tina. "Please raise your right hand. Do you swear that your answers will be the truth, the whole truth, and nothing but the truth, so help you God?"

"I, I do," Tina replied timidly, but that disappeared when she noticed the video camera. "Do I have to have that camera look'n at me?" she complained. "I don't like it."

"Yes, you do," Amanda said. "It's part of the deposition."

Barry began abruptly, "You know that I represent the Lukarillas, whom you've sued in this matter, don't you?"

Tina nodded.

"Answer audibly," he admonished her. "The court reporter might miss a nod of the head. Answer yes or no."

"Okay, the answer is yes."

"You're under oath. I'm going to ask you some questions about yourself, what you claim happened, and several other matters. I expect you to answer those questions truthfully. Do you understand that?"

"Yeah."

"And you'll have to speak up so Mrs. Mason can hear you."

"Okay," she said in a louder tone.

"It is important that you understand my questions before you give an answer. I know Ms. Johnson has cautioned you about this, but I'm doing it, too. So if you don't understand me, please don't answer. Tell me that you don't understand. Do you understand that?"

"Yeah."

"State your full name for the record."

"Tina Marie Angela Marcellas."

"When and where were you born?"

"I was born in 1969, the twelfth of August, in Juarez."

"When did you come to this country, and what is your status here?"

Barry noticed that she was relaxing with the background questions. Confidently, she replied, "Juarez is next to El Paso. I was in and out as a kid. My family came to California when I was thirteen. I got a green card."

"Are you single or married?"

"Single."

"Have you ever been married?"

"Nope."

"Do you have any children?"

Tina stiffened, shifted in the chair and looked at Amanda. Getting no help, she looked askance and said, "I had a girl, when I was seventeen, but she lives with my ma down in LA."

"Who's the father?"

Looking down, she replied, "I don't know his name, but I'm pretty sure it's a guy I slept with one night in Fresno."

Barry decided to ease off temporarily. "Tell me about your family. Who are they and where do they live?"

Again she relaxed and brought her eyes up to meet his. "My father's Juan, my mother's Maria. They work in the fields. I got three brothers and two sisters. They's younger and live with my parents."

"Where do you live?"

"We rent the upstairs in a house across the river in Sellwood, it's at 1572 Southeast Umatilla."

"Who's the 'we,' and how long have you lived there?"

"I been there since the end of July, last year. I live there with Peg. We came up here together."

"You say you came up here together. Where did you come from and how come you came up here?"

"Well, Ginny, Peg and I worked for a catering outfit south of LA. Del Mar Catering, it's called. The guy that owned it had an in with lots of important people, so we catered at some fancy places. We did a bunch of work around Christmas an' New Year's time for the newspaper down there, *The Express*, an' for Angie. We was at a party at Angie's condo in June, an' she tol' us she had a friend who bought a catering business in Portland. She needed help. She wanted to know if we'd be interested. She introduced us to Marlene, we took the job, an' that's how we got here."

"Who's Angie?"

"She's Angie Lawrence. I think she runs the paper."

"Is Marlene, Marlene Smyth?"

"Yeah."

"What was Marlene doing when she was in LA?"

The conversational mode suited Tina. She continued to be helpful. "I think she was a greeter at some club. Her husband had ta come to Portland 'cause of his job. She came up here with him, an' then I think he left her. She was buying a catering service in Portland, an' she needed help. She called us, offered us jobs, an' we took 'em."

"Let's go back to Los Angeles for a minute. What kind of work did you do there, other than this catering job?"

"Well, let's see. I worked in some bars an' restaurants. When I was real young, I worked in the fields an' did some cleaning. That's 'bout it."

Now that he had her relaxed, Barry asked, "Did you ever do any prostituting? You know what I mean by that, don't you?"

Tina stiffened, clearly surprised. Her face started to redden. "I know whacha mean, and no way!" she exclaimed.

Locking on her eyes, Barry challenged, "You're testifying under oath that you never had sex for money?"

He saw Amanda look closely at Tina. He knew what Amanda was thinking: *The way he asked that question he knows something that'll prove she was lying.*

Tina answered, "Yeah, that's what I'm saying!"

Barry returned to questions tracing her jobs and the places where she'd lived before coming to Portland. He wanted the information so Pam Hall could check on her later. She was still shaken, but she gave fair estimates as to the times, but was pretty vague on the exact locations.

Again treating her mildly, he asked, "Since you've been in Oregon, have you lived with Peg at the address in Sellwood the whole time?"

"Yeah."

"Where does Ginny live?"

"She lives with Marlene in the house next to the business, there wasn't room for all of us."

"Do you have any boyfriends or guys you go out with?"

"I met a guy called Weasel, his real name is George, up at the Sellwood Inn. It's a tavern on seventeenth. I see 'im once in a while."

Barry asked, "Do you sleep with him?"

Tina's face was flushed and her eyes flashed. "Why the hell you ask that? I'm not sharin' my sex life with you, mister!"

Ginny and Peg laughed, but Barry saw that Amanda was not amused. "Calm down, Tina. Let's take a break," Amanda said.

Amanda took all three girls to her office, where she tried to calm Tina down. "If he asks a question that's not proper, I'll object, and you won't have to answer. But if I don't object, answer the question. Don't argue with Mr. O'Shea. Your job is to listen to the questions and answer them without further comment. Do you understand?"

"I guess so," Tina answered.

"And for Godsakes, don't get mad. He's got you, if you do!"

When Amanda and the girls returned, Barry continued.

"Do you want the question read back, or do you have an answer now?"

Tina was still furious despite Amanda's consoling. She stared at Barry with her brown eyes ablaze. "You bet I've slept with him. He' a stud, an' treats a woman like you wouldn't know how."

Barry locked on her eyes. "Did you charge him?"

"Why don't ya get your mind outta the gutter?"

Barry's glare never left her. "Well, did you?"

Tina looked toward Amanda, but she couldn't help. Tina looked down and answered softly, "I did the first time."

"How much?"

"A hundred," she muttered.

"Is that the first time you ever charged?"

Tina was broken. She began to cry. "I'm not telling ya, and that's that."

Amanda interrupted and cautioned, "Calm down, Tina, just answer the question." Then, rethinking, Amanda added, "We need another break."

They left the conference room again and went to Amanda's office. Amanda put her arm around Tina's shoulders. "Okay, take it easy," she said. "I know this is tough, but you have to answer these questions. I wish you'd told me about this before. I could have prepared you better. But we're where we are and getting mad or refusing to answer won't help. The quicker you answer the quicker we get this over."

Still sobbing, Tina said, "I don't care. I won't answer any more questions like that."

"You have to, or he'll take this before Judge Lloyd, and the judge'll make you."

"I don't care. Let 'im do it, if he wants."

"All right, but I warned you. Let's go back and get this over."

When they returned, Barry asked Ruth Mason to read the last question.

"Is that the first time you ever charged," she read.

"What's your answer?" Barry asked.

"I won't answer," Tina said firmly.

"We'll see about that later," Barry said. "What are the names of other guys you've dated or gone out with since you've been in Oregon?"

"None!" she replied.

Barry didn't believe that, but decided to change course. Pam Hall would find out who her other boyfriends were. "Tell me how you happened to be at the Lukarillas' retreat in September."

The change surprised Tina. She paused, then said, "We was working for West Portland, an' one day Marlene says we got a job over the weeken' someplace in the mountains. She wanted to know if we could get away for the weeken'. She told us it was a retreat that a bunch of important guys had each year at a place on the way to the coast. We'd go up Friday an' prepare. They'd get there later Friday, an' we'd serve 'em meals Friday night, Saturday, Sunday an' Monday mornin. We'd get time an' a half an' free room an' board. It sounded great, so we all got on board. Marlene an' Ginny drove up in the big West Portland truck, an' Peg an' me followed in the pickup. It was real pretty up there. This camp was in huge trees an' on a neat river. Only people there, when we got there, were Sven an' Emma. They take care of the place. Thor an' Judy work there too. We moved into a cabin, an' then went to the mess hall an' prepared. The guys started showing up after noon."

"Let's stop here for a moment," Barry said. "I've prepared a little diagram that I'm going to have Ruth mark as Exhibit One. It's not to scale and pretty rough, but I think we can use it to locate a few things at the camp. Then maybe we can use it as we go along."

Ruth put an Exhibit 1 sticker on the diagram. Mary Jo put a copy on an overhead projector so the video camera could pick it up.

"Now, Ms. Marcellas, take a look at Exhibit One. Does that represent, at least in a rough way, the camp and the buildings?"

Tina leaned forward and examined the sketch. "Yep, it does." More composed, she started to tell him more. "Here's the driveway, the mess hall, the cabin we stayed in an' . . . "

Barry stopped her. "Hold on a minute. You're getting ahead of me. You mentioned the mess hall. Write 'mess hall' inside of that building."

Still leaning forward, Tina complied, and Mary Jo did the same on the overhead projector.

"Now, write your names inside the cabin where you girls stayed."

"It's this one next to the mess hall," Tina said, writing their names in the rectangle of that cabin.

"Okay, do you know which cabin Mr. Chalmers used?"

"Yeah, it's right here. The congressman they call Smokie stayed there too."

"Put their names in that box."

"Do you remember where the others stayed?"

"I sure as hell know where Alex, Abe an' the senator were. That's where we got raped!" she said.

That got the attention of Ginny and Peg. Barry glanced at them and saw broad smiles across their faces.

"We'll get to that, but show me where they stayed."

"Right here," Tina responded, writing Alex, Abe and Senator in one of the boxes.

"What about the others?"

"Lemme see." She paused and looked toward the ceiling. Bringing her eyes back to Barry, she replied, "Max, Steve an' that black actor fella . . . what's his name, it's a funny one, like a place, Park, that's it, they was down here, next to the stables. The other senator was in the cabin next to them. An' the ex-basketball guy, they call him Hook, he was in the cabin next to the road, but I'm not sure where the rest was."

"Write in those people and show where the stables are."

As she was writing, Tina remembered, "They called the other senator Julian."

Barry decided it was time to switch to short rapid questions. "What did you do on Friday?"

"Well, we set the table an' gave 'em dinner. They had drinks outside first. We served 'em. Thor was the bartender."

"What happened after dinner?"

"Nottin, we just cleaned up an' went to our cabin."

"How did you meet the men on Friday?"

"We did'na meet 'em. We just served 'em drinks, an' sometimes they'd say something to us, that's all."

"What did they say? Start with the first one who talked to you and continue."

"Well, it wasn't like that. I 'member Senator Shepard, they called him Shep, he wanted to know my name. I tol' him. Then he asked how I got up here. I tol' him, I moved up from Fresno. Then Alex also asked my name, an' I tol' him. He wanted to know if I was married. I also talked to Steve, Abe an' Hook, but I can't remember who said what. That's about it."

"How'd you know who the others were?"

Tina was caught up in the rapid pace. Her answers were shortening. "Oh, we talked later, either at dinner or the next day."

"Do you remember any other conversations before Sunday night with any of the men?"

"Not really. There was lots of kidding, but I don't 'member anything exactly."

"I don't mean exactly, tell me the substance of what this kidding was about."

"I really can't 'member now."

"What'd you girls do Friday night?"

Tina stiffened. She glanced briefly toward Ginny.

Barry followed her eyes and saw Ginny's shut-up stare.

"Noth'n," she replied, "we just read and talked."

Barry paused, looked again at Ginny and then back to Tina. "Are you sure about that? Remember, you're under oath."

She looked down. "Yeah, I'm sure. Nothin' happened Friday or Saturday night."

"I didn't ask you about Saturday night, but thank you. I'll assume, unless you tell me otherwise, that I don't need to ask you any more about that night. But to make sure we understand each other, did you sleep with any of the men, I mean have sex, either Friday or Saturday night?"

"I did not!"

"How about the other two girls? Do you know if either of them had sex with any of the men either Friday or Saturday night?"

Looking away, she replied, "I know they didn't."

"How do you know that?"

Still avoiding Barry's eyes, she said, "Because we were always together both of those nights."

"I want to be sure what you're saying. You're testifying under oath that neither Ginny nor Peg left you Friday or Saturday night, is that correct?"

Looking at Ginny for assurance, she said, "That's correct, damn it."

"Were you in any of the men's cabins at any time before Sunday night?"

"No!"

"Were either Ginny or Peg in any of the men's cabins at any time before Sunday night?"

"Same answer, damn it!"

"You're sure of that?"

This time she yelled. "I'm damned sure!"

Joan's local whispered, "I'm glad those answers are recorded on the video. The jury will see her just as we have."

Barry shifted to the events of Sunday night, which Tina related. She told the story just as Ginny had done on Dorothy Watters' show.

"Speaking of Sunday night," Barry continued, "did you say anything to anyone at the camp about what happened after you left their cabin?"

"We tol' Marlene right after we got back to our cabin."

"What did she do?"

"Noth'n. She said we should keep quiet about it. These was important people, an' if we made a fuss while we was still here, no tell'n what would happen to us."

"Did you say anything to anyone that night or the next day?"

"Nope."

"You saw Sven, Emma, Thor and Judy the next day after the men had left, didn't you?"

"Yep, while we was cleaning up."

"Did you tell any of them what had happened Sunday night?"

She knew how to answer that. "Nope, we was afraid to."

"Have you given a statement to anyone, where you told what you claim happened that Sunday night?"

"Just to the cops, and Amanda."

"What about EBC?"

"Yeah, to them too."

"Anyone else?"

"Nope."

"Tell me how you happened to talk to EBC. I want to know who you talked to, how it came about, and what was said."

She told him about the visit of Susan Silver.

"How'd you happened to hire a lawyer?"

"Susan said we should, and Marlene agreed. In fact Marlene kept at us, till we did it. She sent us to Amanda. She and Oscar'd worked fer her before."

Barry asked some cleanup questions, and the deposition ended.

Amanda met with the girls in her office. Before Amanda could say anything, Ginny couldn't contain herself. "Goddamn it, what does this guy know?" she asked.

"You tell me," Amanda answered. "What does he know? I didn't like the questions either, especially if you're holding back on me. Did something else happen at that camp? What were you doing on Friday and Saturday nights? You'll blow this whole case if you don't tell me what went on. Tina's already got herself in a jam by not warning me in advance. Let's cut the bullshit and come clean. What you tell me is privileged. I'm bound by ethics not to reveal anything. But I can't help or protect you if you're not honest with me. I hope you understand that. Now what do I need to know?"

Peg and Tina were scared, but before they could say anything, Ginny took the lead. "We've told you everything. Nothing went on anytime up there except Sunday night. I don't know where O'Shea was coming from. I just didn't like the sound of his questions."

Amanda didn't know whether to believe her. All she could do was issue a warning. "You'd better be right."

Then she switched gears. She turned to Ginny and Peg and asked about their sex history. "What have you two got to tell me about your sex backgrounds? I assume you've each had your affairs, but what about prostitution?"

They both emphatically denied it.

"How about when you were in LA? Everybody knows that producers and casting gurus take advantage of gals wanting to be starlets. What about you two? Did you ever trade a fuck for a job?"

"Frankly, if I'd had the offer, I probably would have, but I was never so lucky," Ginny replied. "The answer is no."

Peg, however, admitted, "I did, a couple of times, but that's not prostitution."

"You can make that distinction if you want, but if he gets specific enough, like I did, for God sakes don't lie. Don't volunteer it, but don't lie. Am I clear?

"Yes."

Chapter 16

Tuesday afternoon

Peggy House took the chair to Ruth Mason's left. Barry saw a confidence that had been lacking in Tina. She looked like the student who knew the answer before the teacher asked the question. Amanda had done her job over lunch.

Ruth Mason administered the oath and asked Peg to state her full name.

Peg responded, "Peggy Ann House."

"Tell me about your background, where you're from, and things like that," Barry asked.

"I was born in sixty-five, October thirty-first, in Redlands, California. I was raised and went to school there. After high school I went to hairdresser's school and got a job in a Hollywood beauty parlor. Being where I was, for about five years I tried out for bit parts in the movies. I got a couple. Since then I pretty much worked in the restaurant business, a bar maid or waitress, until I got the job with Del Mar Catering." She confirmed the contacts with Angie Lawrence and Marlene Smyth.

"You were here throughout Ms. Marcellas' deposition," he said. "Would you agree with her version of the drawing, Exhibit One?"

Peg had examined it over lunch. "Yes, and I know who else was in those last two cabins. Bill and Ezra were in the cabin with Senator Epstein, and Cece Upshaw and Nels were with Hook. She turned and gave the camera a smirk.

"How did you get acquainted with the men?"

"Like Tina said, we chatted Friday night while we were serving them drinks and dinner. I don't remember what was said, but it was just chitchat, and I suppose in hindsight I'd say some of them were a little forward."

As Barry expected, her phony confidence was producing expanded answers. She was violating the second cannon of deposition preparation - *don't volunteer.* He asked, "Who was a little forward?"

"Well, certainly Abe and Shep, and probably Hook, Steve and Max. But no one was out of line."

"Not out of line, you say. Then tell me how they were forward," he asked.

"Abe offered me a drink after dinner Saturday night. Actually, so did Steve and Max."

"Where were they going to give you the drink?"

"In their cabins, I suppose, but I didn't take 'em up on it."

"Any other little forward remarks?"

"I can't think of any, but the guys were always chummy."

Barry sensed that Amanda was uncomfortable. No lawyer can sit quietly very long when a client is expanding consistently.

She interrupted, "Just answer the question, Peg."

Barry continued as if he hadn't heard her. "What about Friday night? Was anyone chummy then? Did anyone offer you a drink then?"

She answered quickly – too quickly, "No, nothing happened Friday night."

Barry pressed her. "Ms. House, you were in one of the men's cabins early Saturday morning, weren't you?"

"I was not!"

"You're under oath. Are you sure that's your answer?"

"Yes, I'm sure! You don't have to tell me I'm under oath. I don't give a damn if you believe me."

"I just want to be sure that you understand the meaning of your answer."

"Well, the answer is, 'I was not!'"

"How about Saturday night or Sunday morning, did you visit any of the men's cabins then?"

"No, I did not!"

"You're not married, are you? Have you ever been married?"

Scowling, she answered, "Answer's no, to both."

Just as abruptly, he asked, "Have you ever had any children?"

"No."

"Have you had any abortions or miscarriages?"

Peg eyed him coldly and responded, "I don't know why you gotta know this, but yeah, I had an abortion once."

"When did it occur, and how did you get pregnant?

"How did I get pregnant? You gotta be kidding. I got pregnant 'cause I got fucked, that's how. I was a sophomore in high school. My mom didn't want me to have a kid, so we went to the public health clinic. They did it there."

Ginny and Tina snickered, but stopped when they saw Amanda glaring at them.

Barry asked, "What's the status of your sex life today?"

She almost rose out of her seat. "What the hell do you mean *status*?" She sneered. "I do okay, if that's what you're after."

"That is what I'm after. Do you have a boyfriend or someone you usually go with?"

"Not really. I pal around with the guys at the Sellwood Inn."

"Give me the names of the guys you've palled around with."

She grudgingly complied. "Well, there's Pete, uh, I think his name is Cross, and Junior Rich, and Leo, I don't remember his last name. That's about it, there might be another one or two."

"Where did you meet Pete?"

Condescendingly she said, "I met them all at the Sellwood Inn. I just told you that. All those guys live or work around Sellwood. They're in the tavern a lot."

"Have you had sex with any of them?"

"That's none of your damn business. But I know Amanda'll make me answer, so the answer's yes."

"With whom?"

"All of 'em. How's that!"

"Do you charge for sex?"

"Absolutely not!"

"Have you ever taken money for sex?"

"Money, no."

"Does that mean that you've given sex for something else?"

"I don't know what you mean, something else."

Barry glanced at Ginny. She was glaring at him. "There's nothing confusing about that," Barry replied. "Did a man ever offer you something in return for sex?"

She slouched in her chair and answered, "Yeah."

"Tell me about it. What happened?"

Still slouching, she said, "When I was in Hollywood trying to get into the movies, there were a couple of times when the guy doing the interviewing told me, if I'd fuck him I'd get a job. Another time a guy wanted me to go down on him. I got the jobs, so you take it from there."

"You're telling me you fucked the first guy, and went down on the other one, is that true?"

Ginny whispered, "You bastard."

Barry ignored her. Peg answered, "That's right, genius."

"Were there any other times that you gave a man sex for something?"

"No!"

He then moved on to the events of the weekend at the Lukarillas' camp. This relaxed her. Her testimony mimicked Tina's, and she described the events Sunday night just as she had to the EBC camera. She had the same explanation for not saying anything the next day about the alleged attacks.

To clarify and connect the testimony, Barry asked, "When you said a guy wanted you to 'go down on him' a minute ago, were you taking about what you say Abe tried to make you do?"

"That's right."

Barry had an idea. "We didn't ask Tina this," he said. "But let me ask you. Did you know, or had you ever met, any of the Lukarillas guys before? I'm not talking about seeing them on television. I mean meet in person."

She looked surprised, and cautiously, she answered, "Yes."

"Who had you met before?"

"Damn it," she whispered to Amanda. "I didn't listen to the question." She turned back to Barry and qualified her answer. "Met is probably not right, so I should have said, no."

"Why did you say yes, first?"

"Because I've waited on two of 'em before."

"Who are you talking about, and how come you waited on them?"

"Well, when we was at Del Mar Catering we did some work for Angie Lawrence. Max Pepper was usually there when Angie threw a party. I served him drinks and chatted some. Once or twice, Park Price was there with the TV sports gal Rachel Jacobs. I chatted some with him too."

"Do you know if Ginny and Tina knew or chatted with them as well?"

Barry glanced at Ginny and Tina. They both nodded.

"Well, I'm sure they knew Max," Tina said, "and Park was there too, and I'd guess they served them both, but that's all I can say for sure. Wait a minute . . . I remember I've seen Ginny talking to Pepper before. Actually, she seemed to be pretty friendly with him."

"Did they seem like friends?" he asked.

"Yeah, kinda," she replied, "but that's just my impression. I don't know if they were."

Peg's deposition ended at about three.

Amanda asked for a break before Ginny started.

Amanda and the plaintiffs retired to her office.

Ginny was fit to be tied. The door was hardly closed when she took after Amanda. "Goddamn it," she exploded, "why are you letting him do this? What kind of a lawyer are you anyway? That shyster's getting away with murder. We're getting hung out to dry. Why are you lettin' him get away with those questions? Are you gonna let him do that to me, for Chrissakes?"

"Hold it right there!" Amanda said angrily. "I warned you before we started that there would be questions like this. We're in a sex case. You've charged their clients with rape and sodomy. You've got to expect they're going to try to make prostitutes out of you, if they can. Settle down for a minute, so we can talk about you.

"And before you explode again, let me tell you a few things. I've got a pretty thick hide, but you've asked what kind of a lawyer am I, so I'll tell you. I'm a tough lawyer, and I can play just as nasty as the next one, but I don't break the rules. The questions he asked are proper. If I interrupted or instructed Peg not to answer any of those questions, the judge would be all over me. I'd be breaking the rules, and worse, I'd be getting on the wrong side of the judge before we've finished the first quarter mile of this race. I'm your lawyer, and I'll fight for you, but I'm not stupid."

Ginny realized she'd made a fool of herself. "I'm sorry, but I'm still mad, and if I get a chance, I'm going to ream that asshole if he asks me questions like that!"

"I understand, but watch yourself," Amanda cautioned. "Getting mad and fighting back will cost you. Take my word for it. And let me say one more time, if you've got anything you're hiding, let it out. We're beyond keeping secrets now."

"I'm not hiding anything. I told you that before," Ginny said.

Amanda still wasn't convinced, but she said, "All right, but we'd better not start your deposition until tomorrow morning. The way he's going, he should be able to finish you and Marlene by noon. That'll give you tonight to calm down, and you'd better do that, if you don't want to make a mess of your deposition. Is that clear?"

Reluctantly, Ginny replied, "Yes."

The depositions were recessed until nine the next morning.

Chapter 17

Wednesday morning, February 19

When Amanda and her clients came into the conference room, without instruction, Ginny took the witness chair.

After Ginny was sworn to tell the truth, and before Ruth Mason could tell her to state her name, Barry said abruptly, "State your full name."

Surprised, she answered, "Virginia Meadows Lane."

"Meadows your maiden name?"

"Yeah"

"How old are you?"

"Thirty-four."

"Where were you born?"

"In Glendale."

"Where were you raised?"

"In various places in the LA area."

"You're single, but have you been married before?"

"Yeah, twice, the first time when I was seventeen and again at twenty-five. The first one didn't last a year. I got divorced from the second guy when I was twenty-eight. I got no kids."

"How about your schooling and job history," he asked.

"I finished high school in Glendale, and I wanted to get in the movies, but I didn't have the dough it takes to go that way with schooling, so I moved near Hollywood and took what jobs came my way. I worked mostly in bars, first as a barmaid and then later as a bartender. I did get a few parts as an extra. My second husband was a sergeant in the Marines, so I moved in with him near Camp Pendleton and worked in a local tavern. After I divorced him, I went back to LA, where I bummed around for a couple of years before joining Del Mar Catering in Corona del Mar."

"Tina told us how you three happened to join West Portland Catering. Do you have anything to add?" Barry asked.

She was getting comfortable and wanted to talk more. "No, 'cept I was the one who was the friend of Angie Lawrence. I met her through Rachel Jacobs. I'd known Rachel since before my second marriage. I used to date some LA Stars players. Rachel had kind of a thing about covering that team. Anyway, we used to talk. After I'd been at Del Mar for about three years, I started doing some networking. I'd call around to people I'd run into with dough. I called Rachel, thinking we might get some television business. We didn't, but she referred us to Angie. That's how Del Mar got jobs with her."

"Have you ever been involved with prostitution?"

"I've been waiting for you to ask that," she said. "I'm not a whore or a madam and never have been. Does that answer your chicken-shit curiosity?"

Amanda shook her head. "Take it easy, Ginny," she cautioned.

"Madam, you're the one who put prostitution into this case," Barry said sternly. "You told the television audience that the defendants accused you of prostitution. I'm trying to find out if it is true. I take it your answer is no, but I assume you've had sex with men, other than your husbands. That's true, isn't it?"

Her face reddened. "What the hell's wrong with that?"

Looking straight at her, Barry said, "Just answer the question."

"Yeah!"

"How many would you say, five, ten, twenty or more than that?"

"Oh' for God sakes, I don't know, maybe ten or fifteen, I didn't keep count."

"Did you ever do that for favors?"

"Yeah, I fucked some movie guys to get in films, but that's all!"

Barry noticed that Amanda seemed surprised with that answer. "No other times?" he followed.

"No other times."

"How many times were you in one of the men's cabins that weekend?"

"I didn't say I was in one of those cabins more than once."

"You didn't say it, but you were, weren't you? You were in Max Pepper's cabin early Saturday morning?"

She looked quickly at Peg and Tina and demanded, "Who told you that?" Then, catching herself, she quickly added, "I was not!"

Noticing where she'd glanced, Barry asked, "Well then, which one of the other girls was in that cabin that night?"

Recovering, she said, "None of us were."

"You're swearing to that under oath?"

"You're damn right I am!"

He asked about Sunday night and got the same story Ginny told on Dorothy Watters' show. He also got the same pat answer about why the girls didn't say anything about the alleged attack on Monday, after the men had gone.

Barry changed directions again. "Where are you living now?"

"With Marlene," she said. "She's got a house 'bout four or five blocks from the catering office."

"Why aren't the other two living there also?"

"Not enough room. Marlene found them the apartment in Sellwood. Tina told you that."

"Who have you been hanging around with since you've been up here?"

"Oh, a bunch of people, but I suppose you want to know the names of some guys," she answered. "I didn't date much when we first got up here, but I've been going out a lot lately with a guy named Joey Buccanan. He's a bartender at a tavern we go to a lot in Multnomah. It's called Come-on-Inn."

"Do you sleep with him?"

"God, your mind's in the gutter. Yeah we're fucking buddies!"

Amanda said, "Come on, Ginny, just answer the questions, or we'll never get this over."

"Okay, he's got my answer. It's yes, yes, yes!"

Amanda called for a break.

In her office Amanda faced Ginny. "Goddamn it, do what I tell you. Just answer the questions. Keep your smartass cracks to yourself." Then she turned to the Max Pepper cabin visit. She knew the import of the answers Ginny had given. "I want a straight answer. What were you doing in Pepper's cabin?"

Ginny answered, "We weren't in there, I swear. He got me confused and upset. I don't know why I answered that way."

Amanda told her, "Well, you'd better think about it, because I'm damn sure there's someone out there who's going to say you were."

"If they do, they're lying."

When Amanda and the plaintiffs returned, Barry asked, "You've just conferred with your lawyer. Have you understood all of my questions today?"

"Yes."

"Is there any answer you've given that you want to change?"

"No."

He gave her one more chance. "You're sure of that?"

"Yeah, I'm sure," she replied, glaring back at him.

"And you understand, don't you, that a false answer on this deposition can be the basis of a criminal charge of perjury?"

"You threatening me, you bastard? Well, you ain't gonna make me change my answers."

"Very clever, Ms. Lane," he said calmly. "That's all I have for now."

Amanda told Ginny to move over next to Peg, and she brought Marlene Smyth in from another room.

Becky had joined them, and she changed seats with Barry. After Marlene was sworn and had settled in, Becky began by getting background information and some personal details. Then she asked, "Tell me how you happened to come to Oregon and how you acquired West Portland Catering."

"My husband worked for Liberty TV Cable in LA," Smyth said. "They transferred him to Portland the beginning of ninety-one. We moved up here, and about a month later we split up. It'd been coming on for some time. I don't know why I came up here. I thought maybe we'd get a fresh start. I was working at Tualatin Golf Club at the time. I think it was late April or early in May. I was talking to Bill Lattanzi at the club about a catering service he owned and wanted to sell. He told me about the great customers he had, lots of wealthy people, like Hugh Chalmers. He told me about the retreats he did for Chalmers every September. I was real impressed, especially with the kind of people Chalmers got to his retreat. I wanted to buy it, but no way I could swing it financially.

"Then I remembered Angie Lawrence had told me about a guy who had a catering service she used down in Orange County. I thought maybe he'd be interested in expanding up here with me as the working partner. So I called Angie to get his name. I explained the deal to her. I told her that if I could close the deal this summer, I could do the Chalmers' retreat and make an impression on some real important men. Angie said she'd get back to me.

"The next thing I know, she calls back in a couple of days and says she's got an investment company that'd be interested in backing me. She told me to get the details and call her back. I did, and we made a deal. It really went fast. I was the owner, or part owner, I should say, by June first."

"What's the name of the company?" Becky asked.

"It's called J & L Investment Company."

"Where's it located?"

"It's out of Orange County. Its address is in Newport Beach, in one of those new office buildings out by Fashion Island. I don't have the address, but I can get it."

"Please do that and give it to Amanda," Becky told her. "Do you know who the owners of J & L are?"

"No, I don't. Angie talked to them and got their cashier's check to close the deal."

"How much did you put up?" Becky asked.

"Nothing," she replied. "All the cash came from J & L. My part was to run the business."

"Did you say that you started the business June 1?"

"That's when we took over as owner," she replied. "We didn't actually start then. I didn't have a staff. That was a problem with the business. Bill told me that a cook had left him and had taken most of his staff to another job. That was one of the reasons he wanted to sell, and it caused me to think of the guy Angie knew in Orange County, 'cause he would probably have some staff or know where to get some. I told Angie that when we first talked. When she called back about J & L, she said she'd talked to one of the gals at that catering company, and she was interested in coming to Portland if we bought the business. Turns out the gal was Ginny, and she or Angie arranged for Peg and Tina to come too. So after June, I started using Bill's customer list to line up business, and by the time the gals got here in July, we was off and running."

Becky moved on to the problem at hand. "You told Susan Silver of EBC that Ginny, Peg and Tina would never have worked for you if they'd ever sold themselves for sex, do you remember that?"

"Yeah, I think I said that."

"Well, what did you know about their backgrounds before you hired them?"

Tapping her fingers, she said, "I guess not much, except Angie vouched for them."

"How did Angie vouch for them?"

"I don't know. Maybe she didn't say anything, but she recommended Ginny, so I guess I just assumed she vouched for them."

"Did you do a background check on them?"

"No."

"Did they fill out an application or give you any written background information?"

"God, no," Smyth answered. "I didn't have formal papers to give them. I just hired them word-of-mouth."

"So you don't know if any of them had a history of prostitution or doing sex for money or favors, do you?"

"I guess I don't," she said, "but I believed them when they said they didn't."

"They didn't tell you that before you hired them, did they?"

"No."

"Then when did they tell you that?" Becky asked.

"Last October," Smyth said, almost whispering.

Loudly, Becky repeated, "Last October? Where and how did that conversation occur?"

"In my shop, when Susan Silver talked to us," Smyth said softly.

"You mean Susan Silver asked them if they'd ever done sex for money or favors, and they denied it, is that what you're telling me?"

Again softly, she replied, "Yes."

"So when you hired them, you didn't know whether they'd sold themselves for sex before, did you?" Becky asked.

"No."

"Do these girls still work for you?"

"Yes, they do."

"How many times have you talked to Susan Silver?"

"Twice."

"Tell me about those times. When were they, where were you, and so forth."

"She and the McCormick gal from KPOR came to my office in October, like I just said, and talked to me and the girls. We told them what had happened, just like we did on television. Then in November, they came back with a TV crew and interviewed us again with the cameras."

"On the television program it sounded like Ms. Silver interviewed the girls live in the EBC studios in New York, and that she interviewed you earlier at your business. Is that the way it happened?" Becky asked.

"That's the way it came out, but we all did camera interviews in Portland in November at West Portland Catering. Then for some reason they decided to take the girls back to New York for the program."

"Have you given a written or recorded statement about this at any other time or to anyone else?"

"I talked to Amanda about it, but no written or recorded statements."

"Have you spoken to Mr. Chalmers or any of the other men who were at the retreat since September 1991?"

Smyth was twitching and tapping again. "Not to any of them personally."

"What do you mean not to them 'personally'?"

"I meant not to them," she said.

Becky had one more step to go. "Okay, then you talked to someone on their behalf?"

She finally opened up. "Yeah. Right after the first of the year I got a call from some lawyer in LA. He said he worked for Max Pepper, and he wanted to know how he could reach Ginny and Peg. I gave him their phone numbers. That's it."

"Do you know if he or Mr. Pepper talked to Ginny or Peg after that?"

"No, I don't. I never talked to them about it. Fact is, this is the first time I ever told anyone about the call." Becky looked at Amanda, who nodded.

The deposition ended just after noon.

⚥

Wednesday afternoon

The defense lawyers returned to Swift, Wyman & Wiggens and made a conference call to Joan and Miles. Shumanski was in trial. Barry laid out plans to follow up on the depositions. "Our *sub rosa* investigator is waiting for directions," Barry said. "We'll get transcripts this afternoon, and you'll have them by tomorrow afternoon or Friday morning. Please review them immediately and give me your suggestions," Barry said. "As soon as I hear from you, I'll put her to work."

Then Barry switched the discussion to the depositions scheduled in New York. "Remember, Becky and Mary Jo will be representing the Lukarillas. Lou, will you be attending?"

"I'll be there," Miles replied.

"I've talked to Paul," Joan said. "He wants us to go ahead without him. We've also identified the EBC investigator. He's Julius Sanchez. We're going to subpoena him."

"I'll notify Amanda this afternoon," Barry said. "On another subject, I'm concerned about this Pepper thing. When we learned that Ginny and Peg had been in his cabin, I had Hugh call Pepper, Price and Weinstein to get their versions. He got stonewalled. They wouldn't talk. Then we had Hugh contact the rest of the Lukarillas. Several confirmed that some of the girls were in that cabin earlier. He also found out that Weinstein hired a lawyer, and that's why he won't talk. Now we're told that a lawyer representing Pepper has apparently talked to Ginny and Peg. Pepper must have told him about the Friday night visit. Too bad we didn't know about that when I deposed the plaintiffs, but that's water over the dam now. The question is how do we get to Pepper, Weinstein and Parker? We've got to know what they know."

"I think we should have someone talk to Livingston," Becky suggested. "Why don't each of us talk to our clients and ask them what's the best way to approach him. He's in Atlanta. Maybe Joan or someone in her firm could go down there and talk to him."

"Good idea," Joan agreed. "Barry, I assume you'll talk to Chalmers and get his ideas."

⚤

Later that afternoon, Barry called Hugh Chalmers about talking to Livingston.

Chalmers had a good idea. "Whoever's going to talk to Ezra should talk to J.Q., as well," he said. "After I got Ezra's reply, I checked to see who had recommended Weinstein. I knew he was a relatively new member. Looking over the list, I realized he took Ben Grieve's place. Ben was an investment banker in Miami and one of the original members. Then I remembered, Ezra, Julian Epstein and J.Q. Ames sponsored Weinstein. J.Q. is a good friend of Steve's. J.Q. just might be able to get Steve to open up."

Barry thanked him. Barry then sent Joan a fax reporting on Chalmers' call and suggesting that she talk to Ames, since he was in North Carolina.

Thursday afternoon, February 20

Barry received faxes from Joan, Miles and Shumanski with follow-up investigation suggestions. Mary Jo stopped by his office just before he left for the evening. She had the depositions in her computer and had summarized them. She copied the pages of her summaries and of the depositions where the plaintiffs discussed their backgrounds and identified people, places and events and handed Barry the copies.

That evening Barry and Sarah were in their den relaxing. Barry had just poured two vodkas on the rocks, and as he handed Sarah hers, he said, "We're ready for more work from Pam." He gave Sarah the pages of the depositions and summaries Mary Jo had copied. "These are the parts of the plaintiffs' depositions and Mary Jo's summaries that Pam should review. The guys the plaintiffs have been seeing are ID'd there. Have Pam start with them. I want to know what they say about the girls. Also have her interview Bill Lattanzi, the former owner of the catering company. He probably won't have much to add, but you never know. Then have her check the plaintiffs out in LA. I think she has contacts down there."

"She does," Sarah replied.

"Okay, then have her get the owner of Del Mar Catering interviewed. The movie studios are a long shot, but two of them worked there, so tell her to have her contacts check it out. Of course, find out about J & L Investment Company and who's involved. I've got my suspicions about where the L comes from.

See what she can dig up about Max Pepper and Parker Price. They're both Lukarillas, and the girls apparently knew them before the retreat. Is that just a coincidence? Seems like we've run into a lot of coincidences. Is it just a coincidence that Rachel Jacobs dates Price? Is it just a coincidence that Pepper dates Angie Lawrence? Answering those questions is just the kind of challenge Pam likes.

"In the process don't let her overlook both Lawrence and Jacobs. I'd like to know if any of these people know

Susan Silver or any EBC executives. We don't have a lot of time. Becky is going to New York for depositions of Silver and her investigator. They start March tenth, so we'd like to know as much as we can by then. Have Pam report in by Thursday the sixth or Friday the seventh. Tell her to use as many investigators in as many places as she needs."

Sarah was excited to be involved. "I'll find Pam first thing in the morning. She's been waiting to hear from you, so I know she'll get right on it. I'll tell her to do better than March sixth. I'll give you reports as she progresses. For sure you'll have a report by a week from tomorrow."

Barry turned on the television, they sipped their drinks and picked up on the evening news in progress.

Chapter 18

Friday, February 21

Sarah had Pam Hill on the job first thing in the morning. Hall reviewed the summaries and then concentrated on the depositions themselves. She was pleased when she saw the involvement of the Sellwood Inn as she knew the tavern and its owner, Lou Wise, well. She knew he would be there by ten, and she called him shortly thereafter.

"Lou, Pam Hall here."

"Hi, Pam, how ya doing?"

"Great, and I could use a favor. I'm on a job, and I need some information. I'm investigating two women named Tina Marcellas and Peggy House. My information is that they are customers of yours. Am I right?"

"They sure are," Wise said. "They've been hanging around here for, let's see, at least six months. I think they live close by. They're not in every night, but they seem to come in looking for men. Their M.O.'s sitting at the bar and waiting for some guys to offer 'em drinks. What ya checking on 'em for?"

"They got a lawsuit going. They claim they got raped at a retreat up in the Coast Range last September. Maybe you heard about it."

"Yeah, seems like I do remember something like that. Hard to believe those two would be involved in a rape, unless they was doing the raping," Wise said.

"That's what our clients think. I want to talk to some of the guys they run with, ones who'll talk about the kind of girls they are. You know what I mean."

Wise said, "I don't want to get any of my regulars in trouble."

"Don't worry, you know how I operate, and there's nothing criminal involved here. We just want some information. The worst that could happen is they might have to testify in a civil case."

"What you want to know is their names, right?"

"Actually, I've got some names," Hall said. "One's called Weasel or George. Then there's a Pete Cross, a Junior Rich and a guy named Leo."

"I know who you're talking about," Wise said. "Weasel and Tina hang together quite a bit. Pete's probably been with both of 'em. Junior's with Peg a lot. The only Leo I can think of is Leo Santini. He's in here regularly after work. Come to think of it, I do remember him picking up Peg."

"It'd really help me if I knew where to find these guys, and any others you can think of."

"Well, there're two you haven't mentioned, who I'd put at the top of my list," Wise answered. "I'd bet my bottom dollar Tina's screwing Todd Smith. She plays around with Weasel when Todd's not around, but when he is, she's always hangin' with him, especially after about seven. That's when they leave together. The other one's Bruce Walker. He's always lookin' for Peg. I'm sure she fucks him, the way he smells around her. Todd lives just up the block from my place, but he's in here most of the time when he's not workin' or fishin'. Bruce also lives in Sellwood, but I'm not sure where. I know he drives his rig here.

"Why don't you come by about five? Todd or Bruce, or both of 'em, should be in. If the girls aren't here, you can introduce yourself and see if they'll talk. One of those others might be here, too. I can give you some leads on the others when you get here."

"Great, see you then."

The Sellwood Inn was your garden-variety tavern, long bar with stools along one wall, metal tables and chairs, some booths and several game machines. When Hall came in out of the rain, she saw five or six guys spaced out at the bar and two guys and a gal in one of the booths.

Lou Wise was taking care of the place alone. He was behind the bar talking to one of the customers.

Hall hung her raincoat on a peg, sat at the bar some distance from the others and casually surveyed the place.

A few minutes later Wise came over. "Hi, Pam, what'll ya have?"

"How about a draft, Coors Light."

Wise poured the beer and returned. "That's Todd, who I was talking to when you came in. Bruce is the guy down at the end of the bar. Weasel and Leo are with the girl in the booth. I was talking to Todd about you. You'll probably kill me, but I was honest with him, and told him you was checking into Tina, cause she's sued your client for rape. I told him she was one of those gals involved in the scandal up in the Coast Range that was on TV last September. He remembers it. He can't believe Tina was involved or that anyone could rape her. I told him you'd like to talk to him. He said, 'She's nothing to me, just a good fuck. Sure I'll talk to her.'"

Hall said, "You're right. You shouldn't have gone about it that way. But, what the hell, it worked. It's kind of blown my cover for the others, but I guess for once I'll just have to tell them what I'm really up to and see how it goes. Should I just go over and introduce myself?"

"No, come on over. I'll introduce you."

Hall stood next to Smith, and Wise said, "Todd this is Pam Hall, the gal I told you about."

"Hi," Smith said. "Lou says you want to talk about Tina."

"Yes, I'd like to," Hall answered.

"I don't mind. She's a hot number. Why don't we go over to that booth where it's more private? I'll buy you a beer, and you can ask away."

They went to a booth back toward the end of the room, away from where the two men and the woman were sitting.

After they were seated, Hall asked, "Lou tells me he told you who I am and what I'm doing. I want to find out as much as I can about Tina Marcellas. I'm trying to find out if she's telling the truth. Was she really raped?"

"Yeah, Lou told me she's one of those gals involved in that Lukarilla thing or whatever it's called. I remember the TV show. I didn't see it, but heard about it. There was talk about it in here. I can't believe Tina was one of them girls. She's been here when we was talking about it, and she never said a thing. But I know one thing. If she'd been at that retreat, she'd have been the aggressor, not the victim."

"Why do you say that?"

"How I first met her will answer that. It was in here. She and her friend, Peg, was sitting at the bar when I came in after work. Around the end of last summer. It was warm and Lou had the door open. I don't know if you've seen Tina, but when she wants to, she can look damn sexy, and that's the way she and her pal looked sittin' up at the bar that night, low-cut blouses and tight skirts. She seemed to be inviting, so I sat next to her and ordered a beer. After a while we started talking, and, as I thought, she wanted company. I bought her and her pal a couple of beers, then Peg got interested in Leo, who had sat on the other side next to her. So Tina and I kept on talking.

"Next thing I know she says, outta the blue, 'Want to screw?' I been around a lot and had that happen before, but never in here. So I thought I'd pull her leg, and I said, 'What's it going to cost me?' 'How 'bout a hundred,' she says. Still joking, I said, 'Make it fifty and you got a deal.' She says, 'Fine, where's your place?' Now I know she's not kidding. We just made a deal. I tell her I live just up the block, so we leave. What a night and for a measly fifty! Doesn't sound much like a victim, does she?"

Hall replied, "I guess not. Did you see her again?"

"You bet," Smith answered. "She started coming in here regular, and she always came lookin' for me. Only after that it didn't cost a dime. She's actually a pretty good chick, but I wouldn't want her around all the time. She's fun to talk to sometimes and great in the sack. But she'd never have to be forced."

"Are you still seeing her?"

"Not much of late. She hasn't been around here for at least a month. I've been wondering if she'd moved on. Peg hasn't been here either. They rented the upstairs in a house a few blocks away, and I haven't seen them around there either."

Hall asked, "Did she go out with anyone else around here?"

"Yeah, I think she took on Weasel a few times. I didn't see it, but Bruce told me that when I was out of town fishin', Tina kind of 'tached on to Weasel in my place. But I've never talked to him about it."

"Anything else you can tell me?"

"Can't think of anything," Smith said, as he got up and went back to his place at the bar.

Hall looked back at the bar and saw that Bruce Walker was gone. She asked Wise if Walker was coming back.

Wise looked disappointed, and replied, "I talked to him. He seemed real nervous, but he said when you got done with Todd, he'd talk to you. Then a few minutes later he told me that there was nothing he could tell you, and he left. I don't think he's coming back tonight. The way he acted, I think he was afraid to talk, but I don't know why. After you and Todd went over to the booth, I also talked to Santini, when he came up for refills of their beers. He said Sue, that's the girl they're with, has to leave in about half an hour, and he and Weasel will talk then."

Hall stayed at the bar talking with Wise until Santini came up.

Santini didn't look particularly friendly, but Hall was encouraged when he asked, "You want to talk to us?"

"I sure do. Can I join you at your table?" she asked.

Santini stared at her, and then said, "I guess so, come on over."

Hall followed him, pulled up a chair and sat down.

"What ya wanna know?" Santini asked.

"I'm interested in Tina Marcellas and Peg House. I understand you know them."

Weasel waved Santini off and took over the conversation. He looked irritated. "Yeah, we know 'em. What about it?"

"I'm trying to find out what kind of girls they are. Do they go for sex, that kind of thing?"

Weasel challenged her, "What's it to you?"

Hall explained about her client and what the girls were claiming. She told them she was checking on them because they'd filed a lawsuit.

"Yeah, I know Tina better'n Peg. She's a great girl, but

she's been through a lot in the last few months. The Lukarillas fiasco's done her a lot of damage."

"What do you mean, a lot of damage?" Hall asked.

"She's not the same girl. A lot shyer, loses her concentration, gets angry at little things. I used to go with her a lot, and we had fun. She still talks a lot with me, but we don't have much fun anymore."

"Did the fun involve sex?" Hall asked.

"Yeah, we did some screwing from time to time, but it wasn't cheap stuff. We like each other a lot, and it kind of came natural, you know."

"I understand the first time, she charged you a hundred bucks for it. Is that true?"

Weasel looked at her askance. "I don't know who told you that, but yeah, but it was just a joke. I met Tina here one night, and we talked and hit it off. We were joking with each other, and I told her I'd like to go home with her, if she didn't charge. She laughed and said no one gets near her for less than a hundred bucks. I told her I didn't have that kind of cash, and if I gave her a check, it'd bounce. She laughed and said, 'I'll take the check. Let's go to my place.' I gave her the check and that was our first night together. She still has the check. She kids me about it all the time."

"Do you believe what she claims about the Lukarillas' retreat?" Hall asked.

"I sure as hell do. She's not the kind to initiate a problem like that. Those guys took advantage of her, that's for sure."

Hall then turned to Santini and asked, "I understand you've been pretty friendly with Peg House, what can you tell me about her?"

He was slouching and mumbled, "Kind of the same as Weasel says about Tina." Then he spoke clearly. "She's a great gal, and before the Lukarillas thing we had some great times."

"She says she's had sex with you, is that true?"

Santini eyed her and said, "Yeah, so what?"

"Well, tell me about it."

"You mean how we did it? I hope you're not that stupid," Santini said. "But if you're asking if she solicited it, no. We met here and just hit it off. Lots of times we went to her place, with Weasel and Tina, and spent the night."

"All four of you spent the night together?" Hall asked.

"Come on now, you're a gal. You should know better than that. The girls had separate rooms."

"Do you know if Peg was having sex with anyone else?"

"No, I don't."

"Do you know Pete Cross and Junior Rich?"

"Yeah, I know them. You think she was fuckin' them too? I don't think so!"

"You ever talk to them about her?"

"No, I don't know them that well. I just seen them in here. We talk sometimes. That's about it."

"You said you had great times with Peg before the Lukarillas thing. What did you mean by that?"

Santini seemed to want the question. "She's not the same girl now. They took all the spunk out of her. She's afraid to let her hair down."

"How long did you know her before that happened?"

"Maybe a couple of months."

"How much have you seen her since it happened?"

"Maybe a couple times a month."

"I take it she told you what happened?"

Santini stared at Hall and said, "She sure did, and I believe her."

Hall asked Weasel how long he'd know Tina.

"Same as Leo, a couple of months, and same as him for how often I seen her since."

"When is the last time you saw these girls?"

"Last night," they answered together.

Hall asked, "Where did you see them?"

Santini answered. "Peg called me and asked me to come over to her place. When I got there, Weasel was there too. I guess Tina had called him. They told us about the depositions they just had. How bad it was, and how they told the lawyer about us. We told them not to worry. We'd stand by them, and we are, aren't we?" he said proudly, looking at Weasel.

"You bet," Weasel confirmed.

"Do you know if Tina dated Todd Smith?" Hall asked.

Weasel answered that one. "Yeah, she has. I saw you talking to him earlier. I wouldn't believe a thing he told you. I kind a like Todd, but he's a real bullshitter. Likes to brag about his doings with women, and I'll bet not much of it's true. I'm sure, if he told you anything bad about Tina, it's a bunch of crap."

"Has Smith been seeing Tina since the Lukarillas thing?" Hall asked.

Mildly disgusted, Weasel replied, "Yeah, I think so. She likes him and his line of shit. Don't ask me why."

Hall asked Santini if Peg went out with Bruce Walker.

Santini answered directly, "I think she might of. But Bruce won't run her down. I talked to him earlier tonight about Peg's deposition, and he feels sorry for her."

"Did you tell him not to talk to me?"

"No way, you weren't even here then," Santini answered.

Hall went back to the bar and talked with Wise. She told him what Weasel and Santini said about being summoned to Tina and Peg's house the night before.

That didn't surprise Wise. "Those two could be on the take, as far as I'm concerned." He handed Hall a piece of paper. "Here's Todd Smith's and Bruce Walker's addresses, and also the addresses of Pete Cross and Junior Rich," he said. "They all live in Sellwood. You might come back Friday, because Cross and Rich usually come in on Fridays. Come around five again, because if Tina or Peg show up, it wouldn't be before six."

Friday, February 21

Midafternoon Hall entered the Come-On-Inn. The place was empty, except for Joey Buccanan behind the bar. It was a small tavern, with a long bar, plenty of stools, and three or four pinball machines. Some chairs were scattered around the machines.

Hall introduced herself and began the conversation. "I've been told you're a friend of Ginny Lane. I'm doing a background check for a client who's thinking of hiring her. Could I ask you a few questions?"

Buccanan looked at Hall. "I suppose you can, but I don't know what I can tell you. She's a customer, and I've taken her out a few times."

"Do you know anything about her background?" Hall asked.

"Not really. She told me she came up here from California to work in a local catering business. Apparently she was in the same kind of business down there."

"When did you first meet her?"

"Her boss, Marlene, started coming in here last summer. She bought the catering business from Bill Lattanzi. He's in here a lot. He brought her in for lunch. After that she would drop in every now and then in the evenings. She got to know my crowd, and I think she even dated a couple of the guys.

"Sometime towards the end of the summer, Ginny came in with her. It was a slow night, so I shot the bull with them. We were talking about a new golf course out by Hillsboro. I'd played it. Ginny said she was into golf. Her husband got her interested, but she hadn't played since her divorce. I asked her if she was going to take it up again, and she said she'd like to. I told her I'd take her out to the course sometime when we were off work. Maybe a week or so later, she came in, alone this time. She said she had the weekend off and wondered about the golf game. I didn't work Sundays, so we made a date. After the golf, I took her to dinner. I've dated her a few times since."

"If I've got my mental calendar right, when you played golf and went to dinner, it would have been late summer, is that right?"

"It was the weekend after Labor Day," Buccanan said.

"When were the other times you dated her?"

"I suppose a couple more times in September, and maybe once in October, but not since then. I don't think I've seen her since late September or early October."

Hall decided that it was time to ask about the retreat. "Are you aware of publicity last fall about three girls who claimed they'd been sexually assaulted at a retreat in the mountains by some well-known men? It involved an outfit called the Lukarillas?"

With hesitation, Buccanan replied, "Yeah, I remember that. I remember it was a big thing."

"Did you ever hear that Ginny was one of those girls?"

Buccanan was surprised. "No," he replied, and then asked, "Was she?"

"She's filed a lawsuit, saying that she was," Hall answered.

"That's the first I've heard of it. As I say, I haven't seen her in here for some time."

"Then I'm confused," Hall said. "The other day in a deposition she said she's been going out a lot with you lately. You're telling me that's not true?"

Buccanan thought for a moment, and then said, "I'm not going to call her a liar, but I haven't seen her since last fall. The last I knew, she was hot and heavy with Mike Pritchard."

"Who's Mike Pritchard?" Hall asked.

"He runs the Mobil service station up on Barbur near Capitol Highway. Back in ninety-one he came in here a lot. I wasn't active enough for Ginny, so in late September or early October she started playing up to Mike. Wasn't long before they were leaving together. Toward the middle of October, I got in a beef with Mike over a sports bet we'd made. We both thought we'd won. It never got resolved, and I haven't seen either of them since."

"What do you mean you weren't active enough for her?"

Buccanan gave a sheepish grin. "I shouldn't have said that. But, if you gotta know, I was sleeping with her. She's real active, demands a lot. Frankly, I had a hard time keeping up. She likes to start by going down on you. Then she wants to fuck. Wants you to keep it up most of the night. And in the morning she wants more. It was awesome the first time, but every time? I need my sleep."

"Are you kidding me?" Hall asked.

Buccanan was serious. "No, she's got hot pants, if you know what I mean."

⚥

Later that day Hall talked to Bill Lattanzi on the telephone.

"I can't tell you much other than I sold the business to Marlene Smyth," Lattanzi said. "I met her when she was working at the bar in the Tualatin Country Club, where I belong."

Hall tried to reach Mike Pritchard, but he was away for a month in California.

That evening Hall followed up on Wise's suggestion and met with Cross and Rich. They had an almost identical tale to tell about Peg as Santini's. It seemed that they were also summoned to Peg's place after the deposition.

Saturday, February 22

When Barry arrived home after a long morning, Sarah was waiting with good news.

"Pam's called me," she said. "She's had quite a day here in Portland." Then Sarah relayed what Pam had learned.

Chapter 19

Monday, February 24

Pam Hall called Ron Lemery in Los Angeles. She'd known him for over ten years, and she'd done good work for him in Portland, so she knew he'd help. She got right to the point. "I'm working on a case up here that needs some investigation down your way. Are you available?"

"That depends," Lemery answered. "What's it about? What'd you need?"

Hall told him about the girls' lawsuit and the Lukarillas. She explained that the girls had been deposed, and she gave him a synopsis of their testimony. "I've been hired to check out their stories and investigate some people in your area. They might be behind the scenes. Their names are Max Pepper, Angie Lawrence, Rachel Jacobs and Parker Price. Pepper's a partner at Newman & Levine, and Lawrence is president of Citrus Publishing. You know who Jacobs and Price are."

"Yeah, I know Rachel and Price," Lemery said. "They're practically engaged, you know. I've met Pepper and Angie Lawrence too. I've got a buddy who's a partner in Pepper's firm, and I've been to parties thrown by Angie Lawrence. Would you believe that Rachel and Park got me my first invite?"

Hall told Lemery what she knew about the four and how their names came up. She also told him about the girls being in the Pepper-Price-Weinstein cabin two nights before the alleged scandal. "If you agreed to help," Hall said, "I'll get you in touch with Hugh Chalmers for more background on the Lukarillas and Pepper's involvement."

"I'm charging a lot more these days," Lemery told her. "But if your client has bucks, I'm available."

"Money's not a problem," Hall replied.

Hall and Lemery talked further about the things Hall's client wanted to know.

"We're on a fast track," Hall said. "More depositions are going to be taken soon, so we need a report by Friday, March sixth."

Lemery called Hugh Chalmers. He learned about the Lukarillas and how Pepper became a member. He started his sleuthing with Pepper, because he played poker with Byron Leech, one of the partners at Newman & Levine.

Wednesday, February 26

Lemery invited Byron Leech for lunch at the Jonathan Club in downtown Los Angeles.

When Leech arrived the headwaiter led him to the table where Lemery was waiting. Leech greeted Lemery as he sat down. "Hi, Ron. What's the occasion? I'm not used to you hosting a free lunch."

"My psyche just needs an injection of your humor every now and then," Lemery answered. "I've been shameless lately, missing our card days, so I thought I better buy you lunch."

Leech cast a doubtful look.

"Okay," Lemery admitted. "I'll be honest. I'm clocking my time, and you might be able to give me a boost."

"I thought so. Who's your client?"

"You know I can't tell you that. Here comes Paul, let's order, and then I'll pump you a bit."

The waiter offered them a drink.

Lemery ordered his usual Grey Goose on the stem, with a half-drop of Vermouth. Leech chose a glass of the house Chardonnay. The house special for the day was pan-fried fillet of sole, with a lemon mustard demiglaze and buttered broccoli, which they both ordered.

After the waiter left, Lemery said, "My client is looking for a lawyer to handle a very senitive matter. Max Pepper has been recommended. However, the client never hires lawyers, accountants or any personal service providers without first knowing everything he can learn about them. You're Pepper's partner, so I told myself, 'I better have lunch with Byron.'"

"What do you want to know?"

"Whatever you can tell me."

"He's been with the firm since eighty-one," Leach said. "He's probably our best courtroom lawyer, and he has a good business practice as well. He's divorced. That happened before he joined us. For about three years he's been going pretty steady with a gal named Angie Lawrence. She's president of one of our clients, Citrus Publishing Company. That's how he met her. Their best friends are the TV reporter Rachel Jacobs and the movie star Parker Price. Jacobs and Price are also a thing."

"The name J & L Investments came up in one of my searches," Lemery asked. "Does he have anything to do with it?"

"He doesn't, but I formed it for his girlfriend. The 'J' stands for Jacobs and the 'L' for Lawrence. It's a corporation I formed for Angie and Rachel, so they could make investments together. They're the only ones who have an interest in it, as far as I know."

"When was it formed?"

"Early last year. They were going to buy some real estate to start, and we decided a corporation was their best vehicle, particularly if they wanted to keep investing in things like that. Then later in about May, they invested in some company up in Oregon."

Lemery shifted back to Pepper. "What about his outside life? What kind of groups, clubs and the like does he belong to?"

"He plays golf at Big Canyon, and I think he also belongs to the LA Country Club," Leech said. "He belongs here, and just recently I found out that he's a member of a very exclusive men's group. I think it's involved in politics. It's called The Lukarillas. I learned about it when EBC, that's the network Rachel's station's connected with, did an expose on them last fall. It involved some sex scandal. Max told me it was a bunch of crap. He said he was a member and was there when it was supposed to have happened. According to him the women are three sluts, trying to cash in with a sleazy lawsuit."

"Anything else you think might help me?"

"No. The only reason I told you about the Lukarillas thing is that I didn't want your client later connecting the television program to Max's membership, without you knowing what he had to say about it."

They finished lunch, talking about friends and their card group. As they were leaving, Leech offered a suggestion. "You know who you might want to talk to? Steve Weinstein. He owns a big chain of stores in the Southeast called S-Mart. It's on the big board. He lives in Miami, but he's got a place out at Rancho Santa Fe and a condo in the desert. Max is his guest in the desert for golf a lot in the winter and spring. I think Weinstein's somehow involved in this Lukarillas thing. He was in our offices last November huddling with Max. Max introduced me to him as they were heading into his office. Before Max closed his door, I overheard Weinstein say, 'What're we going to tell Chalmers?' I assume he meant one of Max's clients, Hugh Chalmers."

Lemery's next step was to interview Skip Morales, who used to be head of the sports department at KEBC. Lemery had heard he'd been pretty thick with Jacobs. He couldn't remember who had dumped whom, but since Morales was now with Fox, Lemery thought maybe Morales would talk. He called Morales. They agreed to meet for a drink at Harry's Bar across from Century Plaza.

Morales approached Lemery's table. "Long time no see," he greeted Lemery. "You must be after information. What can I tell you?"

"Is it that obvious?" Lemery asked. Then he leaned forward and said, "I need some background and a current update on your ex-roommate Rachel Jacobs and her new guy, Parker Price."

Morales gave him a wink. "Boy, you know how to hurt a guy, don't you? I thought Park was my buddy. Rachel dumped me, and all of a sudden she's in his arms. I guess that's life. She met him through me. She ended up liking him more."

"I know you can tell me more than that."

"Well, okay, let's start at the beginning," Morales said. "Rachel came to KEBC in eight-five. She worked for me. Sometimes after work we'd go out for a drink. I was divorced, and she was single, so we got chummier. Pretty soon we were living together part-time.

"I've known Park for at least fifteen years. We met on a golf course. We both love golf and played together a lot. He belongs to Rivera, and I was his regular guest. Being his gracious self, he'd let me pay his way on the public courses I haunt.

"Three years ago last month the station entered me in the Bob Hope Desert Classic. It's a big deal. Park's been a regular for years. They match a pro with a team of four amateurs, and we play four days, one on each course. The pro's score is used to help our team and for himself in the pro tournament, which is going on at the same time. The pros play a fifth day for their championship. Rachel took some vacation time so she could come down and follow my team. It turned out that Park and I were on the same team, so Rachel met Park, and the three of us spent the week together both on and off the courses. Before long, Rachel was spending more time in her own digs and less time with me. Then one evening I saw her on television with Park going into a premiere of one of his movies. I realized I'd been replaced. Rachel started making weekend trips to Phoenix, where Park has a condo, and they seemed to be together whenever he was here in LA. Later that year, I moved to Fox, so it wasn't really that uncomfortable. They're both still friends, at least Park is."

"Tell me about Rachel's run-in with Abe Sumas," Lemery asked.

Morales told Lemery the locker-room story. "I was gone at the time," he added. "I learned most of this from Park on the golf course. He's real pissed at Sumas. Since she's black and so is he, I understood, but I later learned more. Rachel told Price that Sumas had cost EBC its pro football TV contract, and he blew his stack. He got so wound up on the course when he told me about it I had to take him to the bar afterwards to calm him down. Then he told me some stuff that made me realize this was more than a race deal. Apparently Sumas and Price are both members of the same private club or group. Price told me that Sumas knew damn well that Rachel was going with him and that treating Rachel like that was a slap in his face. To make things worse, he said that Rachel had told him the head of EBC Sports, Grant Slade, had tried to get a U.S. senator into the act, because Slade thought the league had canned EBC because of its tough programs about Sumas. The senator stonewalled Slade. Turns out the senator's in the same group with Sumas and Price, so Price thinks the senator slammed him too."

"Do you know if that group's called the Lukarillas?" Lemery asked.

Morales smiled and nodded. "Now that you mention it, that's the name he used. He still talks about how pissed he is at Sumas and that senator."

Morales was so full of information, Lemery kept going. "Did you happen to see the EBC expose on the Lukarillas and three girls who claimed they were sexually assaulted at a mountain retreat last September?"

Pausing and glancing at the ceiling, Morales said slowly, "I think I do remember something about that, but frankly, I didn't connect the name of the group. I probably should have, I guess."

"Has Price said anything about that? Did you know whether he was at that retreat?"

"No, to both."

"Do you know if Jacobs knows that Price, Sumas and the senator are all members of the Lukarillas?"

"I don't know for sure," Morales said. "But, if Park would tell me all this, I can't believe he hasn't told her. In fact, I'd bet Park is stirred up as much as she is, because they've talked a lot about it."

One more try, Lemery thought. "Do you know anything about a company called J & L Investments?"

"Never heard of it."

Morales looked at his watch and got up. "I've got to be going. I've got a dinner date in a couple of hours, and I'd better go home and take a shower."

"Thanks, you've been a big help, Skip," Lemery said. "Remember, I'm always here to give you a hand, if you need one."

Lemery didn't fare as well with the movie studios. He scouted around, but no one admitted to knowing the girls. Then he talked to the owner of Del Mar Catering, who acknowledged that Ginny Lane had worked for him for several years. The other two were more recent employees.

"They seem to hang out together, and Ginny's their leader," the owner said. "I suspected that Ginny wrangled some dates out of some of our jobs, and I started keeping a closer eye on her just before she quit. Actually they all quit together. I don't know much about Tina, but one of my bartenders told me that he'd lost track of Peg at one of Angie Lawrence's parties. He couldn't find her anywhere. Later he saw her come out of one of the first-floor bedrooms with Angie's boyfriend Max Pepper. I was going to confront Peg and find out what was going on, but she was gone before I could. The bartender has since quit, and I don't know where he's gone."

Lemery checked with the manager at the apartment in Irvine, where the girls lived while working for Del Mar.

"Ginny Lane was one of my tenants for about four years," the manager said. "Her roommate moved out the beginning of 1991, and several months later Tina and Peg moved in. Once the three of them were roommates there was a lot more action in the apartment at night. They had men visitors quite often, and there were several complaints about noise from other tenants. At one point I warned the girls that I'd evict them if the noise and partying continued."

Chapter 20

Monday morning, March 9

In New York the wind-chill was in the teens, and a storm was expected. Amanda was getting ready for the EBC depositions, and she was glad she'd brought her leather gloves, a heavy coat and a scarf. She was walking because Levinson & Wood's offices were so close by. Just as she turned to enter their building, snowflakes slowly began to tumble from the sky. It was nine-thirty when she met Susan Silver and Julie Sanchez in Ryan O'Donnell's office.

O'Donnell showed them into a small conference room, where they began deposition preparation.

Both Susan and Sanchez had been deposed before in the Silex/Lovejoy lawsuit, but Amanda explained that she wanted to give them her usual witness preparation advice anyway. After she had completed that, she continued, "Now let's go over the areas I think the lawyers will ask about." With O'Donnell's help they discussed the things Susan and Sanchez had done leading up to the television programs. "Have either of you done any further investigation into this matter since the Dorothy Watters show?" she asked.

"We put our investigation on hold, waiting to see the defendants' answers to the interrogatories," Susan replied. "We conducted background checks on all the Lukarillas members, once we got their names. Of course, I did talk to you and get Ryan involved in helping with the complaint and the discovery."

"I understand that, but you retained me to give you legal advice about your Lukarillas investigation," Amanda reminded her. "So if you get asked the question I just asked, keep that in mind. You can answer that you talked to me, but don't say anything more. Don't say what we talked about. I'll object to your disclosing those conversations, so wait for the objection. Your communications with me may be privileged. I hope the objection works. Some judges will buy it. Others may see it as a cute trick to hide what we're really doing. If this judge sees it that way, you'll probably have to answer."

Susan disagreed. "I don't know that I will. That's like trying to make me reveal my sources."

"I'm afraid not," O'Donnell said. "Amanda's not a source. What we're trying to protect is our working with Amanda to help her clients. That's a different thing, and it may be hard to protect."

The deposition preparation continued until about mid-afternoon. Then Amanda shifted the conversation. "Let's talk about scheduling some depositions of our own."

"Other than the defendants and Hugh Chalmers, whom do you plan to depose?" O'Donnell asked.

"I'd like to wait until we've deposed the defendants, and with the schedule the judge gave us, we'd better talk about the their depositions now. I suggest we schedule them for the first week in April. That'll leave us the rest of April to take whatever other depositions our investigation suggests. We'll have to work fast, but we can do it."

"That makes sense," O'Donnell replied, "but can you get the defendants done that fast? You might have to fly all over the country to depose them."

"I don't think so," Amanda said. "I'm sure Barry'll talk the other lawyers into bringing them all to Portland. He knows the judge will push for that, if we complain. To get things going, why don't we start those depositions on Tuesday, April seventh? That'll give us a day each through Friday, if we need it. How does that sound?"

"Sounds fine," O'Donnell said. "Will you need any help from anyone here?"

"I'd like Susan and Julie there, if that's possible. I won't take them to the depositions, but I'd like them available to confer with as we go along. If we can only have one, Susan should be that one."

"We'll both be there," Susan said. "You can count on it."

⚥

Becky, Mary Jo, and Miles arrived in New York later that day. They met with Joan at her office, and it was agreed that Joan would take the lead in Susan Silver's deposition, and Becky would start the Sanchez deposition. Ruth Mason had come with Becky and Mary Jo to be the reporter. Joan arranged for a local video firm to do the video recording.

⚥

Tuesday morning, March 10

Since Ruth Mason was not a notary in New York, the video cameraman gave Susan the oath.

As Susan sat in the witness chair she was the portrait of a businesswoman, not an investigative reporter. With a navy suit, her dark hair gathered and tied in back, and round black-rimmed glasses perched on her sharp nose, her disguise was perfect.

Joan said, "Will you state your full name for the record?"

"Susan Joann Silver," she answered confidently.

"Ms. Silver, we've met before. I took your deposition in another case, so I know you're familiar with the procedures. I just want the record to be clear. I'm going to assume that when you answer a question you fully understood it. Is that satisfactory with you?"

"Yes, it is."

Then Joan posed a series of questions leading up to Susan's present position with EBC.

"How did you get involved with the Lukarillas matter?"

Susan looked relaxed. She put both elbows on the

table and joined her hands under her chin. She told of the visit to Mike Ballard's office and her meeting with the EBC anchor.

"Tell me what you did in your investigation," Joan asked.

O'Donnell interrupted, "Counsel, that question calls for her to recite a litany of everything she did. Is that really what you want her to do?"

"Mr. O'Donnell, let's not be difficult," Joan replied. "I'm not expecting her to give me a minute-by-minute recitation of her activities. I think she knows what I want. I want her to just give me a synopsis of what she did. She can supplement later, if she needs to. I'm sure I'll have follow-up questions that will supplement it as well. You understand that don't you, Ms. Silver?"

Susan sat back and answered, "I think I do. I went to Oregon with our investigator, interviewed the three women and their employer, and assigned the investigator to do some follow-up work out there."

"Who was that investigator?"

"Julie Sanchez."

Joan then established that Susan had advised the plaintiffs to seek a lawyer.

"Prior to the filing of this lawsuit in December, did you have any conversations with the plaintiffs' lawyers, either Ms. Johnson or Mr. Bellows?"

"Yes, I did."

"When was or were those conversations?" Joan asked.

Susan looked at Amanda and O'Donnell. "I don't think I should answer that. Aren't the conversations privileged?"

"You can tell her when they occurred, but do not disclose what the conversations were, what was said, and so forth," Amanda replied. "They're subject to the lawyer-client privilege."

Susan complied. "About mid-October I called Amanda Johnson. Actually she called me. I was out and she left her number, so I returned the call. We talked at that time. I hired her and her firm to provide legal advice in Oregon concerning our continuing investigation into this matter."

"You said she called you. Do you know why?" Joan asked.

"I suppose because I told the girls that, if they hired a

lawyer, to have the lawyer call me," Susan answered. "I was thinking of retaining a lawyer there, and I thought I might hire the same one."

"Did you talk to the plaintiffs' lawyers at any other time?"

"I talked to Ms. Johnson on the telephone later in October. I was with Mr. O'Donnell. We talked to her together. Then I talked to her and Mr. O'Donnell just prior to this deposition."

Joan knew that the lawyers would object to what was said, but she didn't think a privilege was involved, so she asked, "Let's start with the first conversation in October, what was said?"

Amanda interrupted. "I object to that and instruct her not to answer or to answer any questions about the substance of the conversation between her and me and/or Mr. O'Donnell on the grounds of the lawyer-client privilege."

"I won't agree that the conversations are privileged," Joan said. "She says she hired you to assist in the investigation your network was making, but until I know what was said, I can't tell if the conversations related to that or to this lawsuit. Conversations about this lawsuit wouldn't be privileged. I want to talk to the judge about it."

That was Becky's signal. "I think we can get him," she said. "It's ten-thirty here. If he's in town, the judge is always in his office by seven west coast time. I have the number, so let's see if we can get him. Is this phone on the corner table a speakerphone?"

"Yes, it is," O'Donnell answered.

Joan said to Becky, "You call him. Then I'll present the problem, since they're my questions."

Becky turned on the speaker and placed a call to Judge Lloyd's chambers in Portland.

"Hello, Judge Lloyd speaking."

"Hi, Judge. This is Becky Cohen. We're in New York taking depositions in the *Lane vs. Lovejoy* case. Amanda's made some objections to Joan Dixon's questions to one of the witnesses, and we think you can help us. Joan can explain."

"I'll try. Ms. Dixon, what appears to be the problem?"

Joan explained the problem and suggested that the judge question Susan in private to see what her answers were going to be. The judge did that and was convinced that the conversations were not privileged. He ordered Susan to respond. At that point the deposition was recessed for lunch.

Joan, Becky, Mary Jo, and Miles went to Joan's office. A lunch Joan had ordered awaited them in one of the conference rooms.

"What a break!" Becky exclaimed. "That ruling has really turned this case upside down. We've got EBC right in the middle of it. Joan, your idea was masterful!"

"That's why I suggested the recess. I didn't want to go forward without our talking," Joan said. "And I've got a suggestion. EBC's obviously got it in for Lovejoy and Sumas. If we can show that to the jurors, they may get the idea that this case is really just the network's way to get back at some enemies. I think we should lay the groundwork for that with the rest of this deposition. Since I have been involved in the Lovejoy case, I can lead Ms. Silver right down that line. I know enough about their attack on Abe Sumas to question her on that too. Even if she doesn't have firsthand knowledge about it, the questions are all we want the jury to hear. I'll do this like a perpetuation deposition, so we can use the video at trial."

"She's all yours," Miles said.

Tuesday afternoon

The deposition resumed at one o'clock with the camera back in action. Susan testified to the conversations that occurred between her, Amanda and O'Donnell. She told Joan about O'Donnell's help with the complaint and discovery requests. Joan then went on the offensive and led

Susan through her involvement in the Silex expose, the libel suit by Lovejoy and Silex, and EBC's problems with Sumas over the Rachel Jacobs affair and the loss of the NFL contract. Becky and Miles asked a few questions for clarification and the deposition ended.

Chapter 21

Tuesday afternoon, March 10

Julie Sanchez surprised Becky when he was introduced. She expected an aggressive-looking man, like a cop. He looked more like an accountant to her, and he dressed the part for the deposition.

Becky began asking the usual personal background questions. Then she wanted to know about his October investigation in Oregon.

He told her about his visits to the Lukarillas camp and Astoria and his conversation with Beth Erickson.

Following up, she asked, "Beth Erickson called the DA's visitors 'a couple of slick-looking guys.' Is that what you said?"

"That's right, that's just what she said," he replied.

"Did she give you any other description of them? Did she say what they said?"

"No, to the first question," he answered. "Other than they wore courtroom suits. She told me they talked to the DA, but she didn't hear any of it."

"Have you done any investigation to determine who they were?"

"No."

"Do you plan to?"

"I haven't been asked to do that," he said cautiously.

"So, your answer is no?"

"That's right."

"Have you been given the list of the members of the Lukarillas?"

"Personally, no."

Becky suspected Sanchez had at least seen the list. "Then let me ask it this way. Have you seen the list, and, if so, where and what were the circumstances?"

"Yes. I saw it toward the end of January in Susan Silver's office. Amanda brought it with her when she came to New York to meet with us."

"Was anyone else there?"

"Ryan O'Donnell was there."

"Anyone else?"

"No."

"Ms. Silver didn't mention this conversation, but I'm going to assume that the judge's ruling applies to it as well, so tell what went on at that meeting."

Amanda interrupted. "I don't agree, and I object to his answering that question," she said. "We had to disclose the earlier conversations because the judge found that there was no privilege created by EBC's hiring our office, but now we are getting into my work product on this case, and that is privileged. The judge has put EBC into this case as my assistant, as such my discussions with them or anyone else working with me in the preparation of the case are protected."

"You may be right," Becky agreed. "But I reserve the right to depose him again if the judge rules otherwise. I have no further questions at this time."

After the others had left, Amanda, Susan, O'Donnell and Sanchez conferred.

"I guess we can't cry over spilt milk," Amanda said, "but with you guys exposed as our backers, this is a much tougher case. It'll be a lot harder to get the sympathy plaintiffs need to score big. I'm not sure how we overcome it."

O'Donnell wasn't so pessimistic. "I agree that we got hurt, but now's not the time to get down-in-the-dumps. The defendants have taken the initiative, and we need to get it back. Let's live with what's happened and save our evaluation of your clients' chances until we've got our investigation and discovery done."

"You're right," Amanda said. "I'm sorry for reacting so negatively, but I really didn't expect what happened today. Joan Dixon's a hell of a lot craftier than what I'm used to."

"All right, let's talk about what we've learned so far," O'Donnell suggested.

Susan reviewed what Sanchez had found to date. "I think Max Pepper may be a key," she added.

"That's a good start," O'Donnell said, "and I agree that Pepper's important. You have to depose him. Remember the questions about the girls being in the other cabin earlier. It sounds like they have some information that one or more of them was in his cabin. Also, I'd like to know how Pepper and Lovejoy both ended up in the Lukarillas. If they can't stand one another, how do they get along in a private group like that?

"If the lawyers agree to bring the defendants to Portland and meet your proposed schedule, then why don't you subpoena Pepper to testify in his office in LA on Tuesday the fourteenth? Otherwise, if you have to go to LA for Sumas, then take Pepper's while you're there. I'm talking a lot, but I've got some other ideas. Do you want to hear them now?"

"Sure," Amanda replied.

"Okay, now we know that Pepper's dating Angie Lawrence, we need to interview her, in person. Susan, you were close to her. Go out to Los Angeles and talk to her before Amanda takes these depositions.

"And what about Rachel Jacobs and Grant Slade? Has anyone talked to them lately? Susan, either you or Julie should do that. What Jacobs says might decide whether to depose Parker Price. If we need his deposition, subpoena him for LA when we're there for Pepper. Also either Jacobs or Slade may have other leads.

"Next, shouldn't we depose Weinstein? He was Pepper and Price's roommate. If they know something, he's sure to know it too. But Weinstein's also the one with Mafia connections, so some more investigation into his background might be in order before taking a deposition. Once we're ready to depose him, it'll have to be in Miami. So just in case, I'd set a deposition for around April sixteenth in Miami. If nothing else, that'll make the defense lawyers scramble. They'll have to split up so they can handle Los Angeles and Miami in the same week. If we decide to go ahead in both places, I assume, Amanda, that you can use your partner."

O'Donnell paused, and then added, "I've gotten a little ahead of myself. I meant to talk more about depositions in Portland first. Remember what Tina said, that there were four other people at this retreat. Sven, Emma, Thor and Judy Larson, my notes say. We have to find out what they know. Maybe they're the ones who'll talk about Friday night. Amanda, you better take their depositions in Portland right away, say next week?"

"It's short notice, but we can try," Amanda answered.

O'Donnell continued to address Amanda. "Send out another interrogatory to make sure no one else was on the retreat grounds that weekend. If other people are identified, you'd better depose them too. You've got time on the west coast, so send the interrogatory out today. And also send an amended letter advising them of the additional Portland depositions and the Los Angeles and Miami proposals."

Amanda felt a lot better when O'Donnell finished. "Thanks, Ryan. I agree with everything you said. I'll call my secretary right away and tell her to update my letter and get the interrogatory off. Luckily, I'm not leaving until tomorrow afternoon, so, Ryan, why don't we talk again tomorrow morning? After a good night's rest, we may think of other things we need to do."

"Good idea. Let's meet here at eight-thirty, and we'll talk again."

Wednesday morning, March 11

The weather was improving. It was still cold, but the snow had stopped and the city had adapted to it. Cabs crowded the streets and the airports were open. Amanda met O'Donnell at his office at eight-thirty.

O'Donnell had another suggestion. "There's another guy you better put on your deposition list. I don't know how we overlooked him yesterday. Remember what that secretary in the district attorney's office told Julie. We need to know who the mysterious visitors were. Who'll know that? That's an easy one to answer, the district attorney. I suggest you set up his deposition immediately, because you'll need time to do investigation, after you find out who those guys are. Why not subpoena him for a day next week?"

"You're right," Amanda said. "When I get back to the hotel, I'll call the office and get the subpoena going, and we'll serve it this week. My secretary will notify the defendants."

O'Donnell continued, "That raises another question. Have you got the troops to keep this offensive going? Now that they know EBC's involved, the Lukarillas are going to try even harder to outspend you. Can you do it by yourself? I'm not suggesting that you hire us to help, but since EBC has agreed to help with expenses, shouldn't you hire some temporary help?"

"I think Oscar and I can handle it," she answered. "We have two associates, one with five and the other with two years' experience, and we have four very capable legal assistants. The judge has cut off discovery in May, although realistically I'll bet that gets extended at least until June. So the time crunch is really only about three months. Then we have the summer to do further investigation and get ready for trial. I'm sure we can do it, but let me give it some more thought. We do want your continued input, however."

"We'll help any way we can," O'Donnell said. "Just keep us advised, either directly or through Susan. Is there anything else we can do today?"

"I don't think so."

"You're welcome to use this conference room the rest of the morning," O'Donnell added.

She thanked him, but she decided to do some shopping until the office back home opened; it was only six-thirty there. Then she'd work in the hotel room until it was time to leave.

"Okay, keep in touch," O'Donnell said.

Friday morning, March 13

Barry walked down the hall to Becky's office. "You sure got Amanda's attention," he remarked. "Her fax machine's flying. She's subpoenaed Owen Persell for a deposition on the nineteenth in Astoria, and she wants to do the Larsons on the eighteenth. I was just getting ready to let her know that we'll bring the defendants here for the depositions she wants in April, but now I guess we have more to talk about. I really don't see how we can object, so I'll tell her that we'll have the Larsons here in our offices to start at nine on the eighteenth. If she doesn't finish with them that day, she may have trouble taking Persell's deposition the next day in Astoria, but that's not our problem."

"She'll be prepared for that," Becky said. "She probably already has Oscar lined up to take Persell's deposition."

Barry knew she was right, so he decided to make the same plans. "Okay," he said, "you defend the Larsons' depositions, since you talked to them, and I'll to go to Astoria. I'd like to talk to Persell beforehand, but I better not. We don't want that coming out on his deposition. Get Mary Jo and meet me in my office in an hour. I'm going to arrange a conference call with the other lawyers so we can discuss Amanda's requests with them."

After Becky and Mary Jo joined him, the conference call was placed, and Barry turned on his speakerphone. "You're on the speaker now," he told the others. "Becky and Mary Jo are with me. Glad to have you with us in person, Paul."

"Me too," Shumanski replied. "The judge took a recess for God knows how long. It could last a few weeks or months. Anyway, he knows my trial schedule here, so I'm sure I'll be available in September."

"Great," Barry said. "With these deposition requests flying at us, I thought we should talk. Let me give you our thoughts, and I'll preface it by saying that we don't want to go to the judge for relief, if we can help it. If we can meet Amanda's demands without totally compromising someone's position, we should do it. I recommend we bring all the defendants to Portland for the depositions. We can have the Larsons ready on the eighteenth, so I say let's go for it."

"We're okay too," Joan said. "We'll rely on you for the Larson and Persell depositions, and on you and Lou for what goes on in LA. I can handle Miami."

"That's fine with us," Miles added. "I can be available in LA."

Shumanski concurred, but if he was available, he was going to join Joan in Miami.

⚥

Barry called Chalmers and asked him to call Pepper, Price and Weinstein and get the names of their lawyers.

⚥

Monday morning, March 16

Winter was gone by March in Portland. Trees began to flower in late February, and crocus and daffodils had been in full bloom for better than a week.

Chalmers called Barry. "I finally talked to Max, Park and Steve," he said. "Steve really didn't want to talk, but I told him I'd discussed his situation with Ezra. I also told him the plaintiffs were going to take his deposition, and Max's and Park's too, so it was time for everyone to be up front. He gave me his lawyer's name. He's Lester Solomon in Miami. He didn't have the number handy, but I said we could get it, and you'd call him.

"Max is another story. He claims he wants to help. He says the girls were in his cabin, but there's more to it than that. He's heard about the deposition. One of his partners, John Sheldon, will be representing him. He wants you to call Sheldon and to meet with him before the deposition. At the end of the conversation, he added that he's concerned about Park, and maybe Steve.

"Then I called Park. He was really cool. He knows he may be deposed. He's hired a lawyer in Los Angeles, Claude Skow. He said, 'Talk to him, if you want to.'"

Tuesday morning, March 17

John Sheldon returned Barry's call. "I'm glad you called," he said. "Parker Price told Max that their depositions are going to be taken next month. I don't know how Price found out, but I told Max that we ought to be talking to you guys before he's deposed. He's been troubled that he clammed up with Hugh Chalmers. He knew what Hugh's electronic message back in December wanted, but he wasn't sure what to do. It has to do with the fact that he'd known these girls before they moved to Portland, and in a way he feels responsible for their being at the retreat. I don't want to talk anymore about it on the telephone, because Max is still not sure how much he wants me to tell you. I'm trying to convince him to open up. I think the deposition's going to be on April fourteenth. Could you meet with me the afternoon before in my office, say at two?"

"I sure can," Barry replied.

"Let's do it that way then," he said. "Hopefully by then I can tell you exactly what to expect, and we can talk about how you want to handle Max."

Chapter 22

Wednesday morning, March 18

The depositions of the Larsons began at nine. Ruth Mason was at one end of the conference room table with her steno machine. The cameraman was set up at the opposite end. Amanda took the chair to Ruth's left. Amanda decided to start with Sven, so he took the witness chair. Becky and Mary Jo sat next to him. Emma, Thor and Judy waited in another conference room.

Ruth Mason gave Sven the oath.

Amanda began, "State your full name."

Sven sat erect, looking directly at Amanda. His large forearms rested on the table and he leaned slightly forward. "Sven Gunther Larson."

"Where do you reside, and with whom?"

"I live with my wife, our son and his wife, and their two children," he replied. "Our address is Route 4, Box 87, Elsie, Oregon, but we don't live in Elsie. We live south of town on a county road that goes along the Nehalem River, connecting US Highway 26 to State Highway 53 about two miles from the coast."

"Is Elsie the closest town to you?" she asked.

"It is now."

"What do you mean, it is now?"

"Emma and I've lived in the same house for forty-five years. I built it, and at that time a few miles to the north was a small logging village called Lukarilla. It's not there anymore."

"What happened to the town?"

"It wasn't really a town. It was just a place where a bunch of loggers lived along the river. However, there was a sign there. When the logging industry starting going bad in the seventies, everyone slowly moved away, and the state finally took down the sign."

"I understand that somewhere along that county road is a camp used by the Lukarillas for an annual retreat," she said, and then asked, "Do you have something to do with that camp?"

"I'm the caretaker."

"Whose property is it?"

"Hugh Chalmers'," he said, and then corrected himself. "Wait a minute. That's wrong, it belongs to CFP."

"CFP is Chalmers Forest Products?"

"Yes."

"Where do you live from the CFP property?"

"Right downriver from it."

Amanda passed a document to him and said, "Here's a rough map that an earlier witness drew. It's marked Exhibit One. Can you orient yourself with that map?"

He took the document and examined it carefully. Then placing it to the side, he looked back at Amanda and said, "Yeah, it looks like the Chalmers' place."

"Show us, using that map, where your place is," she asked.

"I really can't," he said. "The map isn't big enough." Then being helpful, he pointed to the exhibit and said, "There's a dirt road along the river that comes onto the Chalmers' property just west of the stables here. And that road leads to our house, maybe three to four hundred yards to the south."

"Draw as much of that dirt road on the exhibit as you can," Amanda said. "You'd better use a red pen, so we know you did it."

"It's right here," he said, drawing two red lines for the outline of the dirt road.

"Mr. Larson, were you on the property during the Lukarillas' retreat in September 1991?"

He was still sitting erect, looking directly at Amanda. He answered, "Yes, I was."

"How many men were there?"

"You mean other than me and Thor?"

"Yes. Just tell me who was there."

He looked at the ceiling, thinking. "Well, there was Hugh Chalmers and Smokie Goodenough. I'm kind of doing this by where they were staying. Then there was Abe Sumas, Senator Shepard, Alex Lovejoy, Max Pepper, Steve Weinstein, Park Price, Senator Epstein, Bill Churchill, Ezra Livingston, Cecil Upshaw, Nels Beecham and Hook Van Dyke."

"Were they staying in the cabins we see on Exhibit One?" she asked.

"Yes, they were."

"Had you known these men for some time?"

"Most of them, some longer than others. I only met Pepper once before. The year before was his first year."

"What was your job at the retreat?"

"No different, take care of the camp. Except Thor and I handled the horses for the guests."

"I understand that the Lukarillas hire catering from an outside source, is that right?"

"Yes."

"Can you tell me who the caterer was?"

"West Portland Catering."

"Was it the same caterer in 1990?"

"The name was the same."

"The way you say that, I gather there was something different in 1991 about the caterer, is that right?"

"Yes."

"Mr. Larson, it sounds like you're following orders," Amanda said. "Somebody probably told you to just answer the question, and no more. Okay, what was different?"

"In 1990 the company was run by Bill Lattanzi," he said, and then he added, "Lattanzi was the cook. He'd been there for several years. He had several different girls working as waitresses. He must of sold out, 'cause in 1991 it seemed to be run by a gal named Marlene. She was the cook. She had three new girls with her, Ginny, Peg and Tina."

"Did you have anything to do with the caterers or the people working for them?"

"Not really."

"Anything at all?"

"No, other than to talk to them, pass the time of the day," he said. But he quickly added, "Wait, I'll change that. We did work together cleaning things up after the men left on Monday."

"You're aware now, aren't you, that my clients claim they were sexually assaulted on Sunday night?"

"I'm aware that that's what they claim."

"Were you aware that they were assaulted?" she asked.

"I was not. No one said anything about that, even on Monday, when we were working together, and the men were gone."

"When was the first time you were aware of such claims?"

"Sometime after it hit the paper and was on television. I don't remember seeing it in the paper, but someone did and told me about that time."

"Who told you?"

"Mr. Chalmers called, after he'd seen the paper, and asked if I knew anything about it. I told him no."

"Do you know if your wife, son or daughter-in-law knew anything about the claims before the newspaper story?"

"They've all told me that they didn't."

"Are you aware, today, of anything else that happened out of the ordinary that weekend?"

"I am," he said, "but not from personal knowledge."

"What are you talking about?"

"I was told by Thor that he saw two of the caterer girls come out of one of the men's cabins early Saturday morning. I was told by Judy that she found condoms in that cabin when she was cleaning on Saturday."

Now Amanda knew the source of Barry's questions, so she wasn't surprised by the answer. She strongly suspected whose cabin it was, but she had to ask, "Whose cabin was it?"

"All I can tell you is what I was told. I was told it was the cabin Pepper, Weinstein and Price were staying in."

"Did any of the Lukarillas men say anything to you about the girls?"

"No."

"Do you know anything that would cause you not to believe what my clients say happened to them on Sunday night?"

"I'm not sure I know exactly what they say happened to them. But no, I don't know one way or the other," he replied. "Except what they claim troubles me. If they'd been attacked, why didn't they say something after the men were gone?"

"Thank you, Mr. Larson, I have no further questions," Amanda concluded.

Thor Larson was next. His deposition went pretty much like Sven's, until Amanda got to Saturday morning. Like Sven he was brief and to the point. Listening to him was almost hypnotizing. He had the same erect posture and ease of composure.

"Your father told me," Amanda asked, "that you saw two of the girls coming out of one of the men's cabins Saturday morning, is that right?"

"Yes, I did," he replied.

Amanda knew what was coming, but it was her job to neutralize him, if she could. She decided to press him. "All right, then tell me what you saw."

Still very erect and looking directly at her, he said, "First, I saw the girl we called Peg come out of the cabin where Max Pepper, Steve Weinstein and Park Price were staying. A little later I saw Ginny come out of the same cabin."

"When was this?"

"At about five-thirty in the morning."

"Where were you, what were you doing?"

"I was feeding the horses."

"Feeding the horses," she repeated. "You mean at the stables?"

"Yes, ma'am," he replied.

"This was the end of September, wasn't it?"

"Yes, it was."

"Well, it's dark out there that time of year, isn't it? What time does the sun come up?"

"I guess I don't know which question I should answer," he said. "But since it comes up probably about seven-thirty or eight o'clock, maybe that answers both."

"So, you agree that it was dark out when you were feeding the horses that morning, isn't that so?"

"Yes, it was."

"And you were inside the stables with the lights on?"

"Well, yes and no," he replied.

"What do you mean by that?"

"I was under the roof, but the stable stalls were open on the north side," he explained.

"You mean you leave the horses exposed to the outside at night that time of year?"

Being an Oregonian, she knew the minute she asked that question that she shouldn't have, because he said, "I don't know where you're from, ma'am, but late September in Oregon is some of the best weather we get. It's warm, and we almost always keep that side of the stables open. We close them up in mid- October."

She tried another avenue. "From where you were in the stables, where was this cabin you claim the girls came out of?"

"I don't claim it, ma'am," Thor said. "That's what I saw. The cabin was next to the river, one of the two closest to where I was."

"How far was it from where you were?"

"I don't know, a hundred, maybe two hundred feet."

"You mean it could have been as much as a city block?" she asked.

"No, it wasn't that far, but it was a ways."

"After Peg left that cabin, where did she go?"

"To her own cabin."

It didn't make sense to Amanda that he could really see that. "You saw her do that in the dark?"

"Yes, ma'am. There's outside lights on the back of all those cabins. As you said, it gets dark early at night and stays dark in the morning. The lights are there so's people can see where they're going."

"So you want us to believe, do you, that it was dark out, with some lights, you're inside the stables, and you're sure you saw Peg, who you just met a few hours earlier, come out of a cabin over one hundred feet away? What I'm getting at is how can you be sure the person you saw was Peg."

Without hesitation, he answered, "Well, ma'am, I guess when you put it that way, I can't be absolute, but there was only six women up there. Two were my wife and my mother, and they were back at our house. I know I saw two women come out of that cabin. That leaves only four choices. I don't think either was Marlene. She's stocky and older, and the first girl was short and thin. Of the three, that described Peg to me. Tina's tall. She wasn't one of them. The second girl was short too, but a little heavier, just like Ginny. I know, when I saw the first girl, I identified her right away as Peg. Same thing when I saw the second one. I thought it was Ginny, and I still do."

"But you agree with me, you can't be sure, isn't that right?"

"All I can say, ma'am, is what I've told you," he answered.

"Did you talk to any of the girls about this?"

"No."

"Were you aware that something had gone on with the girls in one of the men's cabins on Sunday night?"

"No, I never heard about that until the girls was gone."

"Did you have any conversations, or overhear any conversations, with the men about the girls during that retreat?"

"No."

"Did you ever talk to any of the men about what you claim you saw on Saturday morning?"

"Only with Mr. Chalmers, after the newspaper story."

"What did you tell him?"

"Just what I've told you."

"That's all the questions I have at this time."

⚥

Judy's deposition was next. She testified that when she was cleaning the Pepper-Weinstein-Price cabin Saturday morning, she found two condoms in the wastebaskets in the bathrooms. One was in each bathroom. She said that after her husband told her he'd seen two of the girls coming out of that cabin early in the morning, she told him about the condoms.

Amanda made an attempt to weaken Judy's conviction. "You don't look like the kind of girl who'd be exposed to condoms, are you sure that's what you saw?"

"I know what I saw, Ms. Johnson," she answered. "Thor used condoms when we were first married. We couldn't afford kids then. I know what they are, what they're for, and what they look like. They're what I saw!"

Amanda asked Emma whether she had anything to add. Receiving a no, she decided not to depose her.

Chapter 23

Thursday morning, March 19

Barry and Mary Jo arrived at the courthouse in Astoria for Owen Persell's deposition. It was one of those spring mornings locals cherish at the coast, cool and clear. From the hill you could see the sparkling blue mouth of the Columbia River as it approached the bar where it entered the Pacific Ocean.

The deposition of Persell started at nine in his office on the second floor of the courthouse. Ruth Mason was the reporter, and Oscar Bellows was representing the plaintiffs. Although he was merely seeking information with this deposition, Bellows had a video cameraman, just in case.

After Persell had been sworn in and had identified himself, Bellows didn't waste time. "You're the district attorney for Clatsop County, aren't you?"

"Yes, I am."

"How long have you held that position?"

"I was first elected in 1968. I've been district attorney for just over twenty-two years."

"How old are you?"

"Fifty-six."

"So you were, what, thirty-four when you were elected?"

"That's right, I'll be fifty-seven in June."

"All right, now as I understand it, complaints were filed by our clients with your department, claiming that they had been sexually attacked on Sunday, September twenty-second, 1991. My understanding is that the complaints were filed on Tuesday, September twenty-fourth, is that right?"

Persell had a county file in front of him, which he glanced at and responded, "Yes."

"I have a copy of your press release of October second. You said, and I quote, 'I made a thorough investigation into these charges, and I find that there is insufficient evidence to proceed any further with this matter,' isn't that correct?"

Barry knew that Persell, as a lawyer, anticipated what was coming, so it didn't surprise him when he qualified his answer. "Yes, but I said that 'my office' made the investigation."

"All right. Then tell me who made the investigation, what it entailed, and what the findings were."

Looking directly into the camera, Persell spoke with conviction. "Actually, I made the investigation myself. I got ahold of Hugh Chalmers on Thursday. His company owns the property where these assaults were supposed to have occurred. If you don't mind, my memory will be better if I refer to this file." Then reading, he continued. "He told me that he talked to all three men. They told him that they were in their cabin Sunday night playing cards when one of the girls, Peggy, came to the cabin and asked if they needed any ice. He said the other two girls were with her. They asked the girls in for a drink, and, after a few drinks, they had sex with the girls. They said the girls were looking for sex and consented. He also gave me the telephone numbers for the three men. I called them. I talked to Lovejoy and Sumas on Friday the twenty-seventh and took a recorded statement from each of them over the telephone. They told me basically what Mr. Chalmers had said. They each denied emphatically committing any type of sexual assault. I left a message for Senator Shepard, and he called me back on Monday. I took a recorded statement from him. He said the same thing and also denied any sexual assault. I read to each of them the statements that the girls had given me, and each of them told me that the girls weren't telling the truth. Based upon what I had found, it seemed like the typical she-said he-said situation. I found nothing to corroborate the girls' statements. Without corroboration, I didn't see how I could proceed. To do so would be in effect saying that the men had lied to me. I didn't have sufficient evidence to back that up, so I dropped the matter."

"What you've told me is basically what's in your official file," Bellows said, "but the file doesn't reveal that you had two visitors from out of town the day before your press conference. They came to see you about this matter, and they wanted you to drop it, didn't they?"

Persell was startled. "Who told you I had visitors?" he said.

"You're not taking my deposition, Mr. Persell. I'm not at liberty to reveal my source for that information at this time, but I can assure you that I have a source. Now, will you please answer the question? Read it back to him, Ruth."

Ruth Mason read the question back.

"I'd like to take a ten-minute recess," Persell said, and then, before Bellows could object, he walked out of his office.

Clearly irritated, Bellows made a statement for the record. "Let the record show that I didn't agree, and wouldn't have agreed, to such a recess, but Mr. Persell left his office before I could tell him to stay and answer the question first."

Persell went into an office on the first floor and made a long-distance telephone call. About fifteen minutes later, he came back and agreed to resume the deposition.

"What did you do after you left your office fifteen minutes ago?" Bellows demanded.

Reluctantly, Persell answered, "I made a telephone call."

"Who did you call?"

"Mike, Myron is his actual first name, Santana."

"Who is he, and where was he when you called him?"

"He was in San Francisco. He's in the import business."

"Why did you call him?"

"Because he's the one who sent those two men to see me."

Barry wondered when Bellows would remember that his earlier question hadn't been answered.

Coincidentlly, he remembered just then. "We'll come back to that," he said, "but are you now ready to answer the question I asked you earlier, the one the reporter read back?"

Persell faced the camera and addressed it frankly. "Yes, I am. You're right that I had two visitors from out of town on that date, and you're right that they wanted to talk about the complaints."

"Who were they?"

"I really don't know. They introduced themselves as Mr. Jones and Mr. Smith, and they told me that Mike had asked them to visit me."

"What else did they say?"

Still facing the camera, Persell explained, "They wanted to know what I was going to do about those complaints. They said Mike had an interest in the matter, and he didn't want me to proceed unless I had positive proof that the girls' stories were true. They said that Mike suspected the whole matter was a set-up, and that I should be very careful before going forward with criminal charges. I told them that I had already decided not to proceed. They said, 'In that case we'll be on our way,' and they left."

"Is that all that was said? I understood that they were in your office for several hours."

"You understood wrong. They were there maybe a half hour at the most. I've given you my best memory of the substance of what was said. There were some pleasantries about the city, the ocean, the river and the bridge to Washington and other scenery, but that's all that was said about the complaints."

"Tell me how you know Mr. Santana," Bellows asked.

"I've known him for over twenty years. He used to have an interest in a salmon and tuna cannery here. It closed down a few years ago when the fishing industry went sour."

"Did you, or do you, have a business relationship with him?"

"None other than he, along with other local people, helped me financially when I first ran for District Attorney. He may have contributed to my first reelection campaign, as well."

"Tell me how that occurred."

Without hesitation, Persell faced the camera and replied, "Well, back in the late sixties my predecessor was being pretty tough on the fishing industry and their docking rights on the river. The owners of several canneries and some fishing boat owners came to me about running against him. I had a private practice in Seaside at the time. I started there in 1960, when I got out of law school. One of those people was Mike Santana. They told me that they'd back me financially if I'd run. I figured with their backing I might win, so I took a shot at it. You know the results."

"No further questions," Oscar concluded.

It was Barry's turn. "Why would Mr. Santana have an interest in what you were going to do about those complaints?" he asked.

"Frankly, I don't know. That's just what those two men said."

"Was your decision not to proceed with the matter in any way influenced by the visit of those two men, or what those two men said?"

"No."

"I have no other questions," he said.

Thursday afternoon

Bellows got back to Portland at a little after twelve-thirty. He told Amanda what Persell had said.

Amanda called O'Donnell. "Ryan, I have Oscar Bellows here with me. We've now taken the Larsons' and the district attorney's depositions." She and Bellows then summarized what they had learned.

"I don't know what to do about the Larsons," Amanda said. "I've talked with the girls again. Ginny and Peg flatly deny that they were in that cabin. Tina and Marlene can't believe that they were either. They were asleep, but they're sure they would have awoken, either when the girls left or returned to their cabin. We'll send you transcripts. I'd appreciate your thoughts, after you've had time to digest them.

"We need to follow up on this Mike or Myron Santana matter. I'll send our investigator down to Astoria to scout around and see what he can find out about Santana. Someone needs to check him out in San Francisco. I'll bet he's got a connection with a Lukarilla. Santana had more to do with Persell's decision than Persell is willing to admit."

"I agree," O'Donnell said. "But San Francisco is for Sanchez. We'll talk to him today and have him get right on it."

Amanda called for Herb Goodwin, the firm's investigator. He'd been with them since the firm started over nine years ago. When Goodwin arrived, Amanda explained what they'd learned at the Persell deposition. "I know there's a lot more to this, and probably some connection to the Lukarillas," she said. "We want you to check it out, and the place to start is Mike Santana and Astoria. We haven't got a lot of time, so drop what you're doing, get down to Astoria and see what you can find out."

"I've got a better idea," Goodwin replied. "There's still a few of the guys down on the docks here in Portland who used to work out of Astoria back when the canneries were a big business. They loaded ships down there. I'll start by talking to them. They may have heard of this Santana."

That was fine with Amanda. The firm handled a lot of on-the-job injury cases for longshoremen, and Goodwin was their investigator for those cases. The docks were a tough venue, but he got along down there. He looked like a fighter, husky, five-seven and around two hundred pounds. He still had his army crew cut.

When Barry returned from Astoria, he headed for Becky's office, and he told her about Owen Persell's deposition. "I'm going to call Hugh right now," he said, "and see if he knows anything about this Santana guy and Persell's visitors." Chalmers came on the line, and Barry put him on the speakerphone and related what Persell had said. "Have you ever heard of this Santana guy?" he asked. "Did you know about Persell's visitors?"

"Yes and no," Chalmers answered. "No, I didn't know Persell had those visitors, but, yes, I know who Mike Santana is. He was well known in Astoria twenty years ago. He and his cronies, mostly hoods, had a stranglehold on the stevedoring down there. We shipped lumber out of that port back then, and they always got their cut. The district attorney tried to put them out of business, but they got him defeated. That's how Persell got his job. I haven't the slightest idea why Santana would be concerned about Lovejoy, Sumas or Shepard. I know it sounds like he must have some connection with them, or why send those guys to see Persell? But I'd be very surprised if any one of those three had anything to do with him."

"Do you suppose he was trying to protect someone else who was at the retreat?" Barry asked.

"What do you mean by that?" Chalmers asked.

"Don't forget, we've got evidence that the girls were involved with three other Lukarillas, Pepper, Price and Weinstein. Remember those are the three who've stonewalled us. It's probably not Pepper. I've talked to his lawyer and made arrangements to meet with him before the deposition on April fourteenth. I think Pepper's going to cooperate. On the other hand, Price's and Weinstein's lawyers still haven't returned my calls. I remember you told me that Ezra Livingston talked to Weinstein. If it's okay, I'm going to call him. He may know if Weinstein's the connection. I'll also keep after Weinstein's lawyer, Solomon."

"You may be right," Chalmers replied. "Go ahead and call Ezra. I told him you might."

Friday, March 20

Herb Goodwin checked the paper for the ships in town and then headed for Front Avenue, where most of the Friday activity seemed to be going on. He checked in at Terminal One, which was located on the west side of the Willamette River just north of the Fremont Bridge. Two ships were docked there. He examined the crew list and found Eric Sundoval, one of the guys he was looking for. Sundavol was with two other longshoremen. It was raining, and they were standing on the dock under a tarp tent, next to the *Kanga-Tu*, a ship registered in Nigeria, keeping dry and waiting for something to do.

"Hey, Eric, you got a minute?" Herb called out.

"That's all I got is time," Sundavol answered. "Whatcha need?"

"Some information about a guy who used to be involved with the docks down in Astoria. I wonder if you might have known about him. Name's Mike Santana."

"Hell, yes. Everyone on the docks knew Mike. He and his boys ran the place back in the sixties and seventies."

"What do you mean ran the place?"

"You know what the docks was like back in those days," Sundavol replied. "The mob had its fingers in all over the place. They took up the vacuum when Harry Bridges lost his hold on the Pacific Northwest ports. They had money in the canneries, and they ran the docks. The operation was run out of San Francisco, Mike's headquarters. One of his responsibilities was Astoria."

"Was there a time in the sixties when they were having trouble controlling the docks?"

"They never had any trouble with control. The trouble they had was with the DA. He was trying to make a name for hisself. He claimed the mob was holding up the shipping and stevedoring companies, and he was cracking down. Mike and the others backed a young guy in an election and got rid of that DA."

"How do you know Santana had mob connections?"

Sundavol laughed. "How do I know it? Everyone knew it. If you were a longshoreman, you knew who the real boss was and who his enforcers were."

"Is he involved down there now?"

"Nah, there's no shipping out of Astoria since the canneries went south."

"What about up here? Is the mob involved?"

"Funny thing is, they never have been. Astoria, yes, but they never got ahold of Portland-Vancouver."

Goodwin thanked him. "You've told me what I wanted to know," he said. "Be talking to you."

⚥

Goodwin reported back to Amanda. "I really don't see what a trip to Astoria will prove," he said. "I'll go if you want, but it seems to me the next stop should be San Francisco. I've got a few contacts there."

She agreed, but told him, "Hold off for now on San Francisco. I think our EBC friends want to try there first. I'll call them and let you know. Good job." She called O'Donnell and left a message.

⚥

Barry put in a call for Ezra Livingston in Atlanta. He was out, but his secretary promised to give him the message as soon as he returned. Then he tried Lester Solomon again, but he'd left his office. Barry left his name on his voice mail, told him it was important and again asked him to call back. He didn't go to lunch until a little after twelve-thirty.

Probably because he thought Barry would be out, Price's lawyer, Claude Skow, called at twelve-fifteen.

Barry answered the phone himself.

Skow was surprised. "Oh," he said. "I didn't expect you to answer the phone. I'm returning your call."

"I left the number of my direct line," Barry said. "I

understand you represent Parker Price. As I said in my message, I represent Hugh Chalmers and the Lukarillas in connection with a lawsuit in federal court up here. Your client isn't a defendant, but I think he may have some information about the case. The plaintiffs' lawyers think so too. They're going to try to take his deposition in LA on April fourteenth."

"I know about the case and the deposition date," Skow said. "I'm not sure I can help you, but ask away."

"We have information both from interviews and depositions that the plaintiffs paid a visit to a cabin, where your client was staying, the night before they claim that they were assaulted. They've denied the visit in their depositions. Obviously, if they're lying that'll hurt their case. I guess what I'd like to know is what your client will say about this. If possible, I'd like to meet with you before the deposition, so we can talk about how to handle your client's testimony."

"My client's aware of the testimony, but he doesn't want to take sides. He won't allow me to discuss his testimony ahead of time."

The answer surprised Barry. "Might I ask how he became aware of the testimony?"

"You can ask, but I'm not at liberty to discuss that either," Skow said.

"Has he been subpoenaed for the deposition?"

"Yes, and it will be in my office. That's all I'm going to say."

About two hours later, Ezra Livingston returned Barry's call. "What can I do to help, Mr. O'Shea?" he asked.

"Please call me Barry. I need some information about Steve Weinstein." He told Livingston what they'd learned about the visitors to the Astoria district attorney and the connection to Mike Santana. "Hugh told me what you said about why Weinstein won't talk about the retreat. Weinstein gave Hugh his lawyer's name, and I've been trying to reach him with no success yet. So I thought I'd call you and get a little more background on Weinstein. We're wondering how and why Santana got involved."

"I've never heard of Santana," Livingston said. "But let me tell you what I can about Steve. You probably know that I was one of his sponsors for the Lukarillas. The others were Julian Epstein and J.Q. Ames. Ben Grieve, an investment banker from Miami, had been a Lukarilla for years. He died in 1987. We put Steve up to replace him in 1988."

He then talked about Weinstein's background as a businessman. "I told Hugh, when we nominated him, that the only negative I knew was some years back he had some dealings with Joe Boccini, a Miami investor. When Steve first got started with S-Mart, like a lot of others, he expanded too quickly, particularly out of state. He spread himself too thin and got short of cash. He was getting close to bankruptcy in the mid-seventies, when Boccini invested in the company. I'm not sure how that occurred, but the financial problems seemed solved after that. I told Hugh this, because there had been talk that Boccini was connected with a Mafia family in Miami. In fact, I once heard he was the head of it. But the company went public in 1986, so whatever financial control Boccini might have had went away. Both Senator Epstein and J.Q. were sure Steve wasn't tainted with the mob, so he was accepted. You don't think Boccini's the connection to Santana, do you?"

"I really don't know," Barry replied, "but thanks for your help. We need all the information we can get. Hopefully, I'll get through to his lawyer and find out what he's afraid of. Thanks again."

Chapter 24

Monday morning, March 23

It was spring and getting warmer in New York. At eight west coast time O'Donnell called Amanda. "Sorry I didn't get back to you on Friday. We finally got some warm weather, so I took off early for the weekend," he said.

Amanda told him about Goodwin's investigation. "We decided that there wasn't much need to go to Astoria. But someone needs to follow up in San Francisco. I suspect Weinstein's mob friend in Miami knows Santana and has his fingers in this."

"You may be right," O'Donnell replied. "I'll turn it over to Sanchez. I think he has a contact in Miami. The answer may be there. If not, he's done some great work for us out in San Francisco."

"Sounds good. I'll leave the ball in your court. But let us know what you find as soon as possible. We're getting short of time. Weinstein's deposition is scheduled for April sixteenth."

Barry's telephone rang.

"Mr. O'Shea, this is Lester Solomon."

"Thanks for calling," Barry said. "I represent Hugh Chalmers and a group called the Lukarillas. Steve Weinstein's a member of that group. I called because I've been told that you're his lawyer." Barry started to explain about the lawsuit, its allegations and status when Solomon interrupted him.

"You're right, I represent Steve," Solomon said, "but I don't think I can help you. He hired me because he wants to stay out of the lawsuit."

"I understand," Barry continued, "however, you should know a little more about where we are in the case. Our investigation and some depositions that have been taken establish that two of the plaintiffs were in your client's cabin the night before the alleged assaults. The plaintiffs deny this. Plaintiffs' lawyers are going to subpoena your client for a deposition. In fact they may have already done it. Now that he's going to be deposed, he's involved, and we don't want an unfriendly deposition, if we can help it. I'd like to meet and talk before the deposition, so we can know what your client will say ahead of time."

"I understand," Solomon said, "but right now I'm not in a position to help you. I didn't know about the deposition, nor do I know if he's been subpoenaed. I'll call Steve and tell him about our conversation. If he changes his mind, I'll call you."

"Please do it right away."

Susan called Angie Lawrence and made a lunch date with her for next Thursday.

Then Susan called Rachel Jacobs and talked to her about the Lukarillas lawsuit and EBC's ongoing investigation into the district attorney's dropping the case against Lovejoy, Sumas and Shepard. "I need your help with some background on Sumas," she said. "I'm coming out to Los Angeles on business later this week. Could you meet with me sometime either Wednesday afternoon or Thursday morning?"

"Sure, let's make it Thursday morning," Jacobs replied.

That same morning Sanchez called Vince Romero in Miami. "We need a deeper look into Boccini and Weinstein." Sanchez told him about Santana's sending messengers to visit the district attorney in Astoria. "Ask around and see if Santana's name comes up in connection with either Boccini or Weinstein."

"I'll get right on it," Romero replied. "How soon do you want a report?"

"As quick as you can. Things are really moving here. Weinstein's deposition is going to be taken on April sixteenth, so if you find anything, we need to have it before then."

Wednesday, March 25

Romero received a call from an informant.

"Is there any connection between Mike Santana out in SF and Boccini?" Romero asked.

"You gotta be kidding," the informant said. "You want the whole story or just the highlights?"

"Let's try the highlights first."

"Okay," the informant said. "Up until the late sixties, Buzz Nomo had control over all the Mafia clans down here. He owned the longshoremen's union, and Mike and Boccini were his lieutenants, directing union activities. Nomo got cancer, and a scramble began over who'd be his successor. The infighting among the clan leaders got out of control, and a successor never emerged. So, when Nomo died, the mob split up into smaller clans, and Boccini took over one of them.

"About that same time, the union in SF was a mess. Bridges' screwups had the big guys taking cover. Nomo was trying to fill the gap and take control out there. Mike saw an opportunity and moved to SF. He took over Nomo's operations there. However, Mike still kept his contacts in Miami, so if one of Boccini's buddies needed help in Santana's area, it wouldn't surprise anyone that Boccini would call Santana for help."

"Thanks," Romero said. "Hey, will you ask around and see if Boccini had made a call for help with the DA in Oregon?"

"I'll try. I don't know if Santana's got influence in Oregon. But if he does and if Joe called and said one of his friends wanted that DA to cool it, Mike'd go to bat for him."

Thursday morning, March 26

It was going to be seventy-five in Los Angeles today. Susan wondered why she put up with New York. She arrived at KEBC shortly before nine and asked for Rachel Jacobs. Ten minutes later Rachel came out and led Susan into her small office in the sports department.

"Excuse the mess," Jacobs said. "Maybe it'd be easier if we go down to the coffee shop in the basement. This time of the morning we'll have it to ourselves."

They picked up coffee and took a table in the corner. "How can I help you?" Jacobs asked.

"I just want to be brought up to date on the problem with Sumas," Susan said. "Has anything happened since 1990? Before you start, I should say that I know that Grant Slade is real hot under the collar. He thinks Sumas and the Stars are responsible for our losing the NFL contract. He tried for help with Senator Shepard and got nowhere, even though he thought Shepard was his friend."

"Yeah, I know all that. I assume Grant's told you about the investment he made?"

"I don't know what you mean. What are you talking about?"

"Maybe I'm talking out of school," Jacobs said. "But he works with you, so I don't see how it can hurt. Angie Lawrence and I backed the gal who bought the catering service that's involved in the lawsuit. We did it with J & L Investment Company. It's a company one of Max's partners formed for us. Grant and my boyfriend, Park, put up the money."

"You gotta be kidding. How did that come about?"

"I think I better let Grant tell you that," Jacobs replied. "While I'd like to see Sumas take a big fall, it's his agenda, and I've said enough."

"Did you know these girls?" Susan asked.

"No, but I think Angie did."

"Really? I'm seeing Angie for lunch. I'll ask her about it. Thanks for talking with me. By the way, how's your network thing going?" The conversation then turned to Jacobs and her future with the network.

⚥

Thursday, afternoon

After Susan left, Rachel called Angie and told her about Susan's visit and what she'd told her.

"Interesting," Angie responded. "Sounds like Susan's LA trip and our lunch are connected."

At lunch Angie and Susan talked about old times and brought each other up to date. Finally, Susan broke the ice. "I'm still investigating the Lukarillas and the incident we covered last fall. I suspect there's a bigger story, and I could use your help. It concerns a lawyer down here, Max Pepper. I'm told that you and he are good friends."

"I'm surprised. I thought you wanted to talk to me about J & L Investments and the catering service," Angie said. "Rachel called me after your visit with her this morning. Why are you interested in Max?"

Susan should have realized that Jacobs would warn Angie, but she stayed with the subject she'd begun. "In our investigation we learned Pepper and Alex Lovejoy don't get along. We've also learned that Pepper is one of the Lukarillas and that he was at the retreat where the girls claim they were assaulted. First, we're curious how Lovejoy and Pepper could both be members of this close-knit group. Second, in some depositions, employees of the Lukarillas have testified that two of the girls were seen coming out of Pepper's cabin early in the morning the day before the assaults. That's when I decided to come out and talk to you about Pepper, Lovejoy and the Lukarillas connection. I didn't know, until I talked to Rachel Jacobs, that you two were involved with the caterer."

Angie was hesitant. "I don't want to get Max involved."

"Angie, he's already involved," Susan said. "His deposition's going to be taken. If you know something more about his connection with the girls, you should tell me. We're friends. It'd be a lot better for you to tell me what you know than to have someone else dig it out. I won't put a bad light on what you tell me. I want to get the facts in the proper context. Can't you help me do that?"

"I guess you're right," Angie said. "I really don't think Max did anything wrong, but being involved in something like this, that's already hit national TV, isn't good for the reputation of a respectable lawyer. I'll tell what I know, and what I didn't know, as well. Let's start there. I didn't know any of these girls had been in Max's cabin. Do they admit it?"

"No, they've testified under oath that they weren't in any of the men's cabins before the fatal Sunday night."

A little more at ease, Angie continued, "Okay, here's what I can tell you. You're right! There's no love lost between Max and Alex." She related how Alex had blackballed the Peppers in Boston, leading to a divorce and Max's move west. "Max can't stand Alex. Max represents Citrus Publishing. That's how I met him. He's basically my lawyer, although there's more to our relationship than that.

"Hugh Chalmers got him into the Lukarillas." She explained how he had replaced Chalmers' lawyer, Sam Levine. "Max joined the Lukarillas in either 1989 or 1990. I know the first time he went to a retreat was in September 1990. Max and I have discussed our feelings about Alex. We both dislike him, but we think alike, he's water over the dam. We're not interested in retribution, although I suppose someone could try to make something out of J & L's investment into the catering company. Actually, your Grant Slade had more to do with that than anyone."

The Angie paused and said, "Let me back up a moment. Before I say more, you need to know more background. After I came out here and took the Citrus job, Elmer Russell, my boss, introduced me to the community. He sponsored me as a social member of the Big Canyon Golf Club, and his wife got me into the Orange County Town Club, an all women social club in Laguna Beach.

I regularly used the club as a place for business lunches and dinners. One of the first persons I met at the club was the dining room hostess, Marlene Smyth. I'd learned in New York that the hostesses in clubs and quality restaurants could be very helpful business associates. So, although tipping was not allowed at the club, early on I gave Marlene a small envelope that contained my business card and a hundred dollar bill. Marlene reciprocated by acknowledging me when I came to the club. She also made a point to help me meet the important members.

"One day I went to the club for an early lunch. When I arrived at the dining room, Marlene greeted me, and when she realized I was alone, she offered to introduce me to a woman she described as a neat gal, who was sitting alone. The neat gal was Rachel Jacobs. I had lunch with Rachel, and that developed into a close relationship. We agreed to meet again the following week, and the lunches became a weekly ritual. Marlene reserved the same booth for us every Tuesday, but she only held it until 12:30 in case one of us didn't show up."

Angie then told Susan about how she and Rachel got involved with West Portland Catering and the waitresses through Smyth. "I told Max about Marlene's catering idea, because of the coincidence with the Lukarillas," she said. "Later we had dinner with Rachel, Park and Grant. Max had me to tell the others, because Park is also a member. Max and Park both thought it was a good investment for Marlene because they knew the guy who wanted to sell. It was Grant who brought up the idea of backing Marlene. He talked about using the catering company's presence at the Lukarillas' retreats to set up Lovejoy and Sumas. I made it plain that I wanted no part of any revenge plan. I think that's why Max didn't get involved. Rachel wasn't so kind. Grant and Park put up the money.

"And there's another thing I should tell you. After J & L invested and Marlene had the company, she called me." Then she related how the plaintiffs joined the catering company. "I told Rachel I'd done that," she added.

After Susan left Angie, she went back to her hotel to check out. She was scheduled on a red-eye back to New York. Before she left her room, she called Grant Slade. His secretary answered and said, "He's out of town, down in Houston talking to the owner of Sports Cable Network."

"What's that all about?" Susan asked.

"I guess you haven't heard. Tuesday, he got a call to come down there and talk. Apparently they want him to take over as CEO of the network."

"I'll be damned. I sure hadn't heard. I guess I'll have to talk to him when I get back."

"He won't be here tomorrow," the secretary said, "and I've got a hunch he may be working full-time in Houston by Monday. It sounded like a deal he couldn't turn down. There's a shake-up going on at that network, and, as I understood it, if he took the job, he was to go to work immediately."

"Thanks." Susan ended the call and thought, *Now where do I go? I wonder if Grant will even talk to me, if he's gone from EBC?*

Friday morning, March 27

Susan's plane landed in Newark. She went directly to her Manhattan apartment and slept until seven. In her office by ten, she immediately started trying to track Slade down in Houston. Her secretary found him at the Sports Cable Network's offices. "You're harder than hell to find," Susan said when she came on the line.

"I'm not hiding," he answered. "I got a great offer, and I decided to move. What's up?"

"I'm still working on the Lukarillas thing. I need your help. I just found out you invested in the catering company that's involved. What going on, Grant?"

"Nothing," he answered. "Park must have told you about it. We just thought it was a good investment. Besides, we were helping out a friend of Angie's."

"Oh, come off it, Grant. I know how you feel about Sumas and Shepard. I see your sly hand in what happened at that retreat. Before I get the network in too deep, I want to know how you're involved."

"I don't owe EBC anything," he said. "But, Susan, you're barking up the wrong tree. I invested and that's it. I don't know anything about what happened at that retreat, other than what I heard you report. I will say, however, it doesn't break my heart to see Sumas sucking it."

"Somehow, I'm having a hard time with that," Susan said, "but I'll let it drop for now."

Chapter 25

Sunday morning, April 5

Joan Dixon, Alex Lovejoy and Lou Miles arrived in Portland to begin deposition preparations. Sumas and Shepard were to arrive on Monday morning.

Joan and Barry used the video camera to prepare Alex and Hugh on Sunday.

Monday morning, April 6

Miles began the Sumas preparation. "Abe, I want you to try and relax. I'm going to dig into your sex life."

Sumas grimaced.

"I said take it easy! I see that damn temper of yours about to erupt. This is just what plaintiffs' lawyers are going to do in your deposition, so let's lay it on the line between ourselves first. I know you've been married three times. I'm not talking about that. What I want to know is whether you've had problems in the past with women. I'm talking about problems other people know about. I remember hearing about some back when you were playing pro football. Am I right?"

"Yeah, damn it, you're right," Sumas acknowledged grudgingly. "I had some problems, but Jesus those were years ago, before I was married. What've they got to do with this shit?"

"You tell me about the problems, and then I'll answer your question," Miles said.

"Okay," he said, "there was this slut in Pittsburgh back in the late fifties. She claimed I forced her into sex. She gave me a blowjob, and then tried to claim she didn't want to do it. It was a bunch of crap, and the DA dropped the charge, but it did hit the papers." Then he told him about the Baltimore and Philadelphia charges, calling them a pack of lies and boasting that these were dropped too. "I know it makes it sound like I got a thing for blowjobs," he said, "but the truth is that the last two never happened and the first one wanted to do it. That's it. Ask any of my wives. I didn't play around on them. We just weren't compatible as marrieds, so we divorced. We're still good friends."

"What you've told me is relevant," Miles said, "because they're trying to find evidence to corroborate the plaintiffs' version of what happened. Evidence that you've done like things before could do that. The best way to deal with it is to answer up front like you just did."

A similar interview between Paul Shumanski and Senator Shepard revealed no extracurricular sexual problems, according to the senator. Shumanski dug in hard, but the senator consistently denied any problems. The senator said that there are always rumors in any political campaign, but no rumor against him had ever been followed up with any evidence, because there was none.

Miles and Shumanski took Sumas and Shepard through video practices similar to the ones used by Joan and Barry earlier. Barry followed them Monday afternoon with a follow-up session with Chalmers, and Joan did the same with Lovejoy.

⚥

Tuesday morning, April 7

When Barry entered the deposition room with Chalmers, he was surprised to see Oscar Bellows representing the plaintiffs. Barry introduced Bellows to Chalmers, but Bellows saved his greeting until after Ruth Mason administered the oath.

"Good morning, Mr. Chalmers," Bellows said. "We've been introduced and as you know, I represent the plaintiffs in this lawsuit. I'm now going to take your deposition. I assume your role in this deposition has been explained to you, and you're aware of your responsibility to answer my questions. Am I correct?"

"Yes, you are," Chalmers answered.

Bellows started with questions about Chalmers, his personal and business backgrounds and his present situation. He asked a series of questions about the Lukarillas. He established that Chalmers had started the group, that it had a small yet geographically diverse membership, that the members were all business and civic leaders, and that its purpose was the sharing of philosophical and political experiences and ideas. He learned that the original group was composed of sixteen men from business, government, the legal and accounting professions and the entertainment industry. He found out how the group got its name, that it operated very informally, that it met just once a year, and that it maintained no records. He showed Chalmers the map, marked Exhibit One, and had him authenticate it as substantially correct.

"All right, now I'd like to learn about the members," Bellows said. "Let's take them one at a time. Is that okay?"

"That's fine. I assume you're talking about the present members?" Chalmers asked.

"Yes. We've discussed you, so now tell me about Hilton Jones."

From their meetings Barry knew that Chalmers liked the historian role, and as he answered that became apparent. All he lacked was a podium.

"Hilton is the managing partner of Stevens & Sherman," Chalmers explained. "It's a premier law firm in New York. They've got hundreds of lawyers. Hilton's one of the finest business and corporate lawyers in the country. I don't know his exact age, but I'd say he's in his sixties. He joined us in about seventy-three. He took the place of the New York lawyer, who Sam Levine recruited as an original member. That lawyer died a year or two before Hilton joined us."

"Do you know if Mr. Jones or his firm are the lawyers for any other members of the Lukarillas?" Bellows asked.

"I can't say for sure, but I believe that his firm represents Silex Petroleum, S-Mart and Random

Electronics. The heads of those companies are members. Alex Lovejoy is CEO of Silex, Stephen Weinstein is chairman of S-Mart, and William Churchill is president of Random."

"Do you know if Mr. Jones represents any of the members personally?"

"I do not."

"As I understand it, Mr. Jones was not at the retreat last September, is that correct?"

"He was not there."

"Next on the list your lawyers gave us is Max Pepper. And for the rest please include whether each was at the retreat," Bellows asked.

"Max is a partner in the law firm of Newman & Levine in Los Angeles," Chalmers replied. "He's our newest member. He succeeded one of our original members, Sam Levine. Sam died of cancer in February eighty-nine. Newman & Levine have been one of my company's law firms for many years. Sam Levine was the lawyer I used. He helped me put together the original group. After Pepper joined Sam's firm, he became kind of Sam's protégé. When Sam died, I wanted someone from that firm to take Sam's place in the Lukarillas. Max was the only partner there who I knew well. He was now my lawyer, and I trusted him and valued his opinions, so I backed him. Other than CFP, I don't think that firm or Pepper represents any other Lukarillas. He was at the retreat."

"Let me interrupt you there for a moment," Bellows said. "We've done some investigation into the backgrounds of the defendants, and we've found that there's been bad blood between Alex Lovejoy and Pepper in the past. Don't your replacements have to be unanimous? How did Pepper get past Lovejoy to become a member?"

Chalmers winced, but answered calmly, "Yes, they do have to be unanimous, and there was a slight problem, but I worked it out."

"Tell me what happened."

"I called the other members to get their okay, and Alex gave me an immediate rejection. He wouldn't discuss the reason, but he made it plain that he didn't like Pepper. This really disturbed me, as I really wanted Max to take Sam's place, and as you said, I had to have unanimous consent. I couldn't understand why Alex was so closed-mouthed." Then Chalmers explained that he involved Hilton Jones, and Lovejoy finally came around. He concluded, "Max attended his first retreat in 1990. Alex wasn't there."

"How about Cecil Upshaw?"

"He's been with us for some time. I think he joined in either seventy-four or seventy-five. He's the president of the national accounting firm of MJK&L. Frank Boone was the accountant in the original group. He was the head of Benjamin & Boone, CFP's accounting firm. Frank died in seventy-four, and we picked Cece to replace him. Cece was at the retreat." Then he volunteered, "I might add here, though my lawyer told me not to do this, that we've never had a member resign, and we've never asked one to leave. Since the original sixteen, we added four over the years. All the other new members came because of a death." He quickly got himself back on track, saying, "Let's see, you want to know if Cece or his firm represents others. I believe his firm does work for Silex, Random and Universal Airlines. Rex Smith is the president of Universal."

"You're doing great," Bellows told him. "Don't worry if you leave something out. I'll follow-up if I need to. Next is Parker Price."

"I'm sure you know that Mr. Price is a famous pop singer, as well as a movie star. He's not as active now as he used to be. He plays a lot of golf now, competes in a bunch of celebrity events. Let's see. He joined us in seventy-eight, I believe. He took Virgil Connor's place. You're kind of young, so you might not remember him, but Virgil won an Oscar for his acting back in the forties. Mr. Price was at the retreat."

"I know that Edward Thomas is a congressman," Bellows said.

"Yes, he represents Vermont," Chalmers agreed. "I first met him when we served in the Navy together. He'd just served one term when we started, so he's been in Congress for more than forty years. Ed wasn't at the last retreat."

"Julian Epstein is one of Texas' senators, isn't he?" Bellows asked.

"He is, and he's an original member. When I started, I tried to get elected officials around my age, so we'd last a while together," Chalmers said with a chuckle. "So he's been in Congress for over forty years. Ed Thomas recruited him. Julian was at the retreat."

"H.P. 'Smokie' Goodenough, he's also a U.S. Representative," Bellows said.

"Yeah, from Tennessee," Chalmers said. "Originally, we only had one congressman, Ed Thomas. So he's one of the four we added. That was around seventy-seven. Smokie's been in Congress for about twenty years. I know he's chairman of the Interior Committee because we've been involved in some timberland matters before his committee. Smokie was an entertainer before he got into politics, played the guitar and was a country singer back in the late fifties. He was at the retreat."

"You're a good chronologist, Mr. Chalmers. How do you remember all of these things?" Bellows asked.

Barry recognized what Bellows was doing. He wasn't trying to patronize. His compliment was designed to produce a cooperative Chalmers later on.

"It's not hard," Chalmers answered. "The Lukarillas was my brainchild. I started it because I wanted to rub elbows with this kind of guys. There's not many of us, and I've always cherished my association with them."

"Okay, next is Nelson Beecham. He's the governor of Wyoming, isn't he?"

"No, he's the ex-governor. Like Smokie, he was one of the four new guys added in the seventies. I think they can only serve two terms in Wyoming. He finished those terms in about eighty-six. I don't know exactly what he's doing now, except enjoying himself. I know he serves on several Rocky Mountain company boards. He's a great outdoorsman. He was at the retreat, fishing in the river most of the time."

"Vincent Grady, the Governor of Virginia. How long has he been a Lukarilla?"

"He's in our original governor spot. The first one, Harry Roberts of New Jersey, was also recruited for me by Ed Thomas. He was elected in forty-six, and Ed picked him again because he was about my age. I said earlier that no one had ever resigned. That's not exactly true, because our governors passed the baton after each left office. Roberts served until fifty-five, and he nominated Billy Lee

Randolph of South Carolina to replace him. Randolph left us in about sixty-one and was replaced by Guy Westland of Idaho, who was elected in the fall of sixty. Guy's term was up in sixty-nine. Bruce Nessler of Oklahoma was with us for most of the seventies. We had quite a contest over his replacement, but when Vince was elected in eighty-four, he immediately got unanimous approval. He finishes his two terms the end of this year, but my guess is we'll change the pattern and keep him with us for a few more years. He wasn't at the retreat."

"You said Beecham went out of office in nineteen eighty-six. Why hasn't he been replaced?"

"We just haven't got around to it. That's one reason I think Vince might stay on too."

"I understand," Bellows said. "Next is John Quincy Ames."

"He's called J.Q., and he's the chairman of the board of the Southern & Eastern Railroad. It's headquartered in Raleigh-Durham. J.Q.'s an original member. When we started in forty-eight, he was the railroad's vice-president, but most everyone knew he was destined for the top spot. That's why Frank Boone asked him to join us. He's probably one of our most respected and revered members. Even the politicians seek out his advice. He's been invaluable in scrutinizing and evaluating potential new members. He was at the retreat."

"Ezra Livingston."

"Ezra's the chairman of the board of the National Bank of the South. He works in Atlanta. He joined us in fifty-five, after the untimely death of Chancy Turner, who was president of Union National Bank in Chicago. Chancy was killed, along with several other bank officers, when their plane crashed taking off from Denver. Normally we would have looked to that bank for a replacement, but because of the loss of most of its key executives and because Ezra was the rising star in the industry at the time, we chose him. He'd just been made the bank's president at the age of forty-two. He's one of my closest friends. He was at the retreat."

"How about William Churchill?"

"Bill's president of Random Electronics. As you probably know, it's a Silicon Valley company, headquartered in Mountain View, California. Random also has a major plant up my way near Hillsboro, Oregon. We call that area the Silicon Forest. In about seventy-four or-five, Bill took the place of Fletcher Gomes, a San Francisco insurance man. Fletcher was chairman of New Life Insurance Company. Bill was at the retreat."

"Next is Mason Rutledge."

"He's the third of the late-seventies additions. Mason is president of Marion University in Springfield, Missouri. He's one of the country's top political scientists. Before taking the job at Marion, he was a professor of political science at both the University of Minnesota and Harvard. He wasn't at the retreat."

"I know who Hook Van Dyke is," Bellows told him. "I'm a Trail Blazers fan, and I watched Hook terrorize our team before he retired from the Celtics. But you tell me about him as a Lukarilla."

"He was our first athlete," Chalmers said. "He joined us in the early seventies. He took the place of a legendary Boston journalist, Carvel DeZell, who died in about sixty-nine. Hook was there in ninety-one."

"Stephen Weinstein."

"Steve's President of S-Mart. He lives in Miami. He took the place of one of our originals, Ben Grieve, who died in 1988. Ben was another friend of Frank Boone, and he was an investment banker in Miami. I wanted to keep someone from that city, and Ezra, J.Q. and Julie Epstein recommended him. Steve was at the retreat."

"Rex Smith."

"Rex is president of Universal Airlines, and he works in Chicago. Rex's predecessor was Raul Lewis, the founder of that airline. Raul was one of the few older men in the original group. Sam Levine recommended him. Raul passed away in nineteen sixty-nine, if I remember right. Rex took over as president a couple of years later, and we recruited him to replace Raul. That airline is one of a kind, it's only had two presidents. Rex wasn't at the retreat."

"That leaves us with three who we haven't discussed. First, tell me about Alex Lovejoy," Bellows continued.

"Alex is the president of Silex Petroleum," he said. "When he joined the Lukarillas, he was vice-president of New Brunswick Corporation. He replaced the president of that company when he died in nineteen seventy-nine."

"How about Abe Sumas?"

"Abe is our fourth new addition. We got him when he became the coach of the LA Stars. Abe's certainly our most colorful member. He's never at a loss for words. You always know where he stands. He's a master of the expletive, but we put up with it because Abe means well. As you know, he was at the retreat."

"Finally, Senator Shepard."

"Shep is the junior senator from Illinois. When we started Ed Thomas got us two U.S. Senators. We've covered Julian Epstein. The other was Harlan Spock from Kentucky. Harlan passed away in nineteen sixty-four, during the presidential election. We decided not to replace him until the election in November was over. One of those who came to the Senate as part of the Johnson landslide was Lionel Shepard. His military and economic backgrounds were made to order for us. His political career looked long-term, so we recruited him after his election."

Bellows thanked him. "I want to know some more about these men and your organization, so bear with me. When you started out, how did you decide which men to go after? Did you have help in investigating their backgrounds? Tell me just how you did it."

Chalmers continued as the historian. "Yes, I had help," he responded. "I told you earlier what my idea was and the kind of men I needed to make it work. I could have made a list of the top business and political men in the country, but how was I going to round up people like that?" Then he explained how he involved Sam Levine, Frank Boone and Edward Thomas. "After the four of us came up with some potential members, I hired Frank's firm's consulting subsidiary, B & B Consulting, to review that list and make some additions. That's how we landed twelve of the original sixteen members. Frank Boone, Ed Thomas, Sam Levine and I were the other four."

"What kind of information did B & B give you about the prospective members?"

"Their backgrounds and Dun & Bradstreet kind of information, things like that."

"I assume you were interested in the men's education, their personality traits, their habits, their families and marital status and their general reputations, were you not?"

"Yes," Chalmers agreed.

Barry knew that's what Bellows wanted to hear.

"In other words, you were trying to get well-educated men who were at the top of their fields and who were good citizens, is that right?" Bellows asked.

"Yes."

"All right then, when you had to replace a member or when you added the four new members in the seventies, did you go through the same process?"

"No, not usually."

"Why not?"

"By then we had a nucleus of important and influential men. We relied on the recommendations and knowledge of the group. On several occasions we did seek outside input, but it was not our regular practice."

"I assume you sought outside input when something came up about a potential member that needed a further look, is that correct?"

"Yes, that's about it."

"You did, however, continue to try to assure yourselves that new members would meet the criteria you had set up for selecting the original members, did you not?"

"Yes."

"And you continued to consider the personality traits, habits and reputations in the community of potential members important in their selection, did you not?"

"Yes."

With that answer Barry knew the motion to dismiss the Lukarillas that he was planning to file was in trouble.

Bellows moved on. "Mr. Chalmers, were you aware that anything unusual had gone on at the last retreat?"

"What do you mean by 'unusual'?"

"Out of the ordinary, unplanned, anything involving the catering company girls."

"No."

"When did you first hear that the girls had been involved with some of the members?"

"I don't believe that they were 'involved with some of the members,' as you stated. But the first time I heard of a claim to that effect is when I read it in *The Oregonian*."

"For how many years had you catered the retreat?"

"Ever since we started," he replied. "There were a few years when I had to hire the help individually, because there was no caterer who could fit our needs. But most years it was contracted out."

"When you hired a caterer, what was the makeup of the help, males and females?"

"At first they were all males. In the late forties and until the mid-seventies, we used the University Club in Portland. The Club provided a chef and the waiters. The waiters were all Filipinos. By the late-seventies the club had become too busy at that time of year, so we started using the Aero Club. Again it provided a chef and male waiters. I'd say it was in the mid-eighties that we first used a caterer who had female waitresses. He was Bob Lattanzi. He did the cooking, and his helpers were always women. We used Bob every year until 1991, when we contracted with the woman who bought him out."

"So from the mid-eighties, you always had female waitresses at the retreat, is that right?"

"Yes."

"Did they always stay overnight?"

"Yes, we had one cabin designated for the women. Lattanzi used one of the rooms in my cabin."

"Was there ever a time before nineteen ninety-one when the members got involved with the women? When I say 'got involved with,' I mean of a sexual nature, not necessarily intercourse, but playing around, visiting cabins at night, petting, anything like that."

"I never heard of anything like that," Chalmers said. "The women were never involved with the men."

Bellows shifted back to the members themselves. "Hook Van Dyke, you say, joined the group back in the early seventies, when he was playing for the Celtics, is that right?"

"Yes."

"How did his name come to you?"

"Well, as I said, Carvel Del Zell died. He was from Boston, so we were kind of interested in that area. It was my thought to get a well-known athlete, and I was also interested in a black person. I marveled at him when he came to town and played the Trail Blazers, so I suggested him."

"How did you check him out?" Bellows asked.

"I knew one of the Trail Blazers' owners. I also knew the general manager. I had dinner with them, told them about the Lukarillas, and asked them if they thought Hook would be a good addition. They thought he'd be great, and they agreed to talk to Red Auerbach about it. Several weeks later, I got a call from Hook wanting to know what the Lukarillas were all about. We met later that season in Boston, when they were playing Portland. After the season, Hook came to Portland, and I took him to the retreat camp. He fell in love with the place and begged me to let him join. That's how it happened."

"Did you follow Hook in the papers after that while he was still active?"

"Yes."

Bellows grinned. "Then you knew, didn't you, that he had a reputation for getting involved with the women, when the Celtics were on the road?"

"I'm not sure what you mean."

"Well, if you followed the newspapers, you knew that on several occasions women claimed that Hook had sexually assaulted them after a game."

"I think I remember something about that maybe once. But I'm sure Hook was never formally charged with anything like that."

"Well, you certainly knew, didn't you, that things like that were reported quite often about basketball players, when they were on the road? I think the Blazers have had some trouble in the past with some of their players getting overzealous with females, isn't that so?"

"You've asked me two questions." He answered the last one. "I have heard of that in connection with Blazer players one time in the past."

"What about in general?" Bellows asked. "You knew, didn't you, that basketball players, at least some of them, had problems getting involved with the gals?"

"I think I knew it had happened rarely."

"Let's talk about Smokie Goodenough for a minute," Bellows said. "You said he was added in the late seventies as a new member. Who proposed him, and how did you check him out?"

"Ed Thomas proposed him. We thought we needed another congressman and a young one. He was impressed with Smokie. He thought he was perfect for us. Both Julie Epstein and Lionel Shepard agreed that he was a good choice, so we basically took their word. Wouldn't you?"

"I'm not here to answer questions, Mr. Chalmers," Bellows said. "You've answered my question. Let's talk about Smokie's reputation in Washington, D.C. You're aware, are you not, that he has, and has had for a number of years, a reputation for getting involved with his female staff members?"

"I don't know if that's true. I've certainly never heard of it before."

"Have Senators Epstein or Shepard or Congressman Thomas ever told you anything like that?"

"I'm sure they haven't," Chalmers said.

"What about Parker Price? He's a Hollywood figure. Certainly you wouldn't be surprised to know that he has had numerous relationships with the opposite sex, would you?"

"Frankly, I don't know much about Park's personal life."

"But you would agree that it's not unusual for Hollywood actors to be involved with a multitude of women sexually, wouldn't you?"

Chalmers refused to be led. "I don't know if I can agree with that. I know there used to be a reputation in Hollywood for numerous wives. Frank Sinatra had four or five of them, as I recall."

Barry was concerned that Chalmers might be tiring, so he decided to intercede. "Listen to the question, Hugh, and just answer it."

Bellows continued. "Certainly you're aware of the oral sex problems that Abe Sumas has had, aren't you?"

The question irritated Chalmers. "Mr. Bellows, I truly don't know what you're talking about."

"Well, you told me that he was one of your four new additions. I assumed as a new addition, you did a background check on Sumas before asking him to join. Am I correct in that assumption?"

"When Abe took over the LA Stars," Chalmers answered, "Hook called me and suggested that having another sports figure would stimulate our retreats. He said that Abe was colorful and a straight shooter. I polled the members, and they all agreed that another sports figure, especially one like Sumas, would liven up our meetings. Everyone knew Sumas for what he was, a loud, sometimes crude, football coach, who some predicted would be the second Lombardi. With that background, everyone seemed to accept him, and there didn't seem to be any need for further checking. We elected him, and, I might add, he's been a jewel."

With that Bellows bored in. "That may be, but with very little investigation we've found that in his playing days he was one of those athletes who liked the road girls. One ex-teammate told us that there was hardly a night on the road that one of those girls didn't end up in Abe's room. The court records show three charges for forcing oral sex on women, one in Pittsburgh in 1958, one in Baltimore in 1961 and a third in Philadelphia in 1964. I guess you're telling us that you didn't know about these because you and your members just didn't check, is that true?"

Barry knew that Bellows didn't care what the answer was. Any answer would help. His question was what he wanted the jury to hear if he later played the video of the deposition for them.

"I'm telling you that I was not aware of any of that," Chalmers answered, "and, when I say that, I'm assuming what you say is true."

Bellows moved on. "Did you check on Senator Shepard before you asked him to join?"

"I already told you how Shep came to the Lukarillas. His background was public and well known. He had a distinguished war record and educational background. He had worked as a staffer for a noted senator. His election in 1964 was dramatic. There was nothing negative in his background that surfaced in that election. What more checking were we supposed to do?"

"Again, Mr. Chalmers, I'm not here to answer questions," Bellows said. "However, you're aware, aren't you, that after he took office, he's had a habit of offering money for oral sex?"

"I don't know what you're talking about, Mr. Bellows."

Bellows wasn't fazed. He said, "I'm talking about a maid in a hotel in Springfield. I'm talking about at least two female staffers. Weren't you aware that he offered money to those women for oral sex?"

"No, I was not."

"Well, Mr. Chalmers, let me ask you this," Bellows said, raising his voice. "Let's assume, solely for the purpose of this question, that you were aware that four or five of your members had significant histories of offering unwanted sex to women and that all of those men were going to be at your retreat in its remote area, where four unprotected females would also be housed for three nights. Assuming you knew that, you certainly would have kept an eye on those four or five men to be sure that they didn't take advantage of those women, wouldn't you?"

Barry recognized the tactic. The question was an argument for the jury, if the video was later shown. He knew Bellows's point was made no matter what Chalmers said.

Chalmers was still upset, but he tried to stay calm. "Mr. Bellows, I can't answer that question. I did not know then, and I do not know now that any of our members had any such problems."

Barry was satisfied. It was the best Chalmers could do.

With that question Bellows ended the deposition. "Thank you, Mr. Chalmers. That's all the questions I have."

Chapter 26

Tuesday afternoon, April 7

It was Alex Lovejoy's turn. He sat erect and looked at Amanda with confidence.

Amanda asked him about his past. Among other things, Lovejoy told her that he joined the Lukarillas in 1979, taking the place of his boss at New Brunswick. Then Amanda started asking questions about his lawsuit against EBC.

"I'm going to object to questions about that lawsuit," Joan quickly interjected. "His deposition has already been taken in that case. We'll stipulate that you can use any relevant portions of that deposition in this case. I just don't want him subjected to double questions, so I'm objecting to any questions that have already been asked and answered and instructing him not to answer them."

"I understand," Amanda said. "You're suggestion will save us time, but you'll have to tell me when the question has already been asked. I don't have his other deposition with me." Then addressing Lovejoy, Amanda asked, "Did you see any of the television programs about the September 1991 Lukarillas retreat?"

"I did not."

"Have you seen any replays of those programs or any transcripts of them?"

"No."

"Have you seen the September twenty-fifth newspaper story?"

"No."

"Well, are you aware what my clients say happened to them in your cabin on Sunday night, September 22, 1991?"

"Yes, to the extent that I've read the complaint and their depositions."

"Is what they said in their depositions about that night true?"

"Some is," he answered. "But most of what they said is a pack of lies."

"What are the lies?" Amanda asked.

"I'd rather you ask me what actually happened," he said. "The differences between what actually happened and what they say happened are the lies."

Politely, Amanda said, "I'm sorry, Mr. Lovejoy, but you'll have to answer the questions that I ask. Please answer the question."

Joan was pleased because they'd practiced this very scenario.

"I'll try," Lovejoy said, "but if I forget something, I want the opportunity to bring it up later." Then he looked at Amanda. "They lied when they said one of us asked them to play strip poker. They lied about why they were in our cabin. They lied when they claimed that Shep and Abe tried to have oral sex with them. They lied about what I said. And they lied when they claimed they had sex with us because they were threatened."

"All right, what do you claim happened?" Amanda asked.

He looked into the camera. "I've got to go back in time a little. On Saturday afternoon, while Steve Weinstein and I were fly fishing in the river, he told me that Ginny and Peg had dropped by their cabin about midnight. Max Pepper was already in bed. Steve and Park were playing cribbage. One of the girls knocked on the door, and when Steve opened it, Ginny asked if they wanted any ice. Steve told her sure and asked them in for a nightcap. After a couple of drinks, Steve said the girls got horny and wanted some action. He said he and Ginny went into his room, screwed and played around until early morning. It was, to use his words, 'out of sight.' He thought Park and Peg had sex too, but he didn't know for sure, because when he got up Saturday morning around six-thirty, the girls were gone."

"Were all of those cabins set up the same inside?" Amanda asked.

"Yes, all but Hugh's and the mess hall."

She handed him a sheet of paper. "Would you please draw me a sketch showing what the interior of those cabins looked like?" she asked.

Lovejoy drew a rectangle. "The cabins are about in this shape," he said as he was drawing. "There's a long deck in front with stairs in the middle down to the ground. The front doors are here," he said pointing. "There's a long room with a card table and chairs at one end. A fireplace, couch and lounge chairs are at the other end. I may have made the room and porch too long. The drawing isn't to scale. Three bedrooms are in the back like this." He pointed as he continued to draw. "They're connected to two bathrooms. The bedroom in the middle's connected to both bathrooms. I'm putting short diagonal lines to show you about where the doors are. While they may not look that way on the drawing, the bedrooms are all the same size, and each has twin beds. There's a bar with a sink and a small refrigerator under it on the wall opposite the middle bedroom."

"Thank you," she said. "We'll mark this as Exhibit Two."

Ruth Mason put an Exhibit 2 sticker on the drawing.

"Please continue, Mr. Lovejoy," Amanda said.

He turned back to the video camera. "All right. It's now Sunday night. At about nine something, there was a knock at our door. Abe and I were playing gin, and Shep was reading on the couch by the fireplace. Shep answered the door, and all three girls were there. Ginny asked Shep if we wanted any ice. I told him to ask them in for a drink. That's how they got into our cabin. We'd had at least one and maybe two drinks. The girls kinda paired up with us. What I mean is the Mexican girl, Tina, sat down on the couch and was kinda snuggled up to Shep. Ginny and Peg were kneeling on the floor by the card table, Ginny next to my chair and Peg next to Abe's, watching us play cards. Ginny complained that the card game was boring. She wanted more action. I asked her what she meant, and she said, and I can quote her, 'How about a little fucking.' Abe jumped in with something like, 'Yer talking my language, sweetheart,' and he turned to Peg and said, 'You game?' She said 'You bet,' and they went into Abe's room. It was the middle one. Shep took Tina into his room. It was the one down by the fireplace. Ginny and I had sex in my room. That's what happened. No one got assaulted. The girls wanted sex, and so did we. They came looking for it, and we accommodated them."

"Did you tell anyone at the retreat about this encounter?"

"No, I didn't. Neither did Abe or Shep. We decided the next morning to keep it to ourselves."

"To keep it to yourselves, you say. Why did you decide to do that?"

"Because what we'd done was not what the retreats were for, and we realized we shouldn't have gotten involved with the girls."

"Do you know if anyone else knows about what Steve told you?"

"Well, I assume Pepper and Park do," he said, "but truthfully I don't know. I do know it wasn't discussed when we were all together."

"Who else have you told what you just told me?"

"No one but my lawyer," he replied.

"When did you tell them?"

"Joan called me the day after the EBC program in September. I told her then what I just told you. We've talked about it several times since."

Joan nodded.

"Since the retreat," Amanda asked, "have you talked to Sumas or Shepard about what happened?"

"No."

"Have you ever told them the story you just told us?"

He stared at her. "No, and it's not a *story*, it's the truth!"

"Have either of them ever told you his version of that night?"

"I don't like the way you ask that, *his version*, but, no, neither has told me what he remembers."

"Have you ever been convicted of a crime, Mr. Lovejoy?"

In Joan's experience that question usually bothered a witness, but not Lovejoy.

"No, unless you consider a traffic ticket a crime."

"I'm finished," Amanda stated.

Wednesday morning, April 8

Amanda began Abe Sumas's deposition with background questions. Then she covered the facts surrounding Sumas' joining the Lukarillas. Abruptly she changed directions. "What was the name of the girl you had oral sex with in the William Penn Hotel in 1958?"

"How the hell do you expect me to remember that far back?" Sumas answered.

"You were charged with sexual assault by the local DA, weren't you?"

"Yeah, but it never stuck. She wouldn't back it up, 'cause it never happened that way."

"All right, then how did it happen?"

With a grin, Sumas answered, "The way she wanted it. She wanted a hundred bucks to do it. She was a prostitute, that's why she wouldn't testify."

"Then why do you think she made the complaint against you?"

"'Cause after she done it, I wouldn't give her the hundred. I know johns can be charged with prostitution too."

"Well, you don't deny that you and three other Cardinal players tried to force some girls into oral sex at a party in Baltimore in 1961, do you?"

"That's bullshit too. I don't know where the newspaper got that information, but the DA wouldn't press any charges."

She had learned by now that he was well prepared for these questions. "Are you telling us, under oath, that you didn't ask one of those girls to give you a blowjob?"

"I didn't say that," he corrected her. "I said I didn't try to force anyone into giving me oral sex. I said a claim that I did was bullshit."

"Well, did you ask her to give you a blowjob?"

He smirked. "I didn't ask her, but she talked about it. We just never got that far."

"What about the story in the Philadelphia paper that you tried to force a woman to give you oral sex in the back of a bar after a football game in December 1964?" Amanda asked. "You were charged by the DA with sexual assault for that, weren't you?"

"Yeah, I was charged," he admitted. "But like the others, the charge was dropped, 'cause there weren't no evidence."

"You mean it was dropped because they couldn't find the girl to testify against you, isn't that right?"

"You got the damnedest way of asking questions. I don't know what girl you're talking about. I didn't assault anyone then. The charge was dropped. There was a lot of stuff going on in that bar, but oral sex wasn't one of them."

Amanda took advantage of the extra comment. "What was going on?"

He shifted in his chair, showing the first signs of concern. "I don't know, I just said that 'cause your questions said there was."

"Just a minute, Mr. Sumas, forget my question," she said. "You said, 'There was a lot of stuff going on in that bar.' I want to know what stuff."

"Nothing," Sumas said. "I shouldn't have said that."

She continued to press him. "Do you deny, Mr. Sumas, that back in your football days, when you were playing, you were kind of considered an assman by your teammates?"

"Did one of them tell you that?" he asked. Then more reserved, he added with a slight smile, "I guess everyone's entitled to his opinion. I got my share, if that's what you want me to say. But not after I got married. I've been divorced three times, but none of my wives ever claimed that I wasn't faithful to 'em."

Amanda moved to the events at the retreat. His version was identical to Lovejoy's. She ended the deposition.

Wednesday afternoon

That afternoon, it was Bellows' turn again. He deposed the senator. It took about an hour to go through his background. Bellows learned how he became a Lukarilla and that he was a regular attendee at the retreats. "I understand that you have presidential aspirations," Bellows said.

"I don't know where you heard that," the senator said. "I've certainly made no such announcement."

Bellows glared at him, and quietly, in a semi-confidential manner, said, "Senator, we've talked to a woman in the Midwest who told us that in the early eighties she was a maid in a hotel in Springfield, Illinois, where you were staying during a campaign appearance. She says that one morning, when she entered your room to clean it, you offered her a hundred dollars for oral sex. Do you remember that, Senator?"

"I don't remember it, and it didn't happen," the senator answered emphatically.

"Are you saying that she lied to us?"

"I'm not saying anything, except it didn't happen."

"You know Sheila Workman, don't you Senator?"

"I remember that name," he said.

Locking on the senator's eyes, Bellows said, "Certainly you remember her, because she, like the maid, has told us that you made a similar offer to her. Ms. Workman worked for the State of Illinois in Springfield. You used to go out with her when you were in Springfield, didn't you Senator?"

"I . . . don't know what you mean, 'go out with her.' I do remember her. She worked for the party in Springfield, and I had several meetings with her over the years, particularly election years. But I remember the statement you made before you asked that question, and I'm telling you that I did not make any such offer to her! I've never made an offer like that to any woman!"

"Are you telling us, Senator, that you haven't made requests for oral sex from some of your female staffers?"

"That's exactly what I'm telling you!"

"Senator, do you have somewhere the names and addresses of all of the female staffers you've employed since you've been in the Senate?"

"I'm sure we do, somewhere."

Speaking to Paul Shumanski, Bellows said, "Counsel, I don't want to take time now to ask the senator to name these people. His records would be the best evidence. Will you consider this a formal request that we be provided with a list of his female staffers? We need it before the discovery time runs out on May fifth."

"Yes, I'll consider it a formal request," Shumanski answered, "but right now, I can't tell you when we can get it."

"Well, if we don't get it in time to notice some depositions before May fifth, we'll ask for a telephone conference with the judge to get some more time."

"I understand," Shumanski said.

After the deposition, the senator asked to meet privately with Shumanski. The senator was visibly shaken. "We've got to settle this mess, Paul. I can't have questions like that out in public. What'll it take to buy these women off?"

"I don't have any idea, Shep," Shumanski replied. "We haven't had any settlement discussions up to now. I'll talk to Barry about it, but now is not a good time to approach plaintiffs' lawyers. They know how sensitive their questions are, and I'm sure they suspect you may be panicking. To go to them now would play right into their hands. We need to wait a bit. But I'll ask Barry to approach them at an opportune time. I'll also see what the other defendants think about settling and what they might be willing to contribute. You'd better give that some thought yourself. What would you pay to get out of this?"

"I'll think about that," Shepard answered, "but we've got to do something before they try to take depositions of my ex-staffers. You never know what one might say, even though I've never done anything like what's claimed."

"When the timing's right we'll get the other side into settlement discussions," Shumanski said. "They'll probably be unreasonable, but that won't end the matter. We can go to the judge and ask for a settlement conference. In those conferences, the judge'll lean on both sides, and he can even talk directly with the plaintiffs without their lawyers present. Lots of times that's how these cases get resolved. But before we ask the judge to get involved, we need some strong evidence that's bad for the plaintiffs. The judge'll need that to pressure them into being reasonable. We might get that from the Pepper–Parker–Weinstein depositions, so I don't think we can talk settlement with plaintiffs before then. If plaintiffs try to take ex-staffers' depositions, I'll somehow wrangle a settlement conference first."

Later that afternoon, the defendants' lawyers met in the conference room. The depositions had gone well, with a couple of exceptions.

Shumanski explained how nervous his client was. He told them that his client wanted to settle.

Everyone agreed the time wasn't right to approach Amanda, but Barry said that he would do so at a more appropriate time, probably not until after the Pepper–Parker–Weinstein depositions. "My guess is at least one of those guys will make plaintiffs out as sex-hunters, so their lawyers might want out then too. At least it'll be a better time to bring settlement up."

The other lawyers agreed to talk to their clients and see what they'd pay to settle.

Chapter 27

Monday afternoon, April 13

After the morning fog receded, April in Newport Beach was delightful, an azure blue sky and the ocean like crystal. Barry met with John Sheldon at Newman & Levine's Newport Beach offices. Sheldon's office had a spectacular view of Balboa Island and Newport Bay in the foreground and the Pacific Ocean beyond.

"I'm glad we're meeting," Sheldon said. "Since our telephone conversation, I've had several talks with Max. He wants to cooperate, but he needs to be brought up to date on the discovery so far. I hope that's not a problem."

"Not at all," Barry replied.

"Okay, tell me where you are. Max is here, but I don't think he should meet with us. You don't want that coming out on the deposition. I'll report to him and relay what he can tell you."

"It won't make much difference whether the other lawyers know I'm here or that I talked to Pepper," Barry said. "But if he's more comfortable talking through you, let's do it that way." He told Sheldon about the Larsons' testimony and about Lovejoy's conversation with Weinstein. He also told him that the plaintiffs had denied being in Pepper's cabin. "That's the reason I think plaintiffs' lawyers want Pepper's deposition. Price's and Weinstein's depositions are also going to be taken this week. It would help if I knew Pepper's version of that night before his deposition. Also, from our earlier conversation, you mentioned that he had some connection with the plaintiffs in the past. Will he tell me what that was or do I go into that subject during his deposition? I don't want to educate plaintiffs' lawyer, if I don't have to. Of course, anything else he can tell me that'll help the defense would be great."

Satisfied, Sheldon said, "That's what I need. Let me go talk to Max. I'll be back in a few minutes."

Sheldon left. Barry got up, walked to the windows and took in the view.

About fifteen minutes later, Sheldon returned. "First, Max wants you to know about his relationship with the plaintiffs. As you may know, he's a close friend of Angie Lawrence. He met Ginny Lane and Peg House when the catering company Lawrence used for her parties employed them. He says Lawrence treated them almost like live-in help, so he was on a first-name basis with both of them. Next, he told me to tell you about Lawrence's and Rachel Jacobs' involvement with West Portland Catering. A company they own backed Smyth in purchasing that business, but there's more." He told Barry about Marlene Smyth's call to Lawrence looking for financial backers. "Lawrence shared that with Max, Parker Price and Rachel Jacobs one night when they were having dinner with EBC Sports' president, Grant Slade, at the Arches, a restaurant on the Coast Highway. Lawrence told them the name of the business Smyth wanted to buy and that one of its potential customers was the Lukarillas' retreat. Then Slade came up with an idea to back Smyth and use the catering company to get back at Sumas. That excited Price, because he also has a real hard-on for Sumas. Slade tried to get Max involved saying they could fix Lovejoy too." That led to Sheldon's giving Barry the history of the Lawrence-Lovejoy and the Pepper-Lovejoy problems.

"When the scheming started," Sheldon continued, "Lawrence made it very clear that she wanted no part of it, and she made Max agree to stay out of it. That's why he didn't invest. All the money came from Price and Slade, and Jacobs convinced Lawrence to let them use J & L Investment as the vehicle to transfer the money so Price's and Slade's names wouldn't be involved. Max suspects that either or both Slade and Price did something to trigger what happened at the retreat."

Then Sheldon turned to the subject Barry had asked about. "He'll confirm that Ginny and Peg came to their cabin late Friday night. Max says that he went to bed about ten-thirty. Price and Weinstein were playing cribbage. He woke up about midnight and heard Ginny's and Peg's voices in the front room. He went back to sleep. They weren't there when he got up the next morning. However, neither Price nor Weinstein have ever told him that they had sex with the girls that night.

"Max would rather not get into his past relationship with the girls in the deposition. If it comes up, so be it. But if plaintiffs' lawyer doesn't get into it, he'd prefer that you leave it alone. If it becomes important later, he'll make himself available to testify at trial."

Tuesday morning, April 14

Barry met Lou Miles for breakfast at the Four Seasons Hotel. He told Miles about his meeting with John Sheldon. Miles agreed to honor Pepper's request to hold back on questions. After breakfast they went directly to Newman & Levine's offices. Oscar Bellows was there for the plaintiffs, and Ruth Mason came down from Portland to be the reporter. The video cameraman was local.

Bellows started with the usual questions, covering Pepper's legal practice in Boston and Los Angeles and his relationship to the Lukarillas.

Pepper leaned slightly forward in the witness chair with his forearms resting on the table. He admitted to Bellows that he was present at the retreat in September 1991.

"As I understand it, you were assigned to a cabin with Parker Price and Stephen Weinstein, is that right?" Bellows asked.

"Actually, I did the assigning," Pepper said. "I was the junior member and drew the chore of assignments and scheduling."

Lawyers don't make good witnesses, Barry thought.

Then Pepper answered the question. "Yes, I shared a cabin with those two."

Bellows got right to the point. "We've heard testimony in this case, that at least two of my clients visited that cabin either late Friday night or early Saturday morning, do you know anything about that?"

Again not directly answering, Pepper said, "About midnight I heard Ginny and, I think, Peg talking to Park and Steve. I was in bed and had been asleep. I went right back to sleep. They weren't there when I got up the next morning. That's all I can tell you."

"Do you know if either of them had sex or any sexual contacts with Price or Weinstein that night or morning?"

"I do not."

"Tell us why you left Boston."

Pepper removed his arms from the table and glanced briefly at Sheldon. Then he turned back to Bellows and said, "I got an offer from Newman & Levine that, considering everything that was going on, I couldn't refuse."

"What was going on?"

Pepper placed his arms back on the table. "I had just finished a very tough and bitter tender offer case. There were hard feelings generated on both sides. Those feelings spilled over into the community. The problems even affected my marriage. I ended up getting a divorce. Eventually, I started thinking about relocating. I had a law classmate at Newman & Levine, so I called him. A headhunter got involved, I got an offer, and I took it."

"Did the hard feelings involve Alex Lovejoy?" Bellows asked.

"Yes, they did."

"What are your feelings about Alex Lovejoy?"

Pepper turned and asked Sheldon, "Is this relevant, John?"

Sheldon replied, "I'm not sure, but go ahead and answer. Let's see where he's going. I may object if some relevance doesn't show up soon."

Pepper complied. "I don't particularly care for the man."

"I gather the feeling is mutual, is that correct?"

"You could say that."

"I understand that admission into the Lukarillas has to be unanimous," Bellows said. "Given Lovejoy's attitude toward you, why didn't he object to you joining?"

"I really don't know," Pepper answered. "Frankly, I was kind of surprised myself, but Hugh Chalmers wanted me, and he's pretty persuasive."

"Did anything happen between you two at the retreat?"

"No. We didn't talk."

"I have no further questions," Bellows said.

Per their earlier understanding, Barry and Miles deferred.

"Let's come back at one," Bellows suggested. "Parker Price and his lawyer will be here then."

⚥

It was eleven-fifteen in Portland. Amanda was about to leave her office for the airport. Her plane to Miami was the red-eye. Her phone rang. It was Susan Silver.

"I'm glad I got you before you left," Susan said. "I was afraid I'd have to chase you down in Miami. I want to talk about the Weinstein deposition, and what you're going to do about the Santana thing. Ryan and I have been talking, and we think you should follow up with Weinstein to see if he initiated the contact through Boccini."

Amanda was troubled by that suggestion. "I know what you're after, but I need to know if he'll back up the Larsons first. The only reason I can see for his involving Boccini and Santana would be that the girls were in his cabin, and he was afraid of being involved in the DA's investigation. But if he says, as my clients say, that they weren't in his cabin, I'm not going to weaken that testimony by getting him involved in the Santana matter. I realize you'd like that evidence to use in a story exposing the Lukarillas, but I have to think about my clients first."

"We still believe you should ask it," Susan argued. "If Weinstein denies that the girls were in his cabin, then his reason to use influence with the DA has to be to protect The Lukarillas. That'll help your case against them."

"I understand what you're saying," Amanda said, "but I'm afraid that, if I get into it, the implication will be that the girls were in his room. I know what you want and why. Let me think some more about it. I want to see what he says first. I'm sorry but I've got to go. I don't want to miss my plane."

"All right," Susan said, "but remember Weinstein may be our only source to get to the bottom of the Santana pressure on the DA."

Tuesday afternoon

After asking Parker Price about his background and his relationship with the Lukarillas, Bellows got down to business. "Mr. Pepper just told us that he heard Ginny Lane and Peg House in your cabin about midnight Saturday morning, is that correct?"

"I don't know what he heard. I didn't see them."

"Are you saying Pepper's not telling the truth?"

"I didn't say that. I said I don't know what he heard." He added, "About that time I was outside getting some air down by the river. When I got back it was about one, and they weren't there."

"No further questions," Bellows said.

"Mr. Price, how did you first learn that you'd be giving this deposition?" Barry asked.

"I was served with a subpoena."

"When did you receive the subpoena?"

"About the first of the month. Maybe it was an April's Fool," he said with a grin.

"But you knew plaintiffs' lawyers were going to take your deposition and Max Pepper's depositions as early as the middle of March, didn't you?" Barry asked.

"What are you getting at?"

"You told Max Pepper back then that your depositions were going to be taken in April, didn't you?"

Price looked at his lawyer, Claude Skow, for help.

"Answer the question, if you can," Skow told him.

"Yeah, I guess I did. So what?"

"Then let's go back to my earlier question," Barry said. "When did you first learn that plaintiffs' lawyers were going to take your deposition?"

"It must have been around the time I talked to Max."

"How did you learn that?"

Again, Price looked for help from Skow. Skow shook his head and gave a disappointed look.

Reluctantly, Price replied, "Marlene Smyth called me and told me."

"How long had you known Marlene Smyth?" Barry asked.

"I've known her for several years."

"Tell me about that. How and when did you meet her and what was the nature of your relationship with her?"

"Oh, I used to see her at a women's club in Orange County. A gal I go out with took me there to dinner a few times. Marlene was the hostess."

"Who is that gal?"

"Rachel Jacobs."

"Did you or do you have any other relationship with Marlene Smyth?"

He shrugged. "Not really."

"Then why would she call you and tell you that your deposition was going to be taken in this case?"

"I guess I don't know."

"Did you even know about this case before Marlene Smyth called you?"

"Yeah, I knew about it. Hugh called me some time back and told me."

Barry glared at Price. "Mr. Price, you knew the plaintiffs, Ginny Lane, Peg House and Tina Marcellas, before they moved to Portland, didn't you?"

"Why do you say that?"

"Mr. Price, I'm not here to answer questions. You're a friend of Angie Lawrence, aren't you?"

"Yes."

"You and Ms. Jacobs go out quite a bit with Ms. Lawrence and Max Pepper, don't you?"

"Yeah, we go out together some."

"And during the last several years you've been to a number of parties at Ms. Lawrence's home, haven't you?"

"Yes."

"And you know that the plaintiffs often worked those parties, don't you?"

"I'm not sure of that."

"Well, Mr. Price, you know that Ms. Lawrence referred these plaintiffs to Marlene Smyth as employees, don't you?"

"How'd you know that?"

"Again, Mr. Price, I'm not going to answer your questions. What's the answer to my question?"

He shrugged. "I guess I heard that somewhere."

"You heard it from Ms. Lawrence, didn't you?"

He paused and then said, "Yes."

Barry paused as well, and then looking straight at Price, he said, "And the reason Ms. Lawrence told you that is because you're an investor in the catering service owned by Ms. Smyth?"

Another hesitation. Then, "I suppose so."

"Why didn't you tell me that before, when I asked what relationships you had with Ms. Smyth?"

He sat back in his chair, glared at Barry, and said, "'Cause it's not relevant!"

"Who else invested in Ms. Smyth's catering business?"

"A guy named Grant Slade."

"He's the president of EBC Sports, isn't he?"

"No."

"He's not? Since when?"

"Since a week or so."

"But when he invested, he was president of EBC Sports, isn't that so?"

"Yeah."

"Why did you two invest in Ms. Smyth's business?"

"It seemed like a good investment."

"How did you learn about the possibility of this investment?"

"Angie told us."

"Did you know when you invested that the Lukarillas was a client of the catering service?"

"Well, we knew who she was buying from, and I knew Lattanzi had done that for Hugh in past years."

"But one of the reasons that you and Slade decided to invest was that the Lukarillas would be one of Ms. Smyth's clients, isn't that so?"

Reluctantly, he answered, "Yeah, that was one of the reasons."

"Did Mr. Slade have a grudge against any of the Lukarillas?"

Price was beginning to lose control. "Grudge, you say? I don't know about that. All I know is Grant hates Sumas' guts, and so do I, for what he did to Rachel! Is that what you want to hear?"

"So you invested with Marlene to get back at Sumas, is that right?"

Price sat there for a few seconds. Then he looked away from Barry toward Skow, before quietly saying, "No."

"Mr. Price, have you ever discussed this lawsuit or your testimony in this deposition with Mr. Bellows or anyone in his office?"

"Is Mr. Goodwin in his office?"

"Yes, did you discuss these things with him?"

"Yes."

"When and where?"

"He came down here in either late February or early March and talked to me and my lawyer."

"What was said?"

Skow objected. "That's privileged, counsel. I'm instructing him not to answer."

Barry was done. "I have nothing further at this time."

Thursday morning, April 16

Joan and Shumanski arrived at Lester Solomon's office in Miami. They were early for Weinstein's deposition because they hoped to talk to Solomon before it started. However, they soon learned that Amanda got there first. Shortly after the receptionist called Solomon and told him that they had arrived, Solomon came out of the inner offices with Amanda and Weinstein.

Solomon immediately said, "I introduced Amanda to my client in my office, but let me assure you that I didn't allow her to question him."

Weinstein was about average height, but on the heavy side. His dark-framed glasses and rigid expression offered the impression of a serious individual. His deposition began.

"Mr. Weinstein, you are familiar with the lawsuit *Lane v. Lovejoy*, are you not?" Amanda asked.

"Yes," he replied.

"You were at the Lukarillas' retreat in September 1991, were you not?"

"Yes, I was."

"You and I have met, and you know I represent the plaintiffs in that lawsuit, don't you?"

"Yes."

"Are you familiar with what this lawsuit is about?"

"Yes."

"Have you ever talked to me, or anyone from my office, about the lawsuit?"

"No."

"Have you talked to any of the defendants or their lawyers about the retreat?"

He faced her as a businessman ready to deal with the task at hand. "I talked to Ezra Livingston some time back on the telephone, and I talked to Hugh Chalmers on the telephone a few weeks ago. I also exchanged electronic messages with Hugh late last year."

"What did the electronic messages say?"

"As I remember it, he wanted to know if I knew anything about what the girls were claiming, and he asked if I was aware of anything they did at the retreat. I told him I didn't know anything."

"Tell me about your conversation with Mr. Livingston. What was said?"

"It was right after one of those TV shows. He called and wanted to know what I thought of the claims."

"What did you tell him?"

"I told him I couldn't talk about it because my lawyer told me not to. That was all there was."

Then Amanda asked, "How about the telephone conversation with Mr. Chalmers a few weeks ago? What was said?"

"He wanted to know the name of my lawyer, and I gave it to him."

"Why did your lawyer tell you not to talk about the girls' claims?"

Solomon objected. "Don't answer, Steve. The question calls for matters protected by the lawyer-client privilege."

"All right, Mr. Solomon," Amanda said. Then directing herself to Weinstein, she said, "Then I'll ask you what Mr. Livingston asked you. What did you think about the girls' claims?"

"That they were bogus."

"Why did you think that?"

Weinstein turned to Solomon and asked, "Do I have to answer that?"

Solomon asked Amanda, "May I have a minute to talk to Steve privately?"

"It's not proper with a question pending, but if it'll help move things along, okay."

Solomon and Weinstein left the room.

A few minutes later they returned, and Amanda asked Weinstein if he was ready to answer her question.

"Could you ask it again?" Weinstein asked.

"You told me that you thought that the girls' claims were bogus, and I asked 'Why did you think that?'"

"That gets into the reason that he came to see me," Solomon said. "I'm going to instruct him not to answer because the answer will invade the lawyer-client privilege."

"Very well, I'll leave that for a minute," Amanda said. Then she turned back to Weinstein and said, "I understand that you shared a cabin at that retreat with Max Pepper and Parker Price. There's been testimony that two of the plaintiffs were in that cabin early Saturday morning during the retreat. The plaintiffs deny that. What do you say about it? Were two of the girls in your cabin early Saturday morning?"

"Don't answer that," Solomon said. "That again gets into the area of the lawyer-client privilege."

"I don't understand how the answer to that question can be privileged. Maybe we should call the judge."

"That's a good idea," Solomon said. "It's a gray area, and I don't want to waive my client's rights. I won't let him answer these questions without an order to do so."

The deposition was recessed and Amanda placed a call for Judge Lloyd. It was only seven-twenty in Portland, but the judge's clerk was in. She explained that the judge was unavailable. He was on a salmon-fishing trip in Alaska.

"That leaves us in a quandary," Amanda said. "If you don't let your client answer these questions, we'll have to take it up with the judge when we get back to Portland. He'll probably hear the matter on the telephone to accommodate you. You should understand, however, that if he rules in our favor, I'll request that he make your client come to Portland to answer these questions."

"I understand," Solomon said, "but if that happens, maybe he'll let him answer on the telephone."

"I'll object to that," Amanda told him. "I want the answers videotaped, so he'll have to answer them in person. To move things along, are you going to instruct your client not to answer any questions about what went on in his cabin Friday night and early Saturday morning?"

"Yes."

The deposition was recessed.

Chapter 28

It was May five, and discovery was over. But it was time for follow-up and trial preparations. The defendants needed information about Grant Slade and how he might be involved. Pam Hall was out because Barry might need testimony from the investigator. He decided to use Ben Lorenzo.

"We need more information about Grant Slade," Barry told Lorenzo. "I think he's in Houston working for Sports Cable Network. Becky will tell you what we know and suspect. Find out what you can about him and see if he'll talk."

"I'll call Burt Anderson at KPOR," Becky said. "He might know someone at the network who can give you a head start."

Barry then turned to Becky and said, "What do you think about filing a motion to dismiss at this stage? The depositions show that they really don't have much of a case against the Lukarillas."

"I don't think it'll get granted," Becky answered. "But we should file it anyway, just in case. It'll also give the judge an early insight into how weak plaintiffs' case is. That might help at trial. I'll get the motion filed this week."

Amanda filed a motion to overrule Solomon's objections in the Weinstein deposition and to order

Weinstein to come to Portland to answer the questions. The court set the argument on the motion for a telephone conference call on Monday, May eleventh.

Monday morning, May 11

Judge Lloyd began the telephone conference hearing. "Good morning, ladies and gentlemen. I've read the transcript closely and studied your legal briefs. I was in private practice before going on the bench, so I'm very conscious of the need to protect lawyer-client confidences. I totally agree that the witness can't be forced to tell what his lawyer told him or told him to do, so I'll sustain that objection. But, damn it Solomon, for the life of me I can't see how what the witness thinks is protected. That's not involved in his conversations with you. He's going to have to answer that question. The same is true about whether there were girls in his cabin. That question asks for facts, not what you said to your client or what he said to you. That objection is overruled. He's ordered to answer, and he's coming to Portland to do it. Amanda went all the way to Florida to take this deposition. I'm sorry I wasn't here to rule when you called. But she's not going to have to go there again or to take the rest of the deposition on the telephone. You bring the witness to Portland."

Monday morning, June 1

"This is the time set for arguments on the Lukarillas' Motion for Summary Dismissal," Judge Lloyd's clerk said. "Are the parties ready?" the judge asked.

"The Lukarillas are ready, Your Honor," Becky answered.

"Plaintiffs are also ready," Amanda answered.

After brief arguments from Becky and Amanda, and several questions from Judge Lloyd, the judge summed up his feelings. "This is a close question. My inclination is that Ms. Cohen is right when she forcefully argues that this is a case between the plaintiffs and Lovejoy, Sumas and Shepard, not the Lukarillas. But I can't decide this motion on my inclination. I have to determine whether there is *any* evidence from which the jury could conclude that the Lukarillas knew, or should have known, that one or more of these other defendants might sexually assault female workers at this retreat. Even if the evidence is weak, if there's some, I have to deny this motion. I have read the testimony of Mr. Chalmers and the other defendants closely, and I conclude that there is at least *some* evidence that the Lukarillas should have known of some of the alleged propensities of these men. I'm not saying that the weight of the evidence shows that. That's for the jury to decide, even if the evidence is weak. So, I am denying the motion."

Wednesday, June 3

Ben Lorenzo was in Houston. Burt Anderson had set up an appointment for him with an engineer at Sports Cable Network. At Lorenzo's suggestion Anderson told the engineer that Lorenzo was a private investigator hired to do a *sub rosa* investigation of Abe Sumas. When Lorenzo exited the airport he was surprised at the lack of humidity. His cab driver explained that while in the summer and fall the humidity was often so thick you could almost grab a handful, it wasn't usually so in the spring.

"I think there's a guy here at your network who's had a problem with Sumas in the past," Lorenzo said to the engineer. "His name is Grant Slade."

"Hell, he's our new CEO," the engineer said. "He's been with us for about three months now. I don't know him too well, but let me see if I can get him to talk to you."

The engineer dialed his telephone and spoke to Slade's receptionist. He explained that he had a friend in his office who was investigating Abe Sumas and wanted to talk to Slade. After the engineer hung up the telephone, he said, "He'll see you at five this afternoon, if that's all right?"

"My secretary tells me you want to know about Abe Sumas," Slade said to Lorenzo. Then Slade proceeded to give Lorenzo an earful about his feelings. He was so wound up with his explanation that he concluded it by saying, "But I made an investment last year that fixed his clock."

"What kind of an investment?" Lorenzo asked.

"I put some money in a catering outfit that stuck it to him," Slade answered.

Then Lorenzo asked, "You used to be with EBC, didn't you?"

"Yeah, I was head of its sports department. Why do you ask?"

"I was just wondering if your investment had anything to do with the EBC show where it charged Sumas with making a sexual attack on an employee of a catering outfit?"

Slade hesitated. Concerned that he'd told Lorenzo too much, he quickly said, "I don't know anything about that. My investment had nothing to do with that show."

"Well, I assumed that it might when you said you made an investment with a caterer who 'stuck it to him.'"

"It had nothing to do with the EBC show, I told you," Slade said abruptly. "That's all I can tell you. I've got somebody else due in here now, so we'll have to end this conversation."

Friday, July 10

Julie Sanchez had just gotten back to his office when the telephone rang. "Julie, this is Vince Romero calling from Miami. We just had a break in the Boccini matter. My informant talked to Santana. He says that a Miami lawyer named Les Solomon is the one who called Boccini needing help with a criminal investigation up in Oregon. Boccini then called Santana to find out if he knew anyone up that way. When Santana learned that it was the DA in Astoria,

Oregon, he volunteered to handle it himself. Santana told my guy that the DA owed him a lot. He sent a couple of guys up there to lean on him. That's all he'd say."

"That's a hell of a lot," Sanchez exclaimed. "Thanks, you've made my day." Sanchez immediately called Susan Silver.

Tuesday morning, August 11

Sanchez met Sheila Workman in the coffee shop of a state office building in Springfield, Illinois. They got coffee from the cafeteria counter and settled in at a nearby table.

"I'm sure you know why I'm here," Sanchez said. "It's about Senator Shepard and what you told me. We need you for the trial."

"Did you forget what I told you? I don't want to get involved," Workman said.

"I'm not asking you to volunteer. Here's a subpoena." He handed her some papers. "All you have to do is tell the truth. There's a check with it. It's your witness fee and travel expenses. We've got you a reservation at the Heathman Hotel in Portland for September sixteenth and seventeenth. You probably won't need both nights, 'cause you're supposed to testify on the seventeenth, but it's just in case. Take a cab there from the airport. The hotel's just a block from the courthouse. If the check doesn't cover everything, don't worry. I'll call you after it's over, and, if you spend more than that, I'll see that you're reimbursed."

Sanchez left Springfield and drove down the interstate to St. Louis and then on to Evansville, Indiana. He stayed just ahead of the approaching summer storm. He took the city center exit and parked in front of the bar and restaurant where he'd interviewed the maid Senator Shepard had propositioned in the hotel in Springfield.

Entering the bar, he saw that she wasn't there. A man was tending bar. He approached him and asked, "I'm looking for Judy Filcher. I think she works here."

"She owns the place," the bartender responded. "You'll find her meeting customers in the restaurant."

A neon sign directed him to the restaurant through a side door in the bar. He approached a woman who seemed to be in charge and greeted her. "Hi, Judy, you remember me? Julie Sanchez. I talked to you last spring about Senator Shepard."

She eyed him. "Yeah, I remember you."

Sanchez quickly handed her some papers and explained, "The case is going to trial next month in Portland, Oregon. That's a subpoena. You're going to have to come and testify. All you'll be asked is what you told me."

Upset, Filcher said, "I told ya I'd deny what I said."

Sanchez said, "I'm sorry. I know it's an imposition. But I'm sure you won't lie to a federal judge and jury. The jury needs to hear the truth, so we had to subpoena you." He explained the check for expenses and the hotel arrangements that had been made. "Here's my card," he said. "If the check doesn't cover what you're out, then call me after it's over."

When he left he had to run for his car as the storm had hit.

Chapter 29

Steve Weinstein's deposition continued on August thirteenth in Barry's office. Amanda sat behind Barry's desk, and Steve Weinstein faced her. Ruth Mason was set up with her machine. Lester Solomon sat comfortably at the end of the couch next to his client. Joan occupied the other end of the couch, and Miles, Shumanski and Barry were seated around the small conference table on the other side of the office.

Amanda did not hesitate. She immediately took advantage of the judge's ruling. "Mr. Weinstein, why did you think the girls' claims were bogus?"

"Because I knew they wouldn't have to be forced into sex," he replied. Despite the ruling, Weinstein was still the cool customer he'd been before.

"How did you know that?"

"Two of them came asking for sex two nights earlier."

"That answer may have told me the other thing the judge instructed you to divulge," she said. "But let me ask you directly. Were two of the girls in your cabin early Saturday morning?"

"Yes, they were."

"Which ones? Er, strike that," she corrected. "Tell me who was there, how they happened to be there and what happened."

He explained what he'd told Lovejoy while they were fishing in the river. It was almost word for word as Lovejoy explained it earlier. He ended, "Ginny wanted to know where my room was. I showed her, and she said, 'Let's go to bed.' We went in there and had sex."

"What happened to Peg?" Amanda asked.

"I don't know for sure. She and Park were in the living room when Ginny and I left. Park told me later that they went into his room and had sex. When I got up the next morning, both girls were gone."

"You talked to Park about what happened?"

"Yeah, the next morning. I said, 'How was it?' He answered, 'Awesome.' I asked him how long they went at it, and he said Peg had left about five or so. That's the only time we talked about it."

"Mr. Weinstein, when did you retain Mr. Solomon?"

"He's been my lawyer for years," Weinstein replied.

"When did you contact him about the events at the retreat?"

"Thursday, after the EBC program."

Amanda decided to delve into the possible Boccini-Santana connection. "You say Mr. Solomon has been your lawyer for years. Is he S-Mart's lawyer too?"

"He's one of them."

"Was he your lawyer when Julio Boccini invested in S-Mart?"

Weinstein's composure remained the same. He answered in his usual matter-of-fact manner. "Yes, he handled the transaction."

"Then he's known Mr. Boccini since that time, is that true?"

"Yes, it is."

Then Amanda took a gamble. Relying on what Susan had told her about Sanchez's call from Miami, she said, "We've learned that late last September Mr. Solomon talked to Mr. Boccini about the criminal investigation of my clients' claims up in Oregon. You knew about that, didn't you?"

Weinstein looked at Solomon for directions, but got none. "Yes, I did," he answered.

"You know, don't you, that he asked Mr. Boccini if he had any connections out there who could stop the investigation?"

"I don't know what he said to Mr. Boccini."

"Well, you do know that Boccini talked to a Mr. Santana in San Francisco about the investigation, don't you?"

"Yes, I think I knew that."

"And you know that a couple of Mr. Santana's employees talked to the District Attorney up in Oregon and encouraged him to drop those charges, don't you?"

"I've heard that."

"Did you ask your lawyer to get those charges dropped?"

Solomon immediately interrupted. "That calls for communications between us. Don't answer," he said.

"All right, I think the point's made," Amanda said for the video. "Mr. Weinstein, after you heard the EBC program, why did you go to a lawyer?"

"Because when I heard what those girls were saying about Alex, Abe and Shep, I was afraid I might be next."

Amanda knew she'd asked one question too many, so she quit.

After Amanda, Solomon and his client had gone, Barry, Joan, Miles and Shumanski stayed and talked.

"Now's a good time to approach Amanda about settlement," Barry said. "Even though she's discovered some dirt that might hurt the Lukarillas, she now knows that we'll probably prove that her clients are liars."

"You're right," Joan agreed, "but I'm not optimistic that Alex will contribute anything. He thinks the horse is already out of the barn as far as damage to him. He wants to use the trial to rebuild his reputation."

Miles added, "I agree that the timing's right, but Abe feels about the same as Alex, so don't expect much from him either."

"Let's not talk about contributions now," Shumanski suggested. "Barry, you talk to Amanda and see what she says. If we get a figure, then we can discuss it among ourselves. Do you use settlement judges in this district? If you do, I'd like to get one involved before we get any closer to trial."

"We do use settlement judges," Barry replied.

"Then if Amanda won't give us a figure we can deal with, that's what we need," Shumanski said. "Let's find out right away, so we can get to a judge well before trial."

Thursday afternoon

Barry called Amanda. "Have you given any thought to settlement? If it's an option, we probably should talk about it before we get any closer to trial."

"Frankly, it hasn't come up," she said. "But I agree, now's probably a good time to find out. I'll talk to Oscar and the clients and get back to you, at least by mid week."

Monday morning, August 17

Barry received the expected pretrial minute order from Judge Lloyd. In addition to setting times for filing pretrial documents, it set a final pretrial conference with the judge for September tenth.

Tuesday morning, August 18

Thunderheads came from the south along the Cascades. It was raining hard. Barry was staring at the storm as the rain pelted his windows. The phone interrupted his trance.

"I talked to our clients," Amanda said. "They'll settle for seven and a half million."

"You gotta be kidding," he said, "or maybe this damn rain's making you grumpy. If you're serious, why didn't you just say the hell with settling? You gotta know there's no way we'd counter a figure like that!"

"Come off it, Barry," she said. "Nothing's too high to counter. Our clients want two and a half million each, and with the likelihood of punitives, that's the least they've got coming. The demand's reasonable as hell. Any judge would agree."

"Be serious, Amanda. Tell me what it'll really take, so I can have a meaningful talk with the others."

"We're not bidding against ourselves," she answered. "You suggested we talk, so we've given you our demand. If you want to settle, it's your move."

Barry called Chalmers and relayed the demand.

His response was, "Tell her to go to hell!"

"I can't do that, Hugh," Barry said. "Paul wants a settlement judge, so we have to counter. Talk to your members and see what the Lukarillas will offer. I'll call Joan, Paul and Lou and find out what their clients will contribute. Then we'll talk strategy. Get back to me by Friday. Time is getting short."

Barry called Joan. After she answered, his secretary put Miles and Shumanski on the call, and he passed on Amanda's demand. They couldn't believe it. However, they agreed to talk to their clients and get back to him before Friday.

Surprisingly, many of the Lukarillas' members were concerned about the lawsuit and what it might do to their reputations. They wanted out. Chalmers got $850,000 from the seventeen who weren't defendants. Chalmers didn't break down the contributions for Barry, although he did say that three put up more than the others. Steve Weinstein, of course, was one of them.

Lovejoy and Sumas didn't want to settle. They'd put up $25,000 each, solely to cut their costs.

Shepard offered $250,000, so they had over a million to work with.

Thursday morning, August 20

Barry got Joan, Miles and Shumanski on the phone and shared the figures. "Anybody got a suggestion?" he asked.

"I do," Shumanski answered. "We should offer a half a million. It's too damn much, but we need to be credible."

Joan knew Shumanski's idea was colored by the senator's fear of going forward. "Let's think about that," she said. "That offer will probably get Amanda down to five million, but then what'll we do? We haven't got enough authorization left to get her down to reason by going back and forth. So we have to face it. We can't settle without a settlement judge. I think going to a settlement judge with a five hundred thousand dollar offer is too much. It doesn't leave us with enough left over for the judge to work with. How about three hundred thousand, one hundred for each?"

"I'd go lower than that," Miles said. "Fifty for each."

"I've been doing some adding and subtracting on my legal pad as you two talked," Shumanski said. "Joan's right. We need a judge to settle this thing. I've changed my mind. I like Lou's idea of one hundred fifty thousand. We can tell the judge we had to be ridiculous because of the obnoxious demand. That amount is sure to get a 'go to hell' from Amanda. That'll back up our request for the judge."

That seemed to be the consensus, so Barry said, "Okay, I'll make that offer. I'll do it on the phone, so I'm out of reach of her reaction. If I don't call back, you'll know she told me to go to hell. Then, I'll call the judge's clerk and ask for a settlement judge.

"Let's talk about timing. Judge Lloyd won't wait with the trial date so close. He'll find a judge immediately. He'll appoint someone who can get started probably as soon as next week. Warn your clients that the judge'll require them to be physically present at that conference, so they'd better be ready to travel."

⚥

Barry telephoned Amanda right after he hung up. She was in court, but Bellows got on the line. Barry said, "All I could get was one hundred and fifty thousand. We know it'll take more, but if that doesn't bring you way, way down, we want a settlement judge."

"That's just fine with us," Bellows said. "You'll look like hell in front of any of our judges with an offer like that."

"That means you're not going to counter?" Barry asked.

"You're damn right it does. I don't have to go back. The girls said they wouldn't come down if you weren't over a million."

"Okay, I'll call the clerk and tell her we want a settlement judge."

Chapter 30

Friday morning, August 21

U.S. District Judge Kingsley Sommerville was assigned as the settlement judge, and he set the conference for Thursday, August twenty-seventh.

Barry called Joan, Miles and Shumanski. "For your planning and advice to your clients," he said, "you need to know about Judge Sommerville. He's the chief judge of this district. He's been on the federal bench for over twenty-five years, and he's a legend in his own right. A wiry little guy, he's outspoken and accused of being mean, tough and erratic, but no one disagrees that he's smart as hell. He'll be rough on everybody, but that's what we need if we're going to get this case settled."

⚥

Thursday morning, August 27

Judge Sommerville's courtroom was on the sixth floor of the U.S. Courthouse. The courtroom was enormous and the interior was ornate. Oak and marble predominated.

When Becky, Barry and Chalmers arrived, Amanda and Bellows were seated at the table closest to the jury box with Ginny, Peg and Tina in chairs behind them. Becky and Barry joined Joan at an adjacent table. Chalmers and Lovejoy sat behind them. Last to arrive were Miles, Sumas, Shumanski and the senator. They pulled up chairs and gathered with Chalmers and Lovejoy, behind Joan, Becky and Barry.

The judge and his law clerk interrupted hushed conversations as they entered the courtroom. The judge ignored his bench. He and his law clerk pulled up extra chairs and sat down opposite the lawyers and their clients.

"Good morning, ladies and gentlemen, I'm Judge Sommerville, and I'll be conducting this settlement conference. Counsel, please introduce yourselves, your colleagues and clients."

Amanda and Barry responded, introducing the others.

"Nice to meet you all," the judge said, addressing them with a solemn expression. "You should know at the outset that I am not encouraged that this case will settle. I've read your memoranda, and I don't see how you could be further apart. You're obviously being totally unrealistic, all of you. Maybe I can help, and you'll soon see that I intend to try. I expect each of you to try as well. You haven't done that yet. If you seriously want to settle this case, each of you has to wake up and stop playing games. I'm not going to arbitrate a you-come-down and I'll-come-up game. When I talk to you I want straight talk, honest answers. When I ask what you'll take or what you'll pay, I want your bottom lines, not negotiation. Is that clear?"

In order each lawyer answered, "Yes, Your Honor."

"Here's how we're going to proceed," he said. "As I've told you, I've read your memoranda. I don't want any more lawyer statements or arguments. That'll just waste time, and extra time is what we don't have. I'm going to take plaintiffs and their lawyers into my chambers first and see where they stand. Then I'll talk to the defendants and their lawyers. I'll talk to all of them together first, but after that, I'll talk to them separately if I think it's needed. When I'm satisfied that I know what each of you is really thinking, I'll bring you all back together and tell you whether I think it's worth proceeding further. Please, no one leave this floor until I excuse you. Now, Ms. Johnson, will you, your partner and clients please join me in my chambers."

Amanda, Bellows and the plaintiffs followed the judge and his clerk out of the courtroom and into the judge's chambers. They all sat around the large walnut conference table. The judge turned immediately toward Amanda and Bellows and said curtly, "Your clients' demands are ridiculous. I haven't decided yet who I believe in this mess, but, assuming for a minute that they're telling the truth, there's no way any jury in this court is going to give each of them two and a half million. I know you'll have some mind-doctor, or maybe a pair of them, who'll try to sell mental trauma, but who's going to buy it? If you weren't their lawyers, you wouldn't, and neither will six jurors. I know you'll say, 'But Judge, if these guys did what our clients say they did, the jury'll bomb them with punitives.' That's bullshit and you know it.

"I'll tell you what's going to happen. There'll be two totally opposite stories that the jury will have to sort out. Both sides will have some evidence to corroborate their side. You may get a hung jury, because all six won't agree. There's liable to be three that think your way and three who think your clients are lying. I can guarantee there'll be at least two who'll think that. You know you have to get them unanimous to get a verdict. If they get through the debate on who's telling the truth and finally agree to be unanimous, no one's gonna force punitive damages on the jurors who reluctantly went along with your clients. Furthermore, no one's going to force a huge general damage verdict on them either. There'll be a compromise, and that almost always means a low verdict. It'll be a hell of a lot less than two and a half million dollars. Even if your clients are telling the truth, that's the way it'll end.

"But what if your clients are lying? What if the jury doesn't believe them? If they don't, then it's zero. What are the chances of that? From what I've read, I'd say probably at least fifty-fifty. So how much are you going to discount what you think the jury might award, just to avoid that chance? Fifty percent, or maybe more? That's how you folks should be thinking.

"I'll tell you one more thing. I think you should seriously try to settle this case. If you haven't got better than a fifty-fifty chance of winning, it's a pure gamble to go to trial if you can settle. There's no way you're going to do that unless you come down, way, way, way down." Looking directly at Amanda and Bellows, he said, "Are you ready to tell me what your bottom line is, or do you want to talk further to your clients? If you want to talk to them, you can use my library. We can close the doors so it'll be private."

Amanda looked at Bellows.

He said, "We'll talk first."

The judge turned to his clerk and said, "All right, show them into the library." Then addressing Amanda and Bellows, he said, "I'll give you half an hour, then come back in here."

The judge's law clerk ushered them into the adjoining library and closed the door.

While the judge was talking to the plaintiffs and their lawyers, the defendants remained in the courtroom.

"Is it safe to talk in here?" Senator Shepard asked.

"Yes," Barry answered. "And we should." He described what Judge Sommerville would be saying to plaintiffs and their lawyers. "He's going to push real hard to convince them they're being stupid with their demand. I'd be amazed if he doesn't get them to cut their demand down to three million or less. When we get in there, he'll want a figure from us, higher than the one hundred fifty thousand. It should be a tempting figure. One that'll make sense to him and give him the ammunition he needs to put the pressure on the plaintiffs. Anybody got a suggestion?"

Ever since the judge joined them earlier Shumanski had been working again with figures on his legal pad. He was the first to answer. "I've been thinking while he was talking. What if we put together a package that'd get each plaintiff and the lawyers one hundred fifty thousand dollars? That'd take six hundred thousand dollars. I propose we give him that figure and tell him it's got to be divided that way."

"That's the kind of formula he'll like," Becky predicted.

"If you think he'll like it, I'm for it," Joan agreed.

"Does everyone agree?" Barry asked.

Everyone did.

"You be the spokesman, Barry. He trusts you," Miles said.

About twenty minutes later, the plaintiffs and their lawyers came back into the judge's chambers. "The bottom line is two and a half million," Bellows said. "We think our chances are better than fifty-fifty, and we think we've got at least a fifty-fifty chance to get all six jurors without much of a fight. If we do, then they should be mad, and we'll hit big."

"You're whistling Dixie," the judge told him. "But I'm not going to argue with you, Oscar, at least not right now. What I want to know now is whether this is really your bottom line? If you're playing games, you know I'll figure it out sooner or later. So come clean now."

"That's our bottom line," Bellows replied. "I know how you'll work us over later, and you may bend it, but it's our bottom."

"All right, I'll talk to the others."

The plaintiff group came back into the courtroom and told the defense lawyers and clients that the judge wanted them. They went into his chambers and sat around the table.

Standing, the judge was blunt. "I know what the one hundred fifty thousand was. With their demand, I would have done the same damn thing. I told them that their demand was ridiculous. But this is a dangerous case. You all know it. It's dangerous from a dollars-and-cents standpoint, but just airing this mess can do real damage to some of these defendants, particularly the senator. I don't have to lecture you about that." Then addressing Lovejoy, Sumas and the senator, he said, "I know your lawyers have told you about the dangers of this case. Just as I know you're prepared to pay a lot more. So let's cut the bullshit. What'll you pay?"

Barry answered. "Obviously, we've been talking. I don't know where you've got them, but we're willing to make a solid offer that should do it. We've come up with an offer that'll get each plaintiff one hundred fifty thousand, provided Amanda and Oscar will limit their fee to another one hundred fifty thousand. In other words, we'll offer six hundred thousand dollars, if they divide it so each plaintiff gets one hundred fifty thousand."

"Interesting," the judge said, tilting his head. "I like that, and I think you're somewhere near what the case is worth. Let me get them back in here. You guys go back into the courtroom."

After Amanda, Bellows and the plaintiffs were seated, the judge sat down and paused for a moment, looking at each of them. He particularly paused when he looked at each plaintiff. Sternly, he said, "I want each of you to listen closely to what I'm going to say. I've got a pretty damn good offer from them without telling them your bottom line. I didn't tell them what you told me. They've come up with six hundred thousand dollars, with a proviso. They want it divided four ways, one hundred fifty thousand for each plaintiff and one hundred fifty thousand for the lawyers."

"That's not going to do it, judge," Bellows replied. "We might divide that way if the offer was two million, but we're just too far apart."

"Come on, Oscar, get your head out of the clouds," the judge said. "If that's what you really think, I'm going to talk to your clients alone."

"I'm being perfectly honest with you, Your Honor," Bellows said.

So the judge told Amanda and Bellows to go into the library and leave him alone with the plaintiffs.

After they were gone, he said, "Listen you three, I don't always talk directly to the clients, but your lawyers aren't being realistic. Don't get me wrong, you've got good lawyers, but sometimes even the best get colored by how they've prepared a case. When I said earlier that if you get a verdict it'd be a compromise, I was talking about a low figure. You need to know the kind of figures I meant. I'm talking about twenty-five to fifty thousand, not millions. I'm frankly concerned that you aren't telling the whole truth in this matter, but I'll say no more about that. The important thing is that even if you are, you're being offered more than you'll probably get. Do you understand that?"

"I understand what you said, judge," Ginny answered. "But I happen to think you're the one who is whistling Dixie. We aren't as naive as you may think. I've been around, and I'm not taking less than five hundred thousand myself."

The judge didn't expect that. He pursed his lips, narrowed his eyes and said to Ginny, "Young woman, I haven't underestimated you or your girlfriends. I'm well aware that you've been around. That's why I'm having trouble buying your story. If these lawyers do their job, I think the jury's going to have the same trouble. Play hardball, if that's what you want to do, but when this thing is over, just look back to today. You're going to be the saps. I won't whistle Dixie. I'll be satisfied that I've given you a better chance than you probably deserve." He addressed Peg and Tina. "Are you two going to tell me the same thing?"

"Yes, we are," Peg answered confidently, and Tina nodded.

"Fine," he told his clerk. "Get the lawyers back in here." When they returned, he told them, "You've got smartass and stupid clients. Let's go out and tell the defendants that you're going to trial. Do you want me to tell them what your bottom line is?"

"Yes," Bellows replied.

The judge came back into the courtroom, followed by the plaintiff group. "We're not going to settle this today," he said. "Plaintiffs will not go below two and a half million. You should prepare for trial. If you think I can help later, and I'm available, I'll meet with you again. But the way things stand now, you're not going to settle."

The defense group went back to Barry's office.

"What do we do now?" the senator asked. "We still have some money. Shouldn't we offer more?"

"That'd be a bad choice," Barry said. "What the judge was telling us is that the plaintiffs should have taken our offer. He's saying that he told them so, and they wouldn't pay attention. That means they're not going to budge much, and we don't have enough to settle. Later they may feel differently, and we might be able to use the rest of our money, but it'd be a bad tactic to offer more now. I know that probably means going to trial, but I'm afraid that's where we are."

"Barry's correct, Shep," Shumanski said. "We won't settle short of trial, even if we offer all we have."

Chapter 31

Thursday evening

Since February Pam Hall had made a habit of stopping by the Come-On Inn. She varied the days, but she was usually there one evening a week. She was now on a first-name basis with the regulars. Often Marlene Smyth was there, but, while Hall would acknowledge her with a "Hi!" or "How ya doing," she politely avoided Smyth.

It was a hot day, and Hall was cooling off with a beer at the bar and talking golf with Joey Buccanan. Axel Sprague came in and sat next to Hall. He was a regular, and a sometime companion of Marlene.

"Look who's here," Buccanan greeted Sprague. "Where ya been keeping yourself? Haven't seen you in over a month. You must've been shacked up with Marlene. She ain't been around either."

"You're a real comedian," Sprague said. "I haven't seen her. I've been down in Albuquerque visiting my brother. I think she's been at the coast, resting up for that big trial her girls have coming up in September."

"Oh yeah. I'd forgotten all about that lawsuit," Buccanan said. "In September, you say? Where'll it be, here in Portland?"

"Yeah. Marlene's real keen on the case. You'd think she was doing the suing, she and that EBC guy."

"EBC guy?" Hall asked.

"You know, that guy who talked to Marlene and the girls, 'fore they went up to Chalmers' camp," he replied.

Bucannan asked, "What are you talking about?"

"I thought everyone around here knew about that," he said. "Last summer after Marlene bought out Lattanzi, she got a call from an EBC big shot back east. He has something to do with their sports programs, name's Grant something. He wanted to know about her involvement with the Lukarillas retreat. Marlene tells it like she's rubbing elbows with the higher-ups of television."

Hall asked, "Why did he want to know that?"

"I don't know the details. She was always a little coy when it got to the details of her relations with the guy. I do know, though, that he sent another fella out here to talk to her and the girls. Just the way she brags and then clams up, I suspected they was up to something, but maybe not."

Hall asked, "Like he had something to do with what happened at that retreat?"

"I dunno. Probably not, but like I say, she acted like they was up to something."

⚥

Sarah wasn't home when Barry got there that evening. There was a note on the refrigerator. "I should be back by six-thirty, and I've got some news," it read, and was signed "Sarah."

Barry fixed a drink and was watching the television when she arrived home. "I talked to Pam earlier," Sarah said. "She picked up some very interesting information." Sarah told him about the conversation at the Come-On-Inn.

"That does it," Barry said. "I'm sending Lorenzo down to Houston to subpoena Slade for a perpetuation deposition, and I'll have Becky take it."

⚥

Friday morning, August 28

The heat was still on. Barry was glad their building was new and air-conditioned. He remembered how miserable August days were years ago when the firm occupied an early nineteen hundreds-vintage building. He found

Lorenzo and brought him up to date on Pam's evening at the tavern.

"Get a subpoena on Grant Slade for a deposition in Houston," Barry told him, looking at his calendar. "September ninth looks like a good date. We'll want to perpetuate his testimony and use it at trial, so set it up with a video camera in a courtroom in the federal courthouse down there. That'll make him think twice about lying." Then he called Becky in and said, "You take the deposition and be sure to take Ruth Mason with you."

After they broke up, Becky prepared a notice of the deposition and had it served on Amanda that morning.

⚤

After receiving the notice of the Slade deposition, Amanda called Susan in New York. "There's something going on with Grant Slade," she said. "I just got notice that Becky Cohen's going to take a perpetuation deposition of him in Houston on September ninth. You better talk to him right away and find out why they're doing this. Somebody's going to be after him to serve the subpoena as early as later today or tomorrow."

"I'll call him as soon as we hang up," Susan said. "I'll call you tomorrow and let you know what he says. Also, let's talk then about how we can help you at trial."

⚤

Friday afternoon/evening

Susan asked her secretary to find Grant Slade. They left messages for him all over Houston.

He finally called Susan back at her apartment that evening.

She explained what was happening. "What do they want from you?"

"Beats me," he answered. "When's the trial?"

"It starts September fifteenth, and it'll take a couple of weeks," she replied.

"Really," he said. "Then they'll get nothing from me. I'm going out of town on business tomorrow, and I'll be gone for a few weeks. They won't find me before I leave, and I'll make sure no one knows how to reach me."

He was right. Lorenzo was in Houston on Friday but couldn't track Slade down. He spent all day Saturday, Sunday and Monday looking for him. He left the subpoena with a process server on Tuesday, but Slade wasn't found, and the deposition never occurred.

Saturday, August 29

Susan called Amanda. "I found Slade in Houston and asked him why they were taking his deposition. He says he doesn't know what they want, but I'm suspicious because I think he's going to dodge the process server. I didn't suggest he do that, but it was pretty clear that he was going to take off."

"Don't tell me any more," Amanda said, and then changed the subject to EBC's participation in the trial. "We want your help," she said, "but not in the courtroom. I'd like both you and Julie here to meet with us as the trial proceeds. Can you be here on Monday, the fourteenth? We'll be doing final preparations then."

"I'm sure we can," Susan said.

"Okay, I'll get rooms for you. It'll be a place away from downtown. I don't want you staying where you might run into any of the defendants or their lawyers. We'll meet and talk before and after court and during the noon recess. I'd also like to have Ryan available by phone from time to time, if that's possible."

"I'll tell him," Susan replied.

Wednesday morning, September 9

At seven-thirty Becky, Mary Jo and Lorenzo met with Barry in his office. "I just received plaintiffs' witness list,"

Barry told them as he passed copies to each. "I recognize everyone on here except Sheila Workman, Judy Filcher and Jerry Mahoney. Workman has a Springfield, Illinois, address. Filcher lives in Evansville, Indiana, and Mahoney's in Idaho. Have you heard of them?"

No one had. "I'll track 'em down right away," Lorenzo said.

⚥

Amanda and Bellows had a similar discussion about the defendants' list. Amanda called in Herb Goodwin and gave him a copy. "Herb," she said, "get the plaintiffs in here tomorrow and go over the names on this witness list with them. Particularly, find out who Todd Smith, Bruce Walker, George Wershel, Leo Santini, Joey Buccanan, Mike Pritchard and Axel Sprague are. I think they talked about some of them in their depositions. After they tell you who they are, find them and take statements. If they can't identify any of them, you'll have to run those down. I'll bet this is about their sex lives. It's a rush. We'll be in trial in a week."

⚥

Thursday morning, September 10

The lawyers met in Judge Lloyd's chambers. The judge was seated behind his desk as they entered. He rose and invited them to join him around his conference table. Once seated, he said, "I see you've all made your filings. The only motion is to strike the punitive damage claim. I'm not deciding that now," he said. Then directing his remarks to Amanda and Bellows, "But I don't want any comments about the defendants' wealth in the opening statement. I don't want punitive damages or evidence on that subject mentioned until I hear the liability evidence. You know the jury can't award punitive damages unless you have evidence that a defendant is guilty of malicious or reckless conduct. If your clients support what they say in the complaint, you'll have that evidence on the part of Lovejoy, Sumas and Shepard, but you need a lot more than that to have a case for punitive damages against the Lukarillas.

"We'll need a lot more room than my courtroom has, so we're going to use Judge Sommerville's courtroom. I understand you've all been there recently. We'll start promptly at eight-thirty each day and quit at five. Are any of you planning to use any special apparatus in the courtroom?"

Amanda explained that there would be video equipment set up in the courtroom.

"What about a daily transcript?" the judge asked. "If you want testimony prepared for you on a daily basis, you'll have to arrange for the reporters to do it. My reporter, Brenda Michaels, isn't prepared to offer that service."

"Mason and Associates is going to prepare daily transcripts for both sides," Barry said. "We'll coordinate with Brenda on the placement of the other reporter."

"Thank you. Now, I want this case to move along," the judge said. "I won't push you unless I think you're dragging. Have your witnesses available so we don't wait. Is there anything else we need to decide now?"

The lawyers responded that there was not.

"Then we're recessed until eight-thirty Tuesday morning."

Sunday, September 13

The front page of the Sunday *Oregonian* contained a headline that read, "LUKARILLAS TRIAL BEGINS TUESDAY."

Monday evening, September 14

On the *Evening Report* at five o'clock, the anchorman reported that the Lukarilla trial was starting the next morning in Portland. On camera was a distant shot of the federal courthouse. The camera zoomed in on the Southwest Broadway entrance to Dorothy Watters, who was standing on the sidewalk, microphone in hand. She reviewed briefly the background of the case and told the audience that EBC had tried to interview Senator Shepard and Abe Sumas at the airport on Saturday as they arrived in Portland. The scene then shifted to the Delta terminal at the airport, where Dorothy Watters received a "no comment" response from the senator.

In another similar scene Dorothy Watters asked Sumas for a comment on the case, and he responded, "Stick around and you'll see. I'll tell it as it is. I always do."

The segment of the program concluded with another scene at the courthouse, where Dorothy Watters concluded that she would report again after the trial was underway.

Chapter 32

Tuesday morning, September 15

The defense team met in Swift, Wyman & Wiggens' conference room to go over any last-minute matters. In an hour they left for court. When they turned north off Madison onto Broadway, they saw the media. Vans from local and national media were lined opposite the courthouse.

Amy McCormick of KPOR was the first to approach them. She held out a microphone and asked, "Mr. O'Shea, tell us how you plan to answer the plaintiffs' charges."

"No comment, Amy."

She then turned to Senator Shepard. "How will this case affect your presidential ambition, Senator?"

Shumanski stepped in front of the senator and said, "Since the matter's in litigation, we'll make no comment at this time."

Many more questions came their way, but they ignored them and pushed their way through the crowd, taking their places in the line inside the door, waiting to pass through the security arch.

By eight-thirty all the lawyers were seated with their clients in Judge Sommerville's court. Occupying the spectator benches in the back were at least thirty prospective jurors and a few spectators. In the first row were reporters from the newspaper and the television stations.

Judge Lloyd, adorned in his black robe, entered the courtroom from the door behind his bench. Judy Williams struck a gavel on a round wooden block and announced, "All rise, the United States District Court for the District of Oregon is now in session. The Honorable Walter Lloyd presiding."

Judge Lloyd sat and said to the participants and the courtroom audience, "Please be seated." Then he addressed the assembled body, "Now is the appointed time for the trial in the case of Virginia Lane, Margaret House and Tina Marcellas against Lionel Shepard, Abraham Sumas, Alexander Lovejoy and the Lukarillas, civil number 91-5067LL. Are the parties ready to proceed?"

They were.

A six-person jury with two alternates was selected. Juror number one was Shirley Miller, forty-six and a housewife with four children. She and her husband owned a Christmas tree farm just outside of Silverton, south of Portland in the Willamette Valley. Mary Bellman was number two. She was sixty-three and a retired salesperson from the Meier & Frank department store. Her husband was an accountant with the gas company. Glen Overton, a black man, was number three. A widower, he was sixty-nine and a retired high school maintenance superintendent. Juror four was Frances Bishop, seventy, a housewife and an avid outdoors person. Her husband had been an executive with one of the major local banks. Dolores Witherspoon was number five, twenty-nine and single. She worked in the high-tech industry west of Portland. Number six was Ronnie Norstad. He was thirty-four, married and worked as a steamfitter in a local factory. The first alternate was Wyonna Lipton, fifty-four and a widow. She ran a day care center but had no children herself. Jack Smith was the second alternate. He was fifty and worked as a letter carrier.

The judge turned to the jury and said, "We'll begin the trial with an opening statement from the lawyers. What the lawyers tell you now is not evidence. The evidence will only come from the witnesses and the exhibits, which are received in evidence. The media often misdescribes opening statements as opening arguments. That's wrong. The lawyers are not permitted to argue their client's case in an opening statement. The opening statements are merely meant to give you a guideline of the case that each lawyer intends to present. After each lawyer has completed his or her opening statement, we will proceed to hear the evidence. The plaintiffs will present their evidence first. Then each defendant will present his or its evidence. Do not decide this case until you've heard all of the evidence. Withhold any judgments about the evidence until you've heard from all parties.

"Now, it's obvious that this case has drawn the attention of the press. There will probably be stories in the newspaper, and maybe on radio or television, about the trial as we go along. You are not to read any such stories, and, if you hear a report on radio or television, either turn it off or leave the room. Do not follow this case in the press. If a reporter tries to interview you or ask any questions, tell him or her that you will not discuss the case, and immediately report the incident to my clerk."

The judge turned back and faced the courtroom. "Ms. Johnson, we're ready for your opening statement."

Amanda rose, walked up to a lectern that had been placed in front of the jury and arranged her legal pad before her. She was wearing a gray, pinstriped wool suit with a white blouse. Her shoes were black patent leather pumps. "May it please the Court, counsel, and ladies and gentlemen," she began.

"This case is about a secret society that has been meeting for over forty years at an isolated camp in our Coast Range Mountains. It's called the Lukarillas. Hugh Chalmers founded it. He sits over there behind his lawyers," she said, pointing. "He picked the members, and he had definite priorities in making the selections. The members had to be men; they had to be wealthy, influential and important. He chose them from across the nation. He selected corporate presidents from large companies, lawyers and accountants with national firms, politicians holding high state and national offices, and prominent and influential entertainers and sports figures. Not just anyone could join. You had to be invited, and that was almost like winning the lottery, as there are only twenty members. I said the group is secret. That's just what it is and what it was intended to be. No one, not even neighbors in Elsie or along the Nehelam River Road, knew anything about the group or its members. As far as the outside world was concerned, the place where they met was a recreational haunt of Hugh Chalmers and his company, Chalmers Forest Products. The Lukarillas kept no records. They told no one who they were or what they were doing. It was a creed of the members to keep their organization anonymous. According to them they met just once a year, talked, and shared ideas.

"Mr. Chalmers personally checked out each potential member before issuing an invitation. He hired a large national consulting firm to investigate the backgrounds of potential members. He wanted to know all about each one before asking him to join. To qualify he had to have good personal traits and an exemplary reputation, and he had to be intelligent, successful, influential and, of course, a male. Mr. Chalmers told us that his background checks have been so successful that no member has ever been asked to leave. New members almost always succeed a member who has died. There were twenty members as of September of last year. There's never been more. You're now going to be introduced to each of them, and you'll see what I mean about being intelligent, successful, and influential."

Becky felt a tap on her shoulder. She turned, and it was Mary Jo.

"Turn slowly and look who's sitting in the back on the right side," Mary Jo whispered.

Becky turned and surveyed the room. A few of the

potential jurors had stayed, and there were several spectators. Then she saw her and was stunned. Back in the last row on the aisle was Susan Silver. Becky couldn't believe Amanda would allow her within a hundred miles of the courtroom. She turned back and passed notes to Barry and Joan.

⚥

"I've told you about Mr. Chalmers," Amanda said. "He's been a member since the beginning in 1948. These three defendants are also long-time members," Amanda continued, pointing to Lovejoy, Sumas, and Senator Shepard. "My partner, Mr. Bellows, took Mr. Chalmers' deposition several months ago. A deposition is a question-and-answer session, a mechanism the law provides us so we can find out ahead of time what the other side knows. The witness is under oath to tell the truth, just as a witness is in this courtroom. The deposition was videotaped so we could show you parts of it. I'm going to show you a part of Mr. Chalmers' deposition now, so he can introduce the rest of the Lukarillas to you.

Chalmers' testimony, where he identified and gave background sketches of the present members, was then played for the jury.

As the video was ending, Amanda said, "They weren't all at the retreat last year. The ones missing were Hilton Jones, Congressman Thomas, Governor Grady, John Quincy Ames, Mason Rutledge and Rex Smith."

Barry watched the jurors closely. They were totally engaged with the video. They saw and heard just what Amanda predicted.

"An effective use of a video depo," Barry whispered to Becky. "Oscar did a hell of a job."

Amanda then walked around the lectern up to the front rail of the jury box. She cast her eyes back and forth at the individual jurors and said, "What happened at that retreat? I'm about to tell you, but I have to set the stage first. It was held on Friday, September twentieth, Saturday,

September twenty-first, Sunday, September twenty-second and Monday, September twenty-third in 1991. Just about a year ago. The members arrived on Friday and went home on Monday. It was in a remote area south of Highway 26 as it approaches Elsie. You take a narrow road that goes south along the Nehalem River. It's not well traveled. Except for the few people who live down there, a few fishermen and people who want to go to the small camping area four or five miles north of Mr. Chalmers' camp, really no one uses the road. I should further explain that camping area. Spruce Run is its name. It has no facilities except for a few tables and benches. You rarely see more than a car or two there, unless the fishing is good.

"I'm going to put Exhibit One on the overhead; we call it ELMO. You'll probably hear that name as we go along. ELMO's the manufacturer who came up with an overhead that'll project, as I'm doing, on a television screen. This is a rough sketch of the Chalmers' camp drawn by one of the witnesses." She then described the camp, how and why the catering company became involved and how her clients happened to be there. "Because there's no place nearby for the cook and waitresses to stay," she said, "they were assigned one of the cabins. In this case, the one closest to the mess hall – right here," she said pointing to Exhibit One.

"Nothing happened until Sunday night. The plaintiffs had served the members dinner Friday night, breakfast, lunch and dinner on Saturday, and breakfast, lunch and dinner on Sunday. There'd been some chitchat back and forth between the girls and the men over the three days, but nothing other than what you'd expect among eighteen people at a remote camp like this. What happened Sunday night is disputed. Our clients say one thing, these three defendants say the opposite," she said, pointing at Lovejoy, Sumas and Shepard. "But what Ginny, Peg and Tina say is totally consistent. It's what they told their boss, Marlene Smyth, at the time. It's what they told the sheriff and district attorney a few days later. It's what they told the television investigator a month later. It's what they told these lawyers earlier this year, when they took their depositions," she continued, pointing this time at the defense lawyers. "Empire Broadcasting Company videotaped the investigators' interviews, and so you'll know what plaintiffs say happened, I'll show you now that interview of Ginny Lane. What you'll hear is the same thing she'll tell you here in this courtroom, but I want you to see the videotape, because when she talked to the investigator, she didn't have a lawyer to coach her. The investigator was totally independent.

"Herb, run the tape," Amanda instructed Goodwin. "Start where we have it marked." Then she turned back to the jury and said, "This is a videotape of an EBC News Special Report that aired on Friday, December sixth, last year. Susan Silver, the investigator, is interviewing the plaintiffs. They were assigned fake names to protect their identities. Ginny is the Jane Doe you're going to hear from now."

The judge and jury watched the video, starting when Susan Silver asked the question, "Would you please tell the television audience what you told me when we first met?"

It continued through Ginny's version of what happened.

Barry watched the jury as the video was played. They were captured by it.

Becky leaned over and whispered, "Another blow struck by video."

Amanda walked over in front of the jury. "I'm not going to go into any more detail now," Amanda said. "Each plaintiff will tell you what happened. It'll be pretty much what you just heard, but you need to hear it from them. What I am going to talk about, however, is what happened next? The following Tuesday, September twenty-fourth, the plaintiffs reported the attacks to the authorities, the Clatsop County sheriff's office. The sheriff reported it to the district attorney, who talked to the plaintiffs. He got the identical story that you just heard. So what did he do? Nine days later he dismissed the charges! That's what I said - he dismissed the charges! What was his reason? He said 'There was no one to corroborate the plaintiffs' stories.' By this time he'd talked to the defendants, and they denied that they'd attacked the girls. It turns out, however, that his talks with the defendants were three very short telephone calls. No written statement, signed or otherwise. That's all he did to investigate.

"It didn't take us long to find corroboration of what these defendants had done. We checked into these defendants' backgrounds and quickly found that at least two of them have a long history of sexual activities of this kind. You'll hear more about that later. No one could understand why the district attorney had done what he did. That's why EBC investigated. Its people couldn't believe that the charges would be dropped. That's why the plaintiffs came to our office, because the authorities wouldn't do anything. Well, after we got this case started, we took the district attorney's deposition. His name is Owen Persell. We found out what I just told you, that he made no investigation other than to take plaintiffs' statements and make three calls to the defendants.

"But we also found out that just before Mr. Persell held the press conference announcing that he was dropping the matter, he had a visit from some representatives of a Mr. Santana, the head of the longshoremen on the West Coast and reputed to have Mafia associations. Mr. Persell claims that the visit didn't influence him, but he admits the message he got was Santana wanted the case dropped.

"Why did Santana send people to talk to the DA? That's what we wondered. Mr. Persell admitted that he knew Santana. Santana had backed his run for district attorney some years before. That was back when Astoria had a booming fishing industry and Santana's union did all the work loading the ships. Apparently the DA at the time was investigating importation of drugs through the port, and Santana put up a wad of money to get Persell elected to replace him.

"But there's more to the Santana visit than that. There was a Lukarilla involved, Stephen Weinstein, the man you just heard Mr. Chalmers say is the head of S-Mart. A few months ago I went to Miami to take his deposition. It seems that some years ago, when Mr. Weinstein was expanding S-Mart, he got in a load of financial troubles. A Mr. Boccini came in with money to bail him out. Mr. Boccini was a pal of Santana's, when Santana lived and worked in Miami. According to what we found out, Mr. Weinstein became concerned when he heard about plaintiffs' claims on the television in October. He immediately hired a lawyer, Lester Solomon. Mr.

Weinstein told me during his deposition that Mr. Solomon contacted Mr. Boccini for him and had him talk to Mr. Santana about the DA problem in Oregon. Isn't that interesting."

"Your challenge in this case is going to be to decide who's telling the truth, the plaintiffs or the Lukarillas. We're going to help you. I'm not going to go through all of the facts that we'll give you, but suffice it to say, we will produce evidence that at least two of these men had done things just like this before, a number of times," she said pointing at Lovejoy, Sumas and Shepard. "We found out about these activities, and we'll have people here to tell you about them. The evidence will be that if we could find out what these men had been up to, then Mr. Chalmers should have known it as well when he checked their backgrounds. And if he was going to force these women to stay at a camp with these men in this remote area, he should have done something to protect the women from these men."

Amanda paused and walked back behind where her clients were sitting. "The evidence will show that these attacks caused severe emotional injury to each of these plaintiffs," she said placing her hand first on Ginny's shoulder, and then sequentially on the shoulders of Peg and Tina. "After they came to see us, we immediately had them examined by a psychologist, Dr. Martha Bentley. Dr. Bentley specializes in emotional trauma caused by sexual assaults. She will tell you what the plaintiffs are suffering from and how difficult it will be for them to overcome these emotional injuries. Dr. Bentley wanted her diagnosis confirmed before reporting to us, so she had the plaintiffs examined by an eminent psychiatrist, Dr. Alan Schapiro. Dr. Schapiro will tell you that Dr. Bentley is right, and he'll tell you why."

Amanda walked back in front of the lawyers' tables and faced the jury. "That, very briefly, is the evidence that plaintiffs will present to show you that they were maliciously attacked by these defendants," she said, pointing back at Lovejoy, Sumas and Shepard. "It is the evidence that proves the attacks would not have occurred if the Lukarillas had properly checked into the histories of these men. And it's the evidence that establishes that plaintiffs are entitled to significant damages to compensate them for the injuries they've suffered and will continue to suffer in the future. Thank you for your patience. We're confident that when you've heard all of the evidence, you will not hesitate to find for our clients."

"We'll take our noon recess," Judge Lloyd said. Then addressing the jury, he continued, "Ladies and gentlemen, do not talk with anyone about this case and do not discuss it among yourselves. You should not be deliberating in any way about this matter until you've heard all of the evidence. If someone comes up to you and wants to talk, walk away. If the person persists, tell him or her that you'll have to report it to me and do so. It is important that you not talk to anyone. When you go home at night that includes members of your family. No one! Now retire to your jury room, and from there you may go to lunch, but be back in the jury room no later than twenty after one. We will take up again promptly at one-thirty. Everyone please remain seated until the jury has left the courtroom. Thank you. I'll see you all at one-thirty." The judge got up and went through the door to his chambers.

As they were packing up to leave the courtroom, Becky said to Barry, "Did you see the look juror number one, Shirley Miller, gave us when Amanda was telling about Weinstein and his lawyer's talk with Boccini? She was angry."

"I saw her," Barry replied. "The Witherspoon gal didn't look any happier."

Chapter 33

Tuesday afternoon

The trial was ready to resume. After everyone was seated, the judge said, "Ms. Dixon, I believe you're next."

Joan rose and approached the lectern. She wore a black wool dress adorned with a Chanel scarf. "Thank you, your Honor," she started. "May it please the court, Ms. Johnson and Mr. Bellows, and ladies and gentlemen of the jury. As you might expect, our view of this case and the evidence you will hear is quite different from what you've just heard. This is not a case about the Lukarillas, as Ms. Johnson claimed. It's a case about who's telling the truth, the plaintiffs or Alex Lovejoy, Abe Sumas and Senator Shepard. Most of the rest of the Lukarillas are not even peripherally involved with this case.

"There is another interested party, however, and that's Empire Broadcasting Company. It's likely you'll find from the evidence that it's more than an interested party, that it's directly implicated in what happened on that weekend last September.

"Before I get to that, however, let me tell about my client, Alex Lovejoy. You've been introduced to him. He is seated right behind me. He was born in 1934, during the great depression. He's fifty-eight now. He grew up in Texas on a small farm outside of El Paso. Like a lot of other farmers, his parents had a rough time getting through the depression." She told them about his schooling, military service and working life. "Alex is married. He and his wife, Bea, have two grown children, both girls, and three grandchildren.

"Now I want to discuss what I call 'the EBC connection.' It's the network whose news department broke the plaintiffs' story nationally. EBC delivered it on Wednesday, September twenty-fifth last year, as a part of the regular *Evening Report*. Then it used the *Evening Report* on Wednesday, October second, to report to the nation that Owen Persell, Astoria's district attorney, had decided not to proceed further in the matter of plaintiffs' claims. EBC claimed it had a hard time understanding why Persell took this extraordinary action, and it decided to launch its own investigation into these charges and the Lukarillas. Then on December sixth, EBC, Dorothy Watters and Susan Silver broadcast their expose, parts of which Ms. Johnson triumphantly showed you this morning."

Joan turned and pointed to the back of the courtroom. "That's Ms. Silver seated next to the aisle on the left side of the back row. She's that attractive woman with the long black hair in the gray suit. As you can see, EBC's very interested in what's going on here. It sent its star reporter to keep track."

"Damn it," whispered Bellows to Amanda. "I thought you told those two to stay out of here."

"I did," she whispered back. "I don't know what she's thinking."

"But Ms. Johnson didn't tell you that EBC had been involved with this case long before September twenty-fifth," Joan continued. "The evidence will show that in November 1989 EBC did another expose blasting Alex Lovejoy and his company, Silex Petroleum." Joan turned again and looked toward the back of the courtroom and said, "It seems Ms. Silver was a friend of a female executive at Silex who got passed over for the job of chief operating officer in August of that year. Of course, Mr. Lovejoy was the president, and he made that decision. The female executive's name is Angie Lawrence. She quit in a huff and went to Los Angeles, where she's now president of Citrus Publishing Company." Still looking at Silver, she explained, "Ms. Silver was mad. She thought Lawrence should have gotten the job, so she started investigating Lovejoy and Silex. That led to the expose in which she and EBC claimed Lovejoy and Silex were guilty of sexual discrimination and harassment. Mr. Lovejoy and Silex sued EBC for libel, and that lawsuit is still pending in New York. So, you see, EBC had an ax to grind with Alex Lovejoy before September 1991.

"EBC also had it in for Abe Sumas. Back in December 1990, Mr. Sumas got into a dispute with a black reporter from KEBC, EBC's affiliate in Los Angeles. The reporter's name is Rachel Jacobs. EBC Sports' president, Grant Slade, delivered a blistering editorial, charging Sumas and the Stars with gross sexual and racial discrimination on his *Sunday Sport Roundup*. Mr. Sumas went public with counter charges, and, to its deep chagrin, EBC lost its television contract with the NFL the next season. Mr. Slade has publicly accused Sumas of being responsible for that action by the league. He and EBC have been waiting to get even.

"So what? You may ask. Well, the story of EBC's involvement doesn't end there. But first let me tell you about a relationship between some of EBC's friends and two Lukarillas members, a relationship that existed well before the retreat last September. You'll recall that Ms. Johnson told you that Marlene Smyth bought West Portland Catering during the summer before that retreat. That's only partially true. The full truth is that she had financial backers. In fact, those backers put up all of the cash for the deal. Who are the backers? Well, the money came from J & L Investment Company in Los Angeles, and the owners of J & L Investment Company are none other than EBC cohorts, Rachel Jacobs and Angie Lawrence.

"But the intrigue doesn't end there. It turns out that both of those women are chummy with two of the Lukarillas, Rachel Jacobs with Parker Price and Angie Lawrence with Max Pepper. Jacobs and Lawrence learned about the Lukarillas from Price and Pepper, and they also learned that their old nemeses, Lovejoy and Sumas, were members. Actually Price and Pepper have deep-seated problems with Sumas and Lovejoy, as well. Price was going with Jacobs when the Stars incident occurred. He's been furious with Sumas ever since. Pepper's bone to pick with Lovejoy goes back to when he was a lawyer in Boston. He lost a legal fight with Lovejoy, and he thinks Lovejoy blackballed his family with Boston society, resulting in his divorce. I know this sounds like a soap opera, but these are facts.

"And the plot thickens. Marlene Smyth had known Angie Lawrence and Rachel Jacobs for several years. She was the hostess at an exclusive women's club to which they belonged in Newport Beach, California." Then she explained how Smyth moved to Oregon and acquired the catering company. She told them how Smyth had called Angie and how Angie had talked about the catering company over cocktails with Jacobs, Pepper and Price. "Guess who else was having cocktails with them?" she said. "Grant Slade. Remember, he's the EBC Sports executive who got into it with Sumas. Ms. Lawrence told that group that one of the catering company's clients was the Lukarillas' retreat. Of course, Pepper and Parker knew about West Portland Catering, because it had catered earlier retreats. When all was said and done, Slade and Parker decided to put up the money to buy the company and to cover up their involvement by offering the money to Ms. Smyth through J & L Investments. So before this retreat ever started, Lovejoy's and Sumas' enemies, including EBC, were deeply involved."

Barry was watching the jury and the judge for reactions. Joan had their attention. Each time she asked one of her rhetorical questions, each juror seemed to be looking for the answer.

"But there's more," Joan said. "One of the reasons West Portland was for sale was that the previous owner had lost his waitresses. So, Marlene Smyth was in need of helpers after she and J & L made the purchase. Again, she called her friend Lawrence. She knew Lawrence had connections with a catering service in Newport Beach, and she thought she might know where to get help. Surely you can see what's coming next. Yes, Angie Lawrence gave Marlene the names of the plaintiffs, and Marlene hired them. Meanwhile, Pepper was in charge of cabin assignments for the 1991 retreat. And guess how he arranged one of the cabins? He put Abe Sumas, Alex Lovejoy and Senator Shepard together. The cabin assignments were circulated to the members about a month before the retreat. We think you'll find that either Pepper or Price told Slade about those assignments and that he probably made use of that information. Exactly what he did, I'm not sure, but hopefully, we may have evidence that will tell us. So you see, even before this retreat began, EBC and some old enemies of two of the defendants were players in what transpired.

"EBC's involvement did not end with the retreat. It was instrumental in the filing of this suit. When Susan Silver interviewed the plaintiffs for EBC's expose, she told the plaintiffs to find a lawyer and sue, and she told them to have their lawyer call her before she filed a complaint." Looking again at Susan Silver in the rear of the courtroom, Joan said, "And then Ms. Silver arranged for one of EBC's New York lawyers to prepare the complaint and other legal papers for Ms. Johnson. Ms. Silver and Ms. Johnson then laid plans to get maximum impact by having EBC broadcast its expose first, and then follow a few days later with the filing of this case. They tried to keep EBC's involvement secret, but with the help of Judge Lloyd we discovered what was going on behind the scenes when we took Ms. Silver's deposition, and we'll show you later how we found that out.

"Now, I'd like to discuss what went on at the retreat. But what transpired is not what Ms. Johnson and the plaintiffs claim. What actually happened started on either late Friday night or early Saturday morning. Two of the plaintiffs visited the cabin where Max Pepper, Parker Price and Steve Weinstein were staying. It was around midnight. To understand what I'm about to tell you, I should show you what the inside of the cabin looked like. Actually all the cabins were the same, except for Chalmers' cabin. Here on Exhibit Two is a sketch of the interior of the cabins."

Mary Jo put Exhibit Two on the ELMO overhead.

Joan explained the exhibit and continued, "Later on Saturday, while Steve Weinstein and Alex Lovejoy were fly-fishing in the river, Weinstein told Lovejoy what had happened that night. Here's how Mr. Lovejoy described what Steve Weinstein told him. Mary Jo, please turn on the VCR and play the video of that portion of Mr. Lovejoy's deposition."

The portion of the deposition was shown in which Weinstein described to Lovejoy how the two girls asked for and got sex.

Joan's every word had the jury's full attention, Barry observed, but when the videos were shown, each juror seemed transfixed on Lovejoy's image and words.

Joan left the lectern and walked to the jury box. "Both girls were seen leaving that cabin at about five in the morning, and Judy Larson, the caretaker's daughter-in-law, found two condoms in wastebaskets when she was cleaning that cabin on Saturday. Sunday night a similar knock was heard at the door of the cabin where Alex Lovejoy, Abe Sumas and Senator Shepard were staying." She told the jurors what Lovejoy said had actually happened, including showing them a portion of his deposition. "Abe Sumas and Senator Shepard will tell you about the same thing. There were no sexual assaults. Just as two nights before, the girls wanted sex, and they got it. And these were not unusual activities for these women. There will be evidence about their backgrounds that will show that they have a propensity for this sort of thing.

"We will not present any medical witnesses because we believe that the evidence will show that plaintiffs' complaints are completely subjective. In medicine that means the only basis for the complaints is what the patient says. There are no objective findings, such as bruises, the patient's appearance, X-rays, blood tests, and the like, to support the complaints. The evidence will show that the plaintiffs' doctors' diagnoses are solely based upon subjective evidence, what the plaintiffs say, and that, if the events occurred as testified to by defendants, plaintiffs have suffered no injuries at all.

"The judge has told you that the first evidence you'll hear will be from witnesses called by the plaintiffs. Defendants cannot present witnesses until the plaintiffs finish. But some of what I've told you will be developed from plaintiffs' own witnesses, including the plaintiffs themselves. The other evidence will be presented later when it's the defendants' turn. We ask that you wait until you hear all of the evidence before deciding whom to believe. What I have told you are the facts that will be proven by the total of all the evidence. Thank you for your patience.

"Among the defendants' lawyers we agreed that I would make this opening statement first and cover most of the evidence upon which we all will rely. The other defendants' lawyers will now address you briefly on behalf of their clients. Thank you again."

"Who wants to be next?" the judge asked.

Miles and Shumanski made brief statements. They each told the jury about their client and had short portions of their client's deposition shown.

Barry was next. He rose to his feet and went to the lectern. He told the jurors about Hugh Chalmers and his idea that created the Lukarillas. He told them how Chalmers did it, and how successful the idea had become. He described the type of men who made up the membership over the years. Then he left the podium and approached the jury. He spoke clearly but quietly. "As Ms. Dixon has told you, this case is not about the Lukarillas. It's about three defendants and three plaintiffs who shared cabins next to each other during the retreat. It's also about a television network with two vendettas on its mind. Ms. Dixon has already explained the evidence of this, but you'll recall she left the potential involvement of Grant Slade, EBC Sport's president, up in the air. Let me bring that involvement down a little closer to the ground. Recently, we learned some surprising information. I'm not going into it now, but suffice it to say that we may be able to show you that Mr. Slade was deeply involved in what eventually happened at the retreat.

"However, even if we disregard EBC and Mr. Slade's involvement in the retreat and this case, the bottom line of the evidence you will hear is that none of the plaintiffs were sexually assaulted. They were involved in sexual acts, but only ones that they wanted and to which they consented. That's what the more convincing evidence will show. Thank you, ladies and gentlemen. You've heard a lot of lawyers talking so far. Now it's time to hear some witnesses."

It was a little before three, and the judge ordered the afternoon recess. "Ladies and gentlemen of the jury," he said, "remember my admonitions. Everyone in the courtroom remain seated until the jury has left. We'll be back in session in twenty minutes."

Chapter 34

The courtroom was full again at quarter after three. The judge entered and was seated. Turning to the jury, he said, "You have now heard the opening statements of the lawyers, and it's time to hear the evidence. As one of the lawyers told you, plaintiffs will present their evidence first, and then defendants will present their evidence. After you have heard all of the evidence, the lawyers will address you again, this time with final arguments. I will then instruct you as to the law you are to follow in your deliberations, and you will retire, deliberate, and return your verdict. Withhold any judgment, make no decision on the evidence and do not deliberate until that time comes. Call the first witness for the plaintiffs."

After the oath had been given and Ginny Lane was seated, Amanda started by asking her to give her name. She spent several minutes having Ginny tell the jury about herself.

Barry observed that Ginny had been well prepared. She could have been a middle-income housewife. Her makeup was minimal, and she wore blue slacks and a loose aqua cashmere sweater, so her bust was not pronounced.

"How did you happen to come to Portland?" Amanda asked.

Ginny was looking at Amanda when she asked the question. Then she turned to the jury and replied, "A friend recommended me to Marlene." She showed just the right amount of nervousness with the reply. Then innocently, she asked, "Do you want to know who the friend was?"

Clever, Barry thought. *They know Joan would ask that on cross-examination.*

"Yes, tell the jury who recommended you."

"It was Angie Lawrence. She was a regular user of the catering service where I worked. I had known her for several years, and we became friends."

Amanda continued to eliminate some of the cross-examination. "Did you have anything to do with Peg and Tina coming to work for Marlene?"

"Yes, they both worked with me at Del Mar Catering. When I told Marlene that I'd come to work for her, I told her that I could bring two other gals, and she said, 'Thanks, I need help, bring them along.' So I asked Peg and Tina if they wanted to join me. They did. We all went to Portland together."

"Ms. Lane, we understand that West Portland Catering catered the retreat for the Lukarillas the weekend of September twentieth to the twenty-third, nineteen nighty-one. When did you arrive there, and what did you do?" Amanda asked.

"We got there a little after noon on Friday. After we were shown where we were staying and we had put our things away, we worked at getting the evening meal together and ready to serve. We served dinner at seven, and then we cleaned up."

"After you cleaned up what did you do?"

"We went back to our cabin, talked for a while and went to bed. I read for a while in bed."

"Who is 'we'?"

"They've rehearsed this well," Barry thought.

Ginny looked at the jury and said, "Me, Marlene, Peg and Tina. We all stayed in one cabin. Marlene went back to the cabin first because she finished first. The three of us went there about an hour later, when we was done."

Herb Goodwin put Exhibit One on the television with ELMO. "We have two exhibits that were drawn earlier by witnesses, when their depositions were taken," Amanda said. "Can you identify them for the jury? First, will you tell us what Exhibit One is?"

"Yes, it's a sketch of the camp, showing the roads and the buildings, and —"

Amanda interrupted. "May I approach the witness, Your Honor?"

"Certainly," the judge said.

Then she told Ginny, "Here's a pointer, step down closer to the television monitor and use it to describe the exhibit."

Ginny did as instructed. Using the pointer she described the camp scene depicted and where the women's cabin was located.

Goodwin replaced that exhibit with the next one. "Now tell us what Exhibit Two is," Amanda asked.

Again using the pointer, Ginny described the cabin's interiors. "Marlene had the bedroom at this end. I had the one in the middle, and Peg had the one at the other end. Tina used the couch, it had a roll-out bed."

"Did any of you leave the cabin that night or early the next morning?"

As Barry expected, Ginny replied looking directly at the jurors. "I didn't, and I'm almost sure the others didn't either, although I was asleep."

"You can return to the witness chair," Amanda said. "What did you do after dinner on Saturday?"

"The same things we did the night before. Almost identical."

Amanda looked at the jury again. "Did any of you go out of your cabin that night?"

"I didn't, and I'm almost sure the others didn't either."

"Then what happened Sunday?"

"We did the same things that we had done on Saturday. You want me to go into Sunday night?" she asked.

"Yes."

Ginny settled in and turned to the jury. "Well, we cleaned up as usual. It was kind of a banquet that night, with more talking after dinner than the other nights, so we didn't get done cleaning up until after nine. Marlene went to our cabin about seven-thirty or eight. The three of us left the mess hall and were walking back.

"Our cabin's right next to the mess hall, so actually we had just stepped off its porch when Abe came up to us. He was standing outside his cabin when we came out. He said,

'Why don't you girls join us for a nightcap. Tonight's our last night, and you've been working your tails off. You deserve a reward for the way you've treated us.'

"By then we'd gotten to know the guys pretty well. They talked to us a lot at mealtimes. Just joking around, you know. As I told the TV gal, one of us said, 'These are great guys, let's join 'em.' So we went into Abe's cabin. Alex and the senator, who they called Shep, were there. They poured us a drink, and we talked and joked."

Then she explained what happened just as she had on the Dorothy Watters show. "Alex told us to be reasonable and cooperate, and he won't have to tell our boss that we tried to sell them sex. He told us that they'd checked us out and knew that we did this kind of thing for money. 'If you show us you're worth it, we might even pay,' he said. That scared us. We weren't prostitutes, but who'd believe us, if these guys said we propositioned them. We were afraid what they could do to us so we gave in. Senator Shepard fucked me, but I swear I didn't want it!" she said, starting to sob.

Immediately the judge interrupted, "We'll take a ten-minute recess. Mrs. Williams, please escort the jury to the jury room. Everyone else stay seated."

After the jury had gone, as the judge was getting out of his chair to leave, he cast a steely glance at Ginny. Then he turned to Amanda. "We'll resume in ten minutes. Ms. Johnson, get your client under control. I won't tolerate any further displays."

Becky leaned over to Barry. "Damn it, Amanda has done one hell of a job with her. She's Miss Homespun, and I'm afraid the jury may be buying it. I hope Paul can make a dent."

"He will," Barry said. "Since I took her deposition, she'll expect me to question her. When Paul starts, hopefully she'll be confused, and maybe a little shook up. Also don't be too sure every juror is buying her. As you could tell, the judge suspects she's putting it on."

The court was back in session.

"Did you tell Marlene what had happened?" Amanda asked.

Fully recovered, Ginny looked at the jury. "After we got back to our cabin we did. She was shocked, but she said we had to keep our mouths shut till we got out of there on Monday. She told us to say nothing to anyone, including Mr. Chalmers and the Larsons."

"Did you report the attack to the authorities?"

"Yes, we did. We left the camp and drove straight to Seaside. We found the sheriff's office and told them. They took our statements."

"What did you tell the police?"

"Exactly what I just said here," she replied.

"Did you ever talk to the district attorney?"

"You mean the guy in Astoria who dropped our complaint? The answer is no. He never talked to us before he caved in."

"Your honor," Shumanski said. "I move to strike that last comment by the witness. It wasn't responsive, and it was argumentative."

"Objection sustained," the judge ruled. "That last comment will be stricken. You're to totally disregard it," he said to the jury. Then he turned to Ginny. "Ms. Lane, please listen to the question and answer it. I want no more gratuitous statements out of you, do you understand?"

"Yes, Your Honor. I'm sorry."

But Barry believed that she was still steaming inside.

"Have you had any problems physically since that weekend?" Amanda asked.

"I don't have any bruises, if that's what you mean, but I've had lots of mental problems. I can't sleep, my concentration's shot, and I'm on edge most of the time. When I do sleep, I have terrible nightmares. I wake up in a sweat. I'm sure they'll say it's my imagination, but I tell you it's real. I'm a mess." She appeared to be fighting back the tears.

"Nothing further, Your Honor."

Barry knew Amanda quit because she sensed trouble ahead. Ginny was starting to advocate, and she couldn't afford to let her cry. She'd covered everything, so she was wise to end it.

"You may cross-examine," the judge said, addressing the defense tables. Barry saw Ginny sit back, suck it in and look his way, waiting for him to begin.

Shumanski rose and approached the podium. His appearance belied his tough reputation. He was short, about five-seven. He looked to be in his late forties. He was actually over sixty.

"Ms. Lane, when was the first time you saw Max Pepper?" he asked abruptly.

Ginny sat there momentarily. Finally, she responded, "Oh, you mean when I used to see him in California at Angie Lawrence's house?"

Shumanski looked at the jury and then back to Ginny. "I'm not sure what you think I mean, Ms. Lane," he said, "but that's fine, you met him in California. Would you say that by the time of the retreat you two were friends?"

"Yeah, I'd say that. At least I knew him better than the others. Course I'd met Park, I mean Parker Price, at Angie's house in California too. I just didn't see him as often."

"So you already knew two of the men at the retreat and one was a friend, is that right?"

"Yes," she said cautiously.

"And, if I understand your testimony, you didn't say anything to either of them about being attacked Sunday night, is that right?"

"Yeah, Marlene told us not to."

"Did Marlene know you were friends with Max Pepper?"

"I don't know."

"But she didn't tell you not to tell Pepper or ask him for help, did she?"

"She didn't say it that way, no."

"Earlier this year, maybe say in January, you got a call from a lawyer in Los Angeles named John Sheldon, didn't you? He said he was Max Pepper's lawyer."

"Yeah, how'd you know that?"

"Never mind how I knew it," Shumanski said. "He wanted to talk to you about the visit you and Peg made to

Pepper's cabin around midnight Friday night, didn't he?"

"Yeah, that's what he wanted to talk about," she admitted. "But I wasn't in Max's cabin then."

"That's not what you told him, was it?"

"Well, no. What I told him is I wouldn't talk to him. My lawyer wouldn't let me."

"Now just a minute, Ms. Lane. The fact is that your lawyer didn't even know about the call, isn't that true?"

"Ah, well, no, but she didn't want us to talk to anyone."

"You never told your lawyer about the call from Sheldon, did you?"

"No."

"And Peg told you that Sheldon had called her too, didn't she?"

She was still somewhat confused by his approach. "Yeah, she told me he did."

"Didn't she tell him that you two just took ice to the cabin and left?"

"Did she tell him that? She never told me she said that."

Shumanski paused and looked at the jury. He changed the subject to her past. "Let's talk some more about what you did in Los Angeles before coming up here. You were brought up down there, weren't you?"

"Yeah."

"After high school you worked in a bunch of bars, first as a barmaid and then as a bartender, isn't that right?"

Ever since the judge had taken her to task, she'd forgotten her role. She wasn't looking at the jury. She directed her answers at Shumanski, and her attitude was antagonistic. "Yeah, that's right."

"And you tried to get into the movies. You got a few parts as an extra, isn't that right?"

"Yeah, that's right."

"You've been married and divorced twice, isn't that correct?"

"Yeah."

"And during that time you've slept and had sex with maybe ten or fifteen men who weren't your husbands. You didn't keep count, I think you told us, isn't that true?"

"Okay, your pal over there asked me that on the deposition," she said, pointing at Barry. "I said 'yeah' then, and I'm saying 'yeah' now. Are you satisfied?"

Shumanski glanced at the jury and then back to Ginny. "All I want is an answer to my question. I'll take that as a yes. And you actually charged for the sex or got favors for it, didn't you?"

"Okay, that's about enough," she screamed. "I fucked some movie guys to get in films, that's all!"

"You're right, Ms. Lane, that is all," the judge said. "You calm down and answer the question. We don't need your gratuitous swearing. If the question is improper, leave it to your lawyer to object, or I'll stop the lawyer, if I think it's improper. You're the witness. Don't try to be anything more."

"I don't have any more questions, Your Honor," Shumanski said.

Actually, Barry knew he had a couple more pages on his pad of things he could ask. But, like the good trial lawyer he was, he quit at the right time.

"Miss Homespun just got unspun," Becky whispered.

The judge took over. "It's quarter to five. We've had a long day, so I'm going to recess until eight-thirty tomorrow morning. Remember my admonitions, ladies and gentlemen. Don't talk to anyone about this case, even among yourselves or to your spouses. Be back in your jury room by twenty after eight. Have a good evening."

Back in her office, Amanda was not happy. She faced Ginny. "Damn you. How many times did I tell you to come clean with me? You told me you never gave sex for favors. What else do I need to know? And I'm directing that to all three of you," she said.

She got no response. Instead, Tina complained. "Why do I have ta go next? I can't take being asked those shitty questions again, like at the deposition."

"Don't get keyed up," Amanda told her. "You and I are putting in a long night tonight. We're not having a repeat of this afternoon. You'll be ready tomorrow, I promise you."

Chapter 35

The Wednesday morning *Oregonian* reported the beginning of the trial. The article stated that plaintiffs' lawyer, Amanda Johnson, accused the three individuals of sodomizing and raping her clients and said she had evidence that several of them had done things like this before. Finally, the article reported that Ms. Johnson accused the Lukarillas of blocking a criminal prosecution by the Astoria district attorney.

"Tina's the next witness," Barry said. The defense lawyers and clients had assembled in his office before leaving for court. "My guess is that Amanda will only let her stay on the stand to tell her story briefly and to complain of the emotional damage she claims she's suffered. She knows how dangerous she can be. Joan, that should give you a chance to give the jury a true look at Tina Marcellas."

"Yeah," Joan said, "but I'm not going to over-do it. I don't want her to act picked on. I think I can portray who she is fairly quickly."

With her black hair braided and wearing a casual dress, Tina's direct examination took only about a half hour. She claimed Alex threatened them, and that's why she had sex with him. She denied being in any cabin before Sunday night.

"Cross-examination?" the judge asked.

Joan rose from her seat and addressed the court. "Your Honor, may I approach the witness?"

"Certainly," he responded.

Joan picked up Exhibits One and Two from the exhibit table and took them to Tina. Mary Jo put copies on the television with ELMO. "I've handed you Exhibits One and Two. You just identified Exhibit One as your sketch of the cabins. Exhibit Two shows the configuration inside the cabins.

"You wrote the names in the cabins on Exhibit One when we took your deposition. You seemed pretty familiar with their names. You must have become friends with these guys over the weekend, is that right?"

"Yeah," she said. "They talked a lot when we was serving. We talked back and forth."

"Let's look at Exhibit Two. Where did you four sleep?" Joan asked.

Tina told her.

"I want to talk about Friday night. What did you all do after you finished cleaning up?"

"Marlene went back to the cabin first. She was reading when we got there. That was about nine or ten. We kinda talked for a while. I was tired and went to bed 'round ten-thirty."

"Were the other three up when you went to bed?"

"Yeah," she said, and then corrected herself, "but maybe Ginny was in her room reading. Didn't she say that?"

The judge interrupted and cautioned her. "Don't worry about what another witness said. You just answer the question as best you can. Do you understand that?"

"Yes, sir."

"How did you sleep?" Joan asked.

"Okay."

"So I guess you didn't see the others again until the next morning, isn't that right?"

"Yeah."

"So you don't know who went to bed when, do you?"

"How could I? I was asleep."

Barry was watching Tina closely as she replied, and he realized with that answer that she didn't know where Joan was headed.

"Well, what I'm getting at, Ms. Marcellas, is that you don't know if Ginny and Peg left the cabin that night after you went to bed, do you?"

"I do too. I know they didn't."

"How do you know that?"

"'Cause they tol' me so."

"Is that right? When did they tell you that?"

"I don't remember exactly."

"Wasn't it after you three learned that Thor Larson had seen the two of them coming out of the cabin next door early Saturday morning?"

She replied quickly. "You said that, I didn't. I don't remember."

That must have made Amanda a little happier, Barry thought. It was probably as good as Tina could do, but Joan had scored.

"Ms. Marcellas, you've had a pretty active sex life for someone your age, haven't you?"

"Whattaya mean by that?" she answered angrily.

"Well, you told us at the time of your deposition that since you moved up here, you've had sex with a bunch of fellas you met at the Sellwood Inn, isn't that so?"

"If ya say so, I guess that's right."

"That's what you told us, isn't it?"

"I don't remember."

That gave Joan a chance to use the videotape. "Let me show you a little bit of your deposition. It goes from page thirteen, line eight, to page fourteen, line twenty-three. Mary Jo, would you show this to the jury on the television. The person asking the questions is Mr. O'Shea."

The jury saw and heard the portion of Tina's deposition where she was asked about her boyfriends in Portland. She admitted sleeping with Weasel and charging him a hundred dollars, but she refused to answer if that was the first time she'd charged for sex.

The video was turned off. "You remember that testimony, don't you, Ms. Marcellas?" Joan asked.

"Yeah."

"So you did have sex with quite a number of guys, both here in Oregon and before down in California, isn't that so?"

"I didn't say I didn't."

"Then your answer is yes?"

"Yeah, but I'm not detailing it," she said.

"Nobody's asking you to do that. I'm just trying to get a picture of your sex life before you say my client forced you into sex. Let me ask you again about what Mr. O'Shea asked you during your deposition. Was Weasel the first guy you ever charged for sex?"

"Same answer. I won't tell ya!"

The judge broke in. "We're not having any of that, Ms. Marcellas. Your complaint brings your sex life into issue in this case. Answer the question."

He didn't soften her anger, but she answered. "All right, damn it. Yeah, I charged lots of guys. You oughta grow up with nottin'. Livin' in shacks, out in the fields. If men want it, they's gonna pay. I learnt that real early," she sobbed.

The judged stopped her. "We'll take a ten-minute recess. Mrs. Williams, please take the jury to the jury room."

After the jury retired, he again spoke sternly to Tina. "Ms. Marcellas, get control of yourself! I'm not having any more outbursts like that in this courtroom. Do you understand that?"

Still sobbing, she replied, "Yes."

When everyone had returned, Joan asked, "When was the first time you saw a doctor for these complaints you've told us about?"

"I think it was in October or November."

"Why did you go to a doctor?"

"Amanda told us to."

"Did she also tell you what doctor to see?"

"Yeah, she made the appointment."

"I have nothing further," Joan said.

The other defense lawyers had no questions.

Amanda quickly rose to her feet. "You were having problems before I suggested you see a doctor, weren't you?" she asked loudly.

"Yeah, some," Tina answered.

"Nothing further, Your Honor."

The court recessed for lunch.

On the way back to his office, Barry complimented Joan on the job she had done. "You were masterful. She came off as the tramp she is."

"Sometimes it's easier to expose a woman with another woman," Joan said.

"What you did didn't have anything to do with your gender," Barry added. "It was just damn good lawyering."

Wednesday evening

Barry got home too late for dinner. Sarah made him a sandwich, poured them a drink and joined him at the kitchen table. "How'd it go today?" she asked.

He told her about Tina's testimony. "We came out of that fine, thanks to Joan's cross-examination. But then things got worse. Oscar called Owen Persell and really ran him over the coals for his meager investigation. When Oscar got Persell to admit that he never talked to any of the potential witnesses at the camp, the jurors were glaring at him. Later Amanda showed parts of Weinstein's deposition when he admitted that his lawyer, Solomon, had talked to the mobster in Miami and got him to sick Mike Santana's goons on Persell to pressure him to drop the girls' complaints. I have no doubt that at least some of the jurors are suspecting that Persell's actions were caused by Weinstein, and maybe the Lukarillas.

"Plaintiffs ended the day with Hugh and Julie Sanchez. After Oscar got Hugh to tell how important it was to have good citizens as Lukarillas, he raked Hugh over the coals for not discovering that Sumas, Shepard and several other members had sexual problems in their pasts. It was a repeat of Hugh's deposition. I thought Hugh held up fairly well, but Oscar then called Sanchez to show the jury how easily Sanchez found out about these men's past activities. That made Oscar's case that, if these members really had the propensities he claimed they did, then Hugh could have discovered them by a simple investigation."

"What have they got in store for you tomorrow?" Sarah asked.

"Amanda said that we'll have medical testimony in the morning and parts of the defendants' depositions in the afternoon. She and Oscar are moving right along. They'll probably finish this week, so we need to be ready to start our case on Monday. That leads me to something you can do to help. I think Susan Silver's still in town somewhere. See if Pam Hall can find her, so we can serve her with a subpoena. I think if Pam stakes out Johnson & Bellows' office, she'll spot Ms. Silver coming and going."

"How's she going to identify Ms. Silver?" Sarah asked.

"By this photo," Barry said, handing Sarah a photograph he'd had made from the EBC expose.

Chapter 36

Thursday saw a continuation of the Indian summer. An east wind was blowing down the Columbia Gorge, so the mountains in the Cascade Range had no obstructions. Except for its natural glaciers, Mount Hood was bare from the summer sun. Not a day for school or court proceedings. Not a day to be inside.

The jury and the courtroom cast were seated on time when the judge entered and, after the usual gavel presentation, told them to be seated. He started the session. "Call your next witness."

Dr. Bentley came forward with a fold-over briefcase. She took the oath and sat down in the witness chair. She was in her mid-forties and very attractive. She had a pageboy hairdo and wore a tan gabardine suit with a contrasting silk blouse. The rings on her left hand revealed her marital status.

"Please tell the jury your full name and your occupation," Amanda asked.

"My name is Martha Bentley Mercer. I have a doctor of psychology degree, and I'm licensed as a clinical psychologist. I practice under my maiden name, Martha Bentley."

"Where do you practice?"

"Here in Portland. My offices are on Southwest Macadam."

Amanda's next order of business was to qualify Dr. Bentley as an expert witness.

Dr. Bentley faced the jury and went through her medical training and background. "Since 1986 I have directed a great deal of my practice to patients suffering from psychic trauma."

"Doctor, are the plaintiffs in this case, Ginny Lane, Peggy House, and Tina Marcellas, patients of yours?"

"Yes, I first saw all three at your request on November twelfth last year. I saw them separately on that date."

"Tell us what those visits entailed, what you did and what you found."

Opening her files and placing them on the shelf before her, Dr. Bentley looked at the jury and began a recitation that she had obviously performed in court before. "The visits were very similar. Each took about two hours, which is pretty standard. I first had each of them complete a standard questionnaire. Then I interviewed them separately, took what we call histories. That's basically what happened to them, and how it's affected them. I got almost the identical history for each of them, which was not unexpected, considering that the trauma they'd experienced happened to all of them at the same time under the same circumstances." She related an abbreviated story similar to what Ginny and Tina had told the jury earlier.

"In varying degrees, they all expressed feelings of humiliation and degradation as a result of these events, and they were extremely depressed. They each felt anger and frustration, a desire for revenge, guilt, and some shame at their loss of control. Again in varying degrees, they each complained of nightmares and general disturbance of their sleep patterns and of impairment of concentration and memory.

"Next I gave them some standard tests, and I physically examined each of them. As I suspected, and as is usual in cases of psychic trauma, there was nothing abnormal in the testing or the physical examinations. My findings are the same for each young lady. They all sustained psychic trauma as a result of the sexual assaults which they described. Their symptoms are consistent with a diagnosis of post-traumatic stress disorder. That is the type of psychic trauma from which I believe they are suffering."

Amanda stood. "Did you come up with a prognosis and a recommended course of treatment?" she asked.

Dr. Bentley again faced the jury. "Yes, my prognosis is that some of these symptoms in each young lady will be chronic, by that I mean persistent, and will require a course of treatment and counseling. I set up a schedule for each of them, and they have been receiving these treatments and counseling ever since the first visit. The treatment and counseling will continue for several more months. I also felt that, because of the seriousness of their psychic injuries, I should have them seen by a psychiatrist. I made an appointment for each of them with Dr. Alan Schapiro, whom I believe is one of the best in town for dealing with psychic traumas."

Amanda then came forward and stood by the easel. "Dr. Bentley, from your examinations, the histories that you took and your treatments, do you have an opinion, based upon reasonable medical certainty whether any of the injuries sustained by these plaintiffs, as a result of the sexual assaults, will be permanent?" As she asked the question, she wrote with a black grease pencil, **your examinations; their histories; your treatments**.

"I will know better when the treatments and counseling are over," she answered, "but I can say today with reasonable medical certainty that at least some of the symptoms in each of these young ladies will be permanent. I believe that the significant symptoms that will have some degree of permanency are the sleep disorders, the depression, the loss of concentration and the shame at their loss of control. Those symptoms, in patients who suffer from this degree of psychic trauma, tend to stay with the patient to some extent for a long time."

Amanda then completed her writings on the easel with the words **permanent injuries**. "Thank you, Dr. Bentley," she said. "I have no further questions."

Looking at defense counsel, the judge asked, "Cross-examination?"

Barry rose. "Your Honor, before beginning cross-examination, may I be permitted to examine the files Dr. Bentley has with her?"

"Certainly," the judge replied. "We'll take our morning recess a little early, because it may take Mr. O'Shea some time to make that examination and have copied whatever he may want to use as exhibits. Mr. O'Shea, let the clerk know when you're ready to proceed."

After everyone reassembled, Barry began the cross-examination. "Doctor Bentley, you often appear in court in cases where people are claiming emotional injuries and are seeking money damages, don't you?"

"Yes, quite often," she acknowledged.

"Of the patients that you have seen since 1986, when you took up the specialty of psychic trauma, what percentage would you say were involved, like plaintiffs here, in a court case?"

"Do you want the percentage of cases where I appeared in court?"

"No, I want the percentage of your patients who were suing, whether you testified or not."

"Probably most of them," she said.

"Most of them," he repeated. "Doctor, do you know what the symbols ATLA or OTLA stand for?"

"Yes, I do," she replied. "ATLA is the Association of Trial Lawyers of America and the other is the Oregon Trial Lawyers' Association."

"Those are the associations of lawyers, nationally and locally, who represent plaintiffs in personal injury suits, aren't they?"

"That's my understanding."

"And since 1986, how many times have you appeared before those organizations, ATLA and OTLA, and given talks about how to prove psychic trauma in court?"

She hesitated. "I don't know about the way you asked that question, but I've spoken to those groups several times."

"Several times? Let me be a little more specific. You first spoke to OTLA in the fall of 1986, just after you'd decided to specialize in this field, didn't you?"

"Yes, I did."

"The clerk will give you Exhibit Three, and Mary Jo will put it on ELMO. This is a handout that you gave those lawyers at that time, entitled HOW TO PROVE PSYCHIC TRAUMA IN COURT, isn't it?"

"Yes, it is."

Barry was now alongside the television set, looking

directly at the jury. He looked back at the set and then to Dr. Bentley. "So we now see that the way I phrased that question used the exact same language that you used in the title of your talk, don't we."

"Yes, that's right."

"And isn't it fair to say that you've given the same talk, or a similar one, to either OTLA or the national group, at least every year since?"

She thought for a moment. "I think you're correct. I've given the talk several times."

Still standing by the television set in front of the jury, Barry used his fingers to count. "1987, 1988, 1989, 1990, 1991, and 1992, do I count right, that's six times, actually seven counting 1986?"

She looked at Barry. "You count with your fingers very well."

Several jurors snickered.

"So 'several' apparently means seven times in the last seven years, is that correct?" he asked.

"I'm not arguing with your math, counselor."

"Well, let's look at it another way," he said. "Would it be fair to say, doctor, that every time you've appeared in court and testified on this subject, you've been hired by one of those OTLA lawyers?"

"I think that's right."

"Can you tell us how many of those times the lawyers have been Johnson & Bellows?"

"Several, but I can't give you a number."

"'Several' again," he said looking at the jury. "But they've referred you lots of business, haven't they?"

"They've sent me a number of their clients. I haven't kept track of the number."

"Dr. Bentley, while we were in recess, I had several documents from your files marked as exhibits. The first three I want to talk to you about are Exhibits Four, Five and Six. They are identical forms, one applying to each of the plaintiffs. The forms are entitled PATIENT QUESTIONNAIRE. I'm going to have Mary Jo put exhibit Four on the overhead, so we can all see it. It is the questionnaire filled out by Ginny Lane, isn't it?"

"Yes it is," she said, looking down at the exhibit, and glancing at the television set to be sure they were the same.

Barry walked up to ELMO. "Am I correct that you have these filled out before you talk to the patient?"

"Yes, that's right," she replied. "My staff gives these to the patients and instructs them on how to fill them out."

"And that's what happened here with respect to each of these patients, is that correct?"

"Yes."

"Now looking at Exhibit Four, there are a series of questions where the patient puts a check or x in a box for yes or no, is that right?"

"Yes."

"Let's examine some of those questions. Starting right here," he said, using a pencil to point at the document resting on ELMO. "We have the question, 'Have you experienced a sexual assault?' Then that's followed with a series of additional questions." He walked to the easel. "I'm going to write each of them on this white pad with a black grease pencil,

> If so,
> Have you felt humiliated since then?
> Have you felt degraded since then?
> Have you been depressed since then?
> Do you feel anger because of what occurred?
> Do you feel frustration because of what occurred?
> Do you feel guilt because of what occurred?
> Do you feel some degree of shame because of what occurred?
> Do you want revenge because of what occurred?
> Have you had nightmares since then?
> Have you had other sleeping problems since then?
> Have you had problems with concentration since then?
> Have you had memory problems since then?

"I note that Ms. Lane answered yes to all of these questions. Actually, looking at Exhibits Five and Six — please show those as well, Mary Jo — all three answered yes to all of these questions, is that correct?"

Mary Jo slowly replaced each exhibit on ELMO with the next, so everyone could see each of these questions and the checkmarks in the yes box.

"Yes, they did," Dr. Bentley answered without hesitation.

"Where were these plaintiffs when they filled out these forms?"

"I'm not sure, but usually it is done in our reception area."

"When was it done?"

"I'm not sure again. No, I remember. They all came in at the same time. Because after they filled out the paperwork, which included this form, we had to reschedule their exams. I wanted to interview and examine them separately. So I took Ms. Lane right then, Ms. House a couple of hours later, and Ms. Marcellas, as I remember, the first thing after lunch."

"So basically, when Exhibits Four, Five and Six were filled out, the plaintiffs were together in the waiting room, is that correct?" he asked facing the jury.

"Yes, I believe that's correct."

"Was anyone with them supervising the answering of the questions?"

"Certainly not!"

"Dr. Bentley, I wrote down the symptoms that you testified to during Ms. Johnson's examination." He walked back to the easel and turned toward the doctor. He pointed at each of the lines he had written on the white pad. "You gave us these exact same things as the symptoms for each of these plaintiffs, isn't that correct?"

"Yes, I did."

"I'm looking at my notes of what you said earlier. And I'm going to take a green grease pencil and write each of the symptoms you found in the plaintiffs, in the order you gave them, to the left of what I wrote in black earlier." He wrote,

Feelings of humiliation
Feelings of degradation
Depressed
Expressions of anger and frustration
Feelings of guilt
Some shame at their loss of control
Desires for revenge
Complaints of nightmares

Disturbance of sleep patterns
Impairment of concentration
Impairment of memory

"Did I write those down correctly as the symptoms you gave us?"

"Yes, you're basically correct," she replied.

"Doctor, those are the exact symptoms that you ask about in your questionnaire. In fact, on this chart I made, they match up in nearly the identical order, isn't that correct?"

"You're very clever, Mr. O'Shea. I guess, if you want to put it that way, you're correct."

"Then am I correct, that actually your conclusions about these plaintiffs' symptoms are derived from the answers on the questionnaires?"

"Yes," she said, but added, "and from talking to them."

Barry was still standing at the easel. "Doctor, I want to talk about your findings. As I understand what you are telling us, you believe that these plaintiffs are suffering from post-traumatic stress disorder, is that right?"

"Yes, you're right," she replied. "I believe they were exposed to psychic trauma that has caused them to suffer from that syndrome."

"And your conclusions that these plaintiffs suffer those mental injuries are based upon the subjective symptoms you have related, isn't that correct?"

"Not exactly. They are based upon the psychic trauma they reported in their histories and upon those symptoms."

"All right, I see what you mean," Barry acknowledged. "I left out what they told you happened to them. That's fine. I should have included that because it's directly involved with what I'm concerned about. Doctor, what is the difference between subjective and objective findings from a medical standpoint?"

She was more comfortable describing medical matters. She turned to the jury for the first time on cross-examination. "A subjective finding is a medical finding made based upon what the patient tells you, and an objective finding is a medical finding based upon what you, as the doctor, observe from examination and testing."

With the black grease pencil, he wrote in bold on another sheet of paper,

Subjective findings = what the patient tells her

Then under that he wrote,

Objective findings = what the doctor sees from an examination or test

"In other words," he summarized, "an objective finding is like an X-ray showing a broken bone, or a tumor, or a narrowing of a disc in the spinal cord or a spot on the lung. Or it's like a lab test showing a low red cell count, a bacterial infection, high cholesterol or low blood sugar. It's those kinds of things that you find from testing and examinations, isn't that true?"

"Yes, all of those things are objective findings," she replied.

"And the patient has no control over whether those findings are there or not, isn't that true?"

"In almost all circumstances, that's true. The patient can affect the outcome sometimes, like in a blood pressure check. Certain activity will affect the results."

Under Objective findings on the pad, he wrote in bold,

Beyond the control of the patient

He started his next question facing the jury. "But subjective findings are completely and solely in the control of the patient, aren't they? They're what the patient tells you?" He ended the question looking at the doctor.

"You're correct, but a doctor has to rely on what the patient tells her. Otherwise, a great portion of medical science would be useless."

"I understand that, doctor, but just to make sure we are on the samewave length, we do agree that a finding based on subjective symptoms is based solely on what the patient says. That's correct, isn't it?"

"Yes, with the qualifications I stated."

Disregarding her evasion, under subjective findings, he wrote in bold,

Solely in the control of the patient

"And do you agree, doctor, that what the patient tells you can be influenced by many factors, such as what actually happened and what the patient actually feels, isn't that correct?" As he was asking the question, he wrote in bold,

Influences of subjective symptoms

"Yes, it certainly is," she agreed.

And indented under that title, he added in bold,

What actually happened to the patient, and how she feels about it

"And what the patient tells you can be influenced by suggestion, the patient's needs, and the outcome of litigation, can't it?"

"Well, it can, but I take that into consideration when I analyze what the patient says in making my findings."

"I understand that, doctor, but we do agree that those things can influence what the patient tells you, don't we?"

"In a vacuum, yes."

He indented in bold,

Suggestion - Patient needs - Outcome of litigation

"Doctor, would it change your diagnosis, if I asked you to assume that these plaintiffs had sexual intercourse with these men voluntarily and willingly?" As he asked the question he pointed to Lovejoy, Sumas and the senator.

"That's not what they told me," she replied.

"I'm not now asking you what they told you. You and Ms. Johnson have covered that. I'm asking you to assume that the sex was voluntary and willingly entered into. Wouldn't that change your opinion?"

"Well, of course it would," she answered.

"Of course it would," he said and he glanced from one end of the jury box to the other. He turned back to Dr. Bentley. "Then you'd say that the plaintiffs weren't injured at all, isn't that right?"

"On your assumption only, I would agree."

"So it really comes down to whether we can believe the plaintiffs, doesn't it, doctor?"

"Isn't that what we've been saying?"

"Is the answer yes?"

"Yes."

He brought the top sheet of paper on the easel pad back down so his earlier writings faced the jury, and wrote at the bottom of the sheet,

Can we believe the plaintiffs?

Then he turned back to the judge. "I have no further questions, Your Honor."

"Any redirect-examination?" Judge Lloyd asked.

"A few questions, Your Honor," Amanda said. "Doctor, did you find anything in talking to the plaintiffs or in your examinations that would cause you to not believe them?"

"No."

"Since the first visit in November, how many times have you treated and counseled with them?"

"Three times a month since then. They're still coming to see me."

"Have you seen anything, as a result of those visits, that would cause you to even suspect they are not telling the truth?"

"No."

"During your many years of practice have you had occasion to treat and counsel with patients who were not telling the truth?"

"More times than I like to think."

"Are there common signs or signals that show up when you see people who are lying?"

"Yes, it's actually fairly easy to spot, if you're trained to analyze people and their habits."

"And you didn't see any of that in these plaintiffs?"

"Absolutely not."

There was a pause. "Are you finished?" the judge asked.

"Yes, Your Honor," Amanda replied.

"Then we'll take our noon recess. Ladies and gentlemen, be back in your jury rooms at one-twenty. We'll take up again promptly at one-thirty."

While the jury was still in the courtroom, Barry addressed the court. "Your Honor, before we conclude, may I ask the clerk to mark the two white sheets I used during Dr. Bentley's cross- examination as defendants' next exhibits."

He knew Amanda's rehabilitation of Dr. Bentley had been effective, but his writing on the white pad was still facing the jury, and he wanted this reference to it to be the last word.

Chapter 37

Amanda was in her office on Friday at six, ready for her morning report to Ryan O'Donnell. "Yesterday afternoon we had them reeling," she said.

"Tell me about it," O'Donnell said.

"First, we showed the jury Sumas' sorry attempt on deposition to soft-pedal his sexual activities as a football player, then we called his old pal Jerry Mahoney."

"Remind me. Who's Jerry Mahoney?"

"He's a retired football coach from Spokane. Our investigator found him a couple of months ago. He was a teammate of Sumas', when Sumas was with the Cardinals. Reluctantly, he told the jury about the incident in Baltimore when Sumas stuck his penis in a girl's mouth at a party and about his forcing a gal in a bar in Philadelphia to do the same thing. As he was leaving the stand, you could see the darts in the eyes of the jurors as they looked at Sumas.

"We ended the day by showing the jury the parts of the senator's deposition where he denied propositioning Sheila Workman and Judy Filcher for oral sex. I'm sure the jury's now ready for those two tomorrow morning."

"Great job," O'Donnell said.

"We've also ran into a problem. They subpoenaed Susan yesterday. So they may call her live next week."

"How'd they know she was there?"

"Unfortunately, she was in court during my opening statement, and they saw her. I assume they've had her followed since."

The defense group headed for court. The media was still waiting for them, but they were getting used to it. They forged through them without really hearing the substance of the questions shouted their way.

The morning paper featured Sumas, but this time the article was on page two of the Metro section. The headline, EX-TEAMMATE IMPLICATES SUMAS WITH ORAL SEX HISTORY, preceded an article that highlighted Jerry Mahoney's testimony.

Everyone was on time, and after all were seated, the judge began the proceedings. "Call your next witness."

Amanda stood and faced the rear of the courtroom. "Will Sheila Workman please come forward and take the witness stand?"

Barry turned and saw a very attractive middle-aged brunette rise from a spectator's bench and walk through the gate and up to the clerk's table. She wore a dark blue knit dress, which fell just above the tops of her knees, revealing shapely lower legs. She took the oath and, in response to the clerk's request, said, "My name's Sheila Patroni Workman."

Amanda said, "Ms. Workman—"

"It's Misses," she said.

"I'm sorry, Mrs. Workman, are you here pursuant to a subpoena?"

"That's the only reason I'm here."

"Do you know Senator Lionel Shepard?"

"Yes."

"How do you know him?"

"I first met him in the early eighties, when he was running for reelection to the Senate. At that time, I was working for the State of Illinois in the capital, Springfield. During my off-hours, I also worked at the Democratic Party headquarters. I met the senator there. Later, I applied for a job at his Illinois office in Springfield, and I became a member of his staff."

Amanda moved quickly to what she wanted. "While you were working for the senator, did he ever offer you money for oral sex?"

Mrs. Workman didn't expect the abruptness of the question. "I told your investigator that I'd do anything not to have to come here and answer questions like that. But he subpoenaed me, so I guess I have to answer," she said, looking briefly at the judge.

The judge nodded.

"Yes."

"When was that, and what were the circumstances?"

Her eyes started to water, and she looked down at her feet. "Why are you doing this to me?" she said. Then slowly raising her head, she wiped her eyes and began softly. "I don't remember exactly when, but it was after I went to work for him, so it would be about 1985." Then she spoke louder. "We had dated some before I joined his staff. After I joined his staff, he would take me out every now and then, when he was in town. I say every now and then because sometimes when he visited Springfield his wife was with him.

"On one of the occasions, when he was alone, we went out to dinner and then back to his hotel suite for a nightcap. We relaxed, and the kissing and petting started. I had my hand on his crotch, and I felt him getting hard. He whispered, 'It wants a blowjob. Please, Sheila, I'll make it worth your while.' I'm not shocked by oral sex, but the way he said it really upset me. I asked him what he meant by that. I'll never forget his response. I can quote it. 'You know, whatever's reasonable, a hundred, two hundred, you tell me.' I was mad as hell. I jumped up and yelled, 'I'm no prostitute. You go to hell.' And I walked out. That's the last time I saw him in person. I quit the next day."

"Are you aware whether he made similar offers to other women on his staff?" Amanda asked.

"I wasn't then, but I found later that he had. I've been told that at least one of them took his offer," she replied.

The damage was done, but Shumanski got to his feet, as he had to. "Your Honor, that last statement is hearsay. I move it be stricken and the jury advised to disregard it."

The judge turned to the jury. "It's hearsay all right, and it'll be stricken. Ladies and gentleman, that means you're to disregard what the witness said she'd been told. You're not to accept that statement as evidence."

However, they couldn't help but remember it.

"Did you complain to anyone about what he did?" Amanda asked.

"Are you kidding?" she replied, giving the jury a stare of disbelief. "He was a United States Senator. Do you know what he and his people would do to someone like me if I got in that kind of tangle with him?" Tears were finally starting to run down her cheeks.

"Nothing further, Your Honor."

Barry knew that Shumanski had to soften the mood.

"Mrs. Workman, I see tears starting to fall, and I don't want to be the cause of making you cry," he said, "but I must ask you a few questions. Is that all right, or would you like to take a break?"

She gathered herself and wiped her face. "I'm all right. I'm sorry for the tears. This isn't easy. Go ahead."

"Thank you," he said. "Had you had sex with the senator before the incident that you just described?"

"No, just petting."

"Had he ever come on to you like that before?"

"No."

"You know he denies doing what you just said, don't you?"

"Yes, I expect he does."

"Then you're saying he's lying, is that right?"

"No, I'm not accusing anyone of anything," she said. "If he says he didn't do it, then it's his word against mine, and I accept that his word may be better than mine."

"Nothing further, Your Honor."

"Mrs. Workman, you're excused. Call your next witness," said the judge.

Shumanski leaned back and whispered to the senator. "Shep, I'm sorry, but that was the best I could do."

Senator Shepard shook his head. "I know," he whispered back.

"Plaintiffs call Judy Filcher," Amanda said.

Judy Filcher took the witness stand and swore, "I do," to the oath given by the clerk.

Judy Filcher was quite a contrast to Sheila Workman. Stout, with heavy breasts, dressed plainly in a beige blouse and black slacks, she was wearing no makeup. Her brown hair was cut short. She could fit the description of a hotel maid, but she'd be better cast as a bartender, which was what she was.

In response to the clerk's request, she identified herself. "My name is Judy Epson Filcher. I'm married, so I'm a Mrs. also."

"Mrs. Filcher, you are here in response to a subpoena, are you not?" Amanda asked.

"Yes, ma'am," she answered.

"Where do you live, and what do you do?"

"I live in Evansville, Indiana. Me and my husband operate a bar and restaurant there."

"Did you ever work as a maid in a hotel in Springfield, Illinois?"

"When I was younger, yes I did for about three years, before I got married," she replied.

"Did you meet Senator Lionel Shepard when you were working at that job?"

"I don't know if you'd say I met him, at least not formally, but I had dealings with him."

"Tell us about that, if you would."

"Before I do, I want to make it clear that I didn't wanna come here. I didn't want to talk about this."

"We understand," Amanda said. "You're under subpoena, so please go ahead."

She fidgeted in her chair. "He was staying at the hotel while he was in town campaigning. The first time I saw him was when I knocked at the door to his room one morning about seven-thirty. We wait for an answer, then if we don't get one, we go in and check the room to make sure it's vacant. If it is, we come back later and clean it. He was sitting on the bed in his shorts. That's all he had on. I said, 'Sorry' and started to leave, when he asked me to stay for a minute. I didn't know what to do. I knew who he was, and I guess, because of who he was, I stayed. He came over to me and took hold of my arm and said, 'I've got a proposal for you. You look like you could use a few extra bucks. I'll give you a hundred if you'll suck my cock.' While he was saying it, he let go of my arm and pulled it out. It was already stiff. I panicked, turned around and beat it out the door. I never saw him again, but I made a big mistake."

"What was that?" Amanda asked.

"I made the mistake of telling one of the other maids what happened. She wanted me to go to the super, but I told her to forget it, I wasn't getting a US Senator on my ass. Unfortunately, she must have said something, because his opponent heard about it, and he started making noises. When they came to me, I denied it, and the story died. But, if I'd never told anyone, you wouldn't have heard about it, and I wouldn't be here," she said.

"Nothing further, Your honor," Amanda told the judge.

"So you told no one else, is that right?" Shumanski asked quickly.

"Not until the investigator came to see me a few months back."

"Did you tell him what you've just told us?"

"I didn't have to. He basically told me what occurred and asked me if it was true."

"And what did you say?" Shumanski asked.

"I said, yeah, but I ain't going to admit it in court.'"

"Then why are you admitting it now?"

"`Cause he slapped the subpoena on me and basically told me I'd go to jail if I didn't come here and admit it."

"Who was this investigator?"

"I forget his name, but he said he worked for lawyers. He gave me a card. It had their names on it," she said, pointing at Amanda and Bellows.

"So, what you've told us is basically what that investigator told you happened, is that right?"

"Yeah, that's right."

"Nothing further, Your Honor."

The judge then asked Amanda if she had anything further.

"Just one more question, Your Honor," Amanda said. "What you told us is the truth, isn't it, Mrs. Filcher?"

"Yes," she said.

During the noon recess the defense lawyers caucused.

"We knew it'd be bad, and it was. But at least it didn't come at the end of the day," Shumanski said. "Any ideas?" he asked.

"I think you did as well as you could," Barry said. "My hope is they'll use Marlene after lunch. We need EBC in this case, and fast. We can do that with Marlene."

"What have you got?" Miles asked.

"I'm not completely sure, but Pam Hall came up with some last minute stuff that they don't know we have. We may be able to surprise them and get some answers that'll leave the jury thinking hard over the weekend. I don't want to say any more right now."

"Fine, it's your show. We'll just hope," Shumanski said, but, if you do well, I think it'll be time to talk settlement again. At the end of the day I'll take Amanda aside and try to schedule a meeting with her for Saturday morning."

During her years at the Orange County Town Club, Smyth had catered to important ladies, so she didn't lack for confidence. It showed as she walked forward, took the oath, and stated, "I'm Marlene Diane Smyth."

"What is your occupation, Ms. Smyth?" Amanda asked.

"I'm the owner and operator of West Portland Catering," she answered. Responding to Amanda's questions, she told the jury why she had moved to Portland and how she became the owner of West Portland Catering. She described how she acquired financing and hired the plaintiffs. Continuing, she explained that the Lukarillas, and Hugh Chalmers, were clients she acquired with the business. She told the jury that after she was up and running, she followed up with Chalmers. He told her that she could count on the retreat in late September. Amanda's questions then turned to the retreat.

"Where did you stay at the camp?" Amanda asked.

"We had the cabin right next to the mess hall."

"Did any of you visit any other cabin either Friday or Saturday night?"

"No."

"Are you sure that the girls didn't?"

Marlene stared at the jury. "I'm very sure!"

"When were you aware that something had happened Sunday night?"

"About eleven or so, the girls woke me. They were crying and all talking at once about being raped. They were so upset, and at first I couldn't understand what had happened. I poured them each a straight scotch and made them drink it. That seemed to quiet them a little, so I concentrated on Ginny and got the story I'm sure she's told you here."

"Did you ever talk to Mr. Chalmers about what had happened?" Amanda asked.

"No, the police told us not to talk to anyone. They said, 'It's a police matter. The district attorney'll be in touch with you.' But as you know, he never was!"

"I have nothing further," Amanda said.

Facing the jury, Becky stood and walked in front of the table. She looked at Smyth and paused for a moment. "You said you're 'very sure' the girls didn't visit another cabin either Friday or Saturday night. How are you so sure?"

Barry thought Smyth looked like she was prepared for a fight. She gave Becky an icy stare. "Because they told me they didn't!"

"When did they tell you that?"

"After Amanda told us Thor Larson claimed he saw Ginny and Peg come out of Max's and Park's cabin early Saturday morning. The girls told me that he was lying, that they weren't there."

"You slept in the bedroom to the far left as you enter your cabin, isn't that so?"

"Yes."

"When did you go to bed Friday night?"

"Oh, I'm not exactly sure. I went to bed first. I know that because the girls were talking and I wanted to read. I read for about an hour and got sleepy, so I turned out my light and went to sleep."

"Where were the other three when you went to sleep?"

"They were still talking in the other room."

"You don't know when they went to sleep, do you?"

"Well, not exactly."

"So, other than what they told you later, you don't know for sure whether one or more of them left the cabin that night, do you?"

Smyth pursed her lips. She glared at Becky again. "I didn't see them, if that's what you mean, but I believe what they've told me."

"Fine, let's talk about another subject. You had some

financial backers who helped you buy West Portland Catering, didn't you?"

"I don't know about 'some,' a company out of LA called J & L Investments backed me. I told you that earlier."

"And Angie Lawrence is the one who got you that backing, isn't that right?"

"Yes."

"You've since learned that J & L stands for Angie Lawrence and Rachel Jacobs, haven't you?"

"I think I knew that early on."

"Did you also know early on that the actual money came from Rachel Jacobs' boyfriend, Parker Price, and the president of EBC Sports, Grant Slade?"

"I didn't know that as early, but, yes, they put the money up," she replied.

"You also knew that Mr. Price was a Lukarilla, didn't you?"

For the first time since Becky started, Smyth looked at the jury. "Honestly, I didn't know that until I saw him at the retreat."

Becky took a few steps toward Smyth. "But you talked to Grant Slade last summer about your job for the Lukarillas, didn't you?"

A look of complete surprise overtook Smyth. "What, what do you mean?" she stammered.

Becky stared at her. "I mean your investor, Grant Slade of EBC, called you last summer to talk about your upcoming job for the Lukarillas, didn't he?"

She sat there thinking.

The judge interrupted Smyth's thoughts. "Ms. Smyth, do you understand the question?"

"Uh, yes, Your Honor," she replied.

"Then answer it."

"Uh, yes, he did," she stammered again.

"Tell the jury what he wanted," Becky said, looking from the witness to the jury.

"He wanted to know who was going up there with me. I told him. He asked if they were the same girls Angie got for me. I told him they were. He wanted their phone numbers. I asked why? He said, 'Look, I've got a financial interest in this company. I've got a right to know about them.' He told me he had a guy coming out here who would want to talk to them."

"Did you give him their phone numbers?" Becky asked.

"Yes," she replied softly.

"Please speak up," Becky said. "Did that guy come out and talk to them?"

She spoke louder. "I think so, but I'm not sure."

"What do you mean by that?"

"Well, I was going to tell the girls about the call. They weren't there at the time, and I just forgot. About a month later, I was talking to Ginny, and something caused me to remember Slade's call. I asked her if anyone called her. She said, 'Yeah and he came out and talked to us. It was about a job.' Then she must have realized that it sounded like they might be leaving me, because she added quickly, 'Don't worry, he wasn't trying to hire us away.' She dropped it, and so did I."

"So you can't tell us what the conversation was about, other than it was about some job for the girls, is that correct?"

"No' I can't."

"I have nothing further."

Dr.Alan Schapiro verified the testimony of Dr. Bentley.

Barry felt he had made his points well with Dr. Bentley, so he didn't want to tarry with this doctor. He went directly to his hypothetical. "Assume, Doctor, that the plaintiffs accurately reported their present mental symptoms and problems to you. Assume further, however, that they did not actually sustain the sexual assaults that they described. In other words, that they didn't tell you the truth about that. Then under those circumstances, the plaintiffs' present mental symptoms and problems would not be related to a sexual assault, would they?"

The doctor tipped his head back and pondered. Then he looked back at Barry. "Assuming they did not tell me the truth about the sexual assault, you're right," he said.

"And under those assumptions, they are not suffering

from post-traumatic stress disorder, are they?"

"I'll agree," the doctor replied, "but only if you assume they lied to me."

"Nothing further. Thank you, Doctor."

Chapter 38

Amanda turned and leaned back. She told Peg to go up to the witness stand and take the oath.

Amanda stood and asked direct questions. That's how they had practiced. "How did you become acquainted with the men?"

"Well, like Ginny said, we knew Max and Park before. We'd worked some at Angie Lawrence's parties down south, and they were there. The others we met at the camp. They liked to chat, and, looking back, I'd say some of them were a little forward."

"Which ones were a 'little forward'?"

"I'd say Abe and Shep, and probably Hook, Steve and Max, but it was just fun talk, no one was out of line, you know."

"All right, but how were they forward?"

"Like, Abe offered me a drink after dinner Saturday night. Actually, so did Steve and Max."

"Where were they offering to give you the drink?"

"I assumed in their cabins, but I didn't take them up."

"Did anything happen Friday night or Saturday morning?"

"No!"

"Did you go to any of the men's cabins that night or early Saturday morning?"

"I did not!"

"Did Ginny or Tina?"

"Absolutely not!"

"All right, tell what happened Sunday night after dinner." Peg covered the details just as Ginny and Tina had. "Then Abe grabbed me. He shoved my head down to his crotch, took his penis out and forced it in my mouth. I jerked my head out of his grasp and got his cock out. Then I spit. That's about when Alex called 'em off and threatened us. If we didn't fuck 'em, they'd turn us in as prostitutes. Then Abe fucked me. I didn't want to do it!" She tightened her lips, but tears began running down her cheeks.

Amanda sat down and looked at the defense table.

"Who's next?" the judge asked.

"I am," Miles answered. He waited until Peg seemed to have herself under control. He remained seated and addressed her politely. "Ms. House, - it is Ms., isn't it?"

"Yes," she replied with some reluctance.

"That's right, you told Mr. O'Shea at your deposition that you've never been married," Miles said. "But you did have a child, didn't you?"

"No, I told him I had an abortion when I was in high school," she replied angrily.

"As I understand it, you're living with Tina out in Sellwood, and you hang around the Sellwood Inn with her, is that correct?"

"Yeah, it's correct!"

Miles rose and went around to the front of his table, where he leaned back casually. "I'll try to shorten this, Ms. House. You told us in your deposition that you've dated several guys you've met there, and you've had sex with all of them, isn't that true?"

"Yeah."

"And you also told us you got some acting jobs down in LA by giving sex to the men who were doing the hiring, isn't that so?"

She pointed at Barry. "I told him about two, and only one wanted to be fucked. The other wanted me to go down on him," she retorted.

"What do you mean by 'go down on him'?" Miles asked.

"You know what I mean! You want me to say he wanted a blowjob? All right, that's what he wanted, and I gave him one! Does that answer it?"

"And you did it voluntarily, isn't that true?" he asked calmly.

"Yeah, I did it 'cause I wanted the acting job, and I got it!"

Miles paused and went back around the counsel table and sat down. He appeared to be examining his notes, but Barry knew he was waiting for her answers to settle in. Still looking down, he said, "I think that's all, Your Honor."

"You're through?" the judge asked.

"Yes, I am."

"Then we're going to recess for the weekend." Turning to the jury, the judge gave them the cautionary instructions and told them to be back in their jury room at eight-twenty on Monday morning. "Have a nice weekend," he said and then looked forward at the lawyers. "Counsel, please remain after the jury retires. I want to talk with you briefly."

After the jury left the courtroom, the judge addressed Amanda and Bellows. "How many more witnesses do you have?"

"The plaintiffs' case is concluded," Amanda replied. "Except to check our exhibits and make sure they've been offered, we're ready to rest."

"Very well, check the exhibits before you leave. I'll consider plaintiffs to have rested. I'll advise the jury when we commence on Monday. Can I assume that the defendants will want to make some motions?"

"Yes, Your Honor," Barry answered.

"I'll hear them at seven-thirty Monday morning. After that, be ready with your witnesses, so we can start promptly at eight-thirty. Court's in recess."

After the courtroom had pretty much cleared out, Shumanski approached Amanda. "My client's still interested in settling. I'm sure you won't deal with him alone, but I'd like to talk tomorrow, if you've got time."

"Sure," she said. "Why don't you come by my office around eleven, but be sure you bring everything you can offer. We'll give you a final bottom line."

The defense team gathered back at Barry's office. The television was on in the conference room. EBC's anchorman was reviewing the first week of the trial. A jury consultant joined him. She'd been hired by EBC to attend the trial and study the reactions of the jurors.

"The jury's sympathetic to the plaintiffs," the consultant said. "Sheila Workman and Judy Filcher made dramatic impacts, and, while O'Shea did some damage to the doctors, it wasn't enough to help the defendants."

"Makes you wonder why we need juries, when these consultants know so much," Barry commented. "Sometimes I wonder whether they've been watching the same case.

"It's been a long week. We all need a rest. Let's take the night off and meet here tomorrow morning," he suggested.

Before they separated, Shumanski told them about the meeting he'd scheduled with Amanda.

Then Barry issued an invitation. "I'm buying at the club, if anyone's thirsty."

In the downtown club's grille they gathered in a large booth.

"I think we came through okay today," Barry said. "We were in a shitpot of trouble last evening and this morning, but I think the jury paid attention to us this afternoon. What do you think, Becky?"

"I feel better," she replied. "I agree we had a bad day and a half, and I'm not sure we've recovered. A lot is going to depend on what they think about over the weekend, and how we hit them Monday."

"Is there any chance he'd dismiss the Lukarillas?" Miles asked.

"Not a chance," Barry said. "We've got to make the motion, but he told us where we stood when he decided the pretrial motion against us. Within his guidelines, the plaintiffs made a case in court."

Shumanski agreed, but he felt mildly encouraged by the showing they'd made before the jury. "You did a hell of a job with the doctors, Barry, and the jury's got to be suspicious, after Becky shoved it to Marlene Smyth. We made good headway early and late. We've got to be in the ballpark."

"Let's hope so," Barry said. "When we get together tomorrow let's decide who we want to call and when we want to present them. We can't let the case drag. We need to pack a punch, make our sale and stop. The jury'll love us if we let them out of here before the end of next week."

⚤

Saturday morning, September 19

Halfway down the front page of *The Oregonian*, a headline blazed, MAID AND STAFFER REVEAL SENATOR'S ORAL SEX OFFERS. The story then went on to describe Judy Filcher and Sheila Workman's testimony the day before.

⚤

The defense lawyers were in Barry's conference room. The clients were given the day off. They were to return Sunday morning for witness sessions with the video camera.

Barry had the defendants' witness list blown up and pasted on a board. "Let's see who we can eliminate," he said.

"Marlene's one," Miles said. "After what Becky did to her, we've got what we need. I don't see using Lawrence or Jacobs either. We probably couldn't get them here anyway. I'd also drop those Sellwood Inn guys. We've already established all we can sell about the plaintiffs' sex habits. If we push it too hard, we could make someone mad. I'd go with the rest."

"That makes sense," Joan agreed. "We have to call Hugh, Alex, Abe and Shep. They've got some selling to do. We need a few things from Pepper, Price and Weinstein, but I'd use parts of their depositions. The Larsons are a must, as is the deposition of Susan Silver. I'm still not sure what we'd do with her as a live witness. But she's subpoenaed so let her stew. But do we need Buccanan, Pritchard, Lorenzo and Sprague?"

"No," Shumanski replied. "What we wanted from them we've already established cross-examining other witnesses. The only way we get stuff in with these guys is to ask for hearsay, and I don't see having a fight with the judge over that.

"I'm worried, however, about Shep. If he has to testify, they're going to rake him over the coals about Workman and Filcher. Of course he'll deny making the oral sex offers, but he'll have to admit he went out with Workman. That's cheating on his wife. It's going to be tough. I'm not looking forward to witness preparations with him on Sunday. But maybe I'll get lucky when I meet with Amanda."

Barry saw that they had a consensus, but he wasn't ready to give up on Lorenzo so easily. "Let's talk a minute more about Lorenzo. He can tell the jurors how he looked high and low for Grant Slade. They'll believe that Slade's probably hiding and that we did our best to try to get him for them. It'll leave a stronger inference that Slade had something to do with what happened at the retreat."

Everyone agreed, and they moved on to the order of presentation.

Joan had been studying this for several days. "I suggest we put Alex, Sumas and the senator on right away to deny it ever happened. The first witness has to be convincing. They'll make some hay on cross with Abe and Shep, so I'd start with Alex. He's very credible when he tells what really happened. His credibility will get stronger when he brings out what Weinstein told him when they were fishing.

"After the Sumas and Shepard cross, we've got to get back on the offensive. Showing that plaintiffs are lying does that, so let's follow with parts of the depositions of Weinstein, Pepper and Price. They corroborate Alex's testimony about plaintiffs' activities Friday and Saturday night. Then bring on the Larsons. That should put the clincher on who's telling the truth.

"Now's the time to get EBC back into the case. Read them Susan Silver's deposition and use Lorenzo. I'm not sure what Hugh Chalmers can add, but he's a good witness, so if he can give us a clincher at the end, I'd use him. Otherwise, let's end with the EBC stuff."

"That's a good plan," Barry agreed, "but I suggest that we can accomplish the same thing if we read the Silver deposition first and then go to the defendants. That has the advantage of immediately tainting the legitimacy of plaintiffs' case with EBC. Following that with what really happened should give us maximum impact. There's another reason. Silver's description of what EBC did previously to Alex and Abe needs further explanations from them, so it's best for them to follow her."

They had a consensus. Shumanski left to meet with Amanda.

⚥

Shumanski called back just before noon. Plaintiffs' bottom line was two and a half million. He said he told Amanda that he might get together a million, but no more. He said, "They told me to take a hike."

The case wasn't going to settle. They knew that now for sure.

⚥

Sunday, September 20

That evening Barry met with Shumanski, Joan and Miles for dinner at their hotel. "How did your preparation sessions go with Lovejoy, Shepard and Sumas?"

Shumanski answered. "When it became obvious we aren't going to settle, I told Shep we had to deal with his problem head on. He has to admit that some of the Workman testimony is true. He agreed. So I told him we'd bring it out first. I explained that by our bringing it out, it gives him the opportunity to explain what happened in his own words. The damage of the testimony will be much less than if Amanda drags it out of him on cross-examination. He agreed, so that's how I prepared him. He's basically going to confess to cheating on his wife."

"Abe has agreed to do the same thing," Miles said, "but he won't agree with everything Mahoney said. He'll admit that he was pretty wild as a youngster, but he'll stick to the fact that he's not been like that for years, and I don't think they can disprove that."

It was just what Barry expected. Lawyers with the experience of Shumanski and Miles would never let their clients go unprotected into cross-examination. "Well done," he said. "The jurors have already heard the bad stuff, so having Shepard and Sumas be up front with them will make some points in the credibility battle."

Joan had had a good session with Lovejoy. "He knows the importance of his leading off. As you know, he's experienced. He's been there before, but we still spent a lot of time with the video. He's ready. He's wanted his say in this mess for a long time, but he knows the importance of not being too aggressive. He's going to be believed."

Amanda and Bellows met with Susan and Sanchez Sunday afternoon. Amanda told Susan about the meeting with Shumanski that morning. "Shumanski said the best he could put together was about a million," Amanda explained. "We told the girls it wasn't enough, and they agreed. We're not going below two and a half.

"Shumanski gave us a preview of their witnesses for Monday. They want to start with your deposition, Susan. We can't prevent that, unless you want to testify live, and I don't think that's a good idea. The deposition will do what they want, and it's not really that bad. Maybe, if they use the deposition, they won't make you answer the subpoena they served. Is that okay with you?"

"That makes sense, but let me talk to Ryan first," Susan replied.

Amanda took Susan into her office to use the telephone.

In about fifteen minutes Susan returned. "Ryan agrees that I shouldn't volunteer to testify. It'll just emphasize their claim that EBC is orchestrating the case."

Chapter 39

Monday morning, September 21

When the defense group turned onto Broadway, there were some TV vans setting up, but no reporters, so the group entered the courthouse for the first time unmolested. It was seven-thirty on the dot when Judy Williams dropped the gavel, as Judge Lloyd came through the door from his chambers.

"Who's first?" he asked.

"Just me, first and last," Becky said.

"I'll take the pretty ones any time," he joked. "Proceed."

Becky made a motion to dismiss the Lukarillas for lack of evidence. She argued for about five minutes. The judge asked plaintiffs' lawyers if they wanted to be heard, and Amanda did. She went on for about ten minutes until the judge interrupted. "If you go on any more, you might convince me that I should grant the motion. But I'm not going let you do that. Motion's denied," he ruled. "Are there any more motions?"

There weren't, so he recessed until eight-thirty.

The trial resumed. "Ladies and gentlemen," the judge said. "The plaintiffs have now rested their case. We will now hear from the defendants. Please call your first witness."

Joan stood. "Your Honor, the first defense witness will be excerpts of the deposition of Susan Silver."

"Very well," Judge Lloyd said. "Please proceed."

"This deposition was taken in New York City earlier this year, in the offices of the law firm of Levinson & Wood, the attorneys for Empire Broadcasting Company," Joan explained. "Present were the court reporter, a video cameraman, and various lawyers. Ms. Johnson represented the plaintiffs. Ms. Cohen was there for the Lukarillas, and I was present for Mr. Lovejoy. Lou Miles represented Mr. Sumas. Also present representing Ms. Silver was a lawyer from Levinson & Wood, Mr. Ryan O'Donnell. Mary Jo, please start the video."

The video started with Joan's questions about Susan's background. Then it proceeded,

How did you get involved in the Lukarillas matter?

Back in early October, our president, Mike Ballard, called me up to his office. He told me EBC wanted me to lead an investigation into charges that three girls had been sexually assaulted at a Lukarillas retreat in the Oregon. He asked if I was available, and I said I was. That's all there was to it.

Tell me what you did in your investigation.

Ryan O'Donnell interrupted,

Counsel, that question calls for her to recite a litany of everything she did. Is that really what you want her to do?

Mr. O'Donnell, let's not be difficult. I'm not expecting her to give me a minute-by-minute recitation of her activities. I think she knows what I want. I want her to just give me a synopsis of what she did. She can supplement it later, if she needs to. I'm sure I'll have follow-up questions that will supplement as well. You understand that, don't you, Ms. Silver?

I think I do.

The video continued with a recitation of what she and Sanchez did when they went to Oregon in October.

Did you tell the plaintiffs that they should hire a lawyer?

Yes, I did.

Did you make a recommendation as to who they should hire?

I did not.

Prior to the filing of this lawsuit in December, did you have any conversations with the plaintiffs' lawyers, either Ms. Johnson or Mr. Bellows?

Yes, I did.

When was or were those conversations?

I'm not sure I should answer that question.

She then looked at Amanda and O'Donnell, and asked,

Aren't the conversations privileged?

Amanda answered,

You can tell her when they occurred, but do not disclose what the conversations were, what was said, and so forth. They are subject to lawyer-client privilege.

Susan Silver then responded,

About mid-October I called Amanda. Actually, she called me. I was out, and she left her number, so I returned the call. We talked at that time. I hired her and her firm to provide legal advice in Oregon concerning our continuing investigation into this matter.

You said she called you. Do you know why?

I suppose because I told the girls that, if they hired a lawyer, to have the lawyer call me. I was thinking of retaining a lawyer there, and I thought I might hire the same one.

Did you talk to the plaintiffs' lawyer at any other time?

I talked to Ms. Johnson on the telephone later in October. I was with Mr. O'Donnell. We talked to her together. Then I talked to her and Mr. O'Donnell just prior to this deposition.

Let's start with the first conversation in October, what was said?

Amanda interrupted,

I object to that and instruct her not to answer or to answer any questions about the substance of conversations between her and me and/or Mr. O'Donnell on the grounds of lawyer-client privilege.

Joan said,

I won't agree that the conversations are privileged. She says she hired you to assist in the investigation your network was making, but until I know what was said, I can't tell if the conversations related to that or to this lawsuit. Conversations about this lawsuit wouldn't be privileged. I want to talk to the judge about it.

Becky said,

I think we can get him. It's ten-thirty here. If he's in town, the judge is always in his office by seven west coast time. I have his number, so let's see if we can get him. Can I use this phone on the corner table as a speakerphone?

O'Donnell answered,

Yes, it is.

Joan said to Becky,

You call him. Then I'll present the problem, since they're my questions.

The jury heard Becky placing the call. A male voice answered,

Hello, Judge Lloyd speaking.

Hi, Judge. This is Becky Cohen. We're in New York taking the depositions in the Lane versus Lovejoy case. Amanda's made some objections to Joan Dixon's questions to one of the witnesses, and we think you can help us. Joan can explain.

Judge, this is Joan Dixon. Rather than making an argument, I'm going to ask Ruth Mason to read you a portion of the transcript where our problem arose, so you can see what the problem is, if that's all right?

Ruth Mason then read the portion of the transcript in which Susan said she recommended that the plaintiffs hire a lawyer up to the point they stopped to call the judge. After Ruth finished, the judge commented,

Well, I think I have the same problem Ms. Dixon has. How do I know whether what she would say is privileged or not?

Amanda argued,

Judge, you can't. That's always the problem when lawyer-client privilege is raised. The lawyer and the client make the decision whether what they say to one another should be revealed, and here we have decided that it should not be. That invokes the privilege.

Joan then suggested,

Judge, I have a practical suggestion. Why don't you interrogate the witness privately – in the presence of only Amanda and O'Donnell – the rest of us will step out of the room. Then you'll know what was said, it won't be revealed, and you can rule if it's subject to the privilege.

Amanda argued further,

I don't think he can do that. Once we claim the privilege, the matter cannot be gone into.

The judge said,

I don't agree with you, Amanda. I think Ms. Dixon has a novel, but appropriate suggestion. I say novel, because I've never done this before. But there is always a first time for a proper procedure. I'll accept her idea and interrogate the witness in private.

Joan then addressed the jury. "At this point the defense lawyers and the cameraman left the room, so you will not see what transpired on the video. However, the court reporter made a written transcript. We will read you that transcript. Judge, will you please read your portion, and I'll answer as Ms. Silver?" The judge started reading,

Ms. Silver, I want you to understand that I am going to ask you some questions about your conversations with Ms. Johnson. While your answers will be reported by Ms. Mason, they will not become public unless I decide that they do not fall within the lawyer-client privilege. If they are privileged, I will seal the record, and no one will have access to it. Ms. Mason is an officer of the court and may not reveal what was said if I seal the record. Do you understand that?

Yes, I do, Your Honor.

All right then, tell me the substance of all the conversations you had with Ms. Johnson, the first time you talked to her in October.

Joan then read what Susan said she and Amanda talked about. The judge then said,

Then, do I understand right, what you wanted was Ms. Johnson's cooperation to use the lawsuit for your own purposes. She would file on behalf of the plaintiffs and get you information to finish your investigation of the retreat and the Lukarillas?

That's right, Judge, I wanted her help.

And do I also understand correctly that the reasons that you hired Ms. Johnson were to keep the conversations confidential and to help finance the plaintiffs' lawsuits?

Well, I didn't say it just that way, but I suppose you're right.

All right, describe the substance of the second conversation later in October.

Joan then read what Susan, Amanda and O'Donnell had discussed in the conversation, wherein O'Donnell made suggestions of theories to be used in the lawsuit and agreed to draft a complaint and some initial discovery requests for Amanda. The judge then said,

Do you know if Mr. O'Donnell sent Amanda a draft of the complaint and drafts of the discovery requests?

I think he did, but I didn't see them. Mr. O'Donnell dealt directly with Ms. Johnson on that.

Well, let's get to the bottom of this. Amanda, did he send drafts like that to you, before you filed the complaint in this case?

Amanda, now taking her own part, read her answer,

Yes, sir, he did.

There's no way you can show those to me on the telephone, so I'll just ask you directly. Are the complaint on file in the court and the initial discovery requests substantially in the same form and content as the drafts sent to you by Mr. O'Donnell?

Yes, sir.

I see. It seems Ms. Dixon's novel suggestion has unearthed a clever scheme by Ms. Silver and her television network intended to keep their behind-the-scenes participation in this lawsuit a secret. I can see why EBC doesn't want the defendants to know how it's involved, but when it decided to surreptitiously use this lawsuit to promote its business interests, it took the chance that it might be exposed, as it's now going to be. These conversations are not privileged. This portion of the transcript will not be sealed, and Ms. Mason will read it to defense counsel when they return.

Joan told the jury, "The defense lawyers then returned to the room, and the judge explained his ruling to them. Ruth Mason read the transcript to them, just as we have done for you. We will now continue the video."

Ms. Silver, you are aware, are you not, that your employer, EBC, is involved in a libel lawsuit with the defendant, Alex Lovejoy?

Yes.

And that lawsuit arises out of an expose EBC did on Mr. Lovejoy and his employer, Silex Petroleum, where EBC accused them of sex discrimination, isn't that correct?

Yes, it is.

As a matter of fact, you were the one at EBC who did the investigation into Silex Petroleum and Mr. Lovejoy, isn't that correct?

Yes.

You were the one who is responsible for compiling the data that EBC used to make those charges, aren't you?

I guess you could say I was responsible. There were others involved in the investigation, but I was in charge.

Who were the others involved?

Well, principally, Julie Sanchez.

Is Julie Sanchez the same investigator EBC used in connection with the programs about the plaintiffs and the Lukarillas?

Yes.

Actually, weren't you the instigator at the network for the investigation into Silex and Mr. Lovejoy?

Yes.

Why did you want to investigate that firm and Mr. Lovejoy?

Angie Lawrence is a friend of mine. I knew how they passed her over for the job they gave Lovejoy. She also told me some things about Lovejoy and her that to me were sexual harassment on the job. Then he passed her over again. She wouldn't do anything about it, so I thought I'd take a look. The network said, 'Okay,' so I did.

And who is Angie Lawrence?

She was the top woman at the company, before Lovejoy was hired over her. I think her title was vice president, but she was the brains behind the president who retired. Lovejoy was brought in to take his place to the surprise of many.

You know, don't you, that your network made some complaints to the National Football League about defendant Abe Sumas, claiming he mistreated a female reporter of EBC's LA affiliate, KEBC?

Yes.

And you know that the female employee is Rachel Jacobs, who is the J in J & L Investment Company?

Yes.

And, your network also published an editorial by the president of EBC Sports, a guy named Grant Slade, blasting Sumas for removing that female reporter from his team's showers, isn't that correct?

I don't know about your term 'blasting' and the use of the term 'showers,' I think it was the locker room.

But what I said is basically true, isn't it?

Yes.

Has anything further occurred in that matter, is there a lawsuit there too?

There's no lawsuit, but Grant Slade told me that we lost our TV contract with the league after his television show, and he thinks Sumas was behind it.

Did he do anything about that?

He tried to get the Senate Antitrust Committee involved, but they turned him down.

Is that the U.S. Senate, and if so, who did he talk to?

Yes. I understand he talked to Senator Shepard, but he wouldn't help.

You mean Lionel Shepard, who is a defendant in this case?

Yes.

Now, from what you have just told the judge, you and your network are helping plaintiffs in this case with finances, investigation and lawyers, isn't that correct?

I'm not sure I agree with the way you said that. We have done what I told the judge.

And, according to what you told the judge, you plan to continue to use your resources to help the plaintiffs. You plan to investigate the members of the Lukarillas for them, and do other things you haven't thought of yet, isn't that correct?

We plan to do what I told the judge.

One other matter, I've had the reporter mark as Exhibit Nine, a videotape of the Dorothy Watters December sixth, 1991 television show. Your office supplied this to us. Can you identify the tape as an accurate presentation of that show?

Yes, it is.

The video presentation ended.

"We'll take our morning recess," the judge said. "Be back here and ready to go in twenty minutes."

When they got out in the hall, Barry asked Mary Jo, "How'd it go?"

"They were all listening. There's no question about that. Juror number three, Glen Overton, and the second alternate, Jack Smith, seemed particularly impressed. Both of them really liked it when the judge exposed what EBC was trying to do. In fact, Overton turned around to Smith and gave him the I thought so nod."

Chapter 40

Once everyone was seated, Joan announced, "Defendants call Alex Lovejoy, Your Honor." Joan leaned over to Lovejoy and spoke quietly. "Go to the witness stand. The clerk'll give you the oath. Then tell the jury your full name. And remember, watch me when I ask you questions, but look at the jury when you answer. You're telling them what happened. Good luck."

Looking at the jury, as instructed, he said, "My name is Alexander Shipman Lovejoy."

"Where do you live, Mr. Lovejoy?"

"We live just outside of Stamford, Connecticut, a little to the west."

"What is your occupation, and where do you work?"

"I am chairman of the board of directors and president of Silex Petroleum Company, and I work in New York City."

"Are you married?"

Lovejoy sat erect and looked directly at the jury as he answered. "Yes, I've been married to my wife, Bea, since 1956. We have two children, both girls, and they're married. We have three grandchildren."

"Tell us a little about your background."

"I was born in El Paso, Texas, in June 1934. I attended primary and secondary schools there. From high school I went to Texas A & M on an academic scholarship. I received a degree in petroleum engineering in 1956. A & M is also a military school for some students. I was one of them. I was commissioned in the US Army Engineers, as a second lieutenant, upon graduation. I got married and entered the service at that time. When I returned from the Army in 1958, I went to work for Texaco as a petroleum engineer. We were sent to Colombia, where I worked in the oil fields for five years. In 1963 I joined New Brunswick, as an operations manager. I remained with that company until April of 1988, when I joined Silex as the president and chief executive officer. I was president and chief operating officer of Brunswick when I made the change. I became chairman of the board of Silex last year."

"When you were president of Brunswick did you have an occasion to meet Max Pepper?"

"Yes, I did."

"Explain to us how that occurred and the circumstances involved."

Lovejoy then told the jury about the attempted takeover of New Brunswick by a Texas joint venture, which was represented by Pepper. He explained that it was an unfriendly takeover attempt and that it was bitterly contested in both the state and federal courts. He said that during the court cases Pepper aggressively deposed him and that he's disliked Pepper since then.

"Have you been a regular attender of the Lukarillas retreats?"

"Yes, over the years I don't think I've missed more than one or two."

"Tell the jury what goes on at those retreats."

He looked directly at the jury when he answered. "They are probably the most stimulating meetings that I've experienced. There's rarely an agenda. Everyone there has an outstanding background, so just talking with each other is uplifting. We share experiences, thoughts and ideas, and I know we all come away from each meeting enriched. I'm convinced that the meetings have enhanced my intellectual development and my performance as an executive of a public company. I'm sure most of the members feel this way. What we try to do is improve our individual abilities by sharing experiences and ideas. That's the way Hugh originally planned the group, and the success has been astounding. I wish there were some way to have similar meetings with leaders of foreign countries. The world would be a far better place if there were."

"When did you arrive at the camp for the retreat last year?" she asked.

"Late Friday afternoon. Hugh had vans for us at the

Portland airport. I rode up there with Shep, Steve Weinstein and Cece Upshaw. We all came in from the east."

"When did you first meet the plaintiffs?"

"Friday night, when we went to dinner," Lovejoy said.

"Did you have any connection with any of the plaintiffs or Marlene Smyth, other than when they served meals?"

"Well, I chatted with the plaintiffs during the meal service, but other than that, the answer's no, until Sunday night."

"Are you aware whether any of the other members had any other contacts?"

"Yes, I am."

"Tell us about that."

He turned and looked at the jurors. "Saturday afternoon I was fly-fishing with Steve. That's another great thing about the retreat, the trout fishing. They plant rainbows in the river every spring, and the Nehalem still has some natives, so by September there's a chance to catch a big one. Sometimes, that time of year, you may even hook a steelhead salmon.

"Steve told me that Ginny and Peg had dropped by their cabin the night before, actually, he said about midnight. He said that Max was in bed, and he and Park were playing cribbage. Ginny came to the door and asked him if they wanted any ice. He said he told her 'Sure,' and asked them in for a nightcap. After a couple of drinks, the girls, to use his words, 'got horny and wanted some action.' He and Ginny went into his room, had sex and played around until early in the morning. Again, to use his words, he said 'it was out of sight.' He thought Park and Peg had sex too. When he got up around six thirty, both girls were gone."

Joan rose and went to the large television set. "During your deposition, you told us that, except for Mr. Chalmers', all of the cabins were set up the same. You drew us a diagram of the interior, which is now Exhibit Two. Mary Jo has put that on the television set. Is that a correct diagram of the interiors of the cabins?"

"Yes it is."

Joan paused for a minute. "You've heard the testimony of the plaintiffs about what they claim happened Sunday night. Have they told the jury the truth?"

He turned, and this time as he stared at the jury he shook his head. "A little bit of what they said is true. But most of it is *NOT*!"

Joan remained silent for a moment to let his answer sink in. "Tell us what happened."

"We were in our cabin after dinner, that's Shep, Abe Sumas and me. Abe and I were playing gin." He picked up the pointer that was resting on the shelf in front of him, and leaning to the side toward the television he used it to point to the card table on Exhibit Two. "Shep was reading on the couch over there by the fireplace." Again he pointed. "At about nine, there was a knock on the door. Shep answered it, and all three girls were there. Ginny asked Shep if we wanted any ice, just like she did with Steve two nights before. I told Shep to ask them in for a drink. That's how they got into the cabin.

"We all had at least one and maybe two drinks. The girls kind of paired up with us. Tina sat on the couch next to Shep, and Ginny and Peg were kneeling on the floor over by Abe and me, talking to us and watching us play cards. Ginny was kneeling right beside my legs, and Peg was next to Abe. Ginny complained that the cards were boring. She wanted more action. I asked her what she meant, and, to quote her, she said, 'How's a little fucking sound.' Abe said something typical, like you're talking my language, sweetheart, and he turned to Peg and said, 'You game?' and she said, 'You bet.' He got up and escorted her into his room, which was the one in the middle," he said, pointing again at the exhibit on the television set. "Shep and Tina then went into his room, down at the end by the fireplace. Ginny and I had sex in my room. That's exactly what happened. The girls wanted sex, and so did we. I think they came looking for it, and we went along. No one forced anyone."

Joan went back to counsel's table and sat. "While you were there that weekend, did you tell anyone what had happened?" she asked.

This time he answered looking at her. "No. We talked the next morning and decided it was better to say nothing."

"What you've just told the jury is just what you told Ms. Johnson when she took your deposition last April, isn't it?"

"Yes, it is."

"Did you tell this to anyone else before the deposition?" she asked.

"I told you, when you called me the day after the EBC television program the first part of October."

"At the time I was representing you in your lawsuit against EBC, was I not?"

"Yes, you were."

"Did you talk to the district attorney?"

"Yes, he called me. I think it was Monday, the last day of September?"

"What did he say, and what did you say?"

"He told me what Ginny and the other girls reported to the police. I told him it wasn't true. I said I'd had sex with Ginny, but she asked for it, and I agreed."

"Since the retreat, and before preparing for this trial, did you ever talk to either Senator Shepard or Abe Sumas about what had happened that Sunday night?"

"No."

"Mr. Lovejoy, has this case had an effect on your marriage?"

"I object to that, your Honor," Amanda interjected. "What effect it has had on his marriage is totally irrelevant."

"Will you ladies please come forward to the side of my bench," Judge Lloyd ordered. "I want a word in private with you."

Joan, Amanda and the reporter came forward to the side of the bench away from the jury. The judge moved his chair to that side, leaned over and quietly asked Joan, "Why is this relevant?"

"Your Honor," she responded, "the response I expect will tend to establish his credibility. After all, this whole case is about who's telling the truth. So it's relevant."

"All right, with that assurance, I'll let him answer." The judge then addressed the courtroom. "The objection is overruled." He told Lovejoy to answer the question.

Barry knew that the jury wasn't aware that Lovejoy's wife was seated in the back of the courtroom, but they could see that he was visibly upset.

Lovejoy looked up at the ceiling and stared at it for a second or two. Then slowly he lowered his head and turned and made eye contact with the jurors. "Yes, it's affected us," he said softly. "When you tell your wife you've cheated on her, she's understandably upset. Bea was mad. She didn't see the television show." Looking back at Joan, he said, "Thank God you called me, so I could tell her the truth before she heard the lies on that EBC broadcast." Then he looked back to the jury. "She's still upset, and I don't blame her. But we've been married a long time. She's not only my wife, she's my best friend. I think she still feels the same about me. At least she's here and supporting me today, in spite of what I did." Near tears, he pointed to his wife in the rear of the courtroom. Each juror turned as he pointed.

"Mr. Lovejoy," Joan asked after a short pause, "did you see any of the newspaper stories or television programs about plaintiffs' claims?"

"I did not."

"You saw the video of Susan Silver's testimony. What is the lawsuit involving EBC and Silex Petroleum?"

"As you pointed out, Ms. Silver apparently got mad at me when I didn't make Angie Lawrence our chief operating officer, and she decided we were discriminating against women. She claims she made an investigation, and they put her on television, accusing us of sexual discrimination and harassment. I'm sorry, but I get emotional when I talk about it. It was a pack of lies. She talked to several disgruntled ex-employees who'd made complaints to the Department of Labor. EBC couldn't wait for the results of the department's investigation. They put the women on national television, claimed what they said was true, and blasted us as sexual discriminators. We sued them for libel. That's the lawsuit, it's still pending. And incidentally, since the lawsuit was filed, the Department of Labor has dismissed all of those complaints as being without merit, but they're still defending the lawsuit."

"I have nothing further, Your Honor."

Bellows began and ended with one question. "Mr. Lovejoy, you don't have any evidence yourself that Empire Broadcasting Company, EBC, had anything to do with the filing of this lawsuit, do you?"

"I don't have any evidence myself, but I've certainly heard that in this courtroom," Lovejoy answered.

"I'm sorry we ran over a little this morning, ladies and gentlemen," Judge Lloyd apologized to the jury. "We'll recess now and convene again at one forty-five. Be in your jury room at one-forty."

Monday afternoon, September 21

The judge entered and was seated. At his direction everyone else sat down.

Miles rose and addressed the court. "Defendants call Abe Sumas."

Sumas came forward, was given the oath, and took the witness stand, resting back in the chair as he had throughout the trial.

He looked directly at the jurors. "I'm Abraham Sumas."

"Where do you live, Mr. Sumas?"

"In LA."

"What do you do for a living?"

"I'm an owner and president of the LA Stars. I hope everybody knows the Stars play football in the NFL," he said with a broad smile.

"Tell us about your life."

"Okay. I guess I start with being born. That happened on a dairy farm in Wisconsin in 1930. That makes me sixty-two, doesn't it? As a youngster, I went to school in a little burg north of Appleton and west of Green Bay. Our high school was real small. We played in a six-man football league. I was the biggest guy, so I played center and linebacker. I loved hittin' and gettin hit. At least one college scout noticed, 'cause I got a scholarship to go to Wisconsin. I played linebacker three years for Wisconsin, and I made second string on somebody's All-American list the last two. I also got a degree.

"The Chicago Cardinals drafted me, but they had to wait out my military service, till the fifty-six season. I stayed outta most of the Korea thing playing sailor in the

NROTC, so after graduation I had to spend three years in the Marines. I played ten years with the Cardinals before I started coaching. In seventy-six the Stars made me head coach. I did that until eighty-three, when I took over as general manager. During my time with the Stars, I bought into the ownership. They made me president in eighty-six. That's what I am now."

"Are you married?"

"Not now," he replied. "But I've had three wives. I got five kids from my first wife, Edith. The kids are all grown, and actually, I've got seven grandkids too."

"How do you get along with your ex-wives?"

"You know, it's funny," he said. "Edith is probably still my best friend. We get along great. She just got tired of football, and I guess I can't blame her. I wasn't married to the other two very long, but we get along fine too."

"Now, Mr. Sumas," Miles began. "The jury has heard parts of the deposition you gave last April, where you were questioned about three separate incidents that occurred back in your playing days. You recall that?"

Looking somewhat embarrassed, Sumas answered, "Yeah."

"You made a point in the deposition that all of those charges were dropped, but let me ask you this, was there any substance to any of those charges?"

"I asked ya to ask me that," he said facing the jury, "'cause I didn't like the way it looked and sounded on the TV. I admit I was probably looking for sex with those gals, and I might of said something like they claimed. It sounds real bad in today's world. But back in the sixties things was different. We was all single and on the road a lot. Football was fun, but it was a tough game, and when we wasn't practicing or playing, most of us liked to play around. Like Mahoney said, I did my share in those days. There was lots of gals hanging around our locker rooms when we was on the road. Most of them wanted to get laid by a football player, and I gave them what they wanted. I admit I wanted it too. Some of 'em was looking for publicity, and unfortunately I made some offers to them that got me in trouble. Things like that still go on, but times have changed. People just don't look at things like that the same as they did back when I was playing."

He paused for a moment, looked up at the ceiling and then back at the jurors.

Barry had been watching the jurors. They were following Sumas closely.

"But I'll tell you one thing that no one can dispute. When I got married, that all stopped. Never once has anyone ever claimed I cheated on my wives. Even now, when I'm single, I don't go looking for stray women." Then he pointed at the plaintiffs. "What they told you are damn lies! They came looking for us!"

Before the judge or plaintiffs' lawyers could say anything, Miles cautioned him. "Mr. Sumas, calm down. I'll ask you in a minute to tell the jury what happened at the retreat. Just take it easy.

"Then what you're telling us is that you don't deny that back in your playing days you did make some advances to girls like Mr. Mahoney said and like the newspapers reported, is that correct?"

"That's right, *but I never forced a gal to suck my penis*," he asserted. "But I gotta admit that back then I'm sure I asked some to. I'm sure not proud of it, but, as a young ex-Marine, I was pretty crude with my sex life."

"All right, Mr. Sumas, now tell us what happened Sunday night at the Lukarillas' retreat last September."

"Actually, Alex has already told you," he said. "What he said is exactly what happened. I'd had a few drinks, and Peg was sidling up to me, down there on the floor leaning against my legs. When Ginny said she wanted to fuck, it seemed too good to pass up, so I asked Peg what she thought. And as Alex says, she says 'You bet.' We went into my room and had at it. There wasn't any penis sucking, just everyday screwing. And she wanted it. So did I!"

"Did Shep ask Tina to give him oral sex?"

"He did not! Nobody said that. It never came up. Ginny's statement got things started, and that's the truth, so help me God!"

"Mr. Sumas, tell the jury about EBC's television show?"

"Back in nineteen nighty, I was having a problem with one of our running backs. He was skipping practice and under-performing. The press was having a field day, because he'd been an all-star. Rachel Jacobs, who's a black female reporter for their LA affiliate, KEBC, came into our locker room after a game to interview him. We have to allow these gals in there now. I happened to be there. She found out the player was in the shower, so she just took off and started in there. She walked right by several naked players who were drying off. I ran up and grabbed her. I pulled her out of the shower and told her to get out. She cussed me, and I probably cussed back.

"The next day her station and the network complained about my company and me to the league. They called me a racial bigot, among other things. When the league heard my side of it, they just laughed. That pissed off EBC, and they put on a national show, calling the Stars and me racists. How the hell we can be racists when over two-thirds of our players and staff are black is beyond me, but that's what they said. If they'd done their homework, they'd have known that my second wife was black. She's still one of my biggest supporters, goes to most of the games at home.

"Sure, I bad-mouthed them with the league. I wasn't bashful about my thoughts when their TV contract came up for renewal, but I don't make those decisions, and I told the truth. If that got 'em axed, too bad. It's their own damn fault."

"That's all the questions I have," Miles said.

Amanda didn't wait for the judge's invitation. She was on her feet, and from behind the counsel's table, she pointed at Sumas. "So now you admit that you propositioned those girls to give you oral sex, is that right?"

"If you're talking about back in the sixties, what I admit is that I probably asked 'em for it. I frankly don't remember what was said. It's been a long time. But I don't want to mislead anybody. I probably asked for it, yes."

"And, as Mr. Mahoney told us," Amanda said, "you had your penis out of your pants, and you asked the girl to suck it, isn't that correct?"

"I don't remember, but I'm not going to deny it."

"I didn't think you would," Amanda said. "I have nothing further."

"It's a little early, but this is probably a good time to take our afternoon recess," the judge said. "Be back and ready to go in twenty minutes."

Chapter 41

"Call your next witness," the judge said, after returning to the bench.

Senator Shepard rose and walked up to the clerk. At sixty, he was bald on top and gray around the edges. Short and stocky, he resembled a wrestler. Nevertheless, his mien was senatorial. He wore a double-breasted navy pinstriped suit with a neatly folded white handkerchief peering out of his coat pocket. His stride was purposeful. He made up for his slight limp by a positive gait in his highly polished black wingtips. In response to the clerk's direction, he replied, "My name is Lionel Bruce Shepard."

Shumanski began his examination standing in front of the counsel table. He held a legal pad, and he glanced at it occasionally. "What is your occupation, sir? And where do you live?"

Like any politician, the senator loved to testify. He sat erect and turned his head toward the jury. "My residence is in Springfield, Illinois, but I live part of the year in Washington, DC. I am the junior United States senator from the state of Illinois."

"When were you first elected to the United States Senate?"

"In 1970."

"Senator, please tell the jury about your background, your schooling and professional life."

His voice was clear and his enunciation pure. "I grew up in Illinois. We lived in several towns. My dad worked for the post office and got transferred a few times, so I changed schools. I graduated from high school in East St.

Louis. Right after graduation, the Korean War broke out. I enlisted in the Marines and fought in that war. After being discharged in 1953, I used the GI Bill to attend Northwestern University. I picked that school because of its wrestling program. I did a lot of that in high school and in the service. Once I got there, I found I was actually more interested in academics than sports, and, to the surprise of many, I got a degree in political science with honors." He slipped the judge a sly smile.

"I was active in the Young Democrats at Northwestern. Through connections there, I got a job in Washington on the staff of a Democrat Senator from Michigan. While working there, I went to law school at Georgetown at night. I received a law degree, but I've never practiced law. I changed my residence back to East St. Louis, and in 1964 I ran for Congress. That was the year of the Johnson landslide, and I slid in with him. I was in the House of Representatives until elected to the Senate in 1970, and I've been there ever since."

"Are you the member of any Senate committees?" Shumanski asked.

"I'm chairman of the Judiciary Committee," he replied, "and also of its Antitrust Subcommittee."

"Did you receive any decorations while you were in the military service?"

"Yes," he replied. "I received the Silver Star and the Purple Heart."

"The Silver Star is awarded for bravery in action, isn't it?

"Yes."

"And why did you get the Purple Heart?"

"I was wounded in the back and leg by shrapnel from a mortar shell. I still have a little limp."

"Do you have a family?"

"Yes," he replied. "My wife's name is Mildred, but everyone calls her Millie. We've been married for forty-one years. We have three adult children, two boys and a girl, and four grandchildren."

Shumanski returned to his chair and sat. He paused for a moment sifting through the papers before him. He broke the silence and spoke softly. "Senator, you heard Sheila Workman and Judy Filcher testify here last week. They made some very troubling statements about you, which I think we all want you to address. First, did you ever have any kind of a relationship with Ms. Workman?"

The senator turned his head toward the jury. His expression was sincere. "Yes, she was a member of my staff, and I did take her out several times."

"Was there a sexual relationship involved?"

This time the senator looked straight ahead. "Yes. But not the way she told you. We never had oral sex, and I never asked for it." Then he turned to the jury. "We did, however, have a sexual relationship, and I have no idea why she denied it. I've had to make peace with my wife about it."

"What about what Ms. Filcher said?"

"That's a lie," he said. "I've heard about her before. Years ago one of my Republican opponents tried to insinuate what she said, but the whole thing died quickly when Ms. Filcher denied it. I don't know why she now says what she did. It's just not true. As a matter of fact, to my knowledge, the first time I ever saw Ms. Filcher was when she was here last week."

"Have you had sexual relations with other female members of your staff?"

He bowed his head. "Yes, I'm embarrassed to say, I have, but not like Sheila claimed."

Shumanski paused to let the answer set in. "Senator, tell us in your words what happened last September on Sunday night at the Lukarillas' retreat."

"I'm certainly not proud to report what I did that night," the senator said, addressing the jurors. "But I did not do what they said! I did not assault anyone! I did not ask for oral sex! I went to bed with the girl named Tina, and I did have sex with her, but she wanted it. Unfortunately, we both wanted it. I can't blame it on booze, even though I had too much that night."

"Senator, did you tell that to the district attorney?"

"No, he didn't ask for details. I just told him that what she said wasn't true. I told him we had sex, and that it was mutual."

"I have nothing further," Shumanski said.

Bellows came on strong. "You admit having sex with your female staffers, and you admit having sex with Tina, but that's all you'll admit, is that what you're telling us?"

Senator Shepard's demeanor remained calm. "Mr. Bellows, those are your words. I admit just what I have told the jury. And, as I said, I'm not proud of it."

"Why didn't you tell us during your deposition that you'd had sex with Ms. Workman and the others?"

"Because I don't believe you asked me about that," the senator replied. "You wanted to know if I'd asked Ms. Workman and Ms. Filcher to give me oral sex. I said that I did not."

"So you're telling this jury that Ms. Filcher and Ms. Workman lied, aren't you."

"I believe I just said I think Ms. Filcher lied. I didn't say that about Ms. Workman, but what she said about me asking for oral sex is not true."

"So you're calling her a liar too, aren't you?"

"I'm not calling her anything," he said.

"I'm not going to argue with you, Senator. I have nothing further, Your Honor," Bellows said to the judge.

"Then that's enough for today. Be back, ladies and gentlemen, in your jury room at eight-twenty tomorrow morning." He gave them the cautionary instructions and ended the proceedings "We're in recess until eight-thirty tomorrow morning."

Becky, Mary Jo and Chalmers joined Barry in his office. "Becky, what do you think about putting Hugh on?" Barry asked.

"We definitely should," Becky replied. "He makes a great witness and would be a strong person to end with."

"Do you feel comfortable with that, Hugh?" Barry asked.

"Sure," he answered. "But with no disrespect to Becky, I think you should ask the questions. My observation during the trial is that the jury trusts you, and what I say will have a bigger impact if you're doing the asking."

"I'd planned to," Barry replied, "and I think I know just what we'll cover."

Amanda called O'Donnell. "They're going to show parts of the Pepper, Price and Weinstein depositions tomorrow morning. I'm faxing you the copies of the pages from the transcripts that they're going to use. The Larsons and Lorenzo will follow. O'Shea was coy about maybe calling another witness who he didn't identify. All he'd say was she's on the witness list. Maybe it's Susan, she's still under subpoena. I'll work with her in case. The final witness will be Chalmers. It looks like they'll finish tomorrow. I'll call after court and let you know."

Tuesday, September 22

Now the trial was reported in the back of the main section. A headline read SENATOR AND FOOTBALL TEAM OWNER ADMIT SEX AFFAIRS. The article was a fairly accurate summary of Senator Shepard's and Abe Sumas' admissions during their testimony on Monday. The slant was toward Sumas' oral sex proclivities and Senator Shepard's extramarital affair with Sheila Workman.

The morning session went as Amanda had reported to O'Donnell with the video depositions and the Larsons.

Before the court recessed for lunch, the judge asked, "How much more do you have?"

"One or two brief witnesses, then Hugh Chalmers," Barry answered. "He'll be our last witness. We should be done by mid-afternoon. Mr. Chalmers shouldn't take more than an hour," he added, looking over at Amanda and Bellows for guidance.

"We don't have much more to ask him, and we won't have any rebuttal evidence," Bellows said.

"Okay," the judge said. "We'll get this case to the jury tomorrow. I'll hear your motions, after Mr. Chalmers. Then we'll send the jury home, and we'll work in my chambers on my instructions. I'll have them typed out by then. You can look them over." Then with a smile he added, "I don't want any arguments, but if you see any obvious errors, let me know and we'll fix them.

"Be ready to start your arguments in the morning. I'm not going to limit your time, but I've got some suggestions," he said with another of those smiles. He looked at Amanda and Bellows. "You shouldn't go more than an hour and a half total, opening and rebuttal. That gives these four defense lawyers another hour and a half, which they'd be crazy to use, but they can, if they want to take the chance."

Ginny, Peg and Tina met Weasel and Leo Santini for lunch in the bar of a restaurant a couple of blocks from the courthouse.

"How'd it go this morning?" Santini asked.

"Bo-o-oring," Peg answered. "They played a bunch of tapes of Max, Park and that Weinstein guy, but I don't know what they think they proved. Max was asleep when they claim Ginny and I went to their cabin. Oh, he said he heard us in the other room, but Amanda got to him, and he admitted he wasn't that sure. Good old Park said he never saw us. Weinstein tried to get the jury to believe he fucked Ginny, but after Amanda tarred him with the mob, who'd believe him?"

"Yeah," Ginny said, "and then they brought on the goody-two-shoes Larsons with their spying from the stables and condom stories. That Judy Larson wouldn't know a condom from a balloon. And Thor. After Amanda finished with him the jury musta thought he was hallucinating from the fumes of the horseshit he'd been shoveling. No one's going to believe he saw what he said from where he was."

Chapter 42

Tuesday afternoon

"Defendants call Ginny Lane," Shumanski said.

Ginny took the stand, and the judge reminded her, "Remember you're under oath."

"I know that," she replied curtly.

"Ms. Lane, you were in the courtroom when your boss Marlene Smyth testified," Shumanski said, "and you heard her say that Grant Slade of EBC called her. It was after you had gone to work for her and before the Lukarillas' retreat. He wanted your telephone number so a guy he was sending out to Portland could talk to you. You heard all of that, didn't you?"

She didn't respond. She was looking at Shumanski, but she didn't speak, like fear and anticipation had put her in a trance.

"Ms. Lane, did you hear me?" Shumanski asked.

Whether he startled her, or whether the spell had broken, she snapped to. "Yeah, I heard you, and I heard Marlene say that."

"What did that man want?"

"He never showed up," she replied.

"Come now, Ms. Lane," Shumanski said, "we all heard Ms. Smyth say that you told her the man came out and talked to you and that he offered you a job. That's what she said, and that's correct isn't it?"

"No, it's not correct! I just told you he didn't talk to us. I don't know what this Slade guy wanted, but he and his buddy didn't talk to us. Ya got that!"

"Yes, Ms. Lane, I got that. I guess you're telling us Ms. Smyth didn't tell us the truth, is that right?"

"I didn't say that! I don't know what Marlene heard or didn't hear."

"Nothing further, Your Honor," Shumanski concluded.

"No questions," Amanda added.

Shumanski didn't wait for the judge. "Defendants call Ben Lorenzo."

Lorenzo approached Judy Williams, raised his right hand, took the oath, and then said, "My name is Ben Lorenzo."

"Where do you live, and what's your occupation?"

"I live here in Portland, and I work for Swift, Wyman & Wiggens as an investigator."

"Were you asked by Mr. O'Shea to find a man named Grant Slade and interview him?" Shumanski asked.

"Yes, I was."

"Tell us what you did."

"I found him in Houston, Texas early last June. He's now head of Sports Cable Network down there. I talked to him about the Lukarillas and found out he hates Sumas' guts. He told me about his investment in a catering service in Oregon."

"Did you talk to him about the EBC show that reported an alleged assault by Sumas on an employee of a catering service?"

"Yeah, I did."

"What did he tell you about that?"

Bellows was on his feet immediately. "Objection, your Honor. That calls for hearsay."

"Sustained," the judge ruled.

"All right, Your Honor," Shumanski said. "Mr. Lorenzo, did you attempt to subpoena Mr. Slade for this trial?"

"Yes, I did."

"Tell us about that."

"The end of August, Mr. O'Shea told me to subpoena Slade for this trial. I went to Houston and tried to serve it, but I couldn't find him. I knew where he worked, where he lived, and where he hung out. I learned all that when I talked to him in June. I tried all those places. His office wouldn't tell me where he was and all of his acquaintances have clammed up. I know how to find people, even when they're trying to avoid me. I looked high and low. I just couldn't find him. I left the subpoena with a process server, but we've never been able to find him to serve it."

"Thank you, Mr. Lorenzo, no further questions."

"Any cross-examination, Mr. Bellows?" the judge asked.

"Yes, Your Honor, a few questions. Mr. Lorenzo, you said Mr. Slade hates Abe Sumas' guts. Now that's something Mr. O'Shea told you, isn't it?" Bellows asked.

"No he didn't, Mr. Bellows," Lorenzo replied. "Slade told me that, and when I was asking him about the EBC show, he said 'he'd fixed Sumas' clock.' He started to tell me how. Then he clammed up like he'd said too much already."

Bellows quit after that.

Barry watched the jurors and saw that each of them followed Lorenzo as he left the witness stand and walked back through the spectator section and out the courtroom's double doors. He purposely didn't interrupt the silent scene.

Finally, after the doors closed, the judge broke the spell. "Call your next witness."

Barry turned and looked to the back of the courtroom. She was there. "Defendants call Susan Silver," he said.

Murmurs of surprise came from the direction of the plaintiffs' table, as Amanda, Oscar and all three plaintiffs turned and watched Susan Silver come forward to take the oath. She was dressed conservatively, but that didn't detract from the attention this attractive woman received as she advanced toward Judy Williams. She was sworn and took the witness stand.

"Ms. Silver, you are acquainted with Grant Slade, aren't you?" Barry asked.

"Yes."

"He was president of EBC Sports, was he not?"

"Yes."

"And he was part owner of West Portland Catering, was he not?"

"That's my understanding," she replied.

"You were aware, were you not, that we tried to take his deposition in this case last summer?" Barry asked.

"I understood that the deposition was scheduled."

"After you learned that we wanted to depose him, did you talk to him about it and warn him that he might be subpoenaed?"

She paused for a moment and looked at Amanda. Then she responded. "I did call him and tell him that he was going to be subpoenaed."

"And you know that the deposition was not taken because we could not find Slade to subpoena him, isn't that true?"

"I knew the deposition was not taken," she answered.

"Did he tell you that he would avoid the subpoena server?"

"Not exactly."

"All right, then what did he tell you?"

"He told me he was going out of town, and they wouldn't find him."

"Nothing further, Your Honor," Barry said.

Amanda had no questions.

"Call your next witness," the judge said.

"Defendants call Hugh Chalmers, Your Honor." As he said that, Barry knew Chalmers was key to a verdict in favor of the Lukarillas.

Chalmers was ready. He came forward with confidence. "I do," he replied, after being sworn to tell the truth and the whole truth by the clerk.

"State your full name for the jury," Judy Williams said.

"Hugh Winston Chalmers."

Barry picked up his legal pad and walked over behind plaintiffs' table and stood next to the jury box. "Mr. Chalmers," he said, "the jury has already heard from you as a plaintiffs' witness. The jury needs to know a little more about you and the Lukarillas. Please bear with me while I ask some more questions to do that. There may be a little repetition. I'll try to avoid that as much as possible. First of all, tell the jury about yourself."

Chalmers faced the jury. "I'm seventy-two. I'm married. My wife's name is Lucy. We've raised two boys. They're married, on their own and have given us four grandchildren. I grew up here in Oregon, in McMinnville. That's where I went to school.

"My dad started out as a logger in the twenties. He didn't have much money, but he figured out a way to buy timber, even during the Depression. I never quite understood how he did it, but by the time the war came along, he had founded Chalmers Lumber Company and was operating several lumber mills. The company flourished during the war. I worked for him during the summers.

"I went to Oregon State, it was called Oregon State College then, and graduated in 1941 with a degree in forestry. It looked like war was coming, and I wasn't really ready to settle down anyway, so I enlisted in the Navy. They put me in officer candidate school and made me an ensign. I served on a bunch of ships in the South Pacific until I got discharged in 1945. I was a full lieutenant by then. When I came out of the service, I married Lucy and went back to work for my dad. His company was Chalmers Forest Products then, and it still is. A year later I found myself in charge when Dad was killed in a mill accident. I've been in charge ever since."

"Did you see any action in the South Pacific?" Barry asked.

"Lots of it. We were involved in a number of battles and several invasions, the Solomons, the Philippines, Iwo Jima and Okinawa."

"How and why did you start the Lukarillas?"

"It wasn't the Lukarillas at the start," he replied. "The name got attached sometime in the sixties by Virg Conner. You heard about him on the television. He was a real showman and couldn't see us without a classy name. He saw the sign the state had up for the little village to our north, and he just named us after it. But that's not what you asked me. I'm sorry, don't let me wander like that, it's a sign of old age."

From where Barry stood he could watch the jury and not be obvious. They were following Chalmers intently.

"Back in the late forties, I was heading a major lumber company, one that I just fell into. I don't mean I didn't think I was running it all right, but I didn't build it. I wanted to start something on my own. I guess it was sort of a conceit. I also wanted contact with influential men who were shaping the country. I thought I could grow and learn from them. I was grumbling to myself about this when the idea of a meeting with men like this at a retreat at our camp on the Nehalem came to me. Frankly, I never thought I'd pull it off.

"Then one day when I was in LA meeting with our antitrust lawyer, Sam Levine, I mentioned the idea to him over lunch. He liked it and suggested I talk to Frank Boone about it. Frank was my dad's accountant and was one of the founders of the accounting firm Benjamin & Boone. When I was in New York on business later that year I also discussed it with Ed Thomas. He'd recently been elected to Congress from Vermont. We served together in the Navy. Both Boone and Thomas liked the idea, so with their help and that of Sam Levine, we came up with a list of businessmen and a few politicians as potential members. Each of us then wrote personal letters to the ones we knew, explaining the plan.

"I guess I was pleasantly surprised when we got positive responses from twelve. It was those twelve, along with Frank, Sam, Ed Thomas, and me, that attended our first retreat in 1948. The members' names weren't as impressive as they are today, but it was a good start. Since that time the membership had grown in stature and in number to twenty, but that's always been the limit.

"I know there's been some remarks made here about us all being men, but that's the way groups like this worked back then. The men had theirs and the women had theirs. That's changing nowadays. Some men's clubs now include women, but here in Portland, The Town Club still only takes women."

"Has the group held a retreat every year since 1948?"

"Yes, we have, and we've never had fewer than fourteen present," he said.

"How have you supported the retreat over the years, by that I mean what help did you use?"

"I've always had Sven and his family, and we've used outside catering for meals."

"Did that outside catering always involve female waitresses?"

"At first it didn't. I used the University Club in Portland for about ten years. They had the greatest Filipino waiters, and they'd send us one of their cooks. It got to be too much for them. Our retreats competed with football season, which was a big item for the club. We used to have major college games in Multnomah Stadium. After that I started using outside catering companies, and for the most part the waitresses were always women."

Barry saw that his tactic was working. Chalmers was looking both at the jurors and him as he answered. "Over what period of time was that?"

"I'd say for over thirty years."

"And during all those years were the retreats run just like in 1991, four cabins of men and one of women?"

"Yes, they were," he said. "The cabin next to the mess hall was always saved for the women. When the cook was a man, he stayed at my house."

"Over that period of time, Mr. Chalmers, was there ever any trouble between the women and the members? Did any of the men make unwanted approaches to the women? Did any of the men ever get out of line with the women?"

"Absolutely not! There's always been a lot of back and forth banter around the tables during meals, but the members never socialized with the women. It just didn't happen. We weren't there for that. It never dawned on me that it would happen."

"Was there ever any sexual interaction between the men and women? Did any of the men ever have sex with any of the women?"

"The answer's the same. That just didn't happen."

"Thank you, Mr. Chalmers, you may examine," Barry said to Bellows and Amanda as he was returning to his chair.

"Mr. Chalmers, you said 'It never dawned on me that it would happen.' You don't really mean that, do you?" Bellows asked.

"It's never happened," Chalmers replied.

"Well, that's just not true, Mr. Chalmers," Bellows said. "We know it happened just last year, at least four of your members have admitted during this trial that they had sex with plaintiffs at your retreat last year. And there's testimony that another one did too. That's five out of fourteen, more than one third of your members in attendance. I suppose you'll say you didn't know that before our client brought this lawsuit, is that right?"

"You're right. I didn't."

"And I suppose you say that you didn't know that at least two of those five have a history of extramarital sexual encounters with young women? I'm talking about defendants Sumas and Shepard. They've admitted that here in court. Is that what you'd say?"

Barry could tell Chalmers knew Bellows was hurting him, but he had to answer. "I didn't know what I've heard here in court, no."

"Certainly a man of your stature would have discouraged such conduct had you known about it, isn't that true?"

He answered carefully. "I would have discouraged it, yes."

"But you didn't, did you?"

Chalmers stiffened. "No, I didn't! How could I discourage something I didn't know would happen?"

"I'm not trying to make you mad, Mr. Chalmers," Bellows said. "I'm just trying to find out what you would have done, if you had known. You told us earlier that the Lukarillas wanted men with outstanding personal traits and habits. I take it that's still your testimony, isn't it?"

"Yes."

"And if you had people like that, obviously you wouldn't have to worry about them taking advantage of female employees, would you?"

He tried to soften his answer by qualifying. "I wasn't thinking of that when I answered earlier. But when you put it like that, the answer is no."

"Thank you, Mr. Chalmers, I have no further questions," Bellows said.

"Any further questions, Mr. O'Shea?" the judge asked.

There was nothing further Barry could ask without compounding what Bellows had accomplished. "No, Your Honor, the defendants rest."

"Very well," the judge said. "Ladies and gentlemen, that concludes the evidence in this case, but before you can begin deliberations, you will hear the arguments of the lawyers for each party and my instructions on the law that you will apply in this case. The arguments will begin tomorrow morning. They will be followed directly by my instructions. Then the case will be submitted to you. You are dismissed for tonight. Be back in your jury room by eight-twenty tomorrow morning, as we want to start promptly at eight-thirty. It is of the utmost importance that you continue to follow my instructions not to discuss this case with anyone, including amongst yourselves. You must hear the closing argument and my instructions before having any such discussions. Have a good night. We'll see you in the morning. Counsel, please remain after the jury has left the courtroom."

After the jury departed, the judge said, "I'm denying all motions to dismiss, except I am dismissing the civil rights claim and the claim for punitive damages against the Lukarillas. Judy Williams will give you each a copy of the instructions and the verdict form I will give the jury. I will allow the two alternate jurors to deliberate. You'll have eight jurors to convince.

"Have a good night's rest, and I'll see you all, bright and cheery tomorrow morning. Please keep me awake, but not with improper arguments or flimsy objections." The judge chuckled, clearly enjoying his own humor. But it wasn't only humor. It was another of his clever judicial suggestions to keep the arguments brief and to the point.

That night on the EBC *Evening Report* Dorothy Watters reported from Portland. The camera panned on the Broadway entrance to the courthouse and on Watters and EBS's jury consultant, standing just outside the door.

"The defendants ended with Hugh Chalmers, the Lukarillas' founder," Watters said. "He did well until Oscar Bellows faced him again with his failure to discover the past sex lives of Senator Shepard and Abe Sumas. We've had our consultant following the jury's reactions. What's your feeling?"

The consultant spoke into her mike forcefully. "It's been an attentive jury. They still glance favorably at the plaintiffs' table. I'd have to say, plaintiffs came through the defendants' case in good shape."

Chapter 43

The front page of Wednesday *Oregonian* read JURY TO GET LUKARILLAS CASE TODAY.

As the defense group headed down Broadway, the press was waiting, but Amanda and Bellows got there first, so they fielded the questions.

"We feel great," Bellows said. "Get inside. Amanda's about to tell you why."

The back of the courtroom was nearly full. Even without Bellows' invitation, the press had the first row filled.

The judge entered and the last day of trial began. "Ladies and gentleman, you've heard all of the evidence, and now the lawyers will address you with their closing arguments. Some think this is the most interesting part of a trial. It probably is, but I must remind you that what the lawyers say is not evidence. That is not to say that what they say is not important. It is important. It is their duty to address you and tell you what they believe the evidence shows and how it fits into their clients' case. Pay close attention to what they say, and then when you leave the courtroom to deliberate take their remarks and analyze them with the evidence, as you heard it and understand it.

"Ms. Johnson, you may begin."

The lectern had been put back in front of the jury. Amanda went forward and placed her notes on its shelf.

"May it please the court, counsel, and ladies and gentlemen of the jury.

"Tuesday, a week ago, I told you this case is about a secret society that meets this time each year in our Coast Range Mountains. I also told you that this case involves three shameful sexual assaults on our clients and attempts to hide and suppress them by this society and a local district attorney. I told you we would prove this with the evidence, and we've done just that!"

She then proceeded to outline the evidence plaintiffs had presented, somewhat chronologically in the order of the presentation. She used selected portions of the videos of the Chalmers' deposition, the Dorothy Watters Show and Owen Persell's testimony. She had Exhibits one and two blown up on boards, which she displayed on easels.

"There are really only three issues that you need to decide in this case."

Herb Goodwin placed an easel in front of the jury, and Amanda wrote with a black grease pencil,

> **One, did defendants sexually assault the plaintiffs?**
> **Two, is the secret society, the Lukarillas, liable for the sexual assaults?**
> **Three, how much should you award as damages?**

"The primary issue is whether there were sexual assaults, so let me address that first. On this issue there's only one question to answer. Who do you believe? Do you believe that Sumas and Shepard tried to force plaintiffs into giving them oral sex? Do you believe that all three defendants coerced plaintiffs by intimidation into having intercourse with them? If you do, then you'll find these defendants committed sexual assaults.

"How do you make that choice? You've probably heard that in a criminal case, the state has to prove its case beyond a reasonable doubt. This is a civil case, and that degree of proof is not required. After we're done with these lawyers' arguments, the judge will tell you what the law says you are to use in a civil case. He'll tell you how to evaluate the evidence you've heard, and he'll tell you that the plaintiffs, our clients, have the burden to prove that they were sexually assaulted by a preponderance of the evidence. A preponderance of the evidence means by the *greater weight of the evidence.* You take the evidence offered and you weigh it, like on the scales of justice that we're all familiar with.

"We do not have to convince you beyond a reasonable doubt. All we need to show you is that the evidence that plaintiffs were sexually assaulted weighs greater than defendants' denials, that the scales tip in plaintiffs' favor, no matter how slightly. Deciding whether plaintiffs were sexually assaulted is just that simple.

"When you review the evidence, it's even simpler. All three plaintiffs positively say they were assaulted. The defendants say they didn't do it. If that's all we had, and if you had no evidence from which to evaluate the credibility of the people making these claims and denials, you'd have to say, 'I guess the scales are evenly balanced. They don't lean in favor of plaintiffs, so they can't win.' But we presented much more than that. We produced two women, Sheila Workman and Judy Filcher, who have nothing to gain by lying. They didn't want to be here or to testify, but they told you what Senator Shepard did to them, and it was basically the same thing. We brought you Jerry Mahoney, who told you about Abe Sumas' pattern to do this same thing. We showed you that what plaintiffs told you is exactly what they've consistently said over and over again since the assaults. The scales clearly tipped, and not just slightly.

"Ask yourselves, what evidence do defendants offer to tip the scales back? The answer is none. Their whole case revolves around two kinds of evidence, neither of which is on point. First, they try to prove that the television network, EBC, has something to do with my clients' case. Does that have anything to do with whether plaintiffs were sexually assaulted? Of course not. Suppose you find EBC is up to its neck in this case. How does that prove that defendants didn't do just what plaintiffs say they did? It doesn't. That evidence is totally irrelevant to whether plaintiffs were sexually assaulted by defendants.

"Next, defendants claim that two of the plaintiffs had sex with two other Lukarillas two nights earlier. Our clients deny that, but assume it's true. How does that prove that three other Lukarillas did not sexually assault them on a different night? It doesn't. This evidence is also totally irrelevant to whether defendants sexually assaulted plaintiffs. You can line up all of defendants' witnesses, except the defendants themselves, and they fit into one or the other of these irrelevant areas. There were nine of these, Susan Silver, Ginny Lane, Ben Lorenzo, Max Pepper, Parker Price, Stephen Weinstein, Sven Larson, Thor Larson and Judy Larson. The first three were used solely to involve EBC. With the last six they attempted to prove Ginny and Peg had sex with Price and Weinstein. None of these witnesses deal with the key issue; did Lovejoy, Sumas and Shepard sexually assault plaintiffs? They did not tip the scales back, and plaintiffs have met their burden to prove that they were sexually assaulted.

"Actually the defendants' denials don't weigh enough to keep the scales even. The defendants have very talented lawyers, and Lovejoy, Sumas and the senator did just what talented lawyers teach. Admit they've been bad, but not bad enough. They admit they had sex with plaintiffs, but claim it was consensual. They grab onto a story told by their fellow Lukarilla to convince you that plaintiffs show up regularly in the middle of the night with ice to get laid. But even the Lukarillas aren't together on that, because Parker Price wouldn't back up that so-called pattern. And did you notice that the senator did the same thing after he heard Sheila Workman and Judy Filcher? Even though he denied any relationships with them on depositions, now in court it's, 'Well, I had sex, but it was consensual. I never asked for oral sex.' See the pattern. How does that weigh? Not very heavily, I suggest. If you look at the evidence the way the judge will instruct you, it'll be obvious that the plaintiffs were sexually assaulted.

"The next issue you have to deal with is the liability of the Lukarillas. The judge will tell you that in order to find the Lukarillas liable, you first have to find that it failed to discover that some of its members had the propensity to commit sexual assaults on women. Second, you have to find that the Lukarillas failed to ensure that these members would not assault plaintiffs when it placed them among its members in an isolated camp. Again, plaintiffs have the burden to prove this by a greater weight of the evidence. What is the evidence on this point? Again it's not complicated, and this time it's uncontradicted."

She then discussed the evidence they'd presented against the Lukarillas. She reviewed the testimony that Oscar Bellows had drawn out of Hugh Chalmers to show Chalmers' failure to discover the propensities of Sumas, the senator, and several other Lukarillas. She compared that to the simple investigation of Julie Sanchez.

"The defense the Lukarillas offer is that it has held these retreats for over forty years and, to Mr. Chalmers' knowledge, nothing like this had happened before. So how does that balance? You weight the fact that Mr. Chalmers could have found out about his colleagues' propensities and didn't, and the fact that the Lukarillas did nothing to warn plaintiffs or otherwise protect against the fact that sexual assaults against women never happened before.

"Pretty simple isn't it? And the answer is obvious. Instead of protecting the plaintiffs the Lukarillas put defendants Sumas and Shepard in the same cabin, which increased the odds of a problem. There can be no question where the evidence weighs on this issue. The Lukarillas are also liable for the sexual assaults of the other defendants.

"The last issue is whether plaintiffs were injured and, if so, what should you award them as damages. There is no dispute that they have been injured. The plaintiffs have so testified, and two doctors, eminently qualified in the area of traumatic emotional injuries, have confirmed that they have sustained serious and permanent injuries as a result of the sexual assaults upon them. Defendants did not contest this evidence, except to argue on cross-examination that, if plaintiffs were not sexually assaulted, then they weren't injured. Well, we know from the evidence that they were sexually assaulted, so even defendants in effect admit that the plaintiffs were injured.

"I can't tell you how much to award plaintiffs, but it should be substantial. Their injuries are serious and permanent. The problems defendants caused them will be with them for an indefinite time in the future. I won't go over all of those injuries. You heard the doctors. You know what the injuries are.

"Ask yourselves what it would take to compensate you, if you were emotionally damaged as these plaintiffs have been." Amanda went to the easel. "Is one hundred thousand dollars for each enough? Probably not. What about two hundred fifty thousand or five hundred thousand or a million?" She wrote in bold **$100,000,** struck it out and then substituted **$250,000, $500,000 or $1,000,000?** "I don't know, maybe it should be more than that. It's your decision. But please remember, when you make that decision, this case, in this courtroom, is the only chance each of these plaintiffs has to recover for what these defendants did to her. Make sure you give each of them all that she is entitled to," she said pointing back to the large numbers on the easel's pad.

"I was mistaken, there is one more issue that you can consider, if you feel you should, but you don't have to. In cases like this, where there has been an intentional infliction of damage – that's what an assault is - you are entitled to award what is called punitive damages. In this case the judge will tell you that you may award punitive damages against defendants Lovejoy, Sumas and Shepard, but not against the Lukarillas.

"Puntive damages are damages that are designed to punish the persons who committed the assaults, to send them a message not to do this again. Normally, we leave that to our criminal laws, but this case is unique, because the criminal laws didn't deal with Lovejoy, Sumas and the senator as they should have. Plaintiffs performed their duties as citizens. They reported the crimes to the police. But our justice system stopped there. Why? Because the district attorney wouldn't investigate the matter, like we did or like EBC did. Incidentally, that's why EBC is involved in this matter. Its employees couldn't believe it when the district attorney dismissed these complaints so fast and with literally no investigation.

"We really don't know why the district attorney didn't prosecute. He certainly didn't give a very cogent explanation when you heard his testimony. It might have been because of the visit he had from those men from San Francisco sent by Mr. Santana, the same Mr. Santana to whom the district attorney owed his job. Mr. Santana may have been carrying out a favor for a man with Mafia connections in Miami, who was an investor with Stephen Weinstein. Whatever the reason, it is clear that these defendants were never held accountable by the criminal laws. So you have the right to do that here.

"In awarding punitive damages, you should take into consideration the individual defendants' net worth – the judge will tell you what that is – and award a sum that is large enough to make sure these defendants don't commit any further sexual assaults. It's your decision, but if you decide to award punitive damages, don't make it a slap on the wrist. Defendants Lovejoy, Sumas and Shepard are worth a lot. So it'll take a lot to get their attention. Make your award one that these defendants will hear loud and clear.

"Ladies and gentlemen," Amanda said slowly glancing across the jury box and affixing her eyes on each of the eight jurors, "thank you for your patience and the close attention you've given to this case. The service you're giving to this community by participating in our judicial system as jurors is highly commendable. Mr. Bellows and I are confident that you will take this case seriously and see that justice is done, and we genuinely believe that justice requires a substantial verdict for the each of the plaintiffs."

"We'll take a fifteen-minute recess. Be back in your seats in fifteen minutes," Judge Lloyd said.

Chapter 44

After everyone was seated, Judge Lloyd invited Joan to proceed with the defendants' argument.

Joan was conscious of her large New York firm connection, so she left the dark suits that she'd worn most of the trial in the hotel. She felt a more casual look would help get the jury's attention. She wore a lime-green knit dress that fell to her knees. It wasn't tight. It fit her tall, large frame comfortably. She'd already added some props for her argument. There were easels facing the jury on either side of the lectern. On each was a white pad of paper. After reaching the lectern and organizing her notes on its shelf, she began.

"May it please the court, counsel and ladies and gentlemen. I have been chosen to give the primary argument for the defendants. The other defense lawyers will follow me with additional remarks. After we sit down, Mr. Bellows will have the opportunity to address you last. Some feel that he who speaks last has an advantage, but that's not really true. The only reason plaintiffs have the right to the last word is because they have the burden of proof. We hear what their attorney argues, and then we answer that argument and put forth the arguments for our clients. The law then gives plaintiffs the right to answer our arguments. But Mr. Bellows is only allowed to respond to the arguments we make. He is not allowed to re-argue what his partner has already told you.

"The evidence in this case clearly establishes that what happened Sunday night, September twenty-second, 1991, was consensual sex and nothing more. Plaintiffs have not met their burden of proof. They were not sexually assaulted! The verdict form, which you will receive when you retire, asks you a series of questions. I've asked Mary Jo to use ELMO and place a copy on the television monitor, so you can see these questions. As you can see, there are four major questions followed by some questions relating to damages." Using a pointer she said, "These major questions are,

> **Is the defendant Shepard liable to Plaintiff Lane?**
> **Is the defendant Sumas liable to Plaintiff House?**
> **Is the defendant Lovejoy liable to Plaintiff Marcellas?**
> **Is the defendant the Lukarillas liable to plaintiffs?**

"Since plaintiffs have failed to establish that they were sexually assaulted, your answer to each of these questions should be no, and when you answer no, that means that you don't answer the questions about damages. Let me explain further.

"As I told you in my opening statement, 'this is a case about who's telling the truth, the plaintiffs or Alex Lovejoy, Abe Sumas and Senator Shepard.' The rest of the Lukarillas are really not involved. Mr. O'Shea will address that in more detail later. Where one side says one thing and the other says the opposite, the decision about where the truth lies is usually decided by credibility." She wrote CREDIBILITY in bold capital letters on the pad of white paper to the jury's right. "That's the key to the decision in this case. Where does the credibility lie? The answer to that question gives you the answers to the questions on the verdict form. It answers the question Ms. Johnson posed, 'where is the greater weight of the evidence?'

"Ms. Johnson misleads you, however, when she claims that defendants' witnesses are irrelevant. In truth, she knows why these witnesses are very important. You have to test the credibility of the plaintiffs, as well as that of the defendants, to decide who's telling the truth. These witnesses help you make that decision.

"The court will tell you how to evaluate the credibility of witnesses. If I may, let me use another piece of paper to list some of the ways the judge will tell you to test the credibility of a witness." She approached the easel and wrote with a black grease pencil. "He will tell you to **examine the way the witnesses testify.**

"Ask yourselves, 'Do they seem to be telling the truth, or is there something suspicious about what they are saying and why they are saying it?' The judge will tell you to ask **what does a witness have to gain?** That's another factor to consider. I'll mention that again in a moment.

The next factor is a very important one. **Do they always tell the truth?** This factor is very important. The judge will tell you, and I'm going to write this right under the word credibility on this pad over here. **"A witness found to be false in one part of his or her testimony should be distrusted in the other parts of his or her testimony."**

She turned and looked at Amanda. "It's on this very point, Ms. Johnson, that we offered those six witnesses you referred to. During our investigation into this case we interviewed the Larsons and learned that Ginny Lane and Peg House were in the Pepper-Price-Weinstein cabin early Saturday morning. All of the plaintiffs adamantly deny that, even though Ms. Marcellas was asleep at the time. We went further and questioned the occupants of that cabin. One of them had previously told Mr. Lovejoy that Ginny and Peg were in that cabin and that they had sex with them there. Max Pepper told you that they were in the cabin that night. Steve Weinstein told you that Ginny and Peg were in the cabin and that they had sex with him and Parker Price. If you believe all of these witnesses, then the plaintiffs are not telling the truth about what happened early Saturday morning. That false testimony means that they are to be *distrusted* in the other parts of their testimony."

Then Joan turned and looked at Amanda. "Ms. Johnson, the evidence from those six witnesses establishes that credibility lies with the testimony of our clients. It shows that Alex Lovejoy, Abe Sumas and the senator are the ones telling the truth. And, if the plaintiffs lied about where they were Saturday morning, how can you be asked to believe their testimony about what happened Sunday night?

"While we're on the subject of credibility, how do the plaintiffs fare if we test their credibility with the second factor, **what does the witness have to gain?** Ms. Johnson just answered that for us, lots of dollars. What did she say? Five hundred thousand or a million.

"And you also need to test **the way they testified**," she said pointing back to the easel. "I think I can sum that up with a few simple words: they cried, swore and argued. Credible witnesses don't do that. They don't need to!"

Joan paused to let that remark set in. "But in this case someone else's credibility is involved and should be examined. With the help of the judge, during depositions we found out that the plaintiffs are not Ms. Johnson's only clients in this case. Empire Broadcasting Company hired her too, and it's got its own agenda and vendettas." She pointed again to CREDIBILITY on the white pad. "So EBC's credibility is also in issue. The cross-examination of Marlene Smyth, the testimony of Susan Silver, the deposition of Parker Price, the adverse testimony of the plaintiff, Ginny Lane, and the testimony of Ben Lorenzo established EBC's deep involvement in this case. Much of that testimony establishes its dislike, and probable hate, for Alex Lovejoy and Abe Sumas. It had its own agenda.

"**What did it have to gain**?" she said, referring to the bold statement on the easel. "Retribution? Some of this evidence further seems to suggest that EBC may even have set the defendants up for this lawsuit. In any event, EBC's involvement in this case clearly diminishes the credibility of plaintiffs' version of the facts." She turned and again looked at Amanda. "That's the reason for the first three witnesses you referred to, Ms. Johnson.

"Next, let me ask what evidence did plaintiffs offer to show you folks that you should distrust these defendants' credibility? I suppose Mr. Bellows will say, Sheila Workman, Judy Filcher and Jerry Mahoney. But did they really affect Lovejoy's, Sumas' and the senator's credibility? Certainly those witnesses have no effect on Alex Lovejoy's credibility, and, since Sumas and the senator's testimony is basically the same as Lovejoy's, the witnesses really don't affect their credibility either.

"Furthermore, Abe Sumas addressed the jury right up front and admitted almost everything Mahoney said. Again he publicly admitted being oversexed back in those days. Is that what a liar would do? The evidence is undisputed that he hasn't had a problem with women in the last twenty years, except for Rachel Jacobs, and we're not dealing with women in men's showers here."

That drew chuckles and some outright laughter from various places in the courtroom, including the jury box and behind the bench.

"It doesn't sound like his ex-wives think he's a liar. How many divorced men can make that claim?"

More smiles abounded.

"And Senator Shepard admitted having intercourse with Ms. Workman, when she didn't even accuse him of it. But he strongly denied asking her or Ms. Filcher for oral sex. Does that sound like a liar? It's pretty clear that evidence plaintiffs offered, while damaging to the reputations of our clients, surely didn't damage their credibility. What it did was enhance it.

"Let me sum up this point on this pad," Joan said, turning over to a clean white sheet on the easel, writing as she talked. "Let's see how plaintiffs did with their burden of proof. Did the scales tip in their favor? Certainly their testimony didn't do it. They weren't particularly convincing, but, giving them the benefit of the doubt, I'll concede that they left the scales even, so I'll put an even opposite their names.

"Now, let's look at the other witnesses who addressed plaintiffs' truthfulness. Thor Larson's testimony establishes that plaintiffs lied. That's clearly a minus to their burden. Judy Larson's testimony makes the minus larger. The evidence from Max Pepper, Steve Weinstein and Alex Lovejoy again establishes that plaintiffs lied. The minus burden is getting pretty big.

"The testimony of Susan Silver, Marlene Smyth and Ginny Lane all detracted from the plaintiffs' credibility, but I suppose an argument could be made that they left the scales even. But their testimony surely didn't detract from the big minus that we now have before us.

"Next, we have the defendants. Although little was done to detract from their credibility, and they seemed truthful as they testified, to be fair again, let's say they left the scales even. But again the minus is untouched.

"Sheila Workman and Judy Filcher were certainly damaging witnesses to the reputation of Senator Shepard. But did they damage his credibility? As I've pointed out, they did not. In fact, by offering their testimony, plaintiffs gave him the opportunity to strengthen his credibility. And

Jerry Mahoney really didn't damage defendant Sumas' reputation, because he didn't deny what Mahoney said. He had no effect on his credibility. The minus is unaffected.

"That's all the witnesses. Where do we stand? We all know the answer. The credibility scales have collapsed against the plaintiffs. Like the teeter-totter that's lighter on one side, plaintiffs' side falls to the ground. It may sound like I'm teaching a class, but, after hearing Ms. Johnson, there's a lesson to be learned. The lesson's titled *credibility.*

"The charges made against the defendants are serious, and they need to be taken seriously. Plaintiffs have the burden to prove that they were sexually assaulted by means of a greater weight of the evidence, and they've totally failed. As I said earlier, your answers to the questions on the jury form asking whether any these defendants are liable should all be 'no.' And once you've given those answers, the judge will tell you that your deliberations will be over. You won't consider any of the damage questions.

"Thank you, ladies and gentlemen. That thanks is from my client, Alex Lovejoy, as well. Your avid attention throughout this trial is commendable. This case is very important to Alex Lovejoy. His reputation is at stake. I speak for him in saying he feels confident that the case is in your hands."

Joan went back to her chair, and Miles stood and buttoned the jacket of his olive glen plaid suit.

"Ladies and gentlemen," Miles said as he approached the jury, pushing the lectern to one side. "I'm going to be perfectly frank with you when I talk about the EBC involvement in this case. As you heard, that network did a real number on my client for protecting the privacy of his players. The president of their sports network, Grant Slade, called him a racist and a chauvinist on national television, when in truth he's the epitome of the exact opposite. All of Abe Sumas' working life he's been associated, played and lived with black Americans. He was married to a black American, who, although divorced from him, remains a close friend. As you witnessed here in this courtroom, Abe is not at a loss for words, sometimes pretty choice ones, but he is not a racist or a chauvinist. And he's not a liar.

"But Abe's made a couple of powerful enemies. One is Grant Slade, who blames him for EBC losing the NFL television contract. Abe admits that he made his views known to the other owners, so maybe he did play a part in that, but the evidence shows he was justified in his criticism of the network. Slade hates Abe Sumas. Another enemy is Parker Price. His girlfriend is the reporter Rachel Jacobs. She caused these bad relationships by trying to interview a player in the showers.

"And what have these two been up to? For one thing they put up the money for Marlene Smyth to buy West Portland Catering, after, and I underline *after*, they found out that West Portland was going to cater the Lukarillas' retreat. Why did they do that? Price said for an investment. Do you believe that? Finally, reluctantly he admitted that one of his reasons was that the Lukarillas was one of the company's clients. Why did that make a difference? Marlene Smyth may have given us the answer when we called her as a reluctant witness. You'll remember that Ms. Cohen had to get the help of the judge to get Smyth to open up. She told us that before the retreat Slade called her. This was also after the plaintiffs had joined Smyth's payroll. Slade wanted plaintiffs' phone numbers, so he could arrange to have his *guy* come to Portland to talk to them. Then Smyth finally told us that Ginny met with this *guy* to talk about a mysterious *job*. Of course, Ginny denies this, so what the *guy* wanted them to do is still a mystery. But is it really? Did Slade, and maybe Price, want to set something up at the retreat to pay Abe Sumas back? When discussing the retreat with Mr. Lorenzo, Slade said he'd fixed Sumas' clock. What do you suppose he meant by that? Slade won't tell us, because he's apparently in hiding from our subpoena."

At this point Barry saw juror Ronnie Norstad look at Jack Smith with another "I told you so" nod.

"And what about Alex Lovejoy?" Miles said, turning and looking at Lovejoy. "He's an EBC enemy, too. And oh, we mustn't forget about Senator Shepard. He's also on Grant Slade's list, because he wouldn't investigate the loss of the television contract. Doesn't it seem a strange coincidence that the plaintiffs would end up in a cabin shared by these three guys, Lovejoy, Sumas and the senator? Isn't it also strange that after this retreat the network that does an expose branding the three as sexual predators is EBC, the same network that's got a grudge against all of them? That's a lot of coincidences, or is it?

"There's one more very interesting fact that bears on this subject. You might have missed it. I did until I was reviewing the transcript last night. While Max Pepper didn't invest in this catering company, he knew Slade and Price did, and he was the one who made the cabin assignments. I don't mean to suggest that he did so for the convenience of Price or Slade, but he had to inform Price of those assignments, just as he did all of the members. Do you suppose that maybe it was after Price found that out, that Slade called Marlene to get the plaintiffs' telephone numbers?

"We don't know the answer to many of these questions, but there's plenty of evidence here to give rise to them. As Joan Dixon so ably pointed out, the great weight of the evidence establishes that my client and the others did not sexually assault the plaintiffs, so either plaintiffs are lying to get some money, or there was something else going on. We'll probably never know the full answer, but you're entitled to your opinions, based on these facts.

"I apologize for being so frank. But I know you picked up on a lot of what I've said, and someone had to say it. It seemed logical for me, because whatever EBC has been doing in and around this case, it hasn't been to help Abe Sumas. I too thank you, on my behalf and on behalf of Abe Sumas, for the way you have followed this case so closely. We ask that you answer all of the main questions in the negative, particularly the second one."

"Mr. Shumanski," the judge said.

Shumanski came forward and also disregarded the lectern. His gray tweed sport coat was open, revealing the full length of his light green Hastings tie, and he spoke with a soft voice that no one had trouble hearing. "Ladies and gentlemen, I'll be very brief. All I want to emphasize is what Joan Dixon already said for me. If my client, Senator Shepard, was a liar, he never would have admitted on this witness stand what he did. It's fine for Ms. Johnson to try to explain that away by his being advised by talented lawyers, but no politician of the prominence of Senator

Lionel Shepard is going to be convinced by a lawyer to tell the truth if he's willing to lie to protect his political life. My client wasn't willing to do that. He told you the truth about his relations with Sheila Workman, and he admitted having sex with Ginny Lane. Ms. Johnson's claim that he's a liar makes absolutely no sense.

"But maybe Lou Miles has something. Maybe there's more to this case than who's telling the truth. I don't know, but I do know from all the evidence that Lionel Shepard didn't deserve to be here, and he should be dismissed by your verdict. Thank you for your patience."

"You're next in line and last, Mr. O'Shea," the judge said.

"No, your Honor, unfortunately Mr. Bellows will have the last word, but it is my turn. I'll likewise be brief." He stood directly in front of the jury, no lectern or easels. "Ladies and gentlemen, as you know I represent the Lukarillas. I've never been quite sure why the plaintiffs felt it necessary to name my client, but now that I've asked that question, I'm sure Mr. Bellows will tell you. I always like to say something like that so that the plaintiff's lawyer has something to say in rebuttal." He turned and smiled at Bellows.

"Mr. Bellows will tell you again all of the things Hugh Chalmers told him during his deposition. But what it boils down to is the fact that he did bring good quality and important men together in this organization, none of whom has ever molested women, either before or during this retreat.

"Mr. Bellows might play the video again for emphasis. He may even suggest that, while Mr. Chalmers never had this problem before, he cannot deny that at least some of the members had sex with the waitresses in 1991. And he may follow that with a comment that had Hugh Chalmers done the simple job of investigating that Julie Sanchez did, he could probably have predicted that something like this was bound to happen. I'm almost certain he'll suggest that, since Mr. Chalmers did not know that sexual intercourse had gone on in nineteen ninety-one until he read about plaintiffs' claims in the paper, how can Mr. Chalmers know that things like this hadn't been going on lots of times before?

"Well, the answer to all of those arguments, Mr. Bellows, is that for over forty years no claims like those of your clients have ever been made. If consensual sex had gone on before, and of course, there's no evidence of that, and no one complained, how does that put the Lukarillas or Hugh Chalmers on notice that a waitress is going to be sexually assaulted? It doesn't, and they weren't.

"But Mr. Bellows will say that if Hugh Chalmers had done the investigation that Julie Sanchez did, Mr. Chalmers could have easily followed up by questioning Abe Sumas and Senator Shepard. That's a clever argument, Mr. Bellows, but how would that have changed anything? We've all heard what Sumas and the senator would have told him, just what they told us here in this courtroom. That certainly wouldn't have alerted Mr. Chalmers that Sumas and the senator were going to sexually assault waitresses, which, of course, they didn't.

"The bottom line is there's no case against Alex Lovejoy, Abe Sumas and Lionel Shepard, because the weight of the evidence clearly establishes that they *did not,* and I emphasize that, sexually assault anyone! And, therefore, there's no case against the Lukarillas either!

"Mr. Bellows is coming next. He has the last word. He may argue something that the four of us just plain forgot to mention. If that happens, you may say to yourself, 'There's a perfectly good answer to that. Why didn't Mr. O'Shea mention it?' Well, don't give up on that perfectly good answer when you get in the jury room, just because we forgot to mention it. *Get in there and tell the others what the answer is!*

"My client and I extend a repetitious, but genuine, thank you for your patience and attention. No lawyer or client can complain about the quality of this jury. Good luck to you in your deliberations. I'm confident you will reach the right and just result."

"Ladies and gentlemen, we've gone past noon," the judge said, "but we're going to finish without another recess. Mr. Bellows will now finish the arguments, and I will follow with my instructions. We will then send you out for lunch and your deliberations. Mr. Bellows."

"Thank you, Your Honor, and ladies and gentlemen. A good defense lawyer knows he should take as much wind out of the sails of the plaintiffs' lawyer's rebuttal as he can. Mr. O'Shea just did his job.

"Yes, I was going to say everything he said I would. But rather than saying it again, I'll just adopt what he said. The difference is that you can't just pass off, as Mr. O'Shea did, the simple fact that in nineteen ninty-one something happened, no matter whose version you believe. It involved unnecessary and inappropriate sex between the members and these waitresses. And the Lukarillas, with a little investigation, could have predicted it. Mr. O'Shea would have us believe that, since it was consensual, it doesn't matter. Asking Sumas and Shepard about their pasts wouldn't have changed anything. When you hear the judge's instructions on the duty of the Lukarillas, what they should have looked for and what they should have done to protect plaintiffs, I submit that you'll find the evidence warrants a verdict against them.

"Ms. Dixon did an admirable job turning the defendants' red herring evidence into credibility. That fact remains, however, as Ms. Johnson told you before, the only evidence that corroborates either version of what happened on Sunday night is that of Ms. Workman, Ms. Filcher and Mr. Mahoney. That evidence tips the scales, and your verdict should be against all defendants and in favor of plaintiffs in a fair, substantial amount."

Bellows paused, and he took time to look at each individual juror. "Thank you for waiting so long. The plaintiffs trust you'll be fair." He turned and walked back to the counsel table, where he sat down to listen to the judge.

"Ladies and gentlemen," the judge began, "you are the sole and exclusive judges of the facts in this case. I am the judge of the law, and it is now my duty to tell you what the law is that you must apply in deciding this case. You must make your decision based only upon the evidence that you have heard in this courtroom and the law about which I will now inform you. Your verdict must be based upon the evidence and not upon guesswork or speculation."

He then gave them more detailed instructions on how they were to evaluate the evidence and the credibility of the witness, saying everything that the lawyers had mentioned in their closing arguments. He gave them instructions to use in determining whether the defendants would be liable to plaintiffs. They were simple. If defendants Lovejoy, Sumas and/or Shepard did what plaintiffs claimed they did, those things would constitute sexual assaults for which they would be liable.

"The Lukarillas, on the other hand," he continued, "can only be found liable to the plaintiffs, if you first find that one or more of the other defendants did in fact commit one or more acts of sexual assault on one or more of the plaintiffs. However, even if you find that sexual assaults were committed, the Lukarillas can only be liable to plaintiffs, if you further find both of the following things:

That it hired women to perform services at its retreat, when it knew or should have known that they would be subjected to unwanted sexual acts, and

That such knowledge was a proximate cause of any injuries sustained by the plaintiffs."

He told them that they could only consider damages if they first found that one or more of the defendants was liable, using the questions on the verdict form. He put the verdict form on ELMO so they could follow along with him on the television set.

"In other words," the judge said, "if your answer to any of the main questions is no, then you do not answer the sub question on damages. Only consider that sub-question if you first answer a liability question as yes." He told them that it was the plaintiffs' burden to prove that they had been damaged and that the amount of damages, if any, was in their sole discretion. He further explained what punitive damages were, that punitive damages could only be awarded against defendants Lovejoy, Sumas and Shepard and that whether to award them was in their sole discretion.

"Your verdict must be unanimous in all respects. When you reach a verdict, have your foreperson date it and sign it on the lines provided. You are now going to retire to your jury room to deliberate and reach a verdict. After you reach the jury room, Mrs. Williams will take orders for your lunch."

The judge gave the oath to the bailiff and then turned one final time to the jury. "You are now excused. When you have reached a verdict, just knock on your door so Mrs. Williams can return you to the courtroom. If you have any questions for the court, give them in writing to Mrs. Williams."

The jury retired under the care of Judy Williams at one twenty-three.

Chapter 45

The defense gathered in Swift, Wyman & Wyatt's large conference room where they had first met back in January. Mary Jo had arranged for a buffet lunch. They sat around the table eating, talking and trying to relax. Everyone felt the trial had gone as well as it could have. Each of them remembered things he or she should have said, but that was normal. The clients seemed pleased, and even Senator Shepard looked relaxed for the first time in more than a week.

Shumanski was the first to turn philosophical. "I think most of you know I've tried cases all over the country, and I must say, this has been an experience that I will file away as unique. I've never been involved in a case of this magnitude and notoriety that was handled in such an expeditious and judicious manner. In most places a case like this would take months. We tried the whole case in less time than it would take to select a jury in Southern California. Barry, you should be damn proud of your judges and court procedures. And I should include your local lawyers, as well. Something like this couldn't happen without the cooperation of the lawyers. I'm going to write Judge Lloyd a letter in a few weeks and tell him just how proud of his court I am."

Chalmers took over the conversation. "It's time a client said something. You guys and gals did a great job. You had tough competition, but that made you look even better. If you want my prediction, you've won the case."

"Thanks, Hugh, but don't count your chickens yet," Barry said. "I learned a long time ago that predicting what a jury will do after a tough, close case is like knowing when double zero will come up in roulette.

"We're all about to suffer what I call *The Wait*. It's the time between when the jury retires and when it reaches its verdict, and it's spooky. It's a unique wasteland in time. If you're like me, you'll feel a constant uneasiness in your stomach that can't be cured or lessened until the verdict is read. There's no medicine or treatment to soften it. I try to work, but it's at best a twenty-five percent effort. You can't go to a movie or play golf or take a run, because the judge won't let you out of reach. You just wait, sometimes for days. Some say the hardest part about being a trial lawyer is the queasy stomach or jitters you get before addressing the jury or judge, but I think it's *The Wait*."

At four-fourteen a call came from the court. The jury had a question, so off the lawyers went. The judge read the question, "Did Marlene Smyth say what job EBC wanted plaintiffs to do?"

While each side conferred on an answer, the judge suggested one for them. "My inclination is to tell them that I won't give them an answer to a question like that. They heard her testimony, and they have to use their own memories. If we give them parts of one witness's testimony, it gives it undue emphasis."

"We do have the transcript," Amanda replied, "but I think you're right. I'm for giving your suggested answer."

"We agree," Barry said.

"All right, that's what I'll do. Do you want me to bring them in here, or is it okay with you if I just go to the jury room and tell them?" the judge asked.

The lawyers agreed that he could go to the jury room.

Nothing more was heard from the jury that afternoon. The judge sent them home with his instructions at six. They were to be back at eight-thirty the next morning to continue their deliberations.

⚥

At eight-thirty Thursday morning the jury was back. Their deliberations and *The Wait* continued. At twenty to eleven they had another question.

After the lawyers reconvened in court, the judge read the jury's note: "Is there a limit to what we can award as general damages?"

"Wow," whispered Joan.

"This one I've had before," the judge explained. "My stock answer is no. Then I tell them that under the federal system, if I think their verdict is excessive, I can reduce it. Are there any objections to my telling them that?"

"No objection," Amanda answered immediately.

The defense team talked again. Their spirits weren't high now. "He has to say no, but I don't like him saying the rest," Barry whispered. "It sounds to me like at least one juror wants to cap the damages. If he tells them that he'll reduce anything that's excessive, that juror's argument for a cap is gone." The others agreed, so Barry said, "Just tell them no. We object to any further explanation."

"Your objection is noted," the judge said, "but I'm going to give them the instruction I usually give."

When the defense lawyers returned to Swift, Wyman & Wyatt and told the clients what had happened, a gloom set in.

"I know it sounds bad," Barry said, "but I can't count the number of times that I've had a late damage question like this that was followed by a defense verdict. It was a question, not a verdict, so don't get depressed over something that hasn't happened."

Faces still looked unhappy.

At three Barry began to worry. His little speech no longer helped him, because, when he'd had those questions before, the defense verdict came within a half hour. It had now been more than four hours, and he was concerned.

At four-eleven the call came. The jury had a verdict, and the lawyers, this time with the clients, headed across the street. There was no conversation, and that's what Barry expected, because it was always like that when *The Wait* was about over.

The lawyers and their clients were seated. A small crowd sat in the rear, including the Johnson & Bellows staff. Judy Williams brought in the jury. Frances Bishop had a piece of paper in her right hand. She was the foreperson.

The jurors were seated and *The Wait* continued. Everyone waited for the judge to appear. It was quiet, very quiet. The jurors were uncomfortable. They each stared straight ahead. So did the lawyers and the clients. Everyone was acting like strangers. Barry knew Becky had her fingers crossed under the table. She always did.

Finally, the judge entered and took the bench. "Ladies and gentlemen, have you reached a verdict?"

"Yes, we have," Frances Bishop replied.

"Please hand it to Mrs. Williams."

Judy Williams took the verdict form from Mrs. Bishop and handed it up to the judge.

He silently read through it without any expression. "Mrs. Bishop, I see handwriting on the verdict after your findings. Are those explanations intended to be part of your verdict?" he asked.

Barry heard several hushed, "Oh, nos," beside and behind him. He knew that the jury had done more than just check the no blanks. It looked like they'd lost. He looked at the plaintiffs' table and saw smiles appearing.

"Yes, Your Honor, the handwritten words are part of our verdict," Mrs. Bishop explained.

"Very well, is this verdict unanimous?"

"Yes, Your Honor," replied Mrs. Bishop.

The judge asked each juror if this was his or her verdict, and each responded that it was. Turning to the courtroom, the judge said, "By this verdict the jury has found in favor of plaintiff Lane and against defendant Shepard, in favor of plaintiff House and against defendant Sumas, and in favor of plaintiff Marcellas and against defendant Lovejoy."

Barry could feel the deflation in those around him. Someone behind him whispered, "Shit." It had to have been Sumas. Barry saw Ginny turn to Peg and Tina. Her face was covered with a broad smile. She mouthed, yea, and gave a double thumbs-up.

The judge continued. "It has awarded each plaintiff the full sum of one hundred dollars, and the handwriting beside each award says that the sum is 'for services rendered.'"

The emotions at the counsel tables reversed. The senator lowered his head into his hands and uttered a sigh of relief. A broad grin came across Sumas' face as he turned to Lovejoy and offered him a high-five. Barry heard the spectators behind him erupt, a mixture of amazement and laughter. He looked at the plaintiffs. The smiles were gone.

"*You bastards!*" Ginny yelled as she faced the jurors.

Judge Lloyd slammed his gavel on his bench. "That's enough!" he said loudly. "Any more outbursts and I'll clear the courtroom! Ms. Lane, you won't like what I'm going to do if you say one more thing." After calm had been restored, he finished the verdict. "Finally, the jury has found in favor of the Lukarillas and against all three plaintiffs."

Chalmers grasp Barry's shoulder and said, "I knew you'd do it. Thank God you were on our side."

Becky grabbed Barry's hand and squeezed.

"Does anyone have anything further to present?" the judge asked.

There was no response.

"Then the verdict will be entered of record, and this court is adjourned," he said, "but everyone remain seated until all of the jurors have left the courtroom."

Barry turned to watch the jurors leave and was surprised to see Susan Silver seated in the rear of the courtroom.

The last juror to leave was Frances Bishop, the foreperson. As soon as she was through the double doors, Susan Silver quickly rose and slipped out behind her.

When Susan got into the hall, she came up behind Mrs. Bishop. "How could you come to such a ridiculous result?" she asked. "That wasn't a verdict. It was pure character assassination. You might as well have called the plaintiffs whores."

Surprised, Mrs. Bishop turned around and saw that it was Susan Silver who was confronting her. "It might seem that way to you," she said. "But we knew what you and your cohorts were up to. Nothing you did could convince us that those women were innocent victims. We wanted to send a message, and from your comments I can see we did."

The End.

THE CHARACTERS

John Quincy Ames	Chairman of the board of Southern & Eastern Railroad and a Lukarilla
Nelson Beecham	Governor of Wyoming and a Lukarilla
Oscar Bellows	Plaintiffs' lawyer and member of law firm Johnson & Bellows
Mary Bellman	Juror number two
Dr. Martha Bentley	Plaintiffs' psychologist
Frances Bishop	Juror number four and foreperson
Joey Buccanan	Bartender at Come-on-Inn and friend of Ginny Lane
Hugh Chalmers	President of Chalmers Forest Products (CFP) and the founder of the Lukarillas.
William Churchill	President of Random Electronics and a Lukarilla
Becky Cohen	Associate trial lawyer for defendants and partner at law firm Swift, Wyman & Wiggens
Joan Dixon	Lovejoy trial lawyer and partner at NYC law firm Bellman & Swett
Julian Epstein	Senior U.S. Senator from Texas and a Lukarilla
Beth Erickson	Secretary in district attorney's office in Astoria, Oregon
Judy Filcher	Springfield, Illinois hotel maid
H.P. "Smokie" Goodenough	U.S. Representative from Tennessee and a Lukarilla
Herb Goodwin	Investigator with law firm Johnson & Bellows
Vincent Grady	Governor of Virginia and a Lukarilla member
Pam Hall	Swift, Wyman & Wiggens sub rosa investigator
Peg House	A plaintiff and an employee of West Portland Catering.
Rachel Jacobs	Sports reporter for LA TV station KEBC
Amanda Johnson	Plaintiffs' lawyer and member of law firm Johnson & Bellows

Hilton Jones	Managing partner of NYC law firm Stevens & Sherman and a Lukarilla
Mary Jo Knight	Legal assistant at law firm Swift, Wyman & Wiggens
Ginny Lane	A plaintiff and an employee of West Portland Catering.
Judy Larson	Wife of Thor Larson
Thor Larson	Son of Sven Larson
Sven Larson	Caretaker of Lukarilla camp
Angie Lawrence	Vice president of Silex Petroleum and later President of Citrus Publishing Company
Ron Lemery	Los Angeles investigator and contact of Pam Hall
Wyonna Lipton	Second alternate juror
Ezra Livingston	Chairman of the board of the National Bank of the South and Lukarilla member
Judge Walter Lloyd	U.S. Magistrate for the District of Oregon and the trial judge
Ben Lorenzo	Investigator at law firm Swift, Wyman & Wiggens
Alex Lovejoy	A defendant, president of Silex Petroleum and a Lukarilla
Tina Marcellas	A plaintiff and an employee of West Portland Catering.
Ruth Mason	Court reporter with Ruth Mason & Associates
Amy McCormick	Reporter for station KPOR
Lou Miles	Sumas trial lawyer and partner of LA law firm Hopson & Hill
Shirley Miller	Juror number one
Ronnie Norstad	Juror number six
Ryan O'Donnell	Lawyer at law firm Levinson & Wood in NYC
Barry O'Shea	Trial lawyer for The Lukarillas and partner at law firm Swift, Wyman & Wiggens
Glen Overton	Juror number three
Max Pepper	Senior partner of LA law firm Newman & Levine and a Lukarilla

Owen Persell	District attorney of Clatsop County, Oregon
Parker Price	Entertainer and a Lukarilla
Mason Rutledge	President of Marion University and a Lukarilla
Julie Sanchez	Investigator for EBC
Mike Santana	San Francisco Mafia member and union boss
Alan Schapiro	Plaintiffs' psychiatrist
Lionel Shepard	A defendant, the junior U.S. Senator from Illinois and a Lukarilla
Paul Shumanski	Trial lawyer for Shepard and partner in Cleveland law firm Fleming, Rose & Keane
Susan Silver	Investigative reporter for EBC
Claude Skow	Parker Price's lawyer
Grant Slade	EBC Sports producer and investor in J & L Investment Company
Jack Smith	First alternate juror
Rex Smith	President of Universal Airlines and a Lukarilla
Marlene Smyth	Owner of West Portland Catering
Lester Solomon	Steve Weinstein's lawyer
Judge Kingsley Sommerville	Chief judge of federal district court in Oregon and settlement judge
Abe Sumas	A defendant, president of Los Angeles Stars professional football team and a Lukarilla
Edward Thomas	U.S. Representative from Vermont and a Lukarilla
Cecil Upshaw	President of MJK&L accounting firm and a Lukarilla
James "Hook" Van Dyke	Former NBA basketball player and a Lukarilla
Stephen Weinstein	Chairman of the board of S-Mart Stores and a Lukarilla
Judy Williams	Judge Lloyd's clerk
Dolores Witherspoon	Juror number five
Sheila Workman	Former member of Senator Shepard's staff

THE ORGANIZATIONS

Bellman & Swett	Joan Dixon's and Howard Sugerman's NYC law firm
Boldt, Benjamin & Spruce	Max Pepper's former Boston law firm
Chalmers Forest Products (CFP)	A forest products company of Hugh Chalmers and owner of Lukarilla campsite
Citrus Publishing Company	A Los Angeles company and owner of The Express newspaper
Come-on-Inn	Tavern in suburb of Portland, OR
Empire Broadcasting Company (EBC)	Television network
Fleming, Rose & Krause	Paul Shumanski's Cleveland law firm
Hopson & Hill	Lou Miles' Los Angeles law firm
J & L Investment Company	Investment company of Angie Lawrence and Rachel Jacobs
Johnson & Bellows	Amanda Johnson's law firm
Levinson & Wood	NYC law firm for EBC
Los Angeles Stars	A professional football team
The Lukarillas	All male "think tank" that holds an annual retreat at a camp in the Oregon Coast Range mountains
KEBC	Los Angeles TV station affiliate of EBC
KPOR	Portland TV station affiliate of EBC
Marion University	University in Springfield, Missouri
National Bank of the South	Ezra Livingston's bank
Newman & Levine	Max Pepper's Los Angeles law firm
New Brunswick Corp.	Alex Lovejoy's former employer
Orange County Town Club	Women's club in Newport Beach, CA
The Oregonian	Portland, OR newspaper
Random Electronics	Bill Churchill's company
Sellwood Inn	Tavern in Portland, OR
Silex Petroleum	Alex Lovejoy's company
S-Mart Stores	Steve Weinstein's company

Southern & Eastern Railroad	John Quincy Ames' company
Swift, Wyman & Wiggens	Barry O'Shea's law firm
Universal Airlines	Rex Smith's company
West Portland Catering	Catering company employing the plaintiffs

THE COURTOOM CHARACTERS

Judge Walter Lloyd

Judy Williams, court clerk
Brenda Michaels, court reporter

Plaintiff Virginia (Ginny) Lane
Peggy (Peg) House, and
Tina Marcellas
Amanda Johnson & Oscar Bellows
Plaintiffs' lawyers

Defendant Alex Lovejoy
Joan Dixon, trial lawyer
Howard Sugarman, personal lawyer

Defendant Lionel (Shep) Shepard
Paul Shumanski, trial lawyer

Abraham (Abe) Sumas
Lou Miles, trial lawyer

The Lukarillas
Hugh Chalmers, representative
Barry O'Shea, trial lawyer
Becky Cohen, associate trial lawyer
Mary Jo Knight, legal assistant
Ben Lorenzo, legal investigator
Jake Marion, business lawyer

Jury

One
Shirley Miller

Two
Mary Bellman

Three
Glen Overton

Four
Francis Bishop
Foreperson

Five
Delores Witherspoon

Six
Ronnie Norstad

First Alternate
Shirley Miller

Second Alternate
Glen Overton

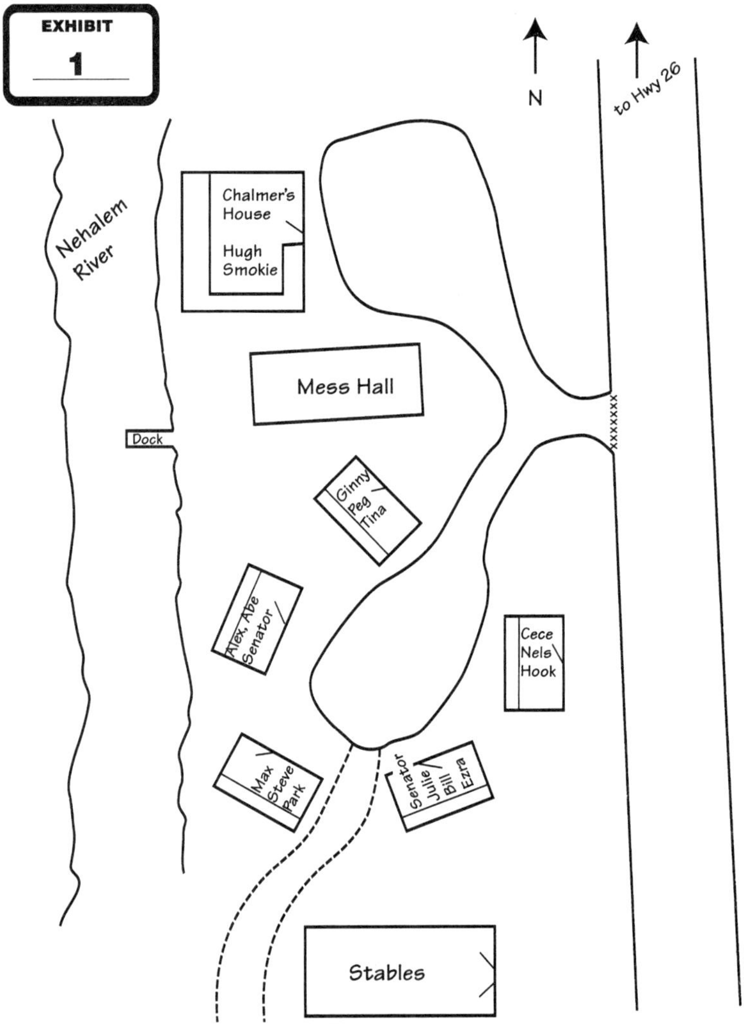
EXHIBIT
1
N
to Hwy 26
Nehalem River
Chalmer's House
Hugh
Smokie
Mess Hall
Dock
Ginny
Peg
Tina
Alex, Abe
Senator
Cece
Nels
Hook
Max
Steve
Park
Senator
Julie
Bill
Ezra
Stables

EXHIBIT

2

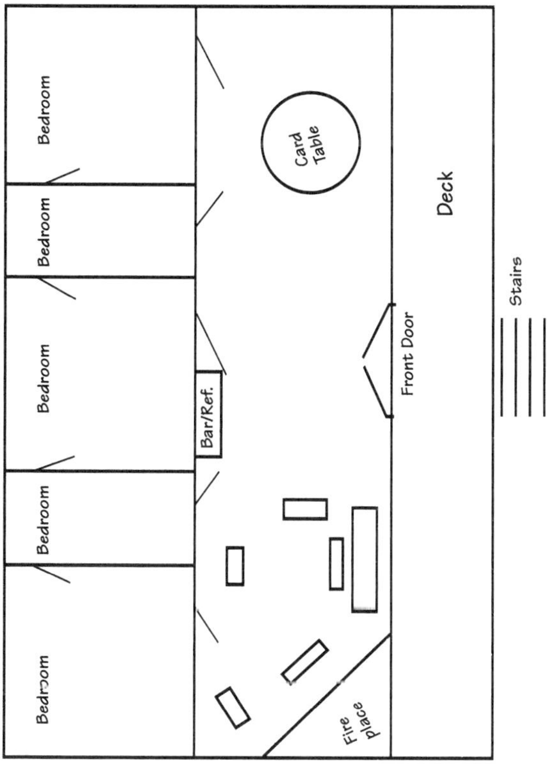
Bedroom
Bedroom
Bedroom
Bedroom
Bedroom
Card Table
Deck
Stairs
Front Door
Bar/Ref.
Fire place

Check out these other fine titles by Durban House at your local book store.

DURBAN HOUSE

EXCEPTIONAL BOOKS

BY

EXCEPTIONAL WRITERS

FICTION

A DREAM ACROSS TIME	Annie Rogers
AFTER LIFE LIFE	Don Goldman
an-eye-for-an-eye.com	Dennis Powell
BASHA	John Hamilton Lewis
THE CORMORANT DOCUMENTS	Robert Middlemiss
CRISIS PENDING	Stephen Cornell
DANGER WITHIN	Mark Danielson
DEADLY ILLUMINATION	Serena Stier
DEATH OF A HEALER	Paul Henry Young
HANDS OF VENGEANCE	Richard Sand
HOUR OF THE WOLVES Völs	Stephane Daimlen-
A HOUSTON WEEKEND	Orville Palmer
JOHNNIE RAY & MISS KILGALLEN	Bonnie Hearn Hill & Larry Hill
THE LATERAL LINE	Robert Middlemiss
LETHAL CURE	Kurt Popke
THE MEDUSA STRAIN	Chris Holmes
MR. IRRELEVANT	Jerry Marshall
OPAL EYE DEVIL Lewis	John Hamilton
PRIVATE JUSTfCE	Richard Sand
ROADHOUSE BLUES	Baron Birtcher
RUBY TUESDAY	Baron Birtcher
SAMSARA	John Hamilton Lewis
SECRET OF THE SCROLL	Chester D. Campbell
SECRETS ARE ANONYMOUS	Fredrick L. Cullen
THE SEESAW SYNDROME	Michael Maddcn

THE SERIAL KILLER'S DIET BOOK	Kevin Mark Postupack
THE STREET OF FOUR WINDS	Andrew Lazarus
TUNNEL RUNNER	Richard Sand
WHAT GOES AROUND	Don Goldman

NONFICTION

BEHIND THE MOUNTAIN	Nick Williams
FISH HEADS, RICE, RICE WINE & WAR: A VIETNAM PARADOX	Lt. Col. Thomas G. Smith, Ret.
JIMMY CARTER AND THE RISE OF MILITANT ISLAM	Philip Pilevsky
MIDDLE ESSENCE-WOMEN OF WONDER YEARS	Landy Reed
SPORES, PLAGUES, AND HISTORY—THE STORY OF ANTHRAX	Chris Holmes
WHITE WITCH DOCTOR	Dr. John A. Hunt
PROTOCOL	Mary Jane McCaffree, Pauline Innis, and Richard Sand.

DURBAN HOUSE FICTION

A DREAM ACROSS TIME Annie Rogers

Jamie Elliott arrives from New York onto the Itish Caribbean island of St. Lucia, and finds herself caught tip in Island forces, powerful across the centuries, which Find deep echoes in her recurring dreams.

AFTER LIFE LIFE Doti Goldman

A hilarious murder mystery taking place in the afterlife. Andrew Law, Chief Justice of the Texas Supreme Court, is the picture of robust health when he suddenly dies. Upon arriving in the afterlife, Andy discovers he was murdered, and his untimely has death has soule some unexpected and far-reaching consequences—a worldwide depression, among others. Many diabolical plots are woven in this funny, fast-paced whodunit, with a surprising double-cross ending.

an-eye-for-an-eye.com Dennis Powell

Jed Warren, Vietnam Peacenik, and Jeff Porter, ex-Airborne, were close friends and executives at Megafirst Bank. So when CFO McAlister crashes the company, creams off millions in bonuses, and wipes out Jed and Jeff, things began to happen.

If you wonder about corporate greed recorded in today's newspapers, read what one man did about it in this intricate, devious, and surprise-ending thriller

BASHA John Hamilton Lewis

LA reviewer, Jeff Krieder's pick as "Easily my best read of the year." Set in the world of elite professional tennis, and rooted in ancient Middle East hatreds of identity and blood loyalties, Basha is charged with the fiercely competitive nature of professional sports, and the dangers of terrorism. An already simmering Middle East begins to boil, and CIA Station Chief Grant Corbet must track down the highly successful terrorist, Basha. In a deadly race against time Grant hunts the elusive killer only to see his worst nightmare realized.

THE BEIRUT CONSPIRACY John R. Childress

At some point every person is faced with a moral dilemma: the right choice or the easy choice. The Beirut Conspiracy is a fast-paced thriller torn from today's headlines. For newly elected US President Roswell Pierce, world peace or uncontrollable global terrorism wait his decision. For drunken and disbarred physician Matthew Richards, his time as a student in Beirut is about to catch up with him, forcing him into an equally difficult choice.

THE CORMORANT DOCUMENTS Robert Middlemiss

Who is Cormorant, and why is his coded letter on Hitler's stationary found on a WWI Nazi bomber preserved in the Arctic? And why is the plane loadedwith Goering's plundered art treasures? Mallory must find out or die. On the run front the British Secret Service and CIA, he finds himself caught in a secret that dates back to 1945.

CRISIS PENDING Stephen Cornell

When U.S. oil refineries blow up, the White House and the Feds move fast, but not fast enough. Sherman Nassar Ramsey, terrorist for hire, a loner, brilliant, multilingual, and skilled with knives, pistols, and bare hands, moves around the country with contempt, case and cunning.

As America's fuel system starts grinding to a halt, rioting breaks out for gasoline, and food becomes scarce, events draw Lee Hamilton's wife, Mary, into the crisis. And when Ramsey kidnaps her, the battle becomes very personal.

DANGER WITHIN Mark Danielson

Over 100 feet down in cold ocean waters lies the wreck of pilot Kevin Hamilton's DC- 10. In it are secrets which someone is desperate to keep. When the Navy sends a team of divers from the Explosives Ordinance Division, a mysterious explosion from the wreck almost destroys the salvage ship. The FBI steps in with Special Agent Mike Pentaglia. Track the life and death of Global Express Flight 3217 inside the gritty world of aviation, and discover the shocking cargo that was hidden on its last flight.

DEADLY ILLUMINATION Serena Stier

It's summer 1890 in New York City. A ebullient young woman, Florence Tod, must challenge financier, John Pierpont Morgan, to solve a possible murder. J.P's librarian has ingested poison embedded in an illumination of a unique Hildegard von Bingcn manuscript. Florence and her cousin, Isabella Stewart Gardner, discover the corpse. When Isabella secretly removes a gold tablet from the scene of the crime, she sets off a chain of events that will involve Florence and her in a dangerous conspiracy.

DESIGNED TO KILL Chester D. Campbell

Award winning author Chester Campbell brings back Greg McKenzie and his wife, Jill, to the glistening white beaches at Perdido Key, Florida. Tim Gannon, son of the McKenzies's closest friends, has been found dead of a gunshot wound. 'Self-inflicted,' says the deputy who investigated, a clear case of remorse over the design flaw in a high-rise beachfront condo that caused a balcony to collapse, killing two people. But, after two thugs work Greg over, he realizes Jill is in danger too, and if this is a murder case, he had better solve it fast.

HANDS OF VENGEANCE Richard Sand

Private detective Lucas Rook returns still haunted by the murder of his twin brother. What seems like an casy case involving workplace violations, the former homicide detective finds himself locked in a life and death struggle with the deadly domestic terrorist group, The Brothers of the Half Moon. A must-read for lovers of dark mysteries.

HORIZON'S END Andrew Lazarus

This wide-ranging international novel presents on man's long haunted pursuit of abandoned values on three continents—North America, Europe, and Asia. Through it all, the wartime sounds of Morse Code signals remind him of his journalist's mission to keep the faith and reveal the truth. Jack Lerner often finds himself in the arms of women who are brilliant, sultry, and enigmatic. He fights his fight facing tough decisions in honest news reporting and contending with a family's survival in a world that refuses to live up to his own personal moral standards.

HOUR OF THE WOIVES Stephatic Daimlen-Völs

After more than three centuries, the Poisons Affair remains one of history's great, unsolved mysteries. The worst impulses of human nature—sordid sexual perversion, murderous intrigues, witchcraft, Satanic cults—thrive within the shadows of the Sun King's absolutism and will culminate in the darkest secret of his reign; the infamous Poisons Affair, a remarkably complex web of horror, masked by Baroque splendor, luxury and refinement.

A HOUSTON WEEKEND Orville Palmer

Professor Edward Randall, not-yet-forty, divorced and separated from his daughters, is leading a solitary, cheerless existence in a university town. At a conference in Houston, he runs into his childhood sweetheart. Then she was poverty-stricken, American Indian. Now she's elegantly attired, driving an expensive Italian car and lives in a millionaires' enclave. Will their fortuitous encounter grow into anything meaningful?

THE INNOCENT NEVER KNEW Mark W. Danielson

When Senator Sam Tinsdale's plane crashes short of the runway during a snowstorm and city-wide power failure, NTSB investigator is sent to Albuquerque to investigate. But when he arrives, he finds the crash site tampered with, evidence removed, and is threatened by men in snowsuits who refuse to provide I.D. When his boss, Ralph Dietz, issues a statement that the Cockpit Voice Recorder and Flight Data Recorder had failed, Stambler smells a cover-up.

JOHNNIE RAY AND MISS KILGALLEN Bonnie Hearn Hill and Larry Hill

Based on the real-life love affair between 1950's singer Johnnie Ray and columnist Dorothy Kilgallen. They had everything—wealth, fame, celebrity. The last thing they needed was love. Johnnie Ray and Miss Kilgallen is a love story that travels at a dangerous, roaring speed. Driven close to death from their excesses, both try to regain their lives and careers in a novel that goes beyond the bounds of mere biography.

THE LAST COWBOYS Robert E. Hollmann

What do you do when you have outlived your time?

Clint and Bubba, two aging cowboys, bodies worn out from rodeos and ranching, whose best days are behind them, try and survive in a citified world. Follow The Last Cowboys as they fight modern society in an attempt to hold on to the way of life they know and love.

THE LATERAL LINE Robert Middlemiss

Kelly Travert was ready. She had the Israeli assassination pistol, she had coated the bullets with garlic, and tonight she would kill the woman agent who tortured and killed her father. When a negotiator for the CIA warns her, suddenly her father's death is not so simple anymore.

LETHAL CURE Kurt Popke

Dr. Jake Prescott is a resident on duty in the emergency room when medics rush in with a double trauma involving patients sustaining injuries during a home invasion. Jake learns that one patient is the intruder, the other, his wife, Sara. He also learns that his four-year-old daughter, Kelly, is missing, and his patient may hold the key to her recovery.

THE MEDUSA STRAIN Chris Holmes

Finalist for Fore Word Magazine's 'Book of the Year'. A gripping tale of bio-terrorism that stunningly portrays the dangers of chemical warfare. Mohammed Ali Ossman, a bitter Iraqi scientist who hates America, breeds a deadly form of anthrax, and develops a diabolical means to initiate an epidemic. It is a story of personal courage in the face of terror, and of lost love found.

MR. IRRELEVANT Jerry Marshall

Booklist Star Review. Chesty Hake, the last man chosen in the NFL draft, has been dubbed Mr. Irrelevant. By every yardstick, he should not be playing pro football, but because of his heart and high threshold for pain, he endures. Then during his eighth and final season, he slides into paranoia, and football will never be the same.

NO ORDINARY TERROR J. Brooks Van Dyke

In this elegant and meticulously researched Edwardian detective story, J. Brooks Van Dyke brings to life the stylized fashions and customs of the time, and weaves across them a story of treason, medicine, and murder. Follow Richard and Emma Watson, nephew and niece to the Watson of Sherlock Holmes fame, as they explore dangerous leads into aristocratic mansions and London's filthiest slums.

OPAL EYE DEVIL John Hamilton Lewis

"Best historical thriller in decades." Good Books. In the age of the Robber Baron, Opal Eye Devil weaves an extraordinary tale about the brave men and women who risk everything as the discovery of oil rocks the world. The richness and pageantry of two great cultures, Great Britain and China, are brought together in a thrilling tale of adventure and human relationships.

PRIVATE JUSTICE Richard Sand

Ben Franklin Award 'Best Mystery of the Year'. After taking brutal revenge for the murder of his twin brother, Lucas Rooks leaves the NYPD to become a private eye. A father turns to Rook to investigate the murder of his daughter. Rook's dark journey finds him racing to find the killer, who kills again and again as Private Justice careens toward a startling end.

ROADHOUSE BLUES Baron R. Birtchcr

From the suii-drenched sands of Santa Catalina Island to the smoky night clubs and back alleys of West Hollywood, Roadhouse Blues is a taut noir thriller. Newly retired Homicide detective Mike Travis is torn from the comfort of his chartered yacht business into the dark, bizarre underbelly of Los Angeles's music scene by a grisly string of murders.

RUBY TUESDAY Baron R. Birtcher

When Mike Travis sails into the tropical harbor of Kona, Hawaii, he expects to put LA Homicide behind him. Instead, he finds the sometimes seamy back streets and dark underbelly of a tropical paradise and the world of music and high finance, where wealth and greed are steeped in sex, vengeance, and murder.

SAMSARA John Hamilton Lewis

A thrilling tale of love and violence set in post-World War Hong Kong. Nick Ridley, a captain in the RAF, is captured and sent to the infamous Japanese prisoner-of-war canip, Changi, in Singapore. He survives brutal treatment at the hands of the camp commandant, Colonel Tetsuro Matashima. Nick moves to Hong Kong, where he reunites with the love of his life, Courtney, and builds a world-class airline. On the eve of having his company recognized at the Crown Colony's official carrier, Courtney is kidnapped, and people begin to die. Nick is pulled into the quagmire, and must once again face the demon of Changi.

SECRET OF THE SCROLL Chester D. Campbell

Finalist 'Deadly Dagger' award, and ForeWord Magazine's 'Book of the Year' award. Deadly groups of Palestinians and Israelis struggle to gain possession of an ancient parchment that was unknowingly smuggled from Israel to the U.S. by a retired Air Force investigator. Col. Greg McKenzie finds himself mired in the duplicitous world of Middle East politics when his wife is taken hostage in an effort to force the return of the first century Hebrew scroll.

SECRETS ARE ANONYMOUS Frederick L. Cullen

A comic mystery with a cast of characters who weave multiple plots, puzzles, twists, and turns. A remarkable series of events unfold in the lives of a dozen residents of Bexley, Ohio. The journalism career of the principle character is derailed when her father shows up for her college graduation with his boyfriend on his way to a new life in California.

THE SEESAW SYNDROME Michael Madden

A terrifying medical thriller that slices with a scalpel, exposing the greed and corruption that can happen when drug executives and medical researchers position thernselves for huge profits. Biosense Pharmaceuticals has produced a drug named Floragen, and now they need to test it on patients to gain FDA approval. But there's a problern with the new drug. One of the side effects included death.

THE SERIAL KILLER'S DIET BOOK Kevin Postupack

Finalist ForeWord Magazine's 'Book of the Year' award. Fred Orbis is fat, but he dreams of being Frederico Orbisini, internationally known novelist, existential philosopher, raconteur, and lover of women. Both a satire and a reflection on morals, God and the Devil, beauty, literature, and the best-seller list, The Serial Killer's Diet Book is a delightful look at the universal human longing to become someone else.

THE STREET OF FOUR WINDS Andrew Lazarus

Paris, just after World War II. A time for love, but also a time of political ferment. In the Left Bank section of the city, Tom Cortell, a tough, intellectual journalist, finally learns the meaning of love. Along with him is a gallery of fascinating characters who lead a merry and sometimes desperate chase between Paris, Switzerland, and Spain in search of themselves.

TAINTED ANGELS Greg Crane

"One of the best mafia thrillers in years."

Tainted Angels tells the story of a Chicago crime family that defeats the Israeli underground's incursion into the New York drug market. After succeeding in New York, Mario Paterlini, with the help of his three sons, expand their narcotics empire in California, where he must deal with the CIA, Mexican drug lords, an Italian narcotics broker, and Los Angeles gangs.

TERMINAL CARE — Arvin Chawla

Billionaire Thomas Poole, Sr., does not believe his son died from an overdose. As he watches the life support being pulled from Michael's body, he wants vengeance, and not on any street-level punks. A fast, scary thriller that will make you think twice about that next hospital stay.

TUNNEL RUNNER — Richard Sand

A fast, deadly espionage thriller peopled with quirky and sometimes vicious characters, Tunnel Runner tells of a dark world where murder is committed and no one is brought to account, where loyalties exist side by side with lies and extreme violence.

WHAT GOES AROUND — Don Goldman

Finalist ForeWord Magazine's 'Book of the Year' award. Ray Banno, a medical researcher, was wrongfully incarcerated for bank fraud. What Goes Around is a dazzling tale of deception, treachery, revenge, and nonstop action that resolves around money, sex, and power. The book's sharp insight and hard-hitting style builds a high level of suspense as Banno strives for redemption.

DURBAN HOUSE NONFICTION

BEHIND THE MOUNTAIN: A CORPORATE SURVIVAL BOOK — Nick Williams

A harrowing true story of courage and survival. Nick Williams is alone, and cut off in a blizzard bchind the mountain. In order to survive, Nick called upon his training and experience that made him a highly successful business executive. In Behind the Mountain: A Corporate Survival Book, you will find the finest practical advice on how to handle yourself in tough spots, be they life threatening to you, or threatening to your job performance or the company itself. Read and learn.

FISH HEADS, RICE, RICE WINE & WAR — LTC. Thomas G. Smith (Ret.)

A human, yet humorous, look at the strangest and most misunderstood war ever, in which American soldiers were committed. Readers are offered an insiders view ofAmerican life in the midst of highly deplorable conditions, which often lead to laughter.

JIMMY CARTER AND THE RISE OF MILITANT ISLAM Philip Pilevsky

One of America's foremost authorities oil the Middle East, Philip Pilevsky argues that President Jimmy Carter's fallure to support the Shah of Iran led to the 1979 revolution. That revolution legitimized and provided a base ofoperations for militant Islamists across the Middle East. A most thought provoking book.

MIDDLE ESSENCE... WOMEN OF WONDER YEARS Landy Reed

A wonderful book by renowned speaker Landy Reed that shows how real women in real circumstances have confronted and conquered the obstacles of midlife. This is a must have guide and companion to what can be the most significant and richest years of a woman's life.

PROTOCOL *(25th Anniversary Edition)* Mary Jane McCaffree, Pauline Innis, and Richard Sand

Protocol is a comprehensive guide to proper diplomatic, official and social usage. The Bible for foreign governments, embassies, corporations, public relations firms, and individuals wishing to do business with the Federal Government. "A wealth of detail on every conceivable question, from titles and forms of address to ceremonies and flag etiquette." Department of State Newsletter.

SPORES, PLAGUES, HISTORY: THE STORY OF ANTHRAX Chris Holmes

"Much more than the story of a microbe. It is the tale of history and prophecy woven into a fabric of what was, what might have been and what might yet be. What you are about to read is real—your are not in the Twilight Zone—adjusting your TV set will not change the picture. However, it is not hopeless, and we are not helpless. The same technology used to create biological weapons can protect us with better vaccines and . CDR Ted J. Robinson, U.S. Navy Epidemiologist.

WHAT MAKES A MARRIAGE WORK? Malcolm D. Mahr

You hear the phrase "marry and settle down," which implies life becomes more serene and peaceful after marriage. This simply isn't so. Living together is one long series of experiments in accommodation. What Makes a Marriage Work? is a collection of fifty insights reflecting one couple's searching, experimenting, screaming, pouting, nagging, whining, moping, blaming, and other dysfunctional behaviors that helped them successfully navigate the turbulent sea of matrimony for over fifty years. (Featuring 34 New Yorker cartoons of wit and wisdom.)

WHITE WITCH DOCTOR John A. Hunt

A true story of life and death, hope and despair in apartheid-ruled South Africa. White Witch Doctor details white surgeon John Hunt's fight to save his beloved country in a time of social unrest and political upheaval, drawing readers into the world of South African culture, mores and folkways, superstitions, and race relations.